If you hurt me, I'll hurt you. Not right away of course, because where's the fun in that?

When an empty passenger plane crashes in the Lake District, Carly Atherton's hopes of getting back together with the man she loves vanish – Luke Emery was one of the two pilots on board.

Solving the mystery of the doomed flight might just be the chance disgraced journalist Carly needs to regain her career, as well as giving her the answers about Luke's death that she desperately wants.

But when she contacts the family of Daniel Taylor, the second pilot, she finds the two women he was closest to – his devoted sister and his loving wife – have very different memories to share.

As Carly delves into the dynamics of a seemingly ordinary family, she uncovers a far darker story than she was expecting.

Because the bonds that shape us can also tear us apart. And sometimes there are monsters living among us, hiding in plain sight...

Also by Carole Hailey

The Silence Project

Scenes from a Tragedy

Carole Hailey

CORVUS

Published in hardback in Great Britain in 2025 by Corvus, an imprint of Atlantic Books Ltd

10 9 8 7 6 5 4 3 2 1

A CIP catalogue record for this book is available from the British Library.

Hardback ISBN: 978 1 80546 153 1
Trade paperback ISBN: 978 1 80546 154 8
E-book ISBN: 978 1 80546 155 5

Printed in Great Britain.

Corvus
An imprint of Atlantic Books Ltd
Ormond House
26–27 Boswell Street
London
WC1N 3JZ

www.atlantic-books.co.uk

[Dedication]

IN PLAIN SIGHT:

The True Story Behind Flight GFA578

by Carly Atherton

Contents

Psychological Evaluation (Excerpt)   1

Introduction   3

Planet Home Article I   13

Notes   15

Izzy's Story 1984–1992   21

Notes   51

Planet Home Article II   56

Notes   60

Izzy's Story 1997–1998   63

Notes   83

Izzy's Story 2001–2003   91

Notes   107

Grace's Story 2005   113

Notes   152

Grace's Story 2005–2006   157

Notes   189

Izzy's Story 2008   197

Notes   210

Izzy's Story 2009–2010   213

Notes   221

Grace's Story 2012–2013   225

Notes   232

Grace's Story 2016   233

Notes   256

Grace's Story 2016   259

Notes   288

Izzy's Story 2017   293

Notes   304

Izzy's Story 2018–2019   307

Notes   330

Grace's Story 2019–2020   333

Notes   352

Izzy's Story 2020   355

Notes   368

Grace's Story 2020   371

The Inquest   389

Notes   397

Grace's Story 9 September 2020   399

Notes   415

The Trial   416

Notes   419

Interview with Fiona Mackie: Part I   425

Interview with Fiona Mackie: Part II   435

Notes   441

Izzy's Story 15 December 2012   443

Final Notes   457

Postscript   461

Psychological Evaluation (excerpt)
prepared by Fiona Mackie, BSc (Hons), MSc, PgDip,
Forensic Psychologist

The client presents as an intelligent, verbally fluent, self-confident individual.

During assessment, the client displayed pronounced antisocial behavioural traits including narcissism, excessive self-esteem, grandiosity and sensation-seeking. Also present was a highly superficial response to others, a pronounced lack of empathy, a ruthless and calculating attitude towards interpersonal relationships, coupled with a relative immunity to experiencing negative emotions, such as phobias, stress, anxiety and depressive symptoms.

The client's presentation is highly consistent with that of a psychopathic personality.

The results of the Psychopath Checklist: Screening Version assessment are as follows: a score of 12 for Part 1 (personality) and 9 for Part 2 (antisocial behaviour). This gives the client a total of 21 out of a possible 24. Scores of 18 or higher offer a strong indication of psychopathy.

It should be noted that 12 is the maximum score obtainable for Part 1 and is a very strong indication of the presence of traits displayed by highly psychopathic individuals.

The client does not view themselves as suffering from a disorder or mental illness and is content with their lifestyle and actions, regardless of the consequences that may result.

[Reproduced with kind permission of Fiona Mackie]

Introduction

My part in this story began with a news alert on my phone one Wednesday evening.

Associated Press

9 September 2020

19:05

<u>Breaking News</u>

Reports are coming in of the disappearance somewhere over the Lake District of an Airbus A320 believed to belong to the Goldfinch Airlines fleet.

More information to follow shortly ...

I had set 'Goldfinch Airlines' as a flag on a news alert service back in 2017 when my brother Jamie began working for them as an A320 pilot. Jamie had been recalled from furlough after Covid had grounded the planes and on 9 September he was due to make his first flight since the start of the pandemic. I was still staring at the first news alert when a second one popped up.

Associated Press
9 September 2020
19:11
<u>Breaking News</u>

The UK's air traffic control agency has confirmed
that shortly after 18:15 this evening it lost contact
with Goldfinch Airlines flight GFA578 which had
departed from Stansted Airport bound for Glasgow.

Jamie usually flew out of Stansted. I fumbled with my
mobile, jabbing at the screen, finally managing to dial his
number. It rang and rang. I hung up and called again.
This time it went straight to voicemail. I left a message.
I've seen the news. Where are you? Call me. I opened my
laptop and searched for Goldfinch Airlines, scrolling
through their corporate website and pictures of the shiny
new planes they had taken delivery of in late 2019, one of
which was now missing somewhere in the Lake District.

One of which my brother was due to be flying.

I drank a mouthful of coffee and immediately wished I
hadn't because I felt sick. I got up from my desk in the
corner of my bedroom, paced around the room, then
checked the BBC News website, but it was just showing
the same information: a missing flight somewhere over
the Lake District.

I tried my brother's number again, and again it went
straight to voicemail. I could hear myself making a weird
high-pitched noise, which I didn't seem able to stop. I
turned on a twenty-four-hour news channel. A ticker ran
along the bottom of the screen.

<u>Breaking News</u>: Reports of missing Goldfinch
Airlines plane over the Lake District ... National Air
Traffic Services confirms lost contact ...

I tried Jamie's phone again and this time it rang. Was
that good? Did it mean he was OK? I willed him to pick
up, but it went through to voicemail. I left another
message. My hands were shaking. Should I ring my
parents?

I turned back to the news. Nothing had changed. The
presenter was talking about the gloomy predictions for
the British economy and I stared at the words rolling past
on the news ticker. Then my phone rang. For a moment I
didn't look at it. I couldn't bear it if it wasn't him. The
phone kept ringing. I picked it up off the desk and held it
to my ear. When I heard Jamie say, 'Hey sis,' I burst into
tears.

My brother wasn't on flight GFA578, but he should
have been. Jamie was supposed to be the first officer,
sitting alongside the captain, but that same morning he
had tested positive for Covid so another pilot flew in his
place. If my brother hadn't caught Covid when he did, if
he'd been asymptomatic and hadn't realised he had it or if
he'd decided to go to work anyway, he would be dead.

From the Head of Communications at Goldfinch
Airlines
10 September 2020
For Immediate Release

Goldfinch Airlines can confirm that the two people
on board flight GFA578 that crashed into the slopes

of Big Crag mountain in the Lake District were Captain Daniel Taylor and First Officer Luke Emery. Both pilots had completed mandatory simulator training in the days before the flight, after returning from COVID-19 furlough.

Goldfinch Airlines wishes to convey its deepest condolences to the family and friends of the deceased pilots. Daniel Taylor joined Goldfinch Airlines in 2016 and had recently been promoted to captain. He was married with an infant daughter. First Officer Luke Emery had been working for Goldfinch Airlines since 2018. Both pilots had exemplary flight safety records.

As has been widely reported, flight GFA578, which was en route from Stansted to Glasgow, was a so-called 'ghost flight' with no passengers or cabin crew on board. In common with other airlines, Goldfinch Airlines has a contractual obligation to utilise landing slots at airports or lose its right to land. The requirement to maintain ghost flights has only recently been reintroduced after being temporarily suspended at the start of the COVID-19 pandemic.

It is impossible to know if things would have been different if the plane had been carrying passengers. What is certain is that flight GFA578 was in the air solely for the purpose of making an utterly pointless journey between Stansted and Glasgow.

My brother is haunted by the knowledge that it should have been him on the doomed flight. He tortures himself by wondering whether he could have prevented what happened or whether, like Daniel Taylor and Luke Emery, his life would have ended that day.

If this was a twisty psychological thriller then a reader might be presented with several questions – Who? How? Why? – and the answers revealed at key points during the story as the writer builds pace, intrigue and tension.

But however much I might wish this story was fiction, it is not. There is no unsolved crime for the reader to puzzle over. You already know who died and how. Very shortly you will know who was responsible. The only question this story concerns itself with is *why*. *Why* did flight GFA578 crash into a mountain, killing two men?

As a journalist, this question has consumed me for the last four years. I have thought of little else because not only was my brother supposed to have been on that plane but also, until eight months before he died, the pilot who replaced him on the flight had been my boyfriend.

My brother and I had known Luke – First Office Emery – since we were kids. Now, Luke was dead. Luke, who cracked jokes that should have been left behind in the playground, who would rather be an hour early than five minutes late, who was chronically messy and unfailingly kind, happy to listen to anyone who wanted to talk. Luke, who, since he was a small boy, had a habit of pinching his lower lip between his thumb and forefinger whenever he was thinking and a slow way of blinking that gave him the look of someone permanently on the edge of sleep. Luke with his red hair and freckles, his love of birthday cards with terrible puns, his revolting homebrewed beer and his not-so-secret obsession with *Strictly*.

Jamie and Luke had gone through school and university together, completed their flying training together, gone to cricket and rugby matches together, had numerous camping trips and been on holiday together, played five-a-side football on the same team. Jamie joined Goldfinch Airlines and a year later Luke left his previous airline and followed him. Three weeks before the crash, my brother had asked Luke to be his best man.

My relationship with Luke was more complicated. As teenagers, he had been my first boyfriend, my first kiss, my first everything. And I was his. But as we got older, our relationship evolved into one of those on-again/off-again situations until in 2018, surprising absolutely no one but ourselves, we decided it should become permanently on. And that's how it remained right up to the moment in January 2020 when I did something that hurt him so badly that, as lockdown loomed, Luke told me he wanted us to spend it apart. He said he wasn't sure he could forgive me, but I knew the separation wasn't permanent. How could it be? We were Luke and Carly. Carly and Luke. We'd be on again soon enough. Everyone knew that.

This is why I needed to understand what had happened. I had to find out for Luke, for his parents, for Jamie, for everyone who had known him. Most of all, though, I had to find out for me. I needed to know why he had died. And why I would never hear him say he forgave me.

In truth, though, that wasn't all. I had another motivation.

In 2020, I was one of the journalists responsible for the publication of a story which made national headlines. It broke during the first national lockdown and, aside from Covid, was the biggest news story for almost a week. I have to be careful about what I say. I can't mention the company involved by name because the litigation is still ongoing, but you'll probably know who I'm referring to when I say that my key source's 'recollections' were a complete fabrication. The backlash was huge. I was accused of inadequate and incompetent fact-checking. Of bringing my employer into disrepute. I was forced to leave my job, and my career as an investigative journalist – the only thing I'd ever wanted to do – seemed to be over.

Which is why I not only *wanted* to find out what had happened on board that plane, but I *needed* to find out. By investigating the story behind flight GFA578 I hoped I could begin to redeem my reputation. I would use the tragic deaths of the two pilots as the focal point for a series of articles about the requirement for airlines to fly entirely empty planes all over Europe. It wasn't the most earth-shattering story – certainly not on a par with the sort of reporting I'd been doing before – but if nothing else, I could try and shine a light on the catastrophic environmental impact of this ridiculous policy and at least I'd still be able to call myself a journalist.

I approached several publications but only the online climate-emergency journal *Planet Home* was interested and, with their kind permission, I have included short extracts from the series of articles they commissioned me to write (which can be found at www.planethome.org).

By the time I'd finished my investigations, I not only had many hours of recorded conversations but had come to realise that what lay beneath the tragedy of flight

GFA578 was a far darker and more terrifying tale than I could have possibly imagined at the outset.

It appeared that I had the makings of a book.

As a first attempt, I spent a couple of months making a misguided effort to fictionalise the story, changing names and situations, but the whole thing felt flat. It was a genuine case of truth being stranger than fiction. My next attempt was to transcribe the interviews word for word, but that didn't work either. Unedited transcribed conversations do not make for an engaging read: there were far too many repetitions, recollections of the same events, questions, prompts and clarifications.

I had been on the point of abandoning the project completely, deciding it was all too complicated to turn into something anyone might like to read, when I happened to go for drinks with a group of friends and found myself chatting to someone I hadn't met before. She was a curator at a small art gallery just off New Bond Street, and as she explained how she went about her job, selecting and arranging the artworks to form a narrative which she interpreted with catalogue notes, I realised I had the solution.

Rather than including hundreds of pages of transcripts, I instead would use them to create a coherent, fluent story, removing repetitions, incomplete sentences, dead ends and random conversational segues. You will find large stretches of this book read almost like a novel: scenes from life, if you will. This is entirely deliberate and was done with the consent of all concerned.

I selected only the most relevant, illuminating content to present in the form that you now hold in your hands: part reportage, part narrative. Other than where it was necessary for the story to make sense, the material appears in the same chronology as it was told to me, and where relevant, I have included news-clippings – although, as the details surrounding the plane crash itself are extremely well-documented online, I have kept these to a minimum.

I fact-checked everything as far as possible – I will not make that mistake a second time – but I should make clear that because significant parts of what happened took place behind closed doors, often with no witnesses, or witnesses who are no longer alive, or ones who were unwilling to speak to me, there are inevitably many things I have been unable to corroborate.

The only exception to my decision not to include transcripts is an interview I conducted with a forensic psychologist in April 2023. She received written permission from one of her clients to discuss their case history (including reproducing the excerpt from the psychological evaluation which precedes this introduction) and I am very grateful to Fiona Mackie for allowing me to include our conversation in its entirety.

Lastly, I have included my own notes, which are collated from notes and recordings that I made during the interviews and investigations and they will show how, initially, I couldn't see what was right in front of me. My desire to get to the bottom of this tragedy meant I allowed myself to get too close and, for a while, I became part of the story. I am prepared for the inevitable criticism that I have not adhered to acceptable journalistic standards.

However, this is not intended to be a piece of journalism and, as much as this book may read in parts as though it is a novel, and as much as you might come to hope it is, this is not a work of fiction.

Instead, it is a cautionary tale. The story of a family that, on the face of it, could be yours. A story in which you may even recognise elements of yourself. But at its heart is a monster. Very early on you will understand *who* the monster is, but until the end you may not understand *how* they did what they did, and even then, you may still ask yourself *why* they did what they did. This book is an attempt to expose how they, and so many others like them, systematically destroy the lives of those they are closest to, even as they hide in plain sight.

Carly Atherton
December 2024

Planet Home Article I

This is an extract from the first of a series of articles investigating 'ghost flights' written by Carly Atherton and published in the online journal Planet Home.

Last October I boarded a train from Euston in London bound for the Lake District. For each kilometre I travelled my carbon footprint was approximately 41 grams of CO_2 emissions, but had I made the same journey on a domestic airline, that figure would soar to 255 grams per kilometre.

I was heading to the northern tip of the Lake District National Park and the slopes of Big Crag, which boasts one of the highest peaks in England. A popular destination for climbers and hikers alike, Big Crag was thrust into the public consciousness on 9 September 2020 when an Airbus A320 smashed into the upper reaches of its south-east facing slope. The only two people on board – both pilots – died instantly.

I was on my way to visit the site of the crash. It was tragic that two lives had been lost, but although

I was thankful that there weren't more deaths, like many others I wanted to know why there were only two people on board flight GFA578. Why was a plane designed to carry 180 passengers flying empty? In the face of the climate emergency, what possible justification could there be for a pointless 600-kilometre flight from Stansted to Glasgow?

In this series of articles I shall be seeking to answer these questions by investigating the mendacious practices of the airport authorities who impose 'use it or lose it' policies on their landing slots, as well as the complicity of governments around Europe who have consistently failed to put an end to this scandal in the sky.

Notes

The inquest into the deaths of Captain Daniel Taylor and First Officer Luke Emery was opened in December 2020 for the purpose of formally confirming their identities, then adjourned to allow the investigators to do their work. It would not be reopened for almost seventeen months.

On 6 January 2021, as England entered its third national lockdown, my brother persuaded an engineer he was friendly with at Goldfinch Airlines to have a Zoom call with me. Before our conversation, I had to agree to two conditions. The first was that I wouldn't reveal the engineer's real name, so here I am calling him Anthony. The second was that I would tell no one what he was going to tell me until the data from the two black boxes on flight GFA578 had been analysed and made public.

On the three-way Zoom, my brother and I listened as Anthony explained how Airbus A320s transmit real-time reports to a maintenance operation centre. I hadn't realised that if a plane develops a fault during a flight the issue is reported simultaneously to both the pilots *and* the engineers on the ground. Anthony said he had been at work on 9 September 2020 and no faults had been reported by flight GFA578.

'There was absolutely nothing wrong with the plane,' he said. 'It was one hundred per cent serviceable.'

'How about if an engine fails and the plane plummets from the sky?' I asked. 'Surely there's not enough time for reports to be sent back?'

Anthony shook his head. 'Impossible. Firstly, if an engine fails, the plane will keep flying without any problem at all. Secondly, planes do not *plummet* from the sky because of some mechanical failure. They just don't. Thirdly, real-time *means* real-time. GFA578 was reporting itself as one hundred per cent serviceable – that's the terminology we use – until the moment it hit the mountain. There was nothing wrong with the aeroplane.'

'So what does that mean?' I asked.

Jamie said, 'That's what you need to find out, Carly. If there was nothing wrong with the plane –'

'Which there wasn't,' said Anthony.

'– which there wasn't,' Jamie continued, 'then something else caused the crash.'

'Why would a perfectly functioning plane hit a mountain?' I asked.

'My first thought was a bomb,' said Jamie.

'It wasn't a bomb,' Anthony said, and Jamie nodded – they'd obviously discussed this already.

'How do you know?' I asked.

'Because, as I said before, the plane was serviceable until the moment of impact. If there had been a bomb, there would have been a catastrophic failure at some point *before* impact.'

'So what else?' I asked. 'Why would a fully functioning plane fly into the side of a mountain?'

'The real-time data lets us know if there's anything

wrong with a plane – mechanical faults, software issues, that sort of thing,' Anthony said. 'The one thing it doesn't tell us is what the pilots are doing. That's the information recorded on the flight data recorder and the cockpit voice recorder, what you'd call the black boxes.'

I stared at Anthony through the laptop screen. I had a horrible feeling I knew what he was getting at. 'So ...?'

'So, we know there wasn't a mechanical failure and there wasn't a bomb. Which only leaves one alternative ...'

We looked at each other, and when I didn't say anything, he continued, 'That plane was deliberately flown into the mountain.'

I sat back in my chair.

'Fuck,' I said.

Jamie was looking down, away from the camera, and I thought he might be about to cry. I knew my brother was thinking of Luke. I was thinking about him too. I swallowed back my own tears. One of us had to hold it together. 'You really think that's what happened?'

Anthony nodded. 'I'm certain. It's not like there were many other planes flying that day, what with the Covid restrictions still in place, so I was monitoring the flight even more closely than I might have at other times.'

'Fuck,' I said again. 'So ...?'

'So,' Anthony said, answering the question I hadn't asked, 'either someone else on board made them do it, which could be possible –'

'But very unlikely,' Jamie said, looking up.

'Why's that?' I asked.

'Because it would mean someone having to evade airport security, stow away on board, force their way into the cockpit through a door that cannot be opened by

anyone except the pilots and make one of them deliberately crash the plane, all without air traffic control having
any idea what was going on.' My brother shook his head.
'I don't see it.'

'I agree,' said Anthony. 'I don't believe it either.'

'So what did happen?' I said.

'One of the pilots deliberately flew into the mountain,'
Anthony said.

Before I could say anything, my brother leaned forward,
his face filling my laptop screen. We spoke at the same
time. 'It wasn't Luke.'

Anyone who knew Luke knew it was inconceivable
that he would have taken his own life. *I'd* seen him at his
lowest. *I'd* been the reason he'd been down there. And,
sure, he was sad, really sad and upset and angry, but never
once had he shown any sign that he might do something
like that.

But if Luke wasn't responsible, that meant Daniel
Taylor – the captain of the aeroplane and father of a young
daughter – had deliberately killed himself and murdered
Luke.

And, until the data from the black boxes was released,
I was the only journalist to know this. I needed a story
and here it was.

This was the story that would get my career back on
track.

The idea of deliberately flying an aeroplane into a
mountain is terrifying. I couldn't even begin to imagine
what sort of person would be capable of doing something
like that. Jamie had flown with Daniel Taylor on many
occasions, and while he described him as friendly, he

didn't consider him a friend. On the occasions they were away overnight, Daniel would always refuse – albeit politely – to join the rest of the flight crew for dinner, preferring instead to eat alone in his room.

My starting point had to be Daniel Taylor's family. I approached his widow, Grace, but she refused to talk to me, as did his father, which is when I contacted Daniel's sister. She had no hesitation in agreeing to meet me, and shortly after the final lockdown restrictions were lifted I arranged to meet Izzy Taylor in a coffee shop near her father's house in Richmond.

I was already seated at a table when she arrived, and my first sight of her was a well-dressed woman standing outside the café checking her reflection in the window, smoothing down her coat and flicking perfectly groomed hair back over her shoulders, before pushing the door open and striding in. Once I'd introduced myself, she removed the coat to reveal a gorgeous cornflower-blue wrap dress, spotless suede pumps and a handbag costing more money than I made in months. She looked considerably younger than her thirty-six years. Right from the beginning, I understood she was someone who did not like being ignored.

She also had an intensity about her. Her speech was rapid and energetic, and I found myself looking down at my notebook more than was necessary in order to give myself a break from maintaining eye contact with her.

Izzy was very friendly towards me in our first meeting, mentioning that she knew my brother was a pilot for Goldfinch Airlines – apparently she had found a picture on social media of me with Jamie in his pilot's uniform.

Over the next few weeks I met Izzy several times, always in the same coffee shop. During those sessions

– and all the ones that followed – I kept my promise to Anthony and did not tell her, or anyone else, that it was almost certain that her brother had deliberately crashed the plane. Instead, I asked Izzy to tell me about her childhood, what life had been like at home, her relationship with her parents and, more particularly, with her younger brother Daniel.

Her memories are collated in the following section.

Izzy's Story

1984–1992

1.

On 4 December 1984, when I was three months old, my parents moved into 72 Silver Street and for the next eighteen years that's where I lived, on the edge of Richmond in south-west London, in a typical 1930s house dominated by large bay windows and spacious, airy rooms.

I'd classify my family as well-off but not rich, certainly not as rich as I would have liked. At the time of my birth my father – a civil engineer, tall, handsome, athletic (he played rugby at county level) – had recently started working for a large construction company. My mother, a nurse, was also tall, also athletic (tennis was her thing), and at the time of our move into Silver Street she was on maternity leave. She wouldn't return to work until my brother and I were both at school.

My earliest memory is of lying in the garden squinting up at an expanse of blue sky. Our house was directly under the flight path into Heathrow and I found it thrilling how the planes appeared above the box hedge at the bottom of the garden, thundering over my head before disappearing out of sight beyond the rooftops on the opposite side of the road. I haven't really considered it before, but it wouldn't be unreasonable to say my life to date has been framed by aeroplanes.

When I think about those first few years before Danny
was born, I remember them as an idyll of only-childness.
Years later, I found out there had been another baby
before me. Daisy lived for sixty-seven days before she
stopped breathing. I can't imagine having an older sister
and I'm not at all sure I would have liked being the second
child. As it was, I was all the more precious to my parents
for surviving when Daisy had not.

One of my mother's nicknames for me was *DoubleP*,
by which she meant not only precious but also precocious. I hit all the usual milestones early, which I know
because they are recorded in my mother's rather childish
handwriting in a pink book with 'Baby's First ...' picked
out in white on the front. I rolled over at four months,
sat up at six, crawled at eight, walked at eleven. When I
began talking at ten months old I immediately spoke in
full sentences and according to my father my first words
were 'I am Izzy'. None of this surprises me. I have taken
several IQ tests and they all rate me as highly gifted/
borderline genius.

Intelligent as my parents both were, there is no doubt
they were at a loss as to how to handle a daughter with
such prodigious talents. I would often look up from a
book or take a break from playing with my toys to find
one or other of them staring at me, although their eyes
would flick away as soon as they saw me looking. There
were whispered conversations behind closed doors, even a
doctor whom they took me to, although that was later on.

Their decision to have another child was primarily for
my benefit – they hoped my sibling would be as gifted as
me and we would be company for each other. Although
Danny didn't really have a chance of matching up to my

talents, it is certainly true that I was his best friend, right up until the time his plane hit the mountain.

Between Danny and I there had been another pregnancy, although I didn't know about it until it was over. I wandered into the bathroom one afternoon to find my mother lying on the floor, shoulders wedged in the space between the toilet and the bath, pants round her ankles, legs slicked with blood. She was crying and snuffled, 'Izzy, darling, go and watch television,' but I stayed where I was. She shouted at me to go away, which was curious because my mother usually wanted me near her – she was forever stroking my hair, covering my face with kisses, squeezing me so tight it hurt. In any case, I didn't move.

Eventually Mum heaved herself off the floor, holding onto the side of the bath for support, and ineffectually rubbed her legs with a towel. She wouldn't look at me, or talk to me, or stop crying. She called my father at work and sobbed her way through enough words to ensure he arrived home as she was being bundled into the back of an ambulance. I was three years old and I can honestly say watching the ambulance turn out of Silver Street carrying my mother away from me was the only time in my entire life I have ever experienced fear. I'm certain it's because the miscarriage got mixed up in my head with the dead fox.

A few days before I found Mum bleeding on the bathroom floor, she and I had been on our way to the local playground. It wasn't far from our house and I used our daily walk to practise my counting – fifty-two steps to the end of our street, turn the corner, thirty-seven steps, cross the road, turn again, and so on. On that particular day, I'd only counted up to forty-one when I saw the fox in the gutter. His eyes were open and his back legs were a bloody mangled mess but his fur was a beautiful deep orange which begged to be touched. I pulled away from my mother's grasp and knelt on the pavement, reaching my hand out.

'Izzy! No!' my mother shrieked. 'Don't touch that thing.' She picked me up.

'I want to stroke it,' I said, as calmly as my dignity would allow, from my position hoisted around my mother's waist.

'Foxes are dirty,' Mum said. 'Riddled with fleas.'

'Why isn't it moving?' I asked.

'It's having a lovely rest,' she replied, but I knew there was more to it than that. Mum marched along the pavement, still carrying me, and after I'd finished playing in the park, we took a different route home.

By bedtime on the day of the miscarriage when Mum still wasn't home, I asked Dad where she was and he said she had gone away for a day or two to have a 'lovely rest'. I understood my mother was never coming home. She was in the gutter with the fox.

I was mistaken, because less than forty-eight hours later my mother did come home. And very soon afterwards, she was pregnant again.

My parents must have read books about preparing a first child for the birth of a second because they threw themselves into readying me for sisterhood. On a daily basis I was encouraged to talk to 'the bump' so it would 'know you're its big sister'. When the kicking started, my hands were forcibly clamped to my mother's stomach to 'feel your baby brother or sister saying hello to you'. When my parents found out they were having a boy the messaging became even more fervent: 'your baby brother is going to be so excited to meet you, Izzy' and 'your baby brother loves you so much, Izzy'. All of which meant that long before Danny took his first breath, it was abundantly clear to me he was *mine. My* brother, *my* baby, *mine, mine, mine.*

I chose his name. My parents presented their proposals and I vetoed several I couldn't pronounce – they particularly liked Stuart but I hated the feel of it in my mouth. Daniel – Danny – was on their list and once I'd heard that name I wasn't interested in any others. *Danny,* I whispered to my mother's stomach, *Danny, my brother, my Danny, my baby.*

He was born on 19 September 1988, two weeks after my fourth birthday. Nan came to look after me. She suffered no fools and her favourite activities were bridge (she had a reputation as a card shark), drinking gin gimlets (once she started drinking, she would only stop when the gin ran out), flirting with men (regardless of their relationship status) and lying.

For Nan, lying was akin to performance art. She was inordinately proud of her talent and would regularly give me tips on perfecting deceit, such as: for maximum *believability* always include some truths with the lies; for maximum *fun*, push your lies right to the brink of credibility and peer into the abyss of impossibility; and if you're challenged on a lie, go on the counter-attack, hard and fast.

On one notable occasion Nan was forced to make an exception to this last rule. She was born on 31 December 1928, but she couldn't bear anyone to know her real age. By the time I was born in 1984, although she was actually fifty-five, she would swear blind she was in her 'late forties', which is where she remained for several more years.

On the final day of 1988, Nan turned sixty and shortly thereafter tried claim her state pension. Unfortunately, because she had consistently lied about her age on so many forms and to so many employers over the years, the Department of Social Security did not recognise her true age, although they did find multiple conflicting records which variously listed her as fifty-seven, fifty-two and forty-nine. Not one record listed her as sixty. She was, the Department insisted, too young to be eligible for a pension. Nan was furious at being denied what was legitimately hers, and her fury was provoked even further when she had to produce, at her own expense, an official copy of her birth certificate and present herself to a civil servant at an office in Croydon to confirm she really was, horror of horrors, sixty years old.

My nan was sharp-tongued but funny with it. Years before I was born, my grandfather died when some scaffolding collapsed as he was coming out of the building where he worked. Nan revelled in recounting the story of his untimely death, then when her audience were stumbling through their condolences she would say, 'He'd have been delighted to die like that – he always loved heavy metal,' then cackle in their faces like a mad woman.

I was Nan's favourite and she was shameless about it: Danny barely existed as far as she was concerned. She treated me as an equal, never talked down to me and when we were together she would ask my opinion on all sorts of things, always contemplating my answers with the utmost seriousness.

'Now then, Izzy, I've got a date with Derek from bridge club,' Nan might say, after describing Derek as lumpy, sweaty and rich. 'What do we think? Green dress or navy trouser suit?' Or, on another occasion, 'I'm considering joining Slimming World, but it'll mean laying off the chocolate. Is it a sacrifice worth making?' We debated at length whether she should accept an offer from Pauline (buxom, snobbish, desperate) to share a cabin with her on a cruise around the Norwegian fjords. 'The most important question,' Nan said, 'is whether I can manage six days in confined quarters with her. What do you think, Izzy?'

These were weighty matters for an almost-four-year-old and I gave them due consideration before proffering my advice (in the above cases: navy trouser suit, no it's not and no you can't). The describe-a-person-in-three-words game was also Nan's invention but we only played it when we were alone because my parents had told Nan she was encouraging me to be superficial in my opinions of other people. Nan said the three words she would use to describe *that* attitude were predictable, unimaginative and humourless and we carried on playing the game.

On the day Danny was born, my mother had dropped me off at nursery as usual, but it was Nan who was waiting for me at the end of the day.

'How was nursery?' Nan asked.

I shrugged. Nursery had been nursery. Right from the start I had never minded going and had never cried when I was left. The other children learned very quickly to let me have first choice of toys, to allow me to select the games we played and take the best position on the carpet at story time. Danny, by contrast, sobbed like a baby every day for weeks when it was his turn to go to nursery. It's funny how different we were.

'Can you guess why it's me picking you up today?' Nan asked.

'My Danny has been born,' I said.

'That's my girl, sharp as a tack,' Nan said. 'Shall we go and meet your baby brother?'

At the hospital, my parents were laughing and smiling and Dad's cheeks were a bit wet. Mum held her arms out towards me but I ignored her.

'Where's my baby?' I asked and all three of them laughed.

I didn't understand the joke so I said again, calmly and politely, 'Where's my baby?'

Dad put his hand on the bassinet beside the bed.

'Danny's in here,' he said but I was too short to see in, so Dad lifted me onto the chair. My baby brother was lying on a blue mattress wrapped in a white blanket. He was wearing a woolly hat and all I could see were puffy red cheeks and a huge forehead. His eyes were tight shut and it struck me how unlikely it was that this unappealing, scrunched-up object would provide me with the lifelong companionship I'd been promised.

'Well, Izzy,' said Mum, 'say hello to Danny.'

I looked around. All of them – Mum, Dad and Nan – were staring at me, waiting.

I looked back at the baby, and at precisely that moment he opened his eyes. Apparently newborn babies can't focus on faces but that's wrong because Danny looked straight at me and I looked straight back at him.

Tiny.

Vulnerable.

Mine.

2.

Throughout our childhood, there was a picture of me and Danny stuck to the top left corner of the fridge door. I was four when the photo was taken and out of the two of us I was always the most striking, never going through a 'puppy fat' stage. To give Mum her due, she always dressed me well, and in my diaphanous pink sundress I'm already lithe and long-limbed, strawberry-blonde curls framing my pretty heart-shaped face.

I've been told people find my gaze very direct – and I was certainly confronting the camera head-on in that photo. I was sitting on the sofa and Danny, who would have been about six months old, was in my lap. In the picture, although I was staring at the camera, Danny – *my* Danny – was staring at me. Even in my brother's first few months, I had assumed my most important role: my brother looking to me for protection while I looked defiantly outwards, ready to fight anyone who came too close.

He wasn't an attractive baby – face scrunched up, hardly any hair, chubby arms waving around – but Danny the baby was exactly the same as Danny the man: devoted to me. Right from the beginning, we only needed each other. Sure, our parents fed and clothed us, kept us healthy, put a roof over our heads, but in all other respects,

we were self-sufficient, best friends, as close as any siblings
can be. I was his big sister, and he was my little brother.

My parents' friends used to comment on how *adorable*
it was to see Danny and I together. It was a refrain I never
tired of hearing, but the truth was that for the first year or
so of his life, my brother was quite boring. He just lay
around, not doing much other than sleeping and eating
and indulging in a lot of crying. So much crying.

Once my brother could walk, I began to get more enjoy-
ment from our relationship. Sometimes, I would run away
from him, fast, so he couldn't keep up, or I'd hide from
him. I always enjoyed hearing him calling my name with
his cute baby lisp: *Ithy, Ithy,* and the catch in his voice as
the tears started. *Ithy. Ithy.* It was the sound of his love for
me, although our mother never understood that.

'It's not nice, Izzy,' she would say. 'You can hear how
upset he is.'

She always seemed determined to twist Danny's and
my relationship, always imputing bad intentions to the
games we played. For example, there was a particular
favourite involving a one-eared teddy bear called Biff. Biff
went everywhere with Danny, who became hysterical if
Biff was ever misplaced. Danny and I used to spend hours
playing a game called Where Is Biff? There were limitless
versions of the game: me hiding Biff in cupboards, me
throwing Biff into bushes in the garden, me trying to flush
Biff down the toilet, but probably our favourite version of
all was the simplest one, which involved me putting Biff
on a shelf just out of Danny's reach. My brother would
marshal his limited powers of concentration, digging his
little toes into the carpet, swaying unsteadily, trying to get
purchase as he reached as high as he could, curling and

uncurling his chubby fingers, desperately trying and failing to rescue Biff.

On one unfortunate occasion, Danny overbalanced and fell, hitting his chin on the bookshelf where I'd put Biff. He started howling and Mum came running into the room.

'What have you done now?' she asked me, unfairly, since I wasn't the one bleeding all over the carpet. She pulled Danny into her lap and rubbed his back in small circles, trying to calm him down.

Later, while Danny was having a nap, I sat outside my parents' bedroom listening to Mum on the phone to her best friend Liz. I always knew when my mother was talking to Liz because she would leave me in front of the television, go upstairs and shut the bedroom door. If I stayed where she left me, I couldn't hear anything, but if I waited a minute then followed her upstairs, I could hear her just fine, and by the time I settled myself outside their room, Mum was already in full flow.

Usually, I enjoyed hearing her talk about me. The words she used most often were: precocious, clever and independent. But sometimes, she said things which weren't as positive and that particular day she was telling Liz how I was a tease and unkind.

'I worry her behaviour is getting worse,' she was saying. 'But Roger refuses to see it.'

There was silence for a minute, presumably while Liz managed to get a word in edgeways, then Mum was off again, sighing dramatically and saying, 'Izzy behaves as if she's much older. You know how self-reliant she is. I mean, I'm all for raising an independent kid, but every now and again it would be nice to feel like she needs me.'

Across the hallway, I heard the hiccupping cry which signalled Danny was waking up. Naptime was over, and my mother's conversation was coming to an end.

Mum was determined to twist everything. She should have been *thanking* me not criticising me. After all, Danny *was* sensitive and pliable and ripe for being walked all over. I couldn't bear the thought of him leaving himself open to being hurt and upset once the time came for him to venture from the safety of our home, and in the absence of my parents doing anything to help him, I took it upon myself to teach him some life lessons. That game with Biff? Not everything my brother wanted would be within easy reach. Sometimes he would have to work for things, and sometimes he might not get what he wanted. That's what the game was about.

The last thing Mum said to Liz before she hung up was, 'Yes, you're right, I'll talk to Roger this evening. Convince him we need to set some clear boundaries for Izzy.'

I beat Mum to it. That evening, when Dad came home from work, I was waiting on the doorstep. I timed it to perfection so my tears started flowing just as he pushed open the wrought-iron gate.

'Izzy, sweetheart,' Dad said. 'What's the matter?'

I turned up the tears and shook my head, indicating that I was too upset to speak.

Dad crouched down so he was level with me and held out his arms. 'Come on, chicken,' he said. 'What's the matter?'

I stepped forward and let him hug me. I sniffed once or twice for good effect.

'There's a good girl,' he said. 'What's all this about then?'

I stepped back to ensure he had a good view of my stricken expression and the tears caught fetchingly on my eyelashes. 'Mummy told Auntie Liz I was a bad girl,' I said.

'Did she?' he asked. '*Has* my little chicken been naughty?'

'No,' I said, squeezing out a few more tears. 'I was tidying up our toys, mine and Danny's. I was trying to *help* Mummy, but then she was on the phone to Auntie Liz and she told her I was bad.'

Dad frowned and pressed his lips together. 'I see,' he said. 'Well, let's go and talk to Mummy, shall we? Sort this out.'

He scooped me up in his arms and carried me into the house. Mum came into the hallway and I buried my face in Dad's neck. Before my mother could say anything, Dad said, 'I found a very upset little chicken on the doorstep. Apparently, she overheard a conversation between you and Liz.'

I turned to regard my mother from the lofty heights of Dad's arms and sniffled a bit.

'Danny cut his chin badly this afternoon,' Mum said.

'It's all been going on here,' said Dad, and I let him give me a kiss on the cheek. He looked at Mum. 'Is the little man OK?'

'He'll be fine. I told him you'd go up and tuck him in.'

'Of course I will, but what about this one?' he said, tugging gently on my ponytail.

'Danny fell over because Izzy had deliberately put Biff on a shelf which was too high for Danny to reach.'

Dad smoothed my hair. 'I think our little chicken was only trying to help you tidy up.'

Mum shook her head. 'You weren't here, Roger.'

Dad kissed my cheek again, then lowered me to the floor, where I reached for his hand, allowing myself a small sob.

'I'm going to go up and say goodnight to our little man, Izzy,' Dad said. 'Do you want to come upstairs with me? Or stay down here with grumpy Mummy?'

Later that evening, after I'd gone to bed, I heard Mum and Dad doing the shouting-not-shouting thing they did when they didn't want me to know they were angry with each other. Our house had a staircase with a ninety-degree turn halfway up, which meant if I sat on the bottom stair of the top half, I could hear everything from downstairs, but no one could see me. By the time I got into position, their argument had already assumed a pattern I was familiar with. Much of what they said was about boundaries. Mum would tell Dad what they needed to do was *set boundaries* for me (which made me sound like a flock of sheep) whereas Dad said I was only *testing the boundaries*, like all kids. Then Mum told Dad he *indulged* me far too much, which Dad said was a ridiculous thing to say because he *refused to baby* me. I was a *very bright girl*, he said, and I needed *stimulation*, not *cosseting*.

'What Izzy *needs*,' Mum said, 'is consistent parenting. And to understand that her actions have consequences.'

Dad refused to be drawn in. 'As I see it, Sarah, poor Izzy was really upset earlier because she heard what you'd been saying about her.'

Then they started on about boundaries again and, confident I wasn't going to miss anything important, I went to bed.

*

As Danny got older, I tried to pass on other life skills to him too, such as showing him where Dad kept an old ice-cream tub into which he dumped his loose change each evening; and how important it was to be selective with the coins we took (too many too frequently and Dad might realise we were helping ourselves to his money); and the art of using those coins to buy a sufficient amount of low-value sweets at the corner shop so as not to arouse suspicion that our pockets were bulging with the higher-value sweets which we really wanted. In other words, the usual sort of stuff which an older sister might be expected to pass on to her younger sibling – in addition, of course, to making sure Danny knew that our relationship, his and mine, would always be the most important relationship of his life.

'Mum won't always be here,' I told him one Sunday afternoon as we were watching *Aladdin* on video for the gazillionth time while our parents drank wine in the garden.

Danny didn't react. He was repeating Princess Jasmine's dialogue, which he had memorised, so I said again, more loudly, 'Listen, Danny, it's important. Mum won't always be here.'

He dragged his attention away from the screen long enough to say, 'I know. Mummy's going to go to work, like Daddy.'

'That's not what I'm talking about, Danny.'

I paused the film and in protest Danny kicked his little heels against the base of the sofa in the way which always made Mum lecture him about *respecting the furniture*.

'You know Mum hates you kicking the sofa, Danny. But soon you won't need to worry about that because she is going to get sick and leave us. She got sick before but then she came back to give me a brother. Next time she leaves, she won't come back.'

I had his attention now, because his eyes filled with tears and he sniffled a bit before saying, 'Where's she going?'

I shrugged. 'She'll be dead, so in the ground, I guess. Then it'll just be you and me.'

'You, me *and* Daddy?' he said, hopefully.

'When mummies go, daddies usually leave too,' I said, although I was hazy on the details.

Danny's tears began to plop onto the sofa. Mum would probably think that wasn't respecting the furniture either.

'I don't want Mummy to go,' he managed to say through trembling lips. 'Who will look after me?'

'I will, Danny,' I said. 'I'll always be here for you. You'll always have your big sister.'

He didn't appear to be as immediately reassured by this as he should have been. '*When* is Mummy going?'

I shrugged. 'Last time there was a lot of blood. That's the sign and I expect it will happen quite soon.'

Some people might consider this wasn't the kindest thing for me to be telling such a sensitive little boy, but I was only a kid myself – a fact which everyone often seemed to forget – and I had to work with the limited information available to me. If Danny spent his early childhood in the mistaken belief that our mother was about to die at any moment, then frankly you have to blame my parents for not explaining the whole miscarriage thing more clearly to me.

In any case, the effect was to bring Danny and I even closer together. I was the point of certainty around which my brother's life revolved. I was the one who would always be there for him and, for all of his thirty-one years, the only person he would ever need.

3.

Filing into assembly on the first day of school, I felt like a conductor who had finally found her orchestra. Entertaining myself with my family had become boring and I was ready for new challenges. I needed more variety in my instruments, as it were, and school provided them in abundance.

For the first couple of years, I confined my attentions to my classmates, honing my talents for engendering rifts between erstwhile best friends. I made it my business to be well-liked and affable, and very rarely did anyone suspect my machinations had anything to do with their volatile and often devastating relationships. I also spent time getting the measure of how things worked in the school, and by the time we began Year 3 I was ready to set my sights higher up the scholarly food chain.

Our teacher, Mr Brown, was tall, energetic and hairy. A mass of wiry blond coils sprung from his head, hairs peered over the top of his collar, crawled over his knuckles, emerged from his cuffs. He even wore hairy jumpers when it was cold, the sort of horribly scratchy things my grandmother who wasn't Nan used to knit for me. I would guess Mr Brown had been teaching for no more than a year or two when he became our teacher. Even to us seven-year-olds he didn't seem very old, although that was at least partly due to his relentless enthusiasm. He would begin each day by clapping his hands and saying, 'Girls and boys, boys and girls, how wonderful it is to see you all looking so bright and cheery this morning,' and somehow he managed to keep up this level of bonhomie throughout the day, circulating around the class like a butler among his underlings, giving a word of encouragement here, a pat on the arm there, a 'well done' over here and a light touch on the head over there.

I worked out early in my school career that the most effective way to navigate this phase of my life was to do as I was told. Not, you understand, because I had any innate desire to be *good*, but being compliant meant I would be awarded the coveted stickers which were handed out to well-behaved children. I didn't care about the stickers themselves, of course, which were hideous primary-coloured stars, but they were stuck onto a class chart and the accumulation of sufficient stars meant the granting of privileges. I wanted those privileges.

Privileges included being chosen to leave class to collect more stationery, or art supplies, or stacks of photocopying from the school office. Or being excused from class entirely in order to help show prospective parents and their offspring around the school. Privileges meant access to parts of the school where other children didn't go, when the corridors were deserted and the teachers all busy. Privileges meant ample opportunity to lurk unseen in places where I wasn't intended to lurk and garner information which wasn't meant for my ears. Gossip about poor Mrs Reed and her *terrible* divorce, for example. Or how Mr Dobson had applied for a head-teacher post and the only person who was surprised when he didn't get the job was Mr Dobson himself.

Many times I never found any reason to deploy the information I gathered – in fact, I often didn't fully understand it – but knowledge is power, and I made it my business to ensure that very little went on at the school that I didn't know about.

By Year 3, then, I was well aware of the connection between exemplary behaviour, stickers and privileges and had successfully garnered myself a reputation for being unfailingly polite, overtly considerate of others and, of course, always coming top in tests.

Each Friday, right after lunch, we had Mr Brown's Quiz of the Week. I suppose it must have taken him quite some time to put together thirty age-appropriate questions about subjects ranging from current affairs (*Who is the president of the United States?* So easy. Clinton, of course, although three of the boys actually answered 'daddy') to geography (*What's the capital of France?* A surprising number of idiots didn't know it was Paris) to animals (*Name three animals which lay eggs.* Give me strength). Mr Brown's Quiz of the Week was the perfect vehicle for me to demonstrate my superior intelligence, and without fail I always came top, receiving two stickers by way of reward. For all that I had no strong feelings about Mr Brown, what's indisputable is that I was his star pupil.

The turning point in our relationship came one Friday when it transpired Mr Brown had, for the first time, failed to put together a quiz. While I had been loitering outside the office waiting to collect swimming-lesson permission slips, I overheard a conversation about how

Mr Brown's mother was seriously ill and he was doing a lot of driving back and forth to visit her. Still. That was no excuse. His Quiz of the Week was my highlight of the week, my opportunity to showcase my intellect to my fellow seven- and eight-year-olds and add to my haul of stickers in the process.

Mr Brown announced that instead of our weekly quiz we were going to watch a film about dinosaurs. He said this as if it was some sort of special treat, and judging by their cheering, the rest of the class appeared to be quite happy about this turn of events.

'What about the Quiz of the Week?' I asked Mr Brown, calmly and politely.

'We'll have a quiz next week, Izzy,' he said.

'I would like to do the Quiz of the Week today,' I replied, still calmly, still politely.

'I'm sorry, Izzy,' Mr Brown said, putting his hand on my shoulder. I turned my head and stared at his fingertips, which were only millimetres from my teeth.

He removed his hand. 'I didn't have time to write a quiz this week,' he said. 'Next week, I promise. But you'll enjoy the film, it's a good one.'

Needless to say, I didn't enjoy the film. I didn't even watch the film. I couldn't see the stupid film through my fury. How dare Mr Brown deny me the opportunity to collect another two stickers? He had stolen those stickers from me.

The whole incident was an important lesson. Leviticus nailed it: an eye for an eye, a tooth for a tooth. None of this 'show the other cheek' bullshit. If you hurt me, I'll hurt you. If I am wronged, my need for justice tastes bitter, like the undiluted lime cordial in Nan's gin gimlets.

Not right away, of course, because where's the fun in that? No. If you hurt me then I shall cherish the wrong you've done me. I'll feed it, nurture it, allow it to flourish, then, when you least expect it, when you have probably forgotten you ever crossed me, *then* I'll serve my own particular brand of justice.

By the time the credits rolled on the film, my fury was gone. Instead, I was working on a plan to redress the wrong which Mr Brown had done me.

Touching, I'd worked out, was both a good thing and a bad thing.

For example, when my mother held her arms out and said, 'Cuddle time,' it meant she wanted to be touched. And if I gave her what she wanted, then she was inevitably more amenable to giving me what I wanted. But if I ignored her, or said 'I don't want to cuddle you,' she would scrunch up her face in a way that meant she was sad and wouldn't let me stay up for an extra half hour of TV after Danny had gone to bed. In fact, it was one of the very first things I ever learned: giving my mother cuddles when she wanted them was a sure-fire way of being able to do more of what I wanted.

I was encouraged to do other touching also considered good touching by my parents. For example, whenever Danny toddled over to me and flung his arms around me, which he did several times a day, Mum and Dad would laugh and smile and talk like babies: 'Aww, wook how your Danny woves you,' and other such nonsense. Since Danny belonged to me, I tolerated his touching, although I wouldn't let his face, almost always covered in dried bits of leftover food, get too close to mine.

I also tolerated giving Nan a kiss on the cheek because, more often than not, it would be followed by her slipping me a coin 'for your money box'. Always mindful of her instruction to 'take whatever you can' from people, on the occasions when she didn't hand over money, I would put out my hand and wait, calmly and politely.

'You, missy, are going to be trouble when you're older,' Nan would say, laughing and reaching for her purse.

But then there was 'bad touching'. I had never actually been told what exactly it entailed, but I had put together enough bits and pieces of information by the time I started school to understand that no one should be touching me without my permission.

At the end of my first day, I came home and recited a list of unwanted touchings: a boy called Mikey had touched my foot with his when we were sitting down for story time, Olivia had bumped my elbow with hers when we were eating lunch, Suzie P had tried to hold my hand at break time and Suzie L, who had the longest hair of everyone in the class, had allowed some of it to brush my arm when we were rifling through the toy box.

'Honey,' Mum said, 'you'll have to get used to that sort of thing. It's going to happen when you're around other kids. You just tell me if any grown-up does it. OK?'

OK, I thought. How interesting. Children touching me was acceptable – even though I didn't particularly like Mikey or Olivia or Suzie P or Suzie L – but adults touching me was not.

I came by another significant piece of intelligence during one of my parents' frequent dinner parties.

I don't remember a time when I didn't eavesdrop on their dinner parties from the bend on the stairs. After all, if they didn't expect me to listen, they shouldn't have invited people round. On this particular occasion, the conversation had been even duller than usual, and I was about to give up for the night and take myself back to my bedroom when someone said, 'What about Darren Patterson, then?'

There was a brief silence, then a jumble of voices.

'I heard the police are involved.'

'They're saying he's been at it for years.'

'I can't believe it …'

'A rugby coach touching boys in the shower. It's disgusting.'

'Let's hope they throw the book at him …'

'And throw away the key.'

'You know his wife's left him?'

'Hardly surprising – I mean, would you stay with him?'

'Those poor boys. It makes me sick.' That last comment was from my dad.

Although I didn't really understand what exactly Darren Patterson had done, one thing was clear: certain touching, bad touching, could have interesting consequences.

Like a maestro rehearsing her orchestra, I needed to get everyone playing from the same score before I delivered justice to Mr Brown.

The first step was to get Abigail Pritchard to start seeing things in a certain way. I chose Abigail because she was considered the prettiest girl in the class. She had recently announced she was in love with Prince Eric and she would be marrying him when she was older. For any lucky individuals who don't happen to know who he is,

Prince Eric is the 'hero' from *A Little Mermaid*, which as far as I was concerned was a stupid cartoon. However, back then some of the girls in my class considered the film a sort of manual for life and Abigail Pritchard was one of a gang of 'Ariels' who spent every break time marauding around the playground, competing to exhibit the greatest knowledge of Prince Eric.

Most of these girls had toy Ariels, but very few had a Prince Eric – presumably their parents drew the line at spending money on a plastic lantern-jawed wastrel – and I happened to know Abigail did not possess a Prince Eric but desperately wanted one. I also knew Olivia *did* have a Prince Eric because she often brought him to school, although, because of the 'no personal toys in school' rule, Eric spent his days hidden in the pocket of Olivia's coat. It was easy enough for me to take a brief diversion on my way to collect some photocopying, pop into the cloakroom and move him from Olivia's pocket to mine.

First step accomplished.

Olivia made a bit of a fuss when she realised her prince was missing, but because Mrs Philips (our headmistress, who was a martyr to her slipped disc, whatever that was) was so strict about the 'no personal toys in school' rule, Olivia was too scared to report Eric as missing.

I waited several days before making my next move, then one break time, I sauntered over to Abigail.

'Hi, Abigail,' I said. 'My nan gave me this but I don't want it and I thought you might like it.'

I brandished Prince Eric with a flourish.

'Oooooh,' she said, practically squealing. 'Really? I can have him?'

'I thought you might need cheering up,' I said.

She was already reaching greedily for her prince, but when I said that, she paused, arm outstretched, looking at me blankly. 'Why do I need cheering up?' she asked.

'Because of what Mr Brown did to you this morning.'

Again the blank look. She really was stupid.

'You know,' I said. I lowered my voice. 'He *touched* you.'

She frowned, trying to recall our teacher's transgression.

'My mum has always said I should tell her if an adult *touches* me,' I said. 'Doesn't your mum say the same?'

Abigail nodded.

'Mr Brown put his hand on your shoulder after register,' I continued. 'And he did it again when we were doing our times tables. And he touched the top of your head right before break time.'

Abigail nodded again, but she seemed a bit uncertain. I obviously needed to spell it out.

'I've been watching him,' I said. 'I know he touches you a lot. He shouldn't touch you, Abigail. I'll go with you if you want to tell Mrs Phillips.'

Of course it was never going to be that simple and I was pleased, really, when Abigail simply shrugged and reached for Eric, pressing the plastic doll close to her chest.

Over the next few days, I told all the girls in the class about how upset Abigail was because of Mr Brown *touching* her. It became the main topic of conversation at break time; people gathered around Abigail and recounted all the *touching* which they had seen him inflict on her. Not to be outdone, some of the other girls started saying he was *touching* them too, and Abigail, never the most robust child anyway, became more and more miserable, until by the end of the week, she had stopped smiling altogether.

Finally, rehearsals were over, my orchestra was tuned, the performance could begin.

We were doing maths. I had finished the questions Mr Brown had set and was twisted round a little in my seat, staring at Abigail, something I'd started to do a few days earlier.

'Why are you always looking at me in class?' she'd asked me.

'I'm making sure he doesn't *touch* you,' I replied.

Following my lead, several others had also started to keep their gaze fixed on Abigail and all the attention made her very uncomfortable, despite our reassurance we were simply protecting her, making sure *he* didn't do any *touching*.

Abigail was rubbish at maths, at everything actually, and on top of the pressure of all the attention, she was also clearly finding the questions difficult. A tear slipped down one beautiful cheek, followed by another. This was perfect, I couldn't have planned it better. Mr Brown was doing his customary circulation of the class and noticed her tears almost immediately.

He bent over a little, looking at her work. 'Oh dear, Abigail,' he said, 'don't cry.'

He lifted his hand and rested his hairy knuckles lightly on her shoulder. He patted her once, twice.

Abigail stood up so fast her chair tipped over backwards. 'You *touched* me,' she said. Then, taking a big breath she screamed, 'You. *Touched*. Me,' and ran out of the room.

It was magnificent. A virtuoso performance.

From that point on, everything fell into place.

Mrs Potter, a Year 6 teacher, came to our classroom a few minutes later and spoke to Mr Brown. Annoyingly, I couldn't hear what she said, but Mr Brown left the classroom immediately, and Mrs Potter continued our lesson.

About an hour later, I saw Abigail's parents walking across the school playground. They were holding hands, leaning into each other, hunched over a little, like they were cold.

During the course of the afternoon, I and the rest of the class were called one by one to Mrs Phillips's office.

'Has Mr Brown ever *touched* you, Izzy?' she asked me.

'No, Mrs Phillips.'

'It's OK to say if he has, Izzy – you won't get into any trouble.'

'But he hasn't, Mrs Phillips.'

Abigail and three other girls who accused Mr Brown of touching them were referred for weekly sessions with a counsellor for the rest of the school year.

As for Mr Brown: we never saw him again and I neither know nor care what became of him.

Notes

Fact-checking the basic details of the first few years of Izzy and Daniel's life was straightforward: the Taylors lived in Silver Street for the entire duration of their childhood. Izzy's father still lives there today. Izzy and Daniel's dates of birth are a matter of public record and I obtained a copy of their older sister's birth and death certificates. Daisy Taylor was born eighteen months before Izzy and lived for sixty-seven days.

From the very beginning, I was puzzled about the memories Izzy chose to share with me. They didn't put her in a great light – in fact, quite the opposite. The situation with her teacher that she claimed to have orchestrated when she was only eight years old seemed so implausible that I spent a great deal of time – more than I should have – searching for a Mr Brown who had taught at Crossgate Primary. Although I managed to establish that both Izzy and Daniel had been pupils at the school, I found no mention of the dismissal of a teacher for inappropriate behaviour, although perhaps that wasn't surprising, given that the alleged incident had occurred many years before.

Meanwhile, it turned out Izzy had been doing her own research.

'You're that journalist who got fired, aren't you?' she said, in one of our early meetings.

'I left by mutual agreement,' I replied stiffly.

She reached across and put her beautifully manicured hand on top of my own stubby fingers, which I curled under my palm, trying to hide my bitten nails and torn skin.

'It was so unfair,' she said. 'I bet it wouldn't have happened if you'd been a man. The whole industry is rife with misogyny.' She squeezed my hand. 'I've been through something similar.'

'Really?' I said. It was difficult to imagine anyone as confident and poised as Izzy being treated badly.

'I had this terrible job in a call centre for an insurance company. Everyone was on minimum wage, toilet breaks were deducted from our statutory break times, no food or drink was permitted at the workstations, and the temperature in the office was kept at 17.5 degrees, so it was like an icebox. People were always being signed off sick and when they returned they would be given the worst shifts – Friday evenings or Sunday mornings – as punishment.'

'It sounds awful,' I said, hoping I would never be so desperate that I had to work somewhere like that.

'It was. I had other job offers, but the way they treated my colleagues was so disgusting that I decided to stick around and figure out how to make them pay.'

'You had another job to go to, but you … stayed?'

She shrugged. 'Someone has to stand up to the bullies, don't they? Stick up for people who can't stick up for themselves. You'd do the same, Carly. I can tell.'

Although I was almost certain that I wouldn't stay in a terrible job for the sake of colleagues I barely knew, I liked the image of myself that Izzy appeared to be seeing.

'So what did you do?' I asked.

'My job involved allocating temporary replacement vehicles for people who'd had car accidents or had their vehicles stolen, and I worked out how to hack the system so that I could authorise loan cars to be used by some of my co-workers, the ones who couldn't afford a car themselves.'

Izzy reached up and tied her hair into one of those effortlessly messy buns that I could never have reproduced no matter how long I tried.

'Wasn't that really risky?' I asked. 'I mean, if they'd found out what you were doing ...'

'Of course, but if it meant someone could go and visit their parents or take their kid for a day out or whatever, then it was a risk worth taking. The company had cars sitting around that were hardly used so it was basically a victimless crime.'

'The thing is,' I said, 'there's no such thing as a victimless crime.'

I knew this because one of the first articles I'd worked on at my previous job had involved interviewing ex-white-collar-criminals who had genuinely believed their crimes were 'victimless'.

'I know, I know,' Izzy said. 'But if the so-called victim is a huge corporation it basically is.'

I didn't agree, but that didn't stop a small part of me admiring her efforts to get one over on an exploitative, bullying insurance company.

'Did you use the cars yourself?' I asked.

'Of course not. I just wanted to help my colleagues. They were so grateful. Someone took his kids to visit the sea for the first time in their lives – can you imagine?'

'You were like a modern-day Robin Hood,' I said.

She laughed and reached across the table again, resting her fingertips lightly on the top of my hand, angling her wrist so the circle of tiny diamonds around the face of her watch cast rainbows on the wall.

'I knew you'd get it,' she said. 'You've got a powerful sense of justice, haven't you? Your commitment to help others and tell their stories shines out of you. If only more people were like us, Carly.'

Even though I'd never have done what she did – by nature I wasn't a rule breaker: I worried far too much about the consequences – I felt a rush of warmth. She was right that I believed passionately in exposing inequality and unfair behaviour. It was why I had become a journalist – to shine an accusing light on the bullies of the world – and I was flattered that Izzy could see that in me.

Izzy clinked her cup of coffee against mine. 'Cheers, Carly. So few people stick up for what they believe in. Look, I know things are tough for you at the moment, but you mustn't give up. The world needs people like you, now more than ever.'

I have no idea how Izzy did it, but in that moment she had said exactly what I needed to hear.

The previous few months had been the most difficult of my life. Not that long ago, I'd had been in a relationship with a man I loved *and* had my dream job. Now I had neither.

I'd spent so much time alone smothered by grief that, at times, I doubted if I would ever be able to find a way through it. I'd have given anything to hear Luke say he forgave me. I hadn't even been able to say goodbye properly. His parents had arranged a memorial service a couple of months after he'd died, but then the second national lockdown began and the service was cancelled. So far, there had been no mention of rearranging it. After all, it wasn't as if there was a body to bury.

It wasn't just my grief that was difficult to deal with. I was struggling to pay my bills, my career was in pieces, and my parents were suggesting I move home, abandon my life in London and get a 'proper job'. I was starting to think that they were right.

But that afternoon, in that café, Izzy saw through my self-pity to the person buried underneath. Listening to her, I remembered why I had become a journalist in the first place. I wanted my words to help people. I wanted to write stories that mattered. And I would start with the story of Daniel and Luke.

Planet Home article II

This is an extract from an article in the series investigating 'ghost flights' written by Carly Atherton and published in the online journal Planet Home.

At a temporary registration station in a car park some three and a half miles from the summit of Big Crag, I am assigned a press liaison officer who introduces herself as Sonya. After a short safety briefing and stern warnings about 'preventing contamination' and 'not removing anything from the site', Sonya invites me to follow her out of the registration station and along a broad, well-worn track.

As we begin to head uphill, Sonya tells me we'll be ascending almost 780 metres to the upper reaches of the south-eastern face of Big Crag. Although the air is chilly, the sun makes brief appearances and stunning vistas begin to open up on all sides. Two fell runners pass us and Sonya explains how the nature of the terrain means that it's impossible to prevent people approaching Big

Crag. Access is only controlled in the area immediately around the crash site.

The grassy moorland gives way to rockier ground and I see why Big Crag's name is so fitting. Huge stone outcrops puncture the land and at times walking becomes more of a scramble. The clouds which had been massing in the distance have arrived overhead and the light has flattened. The wind has picked up and I pull on my gloves and tug my hat more firmly over my ears. The entire area is bleak and grey and I'm grateful for Sonya's company, even as she strides on ahead.

I spend my time trying to prepare myself. I've seen the television footage of the debris, of course, and a couple of days ago I watched a live feed from Big Crag as the residents of the nearby village of Threlwick held a vigil for the dead pilots. But however much I try and imagine what it will be like, the reality of arriving at the site of the crash is so much worse.

From a distance, the debris is indistinct, as if a gigantic bag of smashed and pulverised aeroplane parts has been shaken over the mountain. But as we get closer to where the impact happened, certain things become identifiable. We walk past a wheel, still intact, attached to a solid metal column – an axle, I assume – snapped by the force of impact. But most of the debris is twisted beyond recognition and the scale of the task facing the investigation team seems overwhelming.

On the slope above us, investigators wearing coveralls and headlamps are picking their way painstakingly through the debris. The ground is dotted with bright yellow triangular markers, each with a different number, which give the place the air of a TV crime drama. I ask Sonya about the significance of the markers. She says something but I can't hear her over the sound of the wind, which is now whipping past us, bitingly cold. She raises her voice. 'They mark places where DNA –' she hesitates, searching for the right word '– where DNA *remnants* have been found.'

There's a piece of metal by my foot, marked with a gaudy slash of yellow. Unthinkingly, I bend down and reach for it, until Sonya reminds me not to touch anything. Nothing will be moved until the investigators have finished, she explains, at which point a clean-up team will be brought in to clear the debris. I can't help thinking it'll be impossible to remove everything and I suspect the slopes of Big Crag will become a pilgrimage site for those particularly ghoulish individuals who hunt out tragedy-related souvenirs.

Sonya invites me to pay my respects at a temporary memorial constructed by the residents of Threlwick as a focus for their vigil, and we walk a short way down the slope to a pile of stones surrounded by bunches of dead and dying flowers, unlit candles and soft toys. 'Everyone who has visited has placed a stone here,' Sonya says. 'The local community has been hit hard by what happened. Many of them saw or heard the plane in those final moments.'

After placing a stone, I close my eyes and bow my head, and as the wind screams past my ears, I almost believe I too can hear the sound of flight GFA578 on its final, fatal descent.

Notes

In my *Planet Home* articles, I never mentioned that I knew one of the pilots. Partly this was to maintain a semblance of journalistic impartiality, but also because I did my very best to try and put what I'd seen on my visit to Big Crag out of my mind. Standing on the same slope that would have filled the aeroplane windows in the moments before Luke's death was utterly horrifying. I had difficulty sleeping for weeks afterwards, and when I did, my dreams were filled with fragments of twisted metal.

Izzy had been to Big Crag, too, the only member of Daniel's or Luke's families who made the journey to the crash site.

In one of our meetings, I told her how distressing the experience had been and asked her if she felt able to put into words how it had made her feel to see the place where her brother's life had ended.

'The whole thing was a waste of time,' she said. 'And it didn't make me *feel* anything. Danny was alive, and now he's dead. My brother isn't there. He isn't anywhere.'

She reached into her handbag and pulled out a piece of twisted metal, putting it on the table between us. It was about the size of my thumb and when I picked it up and turned it over there was a slash of yellow paint – the livery of Goldfinch Airlines.

'Did you take this from the crash site?' I asked.

Izzy just laughed.

The more time I spent with her, the more I came to understand that although Izzy was a great conversationalist and a natural raconteur, she was completely resistant to any discussion about her feelings. Sometimes she would use humour to deflect the conversation, but at other times it was as if she didn't understand what I was asking, almost as if I was speaking a different language. All too often, when we were chatting at the beginning or end of our interviews, she would turn the conversation back on me as if there was nothing more important to her than what I might say. She listened. I mean, she *really* listened, never looking around the café or at other people or even glancing at her phone.

'Is everything OK with you, Carly?' she would say, often following it up with something like, 'I know you're struggling. I know you live alone. Lockdown can't have been easy. You must have been lonely.'

I hadn't told Izzy I lived by myself, but she was right. After Luke and I had split up, I'd moved out of our rented flat and into a tiny bedsit with a narrow bed that I had to push up and into a cavity in the wall to give myself enough room to sit at my desk. It was only temporary, I'd told myself. We'd be back together soon enough.

But then lockdown happened and I found it really hard – I'm not good with my own company; I much prefer to be around people. Even when things were opening up again, everyone was still anxious about meeting.

My biggest worry, though, was money. Other than the ghost-flight pieces, I hadn't had anything published for months. My credit cards were maxed out, and I was living on tea and toast. If my parents weren't helping me with the rent, I'd have been homeless, but they wouldn't do it indefinitely. In an effort to move my research along, I'd submitted multiple requests for information to Goldfinch's management team, but so far they were refusing to cooperate and I was running out of ideas.

'You really need this story, don't you,' Izzy said to me, 'after the bastards treated you so badly in your last job?'

I nodded, grateful for her understanding.

'That's why I'm not talking to anyone else,' she continued. 'No other journalists. Only you. I'll help you get your story. I know people. I can make introductions. I'll have a think about who to ask.'

On the recording my 'thank you' is so quiet it's barely a whisper and, as I remember it, that's where our conversation ended. It wasn't until I listened back that I realised Izzy had continued speaking.

'I'll do everything I can to help you because you'll tell it properly, won't you? You'll make sure that everyone knows that I was the most important person in Dan's life. And how he loved me the most.'

I tried again to persuade Grace, Daniel's wife, to speak to me but she refused, as did his father. My brother was trying to line up some of the other pilots from Goldfinch for me to interview, but for the time being, the only person who was prepared to talk to me about Daniel was Izzy, and the next time I met her I asked her if she could remember when her brother first showed an interest in flying.

Izzy's Story

1997–1998

1.

My brother's fascination with planes began in August 1997 – he was nearly nine and I was almost thirteen, and together with our parents we were flying to Portugal for a holiday. The captain of our flight was the brother of a colleague of Dad's and about an hour after take-off one of the flight attendants appeared alongside our seats.

'The captain has invited your children up to the flight deck,' she trilled. This was still pre-9/11 when it was not uncommon for children to wander up to the front of the plane.

'I don't want to go,' I said calmly and politely, turning my attention back to my book. I was halfway through *Catch Me If You Can*, fascinated by the ease with which Frank Abagnale was able to con his way across America. Yes, he may have been caught in the end, but reading the book confirmed what I had already worked out for myself: most people were gullible and deserved everything they got.

Unfortunately, my desire to keep reading was overshadowed by the enthusiasm with which Danny was wriggling in his seat, yelling, 'I want to see the flight deck.'

After a brief discussion between the flight attendant and my father, the gist of which was that Danny was desperate to meet the captain, Danny didn't want to go alone, and there wasn't enough room on the flight deck for Dad to accompany him, Dad turned to me.

'Go on, Izzy,' he said. 'Go with Danny.'

'No,' I replied.

'Please, Izzy,' Danny said. 'Please, Izzy. Please, Izzy.'

I looked at Dad. 'I don't want to see the captain or the flight deck.'

Mum put her hand on my arm, but I shrugged it off.

'Izzy,' Mum said. 'This is exactly what we were talking about yesterday.'

I corrected her. '*You* were talking about it yesterday, not me.'

Mum sighed and held her forefinger up to indicate to the cabin-crew woman that she needed a minute. 'You can't go through life only doing things which benefit you, Izzy. Sometimes you should do things simply to be nice to someone else.'

I didn't agree at the time and the intervening years haven't changed my mind on this point. If I'm requested to do something where there is a clear benefit to me, I will do it cheerfully, happily, willingly. But if there's nothing in it for me, then what's the point? I looked at Dad and shrugged; he dropped his gaze to Danny, who was kicking the seat in front of him in his excitement.

The person sitting directly in front of Danny twisted round, and although we could only see the top of his head, we had no problem hearing his voice. 'Tell that damn child to stop kicking my seat.'

Before anyone else could react, I stood up. The man was old – a lot older than Nan even – and weirdly, given we were on an aeroplane, he had a scarf wound around his neck. His hand, which was splotched with large purple bruises, was clutching his wife's hand. She was equally decrepit. I stood on tiptoe and pushed my head forward. On his cheek I could see a little thicket of stubble which he had missed with his razor. I put my finger on it and lightly stroked it. He jerked his head round to face me. I moved closer so my mouth was only inches from his ear.

'That's my brother you're talking about,' I said, very calmly and politely. 'You may be so old you're practically dead, but he's just an excited little kid.'

The man's breath was sour.

'We're going up to meet the captain now,' I continued, 'while you stay here and contemplate how little time you have left.'

I grabbed my brother's hand, pushing my way past Dad's knees. 'Come on, Danny,' I said.

The flight attendant looked between me, Dad and the man, trying to determine who to give her attention to, but then, taking the path of least resistance, she took Danny's other hand and led us along the aisle of the plane.

I looked back at the man as we passed his seat. 'Your breath smells,' I informed him.

As we continued up the aisle, I could hear Mum talking and recognised her apologising voice, although I had absolutely no idea why she felt the need to apologise. No one, and I mean absolutely no one, insulted my brother and got away with it.

The flight deck was as boring as I had expected.

Two men were crammed into what seemed like an unnecessarily small space. The one on the left – the captain – turned to say hello, full of the fake cheerfulness which some adults put on when talking to children.

Like they're all imbeciles. 'Ahhh, welcome to our office, you two. As you can see, we have the best view in the whole world.'

I rolled my eyes, but Danny seemed genuinely thrilled by the sight of all the screens and buttons and levers which surrounded us. I reached my hand up to flick one of the switches over my head, but the captain said, sharply, 'No touching. Looking is good. Touching is bad.'

I appreciated the truth of that.

While the captain droned on about control columns and throttles and navigation routes and explained how the colourful blobs on the screen in front of him represented clouds from the weather radar, I looked at the first officer, who was handsome, in a sort of older man way. Eventually he turned to look at me. I ran my tongue slowly over first my top lip, then my bottom lip. His face went bright red and he immediately turned back to face the front, pretending to read some information on one of the screens.

Meanwhile, the captain was telling Danny about the autopilot and how it was a 'loyal slave' which always does what it's told. I liked the sound of the autopilot; I thought, I could make use of one of those.

I nodded towards the control column. 'What would happen if you pointed that stick at the ground right now?' I asked.

'We'd start descending,' he said, 'but we'd realise immediately and straighten back up.'

'But if you kept it pointing at the ground. What then?'

'You don't need to worry about that. It won't happen.'

I wasn't worried. 'What if you did?' I repeated, calmly and politely.

'Well,' the captain said, 'if I did then the first officer would stop me and he's a lot stronger than me.' He laughed, although it sounded more like he was clearing his throat.

I looked between the two of them, assessing which one would win in a fight. 'So what would happen if *he* pointed the stick at the ground?'

The captain looked past me, out of the flight deck. 'Lauren,' he called. 'Would you mind escorting these delightful children back to their seats, please?'

When we got back to Mum and Dad, the old man and his wife had moved and I was able to go back to reading without further interruption for the remainder of the flight.

Danny talked about nothing but aeroplanes for the entire holiday and on the flight home Dad bought him a replica of the plane we were flying on. For months he refused to go to sleep unless the stupid thing was beside his bed. At one point it somehow ended up in the wheely bin under all the rubbish, but even that didn't dim Danny's ardour, and it was cleaned off and returned to his bedside, albeit with one slightly bent wing. Barely a week went by without one or other of our parents buying him books with titles like *Amazing Aeroplanes*, or *How a Plane Works*, or *The Little Book of Aviation*. Dad even contacted a local flying club and arranged for him and Danny to be taken up in a plane. No one asked me if I'd like to go.

Sunday afternoons became 'Danny and Dad Time' and they would sit together at the kitchen table and construct Airfix models. While they were gluing tiny bits of plastic together, Danny would interrogate Dad about facts he had memorised about whatever aeroplane they were making.

'Daddy, do you know how many Mk V Spitfires were manufactured in total?'

'No, Danny, I don't.'

'Six thousand five hundred!'

'Wow, that's a lot of planes.'

'And do you know what engines they used?'

'No, what engines did they use?'

'The Rolls Royce Merlin.'

'How interesting.'

Interesting. Really? Who was Dad trying to kid?

If I breathed so much as a word about how much time Danny spent obsessing over the planes (and it definitely was an obsession – within six months there were already fifteen Airfix models hanging from his bedroom ceiling) Mum completely overreacted. After all, I hadn't been entirely serious when I said I might burn the house down to get rid of them.

'This is *Danny's* thing, Izzy,' she would snap. 'Can't you be pleased he's got something of his own?' Occasionally she would suggest I was actually jealous of Danny's *new hobby*, as both my parents insisted on calling it, but they were missing the point, as usual. I had absolutely no reason to be jealous because despite his *new hobby* Danny was still at his happiest when he was spending time with me. We loved being together and, in fact, the two of us would have been perfectly happy not to spend time with any other children.

Our parents went through a stage of pushing Danny and me in the direction of their friends' kids and demanding we *go and play* while the adults drank wine. The only positive to come out of these scenarios was giving Danny and me a chance to play The Game.

I remember the final time we played it. My parents invited the parents of Danny's new best friend to come over for an afternoon. Danny had only been at school a few months at that point and as far as I was concerned Mikey – who was short, nervy and pale – was not a worthy best friend for my brother, who should have been aspiring to more impressive companions. To give little Mikey credit, though, he was an eager participant in The Game, which was played in multiple stages.

First, I lined up three large glasses of water and told Mikey that he, Danny and I were going to have a race to see who could drink their water the fastest. It didn't matter who won or lost this part of the game: the important thing was to make sure little Mikey drank as much water as possible. Mikey guzzled the water, while Danny and I, wise to The Game, made sure we didn't even drink half of ours. Mikey was delighted when he was the winner and I presented him with a chocolate as a prize.

Next, we relocated to the end of the garden behind the shed, where we couldn't be seen from the house. I took a bottle of fizzy drink with us and announced we were going to have a competition to see who could do the loudest burps. Needless to say, like most five-year-old boys, little Mikey found burping hilarious and he willingly drank significant quantities of the fizzy drink. Again, it was irrelevant to Danny and I who won, and we laughed along with Mikey when he burped and once again crowned him the winner.

All of which was really the prologue because it was only then that The Game really started.

'Let's play Pirates and Sailors,' I suggested.

On cue, Danny responded with the requisite enthusi-asm. 'Yes! Can I be the sailor, Izzy? Please?'

I pretended to think about it, then said, 'Mikey's our guest, Danny, so *he* should be sailor.'

Mikey had no idea what we were talking about but his eyes lit up when I produced a £1 coin, which I'd taken from Dad's stash of money. That wasn't enough to persuade some kids to participate in The Game, but I had judged it right with little Mikey.

'You're the sailor and this is your treasure,' I said, handing over the money.

He clenched it in his pudgy hand.

'The pirates want to steal your treasure,' I explained, 'and the sailor's job is to keep it safe. If the sailor manages to hold onto his treasure then it's his to keep.'

'For real?' Mikey asked.

'For real,' I said and set about tying Mikey's hands and feet together with some of Dad's ties that I'd taken from his wardrobe.

Our pirate tactics were simple. All we did was tickle the sailor. We prodded and poked him, not too hard. Hurting Mikey was not the aim – I'm not cruel, after all – we just wanted to make him squirm. At first, little Mikey laughed and appeared to be enjoying himself, keeping his chubby fist curled protectively around his treasure. We kept prodding and poking. Breathless from the tickling, he squirmed. Squirm, squirm, squirm. Then, and I could always tell when it was going to happen, he shouted, 'Stop! I need a wee-wee!'

'Pirates don't stop,' I said, digging my fingers into his little armpits, running them up and down his skinny ribs, prodding his sides. Tickle, tickle, tickle.

'Please. I have to go,' little Mikey shouted again.

'Pirates are merciless. Pirates keep raiding,' I chanted. 'Pirates are merciless. Pirates don't stop.'

Tickle, tickle, tickle.

'Stop, please stop,' Mikey yelled. Then, at last, 'I'm desperate.'

'What did you say, sailor?' I yelled, digging my fingers into the soft curve of his armpit.

'I can't hold it.'

A dark patch bloomed on little Mikey's smart yellow shorts. The Game was over.

I stifled a moan, but when I turned to share the moment with Danny, I realised he was standing a little way off with his back to us. I looked down at Mikey, who had started crying.

'Oh, for god's sake,' I said, 'it's only a game.' I patted his clenched fist. 'And you kept the treasure safe. It's yours *for real.*'

I untied Mikey's hands and feet and went up to the house to tell his parents that sadly their son had wet himself playing pirates with Danny.

That evening when my brother said, 'Will Mikey be OK, Izzy?' I looked at him curiously. I hadn't given his friend a second thought since his parents had bundled him into the car, wearing a pair of Danny's joggers and sitting on a towel. After apologising for how their son's behaviour had curtailed a delightful afternoon, his parents had driven him away.

'Why wouldn't he be OK?' I asked.

'He was really upset about what happened.' Danny looked really upset too.

'Mikey's a cry-baby. You've got to remember you're

very mature for your age, Danny. Maybe you should look for a new friend at school? Someone a bit more grown up. You don't want to be hanging around with cry-babies, do you?'

He didn't reply. Mikey and Danny stopped being best friends, Danny lost interest in The Game and we never played it again.

2.

In September 1998, Danny's obsession with planes meant a mandatory family outing to the Farnborough Airshow. I had recently turned fourteen and was perfectly capable of being left home alone, but my protest at being forced to go along fell on deaf ears. Even Nan had been roped in and was waiting in the car along with everyone else when I slid into the seat next to her.

'What on earth have you got on?' Mum said.

'T-shirt, shorts, Converse ...' I replied.

'Your shorts are so short your bottom's hanging out, and that T-shirt barely covers your chest. Go back in and change, young lady.'

'I don't want to miss the planes,' Danny said.

'Get back inside and put something decent on,' Mum said, her voice rising as it always did when she became too emotional.

'Well, I think she looks like a million dollars,' Nan said. 'What I wouldn't give to have legs like that.'

'Thanks for your input, Clare,' Mum said, 'but it really isn't helpful ...'

'Excuse me for breathing,' Nan replied.

'Let's go,' Danny said.

Dad turned the ignition on. 'We're already late.'

'I don't care. Go back in and change now,' Mum said.

'I think you look great,' said Nan, nudging me with her elbow. 'Lovely long legs. So slim. Definitely takes after our side of the family, doesn't she, Rog?' she said, tapping Dad on the shoulder, but he just said, 'We really need to get on the road.'

'Come *on*.' Danny's voice was strident.

'If you speak like that we won't be going anywhere,' Mum said, then, turning to me, 'I'm not going to tell you again young lady ...'

I shrugged. And they wondered why I never wanted to go on family outings.

Of course I didn't change my clothes. After all, what could Mum do? Physically drag me out of the car and up to my room? I don't think so. Make me stay at home while they went without me? Yes, please.

But as it happened, I was glad I went because it turned out to be a particularly memorable day not only for Danny but also for me.

The whole excursion got off to an unpromising start when were stuck in a queue for a car park for ages and Mum started getting annoyed all over again. Nan was sipping gin out of a hip flask but when I asked her for some she shook her head, nodded towards my mum and mouthed, 'Later.' After we'd finally parked we had to hike across a field, join another endless queue for the entrance, then hike around another field, and at some point, it became clear to me that the plan was to spend the whole day wandering around fields looking at planes while more planes flew overhead.

Danny was thrilled to be there and he ran on ahead yelling, 'This is brilliant.' Years later, I heard him talking about the day at Farnborough and how being among the roar of the planes, the smell of the fuel and the pilots in their uniforms was the moment he realised that when he grew up he didn't have to love aeroplanes from a distance, but he might actually be able to fly them.

For the rest of us, the whole thing was pretty tedious and after a while, when Nan announced she was off to find someone to make her a gin gimlet and asked if I fancied tagging along, I said yes. As we strolled away from the others, she handed over her hip flask – 'Only a sip, mind, to lubricate the pipes.'

Nan always had an unerring nose for finding a bar, and within minutes a young barman was following her instructions for preparing a gimlet ('Absolutely *no* soda, thank you very much'). She handed over a £5 note to the barman and held a £10 note out to me.

'How about you go and see what mischief you can get up to?' she said.

They must have been eighteen or nineteen, too old to be called boys, really, but still too young to be men. They were outside a beer tent and, aware of their gazes wandering shamelessly over my legs, my breasts, my bum, I walked towards them.

'All right?' I said.

'Hi,' one of them replied.

I looked them over, assessing their suitability. Maybe this was the opportunity I had been waiting for. Two of them – including the one who had spoken – were OK-looking in a sort of 'fifth member of a boy band whose name no one remembers' type way. Bland. Boring. Predictable. Not a lot of fun to be had with them.

The third one was more interesting. Blond, greasy hair, a line of pimples along his jawline, he radiated vulnerability, low self-confidence and hunger. Not hunger for food – if anything he was slightly chubby – but hunger for someone, *anyone*, other than his parents to look at him and see the person lurking beneath his needy outer shell.

I put my hand in my back pocket, fingering the £10 note Nan had given me, and looked at him. 'Buy me a drink?' I asked.

He looked round to see if I was talking to someone else, and when he looked back, I smiled, then bit my bottom lip, just a little.

He laid his palm flat on his chest and said, '*Me?*'

I dropped my chin and looked up at him through my eyelashes. 'Only if you've got nothing better to do.'

His two friends were staring at me in absolute shock. Take that you snotty-nose boy-band wannabes, I thought. I took his hand and led him in the direction of the bar.

'What would you like?' he asked, and I scanned the list hanging at the back of the tent.

'White wine.' I knew from my experiments with Mum and Dad's drinks cupboard that wine gave me a buzz more quickly than anything else.

He ordered a beer for himself and a wine for me. The woman serving him glanced in my direction, but she looked completely bored and didn't bother to ask how old I was.

He put his wallet on the bar, and I pointed at his driving licence. 'Great photo,' I said.

He flushed. 'I was going through a bit of a goth phase. Dyed my hair black. Everyone said I looked like a vampire.'

'Can I see it properly?' I asked, and he took the licence out of the wallet and handed it to me.

I pretended to consider the photograph. 'You know,' I said, 'vampires are sexy ...' I gave him a little half-smile. 'I reckon you look like Brad Pitt in *Interview with the Vampire.*'

He took a big gulp of his beer. 'So, uh, d'you like planes then?' he asked, then blushed. This was going to be even easier than I had thought.

'No,' I said. 'My dad, he was mad about planes ... he came to the Farnborough Airshow every year but he ... well ...' I swallowed hard. 'He died a few months ago.'

'Oh my god, how terrible. Shit. I'm so sorry.' He looked stricken.

'I thought I'd come today ... you know ... in his memory ...' I swallowed the rest of the wine in one gulp. 'Shall we have another?' I asked brightly.

The second drink was followed by a third, at which point he ran out of money, and less than ten minutes later we were behind a wall near the car park, kissing. The poor boy got himself very worked up, very quickly. He rubbed himself against me desperately, panting and making a sort of half-moaning, half-squeaking noise. When the friction of his hips against the zip of my shorts started chafing, I reached between us and slipped my hand into his jeans. He moaned loudly and sucked feverishly at my lips and my neck, putting both hands on my bottom, pulling me against him.

'You're so beautiful,' he said, or at least I think that's what he said – his mouth was tangled in my hair, so it was difficult to hear.

'Do you want to do it ...?' I asked.

He pulled his head away from me. 'Really?' he said.

'Sure. Why not?' I rubbed his dick a bit harder. 'You want to, don't you?'

'Oh baby, yeah,' he said, sounding like how I imagined an actor in bad porn film might sound.

I pushed down my shorts and pants, then wrestled with his jeans until they were around his ankles.

'Are you sure about this?' he panted. 'I haven't got ... you know ... a condom ...'

'It's fine,' I said. 'I'm on the pill.' I wasn't, but he didn't need to know that.

His dick jabbed my thighs.

'Oh god. Oh god,' he whimpered. 'This is ... I'm ... oh god.'

I pushed against him, opened my legs wider, letting his penis slide between them. Then I squashed my thighs together, trapping him there. He didn't seriously think I was going to let him put that thing inside me, did he? He thrust awkwardly back and forward against my legs a few times, panting, 'Please ... let me ... Oh god ... I can't hold it ... oh god ... oh god ...'

It was all over.

I pulled up my pants and shorts and looked at him. He was ridiculous. Boxer shorts round his ankles, skinny white legs, penis rapidly deflating.

'Sorry,' he said. 'I've never done that before.' He swallowed, Adam's apple bobbing. 'What I mean is, I've never ... you know ... never had sex.' He looked like he was about to cry. 'I think you're amazing. Can I have your phone number?' he asked.

'I don't think my mum would be happy about that.'

He zipped up his jeans. 'Why not?'

'Because I'm only fourteen.'

He turned ashen; the only colour on his face was his acne. 'But you were drinking wine ...?'

'Yeah, so?'

'And you said you wanted to ...'

I shrugged. 'My teacher said that consent is no defence to statutory rape.'

He looked terrified. 'But I didn't rape you. I mean, we didn't ... I didn't ...'

'Your spunk is all over my legs,' I said. 'And by the time I go to the police, I'll make sure it's inside me too.'

'You can't do that.'

'Can't I?'

'I'm going to university next week. You'll ruin my life. Please ... please don't go to the police. I'm sorry, really, truly, I'm sorry.' He was sobbing like a baby.

'I might or I might not go to the police. I haven't decided. It depends on how I'm feeling, doesn't it, Toby Scheverall?'

When I said his name, he flinched and looked like he might be sick.

'Nice name,' I continued. 'Unusual. Can't be too many Toby Scheveralls around. I'll give you a bit of advice: don't be so quick to flash your driving licence. Also, maybe don't be so quick to try and have sex with underage girls, either. In the meantime, I hope you enjoy prison, Toby ...'

Actual tears were running down his face.

I touched his chin with my finger. 'Acne cream works wonders, you know.'

That day at the Farnborough Airshow was the day Danny decided he would do whatever it took to become a pilot, setting him on a course that ended with his death on the side of a mountain.

As for me ... I didn't report Toby Scheverall to the police. Why would I? Where would be the fun in that?

Because the thing is, as Dad was driving us home that day, I was experiencing the most overwhelming excitement I had felt in my whole fourteen years. And all these years later, I still get a throb of pure pleasure thinking about the weeks, the months, hopefully the years Toby Scheverall spent in a state of terror wondering if today would be the day the police would come knocking at his door.

Notes

I managed to track down Toby Scheverall – or at least someone with the same name. Izzy was right to say it was unusual because I could find only one person called Toby Scheverall. He's an investment banker in London who appears to be the right age to have been in his late teens in September 1998. Although there was no email address listed for him on his employer's website, it was simple enough to work out what it was. I sent Mr Scheverall two emails, both of which went unanswered, so I called the main switchboard and asked to be put through to him. When he answered, I introduced myself and said I was a journalist writing a piece about the Big Crag plane crash.

Mr Scheverall, who had the sort of accent which might be described as 'public school', was polite, although he sounded irritated, and when I told him I had reason to believe he had known the sister of the captain of flight GFA578, he said I must be mistaken. I explained that although he might not have met Daniel Taylor, I believed he had met his sister Izzy at the Farnborough Airshow in 1998.

Mr Scheverall's tone immediately became hostile, and he said, 'I have nothing to say, nothing at all.' When I attempted to reassure him that I was merely trying to gather some background information, he said, 'This is harassment. If you ever contact me again, you'll hear from my lawyer.' Then he hung up. I tried calling him back several times, but I was never again put through to him.

Alongside looking into Daniel's life, I was also investigating whether I could find any evidence to suggest that Luke was responsible for the crash. Even though I was utterly convinced that he would never have deliberately flown a plane into a mountain, if this was going to be the story to relaunch my career then I had to set my personal feelings aside and investigate all angles, wherever they took me.

To that end, I talked to Luke's friends (many of whom were, and still are, my friends too) and, although I didn't find it easy, I spoke with two of his previous girlfriends. As I expected, not one of them gave me a single reason to think that Luke might have wanted to take his own life. I also contacted his parents. I hadn't seen Doug and Mary Emery since before Covid and I arranged to go and visit them at their home in Bournemouth.

I don't want to dwell on the Emerys' grief. Doug's face was grey, skin tight over his cheekbones, and when he picked up a mug of tea, his hand shook. Mary had started crying when she saw me on the doorstep and didn't really stop the whole time I was there. She spent most of her time staring at the wall above my head, tears dripping down her face and gathering at the corners of her mouth. Every so often she'd lower her gaze to mine, wipe her face with the back of her hand and say things like 'I always hoped you two would end up together' and 'he always adored you' and 'I never did understand why you split up'.

I hadn't realised it until that day, but even after I'd hurt him so badly, Luke hadn't told his parents why we'd split up. He hadn't wanted them to blame me. I can't honestly say I would have done the same if it was me. Luke really was the best of us all. How could it be that I would never see him again? That I would never have a chance to turn our off-again relationship back into an on-again one? The guilt was so overwhelming I could barely stumble through the questions I wanted to ask.

Sitting on the Emerys' sofa, I wished I'd never gone to see them – burdening them with my own grief when they were barely coping with their own. Luke's parents were convinced something had 'gone wrong' with the plane and I wasn't going to tell them otherwise. I left as soon as I could without appearing rude.

Over the course of the next few weeks, with my brother's help, I arranged Zoom calls with several Goldfinch pilots. Unsurprisingly, they all described Luke as good at his job, easy-going and personable, great company in the cockpit; they all enjoyed flying with him. Several of them were friends with Luke outside of work, including two who were on the same five-a-side football team as him and Jamie.

Beyond what is mentioned above, I have not included material from my many interviews with Luke's friends, parents or colleagues. In light of what I subsequently discovered, none of it is relevant, beyond confirming what I had known anyway – Luke was, tragically, through no fault of his own, simply in the wrong place at the wrong time.

It is worth noting that my brother was unable to find anyone at Goldfinch who considered Daniel Taylor a friend, and everyone I spoke to confirmed what Jamie himself had told me: there were no concerns about Daniel's abilities as a pilot, but he kept himself to himself and never socialised. I didn't speak to anyone who had spent time with him outside of work. Many people like to keep their private lives separate from their work lives, but I found it sad that not a single person at the airline considered Daniel a friend and I decided to ask Izzy about this.

The next time we arranged to meet, Izzy was almost an hour late, and the only reason I hadn't left the café was because the idea of going back to the silence of my bedsit was too depressing. Instead I nursed a cold cup of black coffee – the cheapest drink on the menu – and got on with some background reading for my next *Planet Home* article.

'You've changed your hair,' Izzy said when she finally arrived. 'It looks fabulous.' She unwound her scarf, unbuttoned her coat, then took the seat opposite me.

'Thanks,' I said, reaching up to touch my fringe. I'd used a home dye kit and wasn't at all sure about the results. 'Do you really think so?'

'You look beautiful.'

'I don't know about that,' I said.

'Seriously. That colour really suits you. It brings out your eyes.'

I've never been good at receiving compliments about my appearance and I could feel myself blushing.

'You know what you need?' she asked and I shook my head, still feeling awkward.

She took her scarf from the back of her chair and settled it on my shoulders. It was wonderfully soft against my neck.

'There,' she said. 'Perfect. It suits you much better than it does me.'

'I can't take your scarf,' I said.

'Sure you can.'

I looked at the label. 'Seriously, I can't. This is cashmere. It must have cost you a fortune.'

Izzy shrugged. 'I've got loads of others. Besides, I'm not taking no for an answer. If you don't take it, then I'm going to get up and leave right now.'

I snuggled the scarf closer. It felt wonderful.

'The choice is yours,' she said. 'Either you refuse to keep it and I'm walking out of here right now, or you keep the scarf and I'll stay and answer your questions. Deal?'

'If you're really sure. It's so lovely of you. Thank you,' I said. 'At least let me buy you a drink.'

'I'll have a caramel macchiato and one of those Danish pastries that they've just brought out of the oven.'

When I returned to the table, I began by asking Izzy if she was surprised that none of Daniel's colleagues had ever spent time with him outside work.

'I'd have been far more surprised if you'd actually found anyone that had,' she said.

'Why do you say that?' I asked.

She shrugged and said, 'You'd have to ask his wife.' She took a bite of her pastry.

'Oh, really? Why's that?'

I waited for her to swallow the food and have a sip of her drink before she replied. 'I shouldn't say.'

'What do you mean? Why not?'

She didn't answer – just carried on eating as if I hadn't spoken.

'Could you persuade her to speak to me?' I asked.

Izzy shrugged again. 'I'd rather not.' She devoured the rest of the pastry in a few bites, brushing crumbs off her silk blouse, apparently unconcerned about the little spots of butter left behind.

'What about your father? Do you think he'd agree to be interviewed?'

'He'll never talk to you – he thinks all journalists are the scum of the earth.'

'Right,' I said. I had no idea how to reply to that.

Izzy put her hands flat on the table, fingers greasy from the pastry. She leaned towards me, and when she spoke, her breath was sickly sweet. 'I shouldn't be saying this, but Grace is very ...' She hesitated for a moment, searching for the right word. 'She's very ... controlling. *Was* very controlling of Danny, I mean. Before my brother met her, he was the life and soul, loads of mates, always out with people. But after they got together ... well ... let's just say she made sure he only had room in his life for *her*.'

'Really?' I said. 'How did she do that?'

'She was always checking up on him. Calling him, texting him endlessly, making sure she knew where he was, what he was doing. If he didn't answer her calls she'd just keep ringing, dozens of times sometimes. Then there was the way she flung her money around. Buying him things, nice clothes, holidays, making him feel indebted to her, so he would always do what she wanted.'

This didn't sound good. Quite the opposite.

'Did it affect your relationship with your brother?' I asked.

'Of course not. I would never have let her come between us. Although sometimes Danny had to lie to her, tell her he was working when really he was meeting me.'

'That must have been hard for him.'

Izzy finished the last of her coffee and stared at me with that intense gaze of hers. I fought the impulse to look away.

She leaned closer. 'I'm telling you, Grace is a toxic, controlling bitch.'

'It must be really upsetting to talk about,' I said, trying to imagine how it would feel to think that way about my brother's soon-to-be wife.

Izzy smiled and sat back in her chair. 'Not at all. I just don't want to talk about *her*. I'm very happy to tell you about my brother.'

Izzy's Story

2001–2003

1.

When I was sixteen and Danny was twelve, Nan came to live with us.

'The Bastard screwed me over,' she informed me after a bottle and a half of Prosecco. The Bastard's name was Gregory Green, and although initially she had described him as bearded, clever and exciting, she later revised her opinion to hairy, fraudulent, scum of the earth. Gregory Green had promised to make my grandmother exceedingly wealthy if she would simply invest in his company which had secured, so he claimed, planning permission to build luxury homes for millionaires somewhere called Thorney Island. As part of his persuasion tactics, he had produced what my grandmother claimed were 'entirely convincing' copies of council minutes, although it was anyone's guess why she thought she could recognise a convincing council minute from a *non*-convincing one, as well as licences, planning permissions, blueprints and even a 1:20 scale model of the site built in fibreglass, complete with tiny millionaires parking their customised Aston Martins, strolling around their lavishly landscaped gardens and gazing at uninterrupted sea views while relaxing in their enormous infinity pools.

'I really thought this was it. My passport to the sort of life I deserve,' Nan said, filling her glass before topping up mine to half full. She didn't like to drink alone, and we had a mutually beneficial arrangement whereby she allowed me to consume fifty per cent of the amount she drank, in return for me keeping her company.

I knew exactly what she meant. I had every intention of living the sort of life I deserved and no intention of letting anyone or anything get in the way of making it happen.

Nan poked a finger into her glass and stirred up some bubbles. 'Champagne not Prosecco,' she said, sighing deeply. 'That's what I should be drinking ...' I decided not to point out that it was only due to my parents' generosity that she was even drinking Prosecco.

My grandmother had given The Bastard every penny she could lay her hands on, racking up debts on multiple credit cards. She'd even taken out several payday loans, convinced she was about to be rich beyond her wildest dreams.

'The Bastard screwed me good and proper,' she mumbled into her glass, knocking back another huge swig.

Privately, I had decided she deserved everything she got after I heard Dad telling Mum that if only Nan had bothered to drive to the south coast and visit Thorney Island, she would have seen immediately that it was a military base.

'They don't even let people walk there,' he said, 'let alone build luxury homes on it. What the hell was she thinking?'

'Your mother has always been convinced she deserves more than she has,' Mum said.

According to the police, The Bastard had left the country not only with all Nan's money but with the life savings of several other equally gullible individuals. Fair play to The Bastard, I thought. He put in the effort, produced all those genuine-looking fake plans, talked a great talk, appealed to the greed of others. That's how to get rich.

However, there was an important lesson in what happened to my grandmother: finding shortcuts to what you want is one thing but being lazy is another thing altogether. All she'd had to do was take one quick drive to the coast and she wouldn't have had to sell her flat and move in with us, '*temporarily*, just while she gets back on her feet,' as Mum said, increasingly desperately, to anyone who asked.

Although our house wasn't exactly tiny, Danny volunteered to move out of his room so Nan could have it. My brother slept in Dad's study on a sofa bed but his only real complaint was being parted from his Airfix models, which still dangled in great numbers from his bedroom ceiling looking like, as Nan said, an aerial graveyard. For his birthday a few weeks later, my parents tried to make it up to him by buying him a very expensive radio-controlled aeroplane. The plane was much more realistic than the Airfix models and complete with actual working elevator, throttle, rudder and ailerons. Or so Danny never tired of telling me. Meanwhile, Mum contacted somewhere called Prior Place which was a twenty-minute drive away and secured permission for him to fly his new toy around one of their fields to his heart's content.

The following month, for my seventeenth birthday, Mum and Dad gave me driving lessons and the promise of a car when I passed my test (which I did only five weeks later). Before they handed over the keys to the two-year-old VW Polo, my parents offered to help with the running costs of my car on one condition: I had to agree to act as Danny's chauffeur.

'Why should I?' I asked.

'Because if you're old enough to drive a car, then you're old enough to start taking responsibility for someone other than yourself,' Mum said.

'Nan should drive him. After all, she's living in our house for free. *She* owes you way more than *I* do.'

Mum shook her head. 'Why does it always come down to who owes what, Izzy? Not everything in life is a balance sheet.'

That was one perspective.

I decided to try a different tack. 'What about my social life?'

'What about it?' I recognised the tone of Mum's voice, which meant I was running out of time to make my point.

'How can I be expected to have a social life if I'm basically operating a taxi service for Danny?'

'Look, Izzy. We've bought you a car, and we'll help you with the expenses. Can't you just, for once, agree to do something without making it all about you? Your brother needs to be driven to Prior Place, he loves spending time with you, why can't you just say, "Yes, Mum, of course, I'd be delighted to help"?'

I spoke to Dad, but for once he sided with my mother. 'We're not actually *asking* you, Izzy,' he said. 'We're *telling* you if you want us to help with the expenses for the car we bought you, then you will need to help your brother out. To be honest, I'm surprised you're complaining, I thought you'd be pleased to have a chance to drive the car.'

I did like having reasons to drive my car, and of course I didn't mind taking Danny, and clearly it was in my interests for someone else to foot the bill for services and the occasional tank of petrol, but I *really* didn't like to be told what to do. In the end we settled on a commitment which meant I would drive my brother and his plane to Prior Place no more than twice per week. Danny, bless him, was just delighted to have the chance to spend time with me.

'It's much better when you take me,' he said on one of our first journeys, his plane resting like a baby on a duvet on the back seat. 'Last time Nan drove me, she kept going on about how I should be more like you.'

'Really?' I said, amused by the idea that Danny could ever be anything like me. 'What was she saying?'

'Oh, you know … just stuff.'

'What stuff?' I asked, glancing across at him. His window was half open and he was running his finger along the top of the glass.

'Danny?' I said.

He looked at me – unlike most people, my brother never had any problem maintaining eye contact with me.

'I'm driving you to this field,' I said. 'Least you can do is tell me what Nan's been saying.'

'She just said I should be more like you.'

'In what way like me?' I asked, although it didn't matter to me in the least. I didn't care what anyone thought of me. I'd long ago decided everyone was far too hung up on what other people thought, wasting their lives worrying about being judged. The only judgement worth making is to ask yourself: am I having a good time? If yes, then great. If no, then do whatever you have to do to make sure you *are* having a good time.

The same wasn't true for Danny. Even at thirteen, he spent far too much of his time worrying about other people and how they *felt*. In his final year at primary school he won the prize for 'Most Considerate Student'. Any new kids who started at the school would be paired up with him because the teachers trusted him to be sensitive, helpful and kind. They might as well have said weak, vulnerable and needy. Or, to cut right to the chase: *victim*.

Because the thing was, unless my brother wanted to spend his life as a victim, he really did need to learn to be a little more like me. I'd be leaving for university the following year and who knew what the future held for him without me around so much to look out for him. Hence my interest in what Nan had been saying to him.

'Spit it out,' I said. 'What did she say?'

'She said I should develop an outer Danny like you have an outer Izzy. She said no one knows the real you.'

'Interesting,' I said.

'I didn't understand what she was talking about. I mean, you're just you, aren't you?'

'Of course.'

'So why would she say that? It's stupid. I mean, I know you, you're my sister.'

'Of course I'm your sister. And you're my brother. Maybe she's going a bit gaga.' I contorted my face, to make it look like I was insane.

When he saw my expression Danny laughed and we didn't talk about it any more.

*

A few weeks after I began driving Danny to Prior Place, we came across the aftermath of an accident on our way home. A car had been overtaking two cyclists on a blind corner, and when a van came from the opposite direction, the driver of the car swerved towards the curb, knocking one of the cyclists off their bike. We must have come round the corner very soon after it had happened. I slowed down, pulled up next to the pavement and Danny and I got out.

The van driver was standing beside his vehicle with his mobile to his ear, shouting, 'Ambulance, send an ambulance.' The middle-aged woman who had been driving the car was standing over the fallen cyclist, who, I could see now, was a young man, not much older than me. He was making a high-pitched wailing noise. The other cyclist – his girlfriend, I assumed – was kneeling next to him, holding his hand and sobbing.

Danny jogged over to the bend in the road to warn any oncoming traffic to slow down. I walked towards the guy on the ground and looked down at him. His girlfriend reached for my arm. 'I'm going to be sick. Can you stay with him?' She got up and staggered over to the grass verge at the side of the road, where she dropped to her knees. The woman who had been driving the car said, 'I've got water. I'll go and get it for her.'

I knelt next to the young man and considered the damage done by the impact. He must have skidded across the tarmac for quite a distance because his T-shirt had been ripped to shreds, as had most of the skin on his right arm. I poked one finger experimentally at the edge of one of the deepest wounds and the volume of the man's wailing increased. I removed my finger and laid my hand on his forehead.

The ambulance took nearly twenty minutes to arrive. Danny and I waited to see the man being loaded into the back, oxygen mask strapped onto his face, his girlfriend ushered in alongside him. The police thanked us for stopping and praised our quick thinking about warning oncoming drivers. They also asked us both to give statements but there wasn't really anything to tell.

By the time we got home, Mum and Dad were really concerned because we'd been gone for so long. When they heard what had happened, Mum started crying which made no sense because Danny and I weren't hurt. But perhaps it wasn't surprising that Danny, with all those sensitive feelings of his, had nightmares for weeks afterwards and often came into my room in the middle of the night to curl up on my big beanbag. "S'OK, Izzy?' he'd mumble, and of course it was fine.

But on the evening of the accident, my mother turned her attention to my wellbeing.

'It's OK to admit you're upset, darling. In fact, it would be good for you to talk about what happened today,' she said, perching on the very edge of my bed, like she didn't want to fully commit to sitting down.

'But I'm not upset,' I said.

'You don't need to be brave, Izzy. It must have been really scary to see an accident like that.'

I didn't understand. There was nothing brave about stopping at the scene of an accident. There was nothing scary about it, either. The whole experience had been exciting and before Mum came in I'd been thinking what a shame it was that the cyclist hadn't smashed his head open so I could have had a look at his brain. I would have liked the opportunity to see where other people kept all these inconvenient feelings that they had.

2.

The summer before I left for university couldn't pass quickly enough. I did not agree with my parents when they said I should get a job and save some money. It was clear what I should do was celebrate the end of school by partying frequently, partying hard, and interspersing that with sleeping as long and as late as possible. That was the best preparation for university, not spending my time pointlessly balancing plates of food on my arm at some local gastropub, sliding them onto tables, then removing them twenty minutes later, before doing it all over again.

Although the nagging quickly became boring, my parents couldn't physically force me to get a job, and thanks to Nan slipping me money every few days (out of the 'allowance' her 'new man' Jeff was giving her), the carelessness with which both my parents left cash lying around and the unlimited drinks for 'favours' arrangement I had with some of the local lads, I managed to get by.

I got my A level results, which were excellent despite all the school-related upheaval I'd been subjected to. In their wisdom, our parents had decided to send my brother and me to private school – or, at least, they'd decided to send *me* to private school, and having done so they felt compelled to do the same for Danny. At age eleven, I sat the Common Entrance Exam, and when I passed it effortlessly I was offered a place at Kew Park School for Girls, which thrilled Mum and Dad. Inexplicably, having made such a fuss about me going to KPSG, they made me move schools again when I was fifteen – the year before my GCSEs. My new school – Lady Goldstone School – was a forty-minute bus ride away. There was no explanation, no apologies, Mum and Dad simply announced I would not be returning to KPSG and would henceforth be attending Lady Goldstone.

As if that wasn't enough, halfway through the final year of school, Lady Goldstone informed me there was no need for me to attend school again except to sit my A levels. Again, no explanation, no apology. Reading lists, handouts and mock exams arrived by email, and I was required to send all homework and exam prep back the same way. It could have seriously jeopardised my chances of getting good grades. Nevertheless, I passed my A levels with flying colours and at the end of September 2003, not a moment too soon, I finally left home to start at Reading University.

But getting back to Danny, I should make it clear that even after I went to university my brother and I remained as close as we'd always been. He visited me often and whenever I came home to Silver Street we quickly fell back into our old habits, which meant I frequently drove him to wherever he needed to be. By then he had moved on from model planes to real planes and more often than not I ended up driving him to a private airfield on the outskirts of London. A strange quirk of the law in the UK means it is possible to fly before you drive: you can take flying lessons from fourteen years old, fly solo at sixteen and get a private pilot's licence at seventeen. As soon as he turned fourteen, my parents started paying for flying lessons for Danny and he flew solo before he had even sat behind the wheel of a car.

I was there on the day of my brother's sixteenth birthday when his instructor Andy climbed out of the little Cessna 152 after he had guided Danny through three flawless take-offs and landings. Watching from a bench alongside the low buildings which served as the flying-club headquarters, I assumed the lesson was over and stood up, putting my book in my bag ready to leave. Mum and Dad were at home getting everything ready for Danny's birthday party and had given us strict instructions to go straight home as soon as the lesson was over. However, when my brother remained in his seat and closed the door of the plane I sat back down. While Andy walked towards me, the plane circled and started taxiing slowly back towards the start of the runway.

'He's ready,' Andy said when he reached me. 'And the conditions are perfect for a first solo flight. He'll remember this day for the rest of his life.' He pushed his sunglasses onto his head and sat next to me on the bench. He was wearing shorts and in the afternoon sunlight the downy hair of his legs was the colour of burnished gold. I assumed one of my most appealing smiles and lifted my gaze from Andy's legs, but he wasn't looking at me. Instead, he was watching the plane which had started to roll along the runway, bumping and jolting over the uneven surface.

'Come on, son,' Andy said as the plane continued to pick up speed. 'You've got this.'

The nose of the Cessna tilted up and for a moment it seemed like the wheels would stay on the ground but then the plane gave a little hop, launching itself into the air then forging up, up and away.

'Yessss ...' Andy said, doing an awkward fist pump before turning to look at me. 'You should be proud of him. Youngest solo pilot ever. He's a natural.'

'Of course I'm proud of him,' I said. 'He's my brother.'

I kept my gaze on Andy's face. His freckles were the colour of cornflakes, and pale spidery white lines spread from the corners of his eyes from too much squinting into the sun. He reached up to his head for his sunglasses, pushing them onto his nose. Then he stood up.

'He'll be about ten minutes,' he said. 'I'm going to head inside.'

I turned my attention back to my book, but I couldn't concentrate. I was reading *Never Let Me Go* by Kazuo Ishiguro which, although classified as a dystopian novel, struck me as aspirational – I'd certainly be very happy to have a clone to donate organs to me, should I need them – but once the little plane disappeared from view Kathy's fate didn't seem all that interesting. Instead, I found myself thinking about my little brother, my Danny, up there alone, his whole life entirely dependent on what his instructor had taught him. What if this guy Andy had forgotten to tell Danny something vital? What if Danny, who had always relied on me to boost his confidence, panicked? What if he wasn't good enough? After all, no one had expected him to be taking his first solo flight today. What exactly would I do to Andy if something happened to my brother? Would my parents still pay for the cost of running my car if I no longer had a brother to ferry around?

Needless to say, Danny landed perfectly. Fortunately for Andy, he *had* taught Danny everything he needed to know to fly solo, and he shook hands with my brother saying, 'Great job, I'm proud of you,' before striding off towards the plane, leaving Danny and me alone.

My brother flung his arms around me. 'That was amazing, Izzy,' he said. 'I was terrified coming in to land, though. Like, what if I forgot what I was supposed to do? But it was brilliant, I loved it. I can't wait to go back up again.'

There is absolutely no doubt Danny was at his happiest when he was sitting at the controls of an aeroplane. For him, being a pilot wasn't a job. It was his life. His entire identity was bound up with flying and except for me it was what he loved more than anything else in the world.

Notes

During this time was Izzy repeatedly offering to help me re-establish myself as a serious journalist. To illustrate this, I have reproduced below a small part of our conversation that I recorded on the afternoon that she told me about her brother's first solo flight. I have included it unamended, save for redacting the name of an individual.

She began by saying she had read my most recent *Planet Home* article and went on to say, 'You're a brilliant journalist.'

'I don't know about that,' I said.

'You are. You're wasted writing stories for dead-end websites.'

'I wouldn't say that. I mean, *Planet Home* is well respected in the climate-emergency field.'

'But someone with your talent should be working for one of the big newspapers.'

'I was, remember? You know why I –' [On the recording, my voice is too quiet to hear my words.]

'I can help you. I know people.'

'Really?'

'Yes. I was with [name redacted] only two days ago.'

'You know [name redacted]?' [The excitement in my voice is palpable.]

'Sure. I got to know her around the time I started my business. She was considering investing. We've become good friends.'

'Oh my god. I love [name redacted]. She's done some brilliant stuff. When I was starting out I emailed her and asked if I –'

'I could ask her if she'd be happy to meet you.'

'Would you really? That would be amazing.'

It's deeply embarrassing to share this, but it's a good example of how Izzy dangled names and offers of introduction in front of me. All I can say is, as foolish as I now feel, at the time I believed she meant what she was saying.

Although I didn't do it immediately, I eventually contacted the schools Izzy had mentioned – Kew Park School for Girls and Lady Goldstone School – but neither of them would confirm or deny what Izzy had said, claiming 'data protection' meant they couldn't disclose any details about previous staff or students, although the email from the administrative office at Lady Goldstone was worded as follows: 'Data protection prevents us from discussing ex-pupils or the reasons why they might have been asked to leave.'

I *was* able to confirm that Daniel was something of a flying prodigy. It took me some time to track down Andy MacLean – his flying instructor – but when I finally got hold of him he remembered Daniel immediately, recalling him as 'a natural', 'completely committed' and 'one hundred per cent focused'.

He also confirmed Daniel had indeed flown solo on his sixteenth birthday, although, contrary to what Izzy had told me, Daniel was not the first or only person to do so.

When I spoke to him, Andy and his partner had been living almost entirely off-grid for five years without access to the internet or a television. Until I told him, he was unaware his erstwhile prodigy had died in a plane crash. I asked Andy if he thought there was any chance that the crash wasn't an accident.

'You mean it might have been deliberate? Why do you ask?'

'I just wondered,' I said. There was nothing more I could say without breaking my promise to Anthony at Goldfinch. 'I guess they'll be looking at all possibilities.'

'I don't know about that,' Andy said. 'All I can say is that Danny was a natural born pilot who loved flying more than anything.'

I'd almost given up hope of speaking to anyone else who was close to Daniel when, out of the blue, I received a phone call from his wife. Grace said she'd heard from her father-in-law that I had been interviewing Izzy. She demanded I stop talking to her. When I refused to give her the assurances she wanted, she became very angry and hung up on me, but a couple of hours later called back and asked if we could meet.

I arranged to see her at a garden centre café not far from where she lived. As I drove there, I went over the little that I knew about her – thirty-three years old, widowed, a mother of a little girl and extremely reluctant to be interviewed – running through likely scenarios for our conversation in my head, but in the end I had to admit I had absolutely no idea what to expect.

Grace insisted we sit outside, even though the weather was chilly. She wore a face mask throughout our meeting.

She also frequently applied hand sanitiser and her hands were chapped and sore. She was wearing several layers of clothing topped with a beige, full-length, padded coat. Her eyes were red-rimmed and she looked pale and tired.

Despite what Izzy had said about her, I felt immense sympathy for Grace. It was impossible not to – she had been widowed with a young child in such a public way – but the truth is that I didn't immediately warm to her. It wasn't that there was anything overtly dislikeable about Grace – certainly there was no immediate evidence of the obsessive, controlling woman that Izzy had described – but she made it clear she was only talking to me under sufferance. She was standoffish and initially very curt. I arrived five minutes after the agreed time, but even though I apologised and explained there had been a diversion because of an accident on the motorway, she gave every impression of being genuinely annoyed.

She had brought her daughter with her, as she did for each subsequent meeting. Beth was almost two and was a solemn, self-contained little girl. Nevertheless, my conversations with Grace were always punctuated by frequent interruptions while she fussed over Beth, often, it seemed to me, quite unnecessarily.

Grace began by again asking me to drop my investigations.

'My husband is dead,' she said. 'What possible benefit is there in talking to a journalist about him?'

I explained that, in my opinion, Goldfinch Airlines, indeed the whole airline industry, should be made to accept responsibility for what had happened.

'Daniel was flying a completely unnecessary flight,' I said. 'That plane shouldn't even have been in the air.'

'He couldn't wait to get back to work,' she said. 'He wanted to be flying.'

I chose my next words carefully. 'Ghost flights are incredibly damaging to the environment. Every month hundreds of entirely empty planes fly from the UK to countries all over Europe, solely to keep hold of landing slots. It's scandalous.'

'I agree, but what's that got to do with Dan?'

'I really hope that by getting to the bottom of what happened it'll bring the ghost-flight scandal to wider public attention and hold the industry to account. Maybe, in this way, your husband's death can bring about some good?'

Grace frowned and I wondered if I'd gone too far. I sat in silence as she unhooked her bag from the back of her chair and pulled out a little Tupperware box full of blueberries. She prised off the lid and set the box in front of Beth, who picked one out, inspected it closely, then popped it in her mouth.

Grace had a sip of her tea then, setting her cup down carefully in its saucer, she took a deep breath and let it out slowly. 'You're not leaving me any choice. If you won't drop this then I'm going to have to talk to you.'

'Thank you, Grace.'

'That doesn't mean I'm happy about it. And, honestly, I couldn't care less about your articles, but if you're determined to write about my husband then I can't allow Izzy's lies to go unchallenged. Someone needs to tell you the truth.'

Grace's Story

2005

1.

I loved Izzy from the moment I saw her.

The first time we met I hadn't long turned sixteen and my grandfather, Jeff, was marrying her grandmother, Clare. It would be the first-ever wedding I had been to, and I was alarmed by the idea of bearing witness to a public display of affection between old people (Clare was seventy-six, while Pops was a sprightly sixty-nine). As far as I was concerned, strong emotions were things you kept hidden inside and did your best to pretend you didn't have. They were most definitely *not* something you flaunted at a grand country house hotel in front of dozens of people. Even more so when the combined ages of the couple displaying their affection was one hundred and forty-five. The whole thing was mortifying.

My mother had her own reasons to be horrified and if she said 'I don't understand why he has to *marry* her?' once, she said it a thousand times. Mum told me Pops was a stubborn old man, and Pops told me Mum was treating him like a child. I suppose they were both right.

At the wedding, Pops gave a speech which began, 'The first time I saw Clare, it was like a brilliantly coloured bird of paradise had flown into my black-and-white world ...' and there was no denying that after he met Clare

Mum and I noticed a change in my grandfather's behaviour. There were the little things, like how he stopped coming round to ours for dinner so often and, although he never forgot to drop off a family-sized box of Maltesers every Friday for our movie night, increasingly he wouldn't stay to watch the film with Mum and me. Entire weekends began to pass without him having time to do the crosswords (easy *and* cryptic) in the Sunday papers. But there were bigger changes too: he bought himself a new car – with a roof that folded back at the flick of a switch; he shaved off his beard and, instead of smelling of himself, he started smelling of Old Spice; he threw away his favourite corduroy trousers with worn, shiny patches and bought a whole new wardrobe including, alarmingly, a leather jacket surely intended for someone fifty years younger than he was.

Then he and Clare started going away for what he insisted on calling 'naughty weekends' and I had to try *very* hard not to think about what they got up to while they were away. They went on a cruise around the Mediterranean and, less than a month later, spent ten days together in New York.

Mum wasn't particularly happy with any of this but tolerated it more or less silently until the evening Pops announced he had asked Clare to marry him.

'You're kidding, right? This is a joke?' Mum said, turning from the pasta sauce simmering on the hob and staring at him.

'Would I joke about something like this?' said Pops. 'Clare and I love each other and we're going to be married.'

Mum turned back to the sauce, stirring it vigorously. 'I thought you were happy with things the way they were.'

She whacked the spoon on the side of the pan, sending a fine shower of tomato sauce over the countertop.

'Marriage is what people do when they're in love. Well, my generation does,' Pops said, winking at me. 'Can't speak for the youngsters, of course.'

'I'm not happy about this, Dad,' Mum said.

'Well, you're not the one she's marrying,' Pops said. 'Your mother died nearly ten years ago. I never thought I'd find someone else. I hoped you might be happy for me.'

'This isn't about Mum,' my mother said, dumping the pasta into a colander so violently that fusilli splattered around the sink. 'Has it occurred to you that Clare might be after your money?'

'First of all, you're talking about the woman I love, so I'd thank you not to be rude about her. And second, do you think so little of me? Someone could only love me for money, not for myself?'

Mum stopped mid-stride, water dripping from the colander. 'Oh, Dad, no, you know that's not what I meant.'

'Well, it's what you said.'

'Any woman would be lucky to have you. I simply meant you're too generous for your own good ... I mean, you've been giving her an *allowance* for goodness knows how long and you know how I feel about *that*.' Mum tipped the pasta into the pan of sauce and started stirring again.

'It's *my* money, Laura,' Pops said. 'I built my business from nothing, I earned every penny, and I can do what I like with it.'

'Of course you can, Dad, but ...'

'Are you worried there won't be any left for you? Is that it?'

'Oh, come on, that's not it at all.'

'You're not very convincing, Laura. But you don't need to worry, there's plenty of money for you. You and Grace.'

Mum carried the pan over to the table and set it down on a metal trivet then snapped her fingers in front of my face. 'Grace! Knives and forks, please. I've asked you twice already.'

She waited for me to get up, then turned to my grandfather. 'This has got nothing to do with money, Dad. I thought you were happy with the way things were. All your meals out, weekends away, holidays, all of that. Why do you have to get married?'

'It's important to Clare. I know she comes across as confident, but deep down she's really quite insecure,' he said. Mum's eyebrows shot up and she opened her mouth to speak, but Pops carried on talking. 'And it's important to me. It's important to us both to show our commitment to each other.'

'Clare's never seemed remotely insecure to me,' Mum said, ladling pasta into bowls and passing them to Pops and me before serving herself.

'You don't know her like I do,' he said.

'And whose fault is that?' Mum asked, pointing her fork at him. 'God knows I've tried. I've lost count of the number of times I've invited her to dinner, but nine times out of ten, she's *too busy*. I mean, what exactly is it she's so busy doing? And when she does make time to come here, she only ever wants to talk about herself. She's not remotely interested in me and Grace. And what about all the times I've suggested we have barbecues in the summer so we can get to know her and her family? There's always some reason why it's not convenient. I mean, don't you think it's a bit strange? You've been seeing her for ages, yet neither Grace nor I have ever met her family.'

'Well, you'll meet them at the wedding. They're lovely people. Her grandchildren are doing so well for themselves. Danny's only sixteen but he's already learned to fly and Izzy's at university. Grace will enjoy meeting them, won't you, darling?'

He looked at me and I shrugged. I was the only one eating and I had just shovelled in another forkful of pasta when Pops said, 'The other exciting news is that Clare wants Grace to be a bridesmaid.'

The pasta in my mouth instantly turned to glue, congealing into a mass which was impossible to swallow. I started choking and gasping for breath. My eyes were streaming. I gulped the glass of water that Mum handed me. Pops thumped me on the back, which hurt and didn't help at all.

When I had finally swallowed my food and stopped coughing, Pops said, 'I knew you'd be excited, Grace, but I wasn't expecting quite such a strong reaction.'

The truth was I could not have been less excited. I might never have been to a wedding, but I knew enough about them to know that as a bridesmaid I would be looked at and scrutinised, my every move examined. All those eyes judging my lank hair, my thighs which rubbed together, that little wodge of fat under my chin which looked enormous in photos and which I couldn't help compulsively touching all the time, hoping against hope it might suddenly disappear.

Mum and Pops were both looking at me.

'Why does Clare want me to be a bridesmaid?' I managed to ask. 'She doesn't really know me.'

'All the more reason why she wants you to do it,' said Pops. 'She's asking Izzy, too. We can't wait for our families to come together.'

Mum gave a little snort but said nothing.

'Besides, it will be a good opportunity for you to get to know Izzy,' Pops was saying. 'Clare's always saying how wonderful her granddaughter is. You're going to love her.'

I looked at Mum, hoping for help, but she had finally begun to eat and apparently had nothing more to say on the subject. After all, Pops was sixty-nine and well within his rights to marry whoever he wished. I had a much more pressing concern. A bridesmaid? How would I survive the ordeal of being a bridesmaid? It was just about the most painfully embarrassing experience I could possibly imagine. I pushed my pasta away. I'd have to confine myself to lettuce leaves from now on. I rubbed my knuckles on the underside of my chin. Maybe it would have firmed up by the wedding.

I didn't meet any of Clare's family until the day of the wedding. Although Izzy and I were wearing matching dresses, our fittings took place at different times because I was visiting my father in Canada when Izzy had hers, then she was back at university when I went for mine.

My anxiety was even greater when I found out the bridesmaid's dress Clare had chosen was a very unflattering shade of green, which had the effect of making me look as if I was only hours from death. The cut of the dress was no better, accentuating my breasts, which I found highly embarrassing, and also my tummy, which tended to bulge alarmingly after so much as a mouthful of food. Mum tried to intervene on my behalf, but apparently Clare had her heart set on that particular dress, in that particular colour.

The night before the wedding, Clare and her family all stayed in the beautiful manor house where the wedding was going to take place, but because Pops was insisting on doing things the old-fashioned way and didn't want to see his 'gorgeous bride before the big day', he, Mum and I spent the night in a Travelodge down the road. Mum grumbled ('If you're paying for everything, why are we the ones stuck in a Travelodge?') but Pops said it was conveniently close, and at the end of the day it was only for one night, so why did it matter?

I didn't care; my anxiety levels would have been sky-high wherever we were.

That evening, after a meal (salad, no dressing, which I barely touched) with some of Pop's friends, I excused myself and went up to my room where I sat on the bed, flicking through the TV channels trying, and failing, to find something to distract me from thoughts of the vile green dress hanging in the wardrobe and the judging eyes of all the guests looking at me the next day.

Mum drove us to the wedding venue, and I was promptly led away from her by a man who was dressed as if he had walked off the set of a period drama. He opened the door at the end of the main hallway and ushered me into a sort of anteroom. Izzy was already there.

My first thought was *That's why we had to wear this horrible dress.* On Izzy it looked so fabulous it might have been designed specifically for her. She was taller than me, slim, with wavy red hair which was arranged in an elabo-rate design (created by a hairdresser paid for by Pops) set off with a circlet of tiny white flowers. I had recently been on a school trip to the theatre to see *Hamlet*, and Izzy looked like Ophelia, except more beautiful.

I realised I was staring at her, and Izzy was staring right back. Her gaze was direct, intense and unblinking, as if she was appraising me. I didn't turn away as I might have done in other circumstances, although I couldn't stop my hand creeping up to check my chin flab.

'I love your hair.'

That was the first thing Izzy ever said to me: *I love your hair.*

I moved my hand from my chin and fiddled with my hair which, despite Mum doing her best, hung as lankly as ever.

'I'd love straight hair,' she said. 'Mine never stays where it's put.'

I stared enviously at her beautiful, lively red hair.

'And you look amazing in the dress, too,' she said. 'It's a lovely colour on you.'

'I love you too,' I said and, immediately realising my mistake, flushed. 'I mean, I love your hair, too. I'd love hair like yours. It's lovely.'

Even Izzy's laughter was beautiful.

'I've been dying to meet you,' she said. 'Nan's told me all about you. She said you're great.'

This was difficult to believe. In the run up to the wedding, I had endured a few awkward dinners with Clare, dominated mainly by Mum's silences while Pops tried his best to find common ground between us all. Other than the occasional uninspired comment about school, I honestly couldn't remember a single thing of any interest I'd ever said to Izzy's grandmother and certainly nothing which would have marked me out as being 'great'.

The uniformed man popped his head into the room. 'Two minutes, girls.'

Izzy walked over to a mirror hanging on one of the walls, smiled, held the expression for a beat, then relaxed. She repeated it several times: smile, hold, relax, smile, hold, relax. I wondered if it was an exercise – I was always looking for new ways to work off the chin flab.

'What are you doing?' I asked.

She caught my eye in the mirror. 'Practising,' she said.

'Practising what?'

But it was time.

Izzy and I lined up behind Clare, who wore an elegant cream dress dotted with Swarovski crystals. I gave my chin a final, sorrowful pat with the backs of my fingers and the three of us began the long walk towards Pops.

Danny must have been there, watching us parade between rows of chairs, but I have no recollection of seeing him. Instead, my only memory is of how terrified I was that the guests' gazes might flick momentarily away from Clare and onto me. I was fat and frumpy, my hair had escaped the clips which were supposed to be holding it in place, and I was certain I could feel my chin bulge expanding and spots spontaneously breaking out all over my face. I looked hideous and I knew what everyone was thinking: *Who is that girl? So lumpy. So unattractive. Is that the sound of her thighs rubbing together? What an unfortunately flabby chin. Such a shame she's a bridesmaid.*

Thanks to Clare's determination to savour every second of the experience, she was walking as slowly as possible, so the whole ordeal went on forever. I briefly wondered if I could pretend to faint, except then everyone would definitely be looking at me. Without breaking step, Izzy laced her fingers through mine, gave them a squeeze, leaned close and whispered, 'You look beautiful.' No one, other than perhaps Mum and Pops, had ever said anything like that to me before and her words electrified me. I instantly felt slimmer, taller and more confident. I put my shoulders back, like Mum was always telling me to do; I lifted my chin, so my neck was taut. I felt good. I may not have felt beautiful, but in that moment I certainly felt almost pretty. It was a wholly unfamiliar experience and I liked it.

Right from the very first day, Izzy made me feel seen, she understood me, she *knew* me. It was as if she had plucked me from the dark, dusty shelf where I'd been hiding and poured herself into the gaping chasm of my self-esteem.

As we took our seats in the front row, I glanced at her. Her smile was exactly like the one she had practised in front of the mirror.

Our families were seated on a long table for the meal and I was at one end, next to Izzy's dad. Roger was kind and kept a lively conversation going with me, asking about my favourite films and TV programmes and the music I liked, but I spent most of my time looking at the other end of the table, where Izzy was, watching how effortlessly she was making the people around her laugh.

I ate everything put in front me. I kept thinking how Izzy had told me I looked beautiful and somehow I was unconcerned about whether my tummy would balloon. The meal went on and on and the speeches were interminable, but eventually we were released from our seats and I made a beeline for Izzy.

'Hi,' I said, bumping my arm against hers in a way which I intended to be casual yet friendly. She turned towards me and for a couple of seconds – it really cannot have been longer – she looked right through me. Then, almost imperceptibly, something shifted, and she smiled and slung an arm over my shoulder.

'Gorgeous little Grace,' she said, 'how about we get out of here for a while? Have some girl time?'

We hid out in the same anteroom we'd been in earlier, sharing a bottle of vodka which she had managed to charm the barman into handing over. Mum occasionally let me have a small glass of wine, which tasted disgusting, and in truth, I thought the vodka was even more disgusting, but I didn't want to admit that. I was terrified of doing anything that might make Izzy like me less or suggest we go back to the party, so when she passed the bottle to me, I kept my lips pressed together and let the vodka wash over them, swallowing only a little of it.

Izzy didn't really talk about herself – instead she asked lots of questions about me and she listened to what I had to say without interrupting. It was an unusual experience to be the focus of someone's undivided attention and that, together with the effects of the dribbles of vodka, meant I opened up to her far more than I would usually. I told her about my Canadian family, my half-sister and half-brother, who lived with Dad in Vancouver, how every summer I went to stay with them, and although everyone was nice enough to me, I always felt like an exchange student, rather than a member of the family. I had kicked up a real fuss about making the most recent trip, and I'd only agreed to go when Mum promised it was the last year she would make me visit. Next year I would be seventeen, she said, old enough to make up my own mind about whether I went or not.

'Dad left Mum when I was seven,' I explained to Izzy. 'He ran off with Mum's best friend.'

'Harsh,' said Izzy, reaching for the vodka bottle, her fingers brushing mine.

'So harsh,' I agreed. 'Anyway, they moved to Canada, and when my half-sister was born, I heard Mum tell Pops how Dad said he was going to do the whole father thing right this time. Mum would be really upset if she knew I knew Dad had said that, but I've never forgotten it. It's also why I will *never* forgive anyone who cheats on me. Never, ever.'

What I didn't say was that I wasn't sure anyone would ever like me enough to be my boyfriend, so having someone cheat on me might never be a problem.

'Ouch,' Izzy said, offering me the vodka.

'I know,' I said, taking the bottle and having a proper gulp. After I finished coughing, I continued, 'It's crazy how much he spoils my half-sister and -brother, but that doesn't really bother me. I've just never understood why he didn't want to do the "father thing" right with me.' I did air quotes with my fingers and immediately felt stupid and patted my chin flub, but Izzy didn't seem to have noticed.

She took a big swig of the vodka and neither of us said anything for a while. I liked how she wasn't trying to make me feel better about my dad, and I drifted off into a vodka-fuelled fantasy where Izzy was my sister instead of spoilt, immature, Canadian Maddie.

'You know,' Izzy said suddenly, 'I've always wanted a sister. And, well, we're related now, aren't we? So, if you'd like to, we could do some stuff together and, you know, hang out …?'

I stared at her, with her still-perfect hair and her still-pristine make-up. She was beautiful and funny and charming and, incredibly, she actually seemed interested in *me*. And, more than that, despite the fact we'd only just met, she'd somehow guessed what I was thinking.

Pops and Clare weren't the only love story that day.

I had no idea how Izzy had done it, but I was hooked.

2.

Shortly before Pops got married he gave me my first mobile phone and, in the days following the wedding, Izzy and I exchanged dozens of messages covering all the crucial subjects such as our favourite Harry Potter characters – Hermione for me and Draco Malfoy for her ('a deeply misunderstood wizard'); the best cleansing regime for oily skin; and the relative merits of Foo Fighters versus Green Day, both of whom Izzy had seen at T in the Park (I was more of a Joss Stone fan, which I kept to myself in case Izzy didn't like her). She always signed off her messages with 'Iz xx' and I got butterflies in my stomach each time my phone pinged with a new message. Needless to say, I was thrilled when Izzy asked me if I'd like to go and stay with her at university for a weekend. Mum, however, was not so keen.

'You barely know her,' she said, 'and I don't like the idea of you hanging out with a load of university students. Plus, the car's going in for a service that weekend. I'm sorry, love, but I won't be able to take you.'

'I'll catch the train,' I said. 'And I won't be hanging out with a load of students, I'll be with Izzy. She said she'll show me round the university. Think of it as research for when I apply for uni next year.'

I was surprised when Mum said yes, but I was sixteen, Izzy was sort of family now, and, probably more persuasively, I had been travelling unaccompanied to Canada to visit my father for several years.

In the end, Mum rang Izzy and spoke to her and extracted several promises: yes, Izzy genuinely wanted me to go; yes, there was somewhere for me to sleep; yes, she would be there to meet me off the train; and yes, of course Izzy would make sure I didn't drink any alcohol.

Although it was only a couple of weeks away, the wait was interminable. I was dying to see her again – we had so much to talk about, she would show me around the university, and she had promised to get us tickets to see *Harry Potter and the Goblet of Fire*, which was being released the day before I was going to visit her and which I was desperate to watch.

Mum gave me some money to buy a new outfit for my weekend away, but I spent most of it on a present for Izzy. It took me ages to decide what to get her, but eventually I chose a friendship bracelet which was the same shade of green as our bridesmaid dresses. There was a genuine silver clasp, which I paid to have engraved with 'Izzy' on the outward-facing side and 'Gx' on the inward facing side (I only had enough money for six letters).

When I showed Mum what I'd bought she pressed her lips firmly together, like she was trying to stop herself saying something, but then she pulled me into a tight hug and whispered in my ear, 'You're a lovely, thoughtful girl, Grace.'

Izzy had agreed with Mum she would meet me off the train at Reading station at 10.35 on the Saturday morning. I felt very grown-up leaving home for the weekend. To begin with, I checked my rucksack every few minutes to make sure the bracelet was still there alongside the new purse Mum had bought me, complete with my train tickets and five twenty-pound notes ('strictly in case of emergency', Mum had said, which meant she expected to get it all back again).

I was trying to occupy myself by rereading *Frankenstein*, which was one of my English set texts. I'd already read it a couple of years earlier and was loving it as much as I had the first time around, underscoring passages which really spoke to me, such as 'I am alone and miserable. Only someone as ugly as I am could love me', but the closer I got to Reading, the more excited I became and the less able to concentrate. In the end I gave up altogether and stared out of the window, wondering what Izzy would be wearing, whether she'd like my dress and polka-dot Dr Martens outfit, whether she'd managed to get tickets for *Harry Potter*, wondering what we'd talk about, whether we'd go straight to the university or back to her house first, whether I'd meet any of her friends and if they would like me.

Reading station was huge. All the people and platforms were overwhelming, but Izzy had said I should follow signs to the taxi rank and she'd meet me outside the front of the station, so I took a deep breath and did exactly what she had told me to do.

When I left the station, the taxi rank was right in front of me, so I knew I was where I was supposed to be. I waited until the crowds thinned out but there was no sign of her. I retraced my steps into the station to see if she was waiting inside but she definitely wasn't there. I went back outside and tried to swallow the panic gathering at the edge of my thoughts. In all the hours and hours I had spent thinking about my visit, I had never imagined Izzy would not be there to meet me.

Finally, it occurred to me that, thanks to my new mobile phone, I could ring her. I was probably worrying for no reason – maybe she was just around the corner. I pulled out my phone and rang Izzy's number but it went straight through to voicemail and I hung up. I tried again and this time I left her an awkward message: 'Hi, Izzy, it's me. Grace. Grace. You know, Jeff's granddaughter. Um. I'm here. At Reading station. Um. Just wondering where you are. Um. Call me? Bye for now.'

Bye for now? I thought. How old was I? Eighty?

Maybe something had happened to her. Should I try and find a hospital? Contact the police?

With tears pricking my eyes, my finger hovered over our home phone number, ready to ring Mum and admit she was right, I *wasn't* old enough to be doing this by myself, I *was* feeling very anxious and, if I was honest, really quite scared. But I knew if I rang Mum she would insist I got the first train home, and I didn't want to do that without knowing Izzy was OK. I prodded my chin fat and remembered how happy I had felt being with Izzy at the wedding.

I put the phone in my pocket, took my purse out of my rucksack, checked my emergency money was still there and joined the queue at the taxi rank. I noticed how, before they got in, everyone spoke through the window, telling the driver where they were going, so when I reached the front, I did the same, reading Izzy's address from a text message, then fumbled with the door handle for far too long, conscious of everyone in the queue looking at me, before I eventually managed to open the door and slide onto the seat.

As the cab pulled out of the station, the driver – who looked old enough to be my grandfather – caught my eye in his rear-view mirror and said, 'All right, love?'

I mumbled, 'Yes,' hoping he wouldn't want to have a conversation, and busied myself counting and re-counting my emergency £20 notes. I had never been in a taxi by myself before and had absolutely no idea how much they cost. Could it be more than £100? What would I do if I didn't have enough money? I stared at the meter ticking over and worried about my dwindling emergency fund.

By the time we got to Izzy's house, the fare had reached £17.50, and I brandished one of the £20 notes at the driver, who took it. He hesitated and I wondered if there was something else I was supposed to do, but then he counted out my change and dropped it into a little groove below the window which separated us.

'Thank you,' I managed, before wrestling with the door and stepping down onto the pavement. With my heart hammering in my chest, I walked up to the front door of an ordinary-looking terrace house and rang the bell. The muffled beat of music was coming from some-where inside. A grubby net curtain was hanging by a single corner in the ground-floor front window. No one came and I rang again. I looked at the peeling plaster on the outside of the house. I wanted to be at home. I wanted my mum.

Suddenly, the door swung open. A tall guy with his back to me was manoeuvring a bicycle out of the hallway. I stepped out of the way of his back wheel and straight into a muddy puddle, soaking my right foot.

'Hi,' I managed to squeak.

He swung round to face me. 'Hi,' he said, then carried on wheeling the bike backwards out of the door.

'Is Izzy in?' I asked.

He shrugged. 'No idea.'

'I've come to stay with her,' I said. 'For the weekend. We're sort of cousins.'

He said, 'Go and see for yourself. Up the stairs, first on the left.'

'Thank you,' I said, squeezing past the bicycle, scraping my calf against the jagged edge of a metal pedal.

Upstairs, the hallway was gloomy – I tried the light switch before realising both light sockets were empty. I hesitated outside the first door on the left, then knocked. I heard a voice and, for the second time in as many minutes, a door was flung open, and there was Izzy. My initial thought was surprise that she was only wearing a towel, and a small one at that. The next thing was how she didn't seem shocked or pleased, or unhappy, even, to see me standing outside her bedroom door. Her expression was completely blank, as if I wasn't there at all or she was trying to see through me to the opposite wall. Then something in her face changed and she flung her arms around me. The towel threatened to drop to the floor.

'Oh my god. You're here! I thought you were coming tomorrow. I'm so sorry, I could have sworn it was tomorrow.'

'I tried calling,' I said.

'Shit. Sorry. My phone's dead. Do you hate me? Please don't hate me. Say you'll forgive me? Please?' She hugged me tighter. 'I'm not going to let go until you say you forgive me. We'll be stuck together forever, which might make things difficult, but I am not letting go until you say you forgive me.'

I laughed; my voice muffled by her shoulder. 'I forgive you,' I said, but she didn't let go.

'Promise you don't hate me.'

'Of course I don't hate you.'

Finally she released me. 'Thank god. I don't think I could bear it if you hated me. Anyway, you're here. That's all that matters. Come in, come in.'

She ushered me into her room, which had a musty, tangy smell, lifted my bag from my shoulder and dropped it on the floor, which was covered in clothes, some of them with labels I actually recognised. My bag lay between a teal-coloured Diane von Furstenberg wrap dress, a shirt from Karen Millen and a green cardigan from Agnes B. I only recognised the cardigan because my mum had the same one in red and would never *ever* have left it on the floor.

I was so busy admiring all her clothes that at first I didn't realise we weren't alone and I froze when I heard the sound of yawning. Izzy followed my gaze.

'I'm going to have a shower,' she said, although it wasn't clear whether she was telling me or the man in her bed.

Before either of us could reply, she left the room. I looked at the guy – other than my dad, it was the first time I'd ever seen a grown-up man with no clothes on. At least, I assumed he had no clothes on under the thin sheet draped over his body. He reached for a packet of cigarettes on the floor by the side of the bed and the sheet slipped, revealing a sparse patch of curly dark chest hair, which narrowed into a thin line running to his navel and,

I imagined, beyond. I pinched my chin flab between my thumb and forefinger, hard, so it hurt.

He held the cigarettes towards me. 'Want one?'

I shook my head, dragging my gaze from his naked body. I looked at the floor and realised my right foot was millimetres away from a condom, slick, wrinkled, with a milky opaque substance in its tip. Oh my god. A condom. With sperm. Right there. By my foot.

I looked back at the guy and, grinning at me, he swung his feet over the side of the bed. The hairs on his legs were dense and his feet were huge – totally out of proportion with his slim body.

'I'll wait outside,' I said.

He shrugged. 'Suit yourself.'

I retreated to the hallway and sat on the floor, knees drawn up in an effort to make myself as small as possible, and bounced my knuckles off the underside of my chin, trying hard to think of something, anything, other than the naked man and the sperm-filled condom on the other side of the door.

'He seemed … nice. Is he your boyfriend?' I asked Izzy, after I had followed her to the pub at the end of her road and we had settled side by side into a booth, her with a vodka Red Bull and me with a lemonade. The drinks had been bought for us by a man wearing a cracked leather jacket and combat trousers. He had a long ponytail and was sitting on a stool at the bar reading a newspaper. Izzy didn't introduce us, although she put her arm around my shoulder and pulled me close, while persuading him he owed her one for 'the other night'. In the end he agreed – I got the impression he wanted us to go away so he could get back to his newspaper – and Izzy asked him to get us both a vodka Red Bull. Although I didn't want to upset her, I insisted I only wanted a lemonade and thankfully the man listened to me.

'So, *is* he your boyfriend?' I said again.

She glanced towards the leather-jacket guy, who was once again absorbed in his newspaper. 'Not a chance in the whole of holy hell.'

Although she had misunderstood me, her vehemence was surprising – the man at the bar seemed innocuous enough and he *had* bought us both a drink.

'Not him,' I said. 'The one in your room?'

She laughed. 'Nah. He's some rando I picked up at a party last night.'

'He seemed to really like you.'

When Izzy had returned from the shower, there had been a heated discussion, during which the guy had been quite insistent that she had promised to go to some art show or other that he had tickets for.

'Grace is here,' she kept saying, as if my presence was the only thing that mattered, and in the end, she walked out while he was still speaking, slammed the bedroom door behind her and took me by the hand, pulling me out of the house, down the road and into the pub.

I sipped my lemonade. 'What's he studying?'

Izzy shrugged. 'Fuck knows. I don't even know his name.'

I had a sudden moment of panic. What was I doing here? Why on earth had I been so insistent about coming? I barely knew Izzy, beyond an afternoon at our grandparents' wedding and a bunch of text messages. Did she even want me here? Had she only asked me to be polite? Was she annoyed when I said yes? Had she been hoping I would change my mind? Maybe she actually wanted to go to the art thing with whatever-his-name-was. After all, having assured both my mum and me that she would be at the station to meet me, she'd – what? Forgotten which day I was arriving? Decided she would rather be having sex with a guy whose name she didn't even know? I should go home, I decided. I could ask her how to get a cab back to the train station. I had enough money to get there and my return ticket. If I left now, I would be back in time to see the Harry Potter film with Mum that evening.

Izzy slid closer to me, her right arm and thigh pressing against me. She leaned her head against mine. 'I'm so happy you're here, Grace,' she said, pulling my hand away from my glass and linking fingers with me. 'I've told *everyone* what an instant connection we had. How I feel like I've found a long-lost sister. I can't wait for everyone to meet you and see how amazing you are.'

She kissed me on the lips. Her mouth was soft. She was the first person ever to kiss me like that. She pulled away and squeezed my fingers tight. 'How about we get you a proper drink, hey? You do know it's basically against the law to be in a pub and drink lemonade?'

She stood up and took a couple of steps towards the bar, then turned back. 'Damn. I've left my purse at home. I don't suppose you've got any money with you, have you?'

I handed over the second of my emergency £20 notes. Izzy went to the bar and returned with two double vodkas and one can of Red Bull. She didn't give me any change and I didn't like to ask if there was any. She split the Red Bull evenly between the two glasses and pushed one towards me. Copying her, I swirled the liquid round with my finger to mix it, bouncing the ice cubes up and down.

She clinked her glass against mine. 'Chin, chin,' she said and immediately knocked back half of the contents.

'Yes,' I mumbled, taking a sip. It was sickly sweet and tasted like a mixture of cherryade and the mouthwash you get at the dentist. In other words: revolting. I was about to ask Izzy if, after we'd had the drinks, we could go and look around the university, when several people piled through the door of the pub.

'Maaaate!' shouted a tiny woman with waist-length braids who came rushing over to our booth and threw herself down next to Izzy. Another two women with identical chin-length bobs squashed into the seat opposite us while, after exchanging a few words between themselves by the door, two guys pulled up stools and sat at the end of the table. All of them were dressed in what my Pops would have called 'civvies', which I had only recently found out meant non-military uniform but was the word he used when he thought people looked scruffy. Their general air of dishevelment seemed studied – there were a few too many coats and shirts buttoned up wrongly, all the sweaters had holes in them, and their deliberately messy hair styles had obviously taken a long time to perfect. I could hear Pops' dismissive tone: *Students in civvies ... it'd take them a lot less time if they simply made a modicum of effort.*

Izzy was the exception. Although she was wearing jeans, her green blouse was silky-soft and ironed, with the buttons correctly fastened. She had large diamond studs in both ears and wrapped around her left ear was a delicate silver filigree cuff. Her hair was in a high ponytail. She looked stunning.

'I'm literally hanging out my arse,' said the woman who had thrown herself down next to Izzy. 'What the fuck did we drink last night? And where the fuck did you get to?'

'Grace, this is Flora,' Izzy said.

I held out my hand. 'Hi, Flora.'

'Oooh, hi.' Flora flashed me a smile, ignoring my outstretched hand and nudging Izzy on the shoulder. '*She's* a cutie.'

Although I willed myself not to blush, I felt the telltale heat flooding my cheeks and ducked my head, letting my hair swing over my face.

Flora reached past Izzy and picked up my drink. 'D'you mind?' she asked. 'Hair of the dog. Essential medicine.'

'No problem,' I said, and she finished it in three gulps, setting the empty glass back on the table.

'These reprobates,' Izzy said, pointing at the two girls opposite us, 'are Sophie and Milly. And those two –' she nodded at the guys sitting at the end of the table '– are Paul and Will. Will's always on the right. Like Ant and Dec. Even in bed. Am I right, boys?'

Paul and Will did identical eyerolls, but I got the impression they weren't doing it to be funny. In fact, Will looked downright miserable.

'So where *did* you go last night?' the one called Sophie asked Izzy. 'Last any of us could remember you were standing on a table, pouring tequila down people's throats like a human fountain. Then you disappeared.'

'Can we get a round in before we do a debrief?' Izzy said.

'Kitty!' yelled Flora, making me jump, and everyone but Izzy and me dug around in their pockets and produced some money, chucking it into a pile on the table. Izzy looked at me. I reached into my purse and withdrew the third of my emergency £20 notes. Izzy squeezed my hand and leaned in close. 'You're a lifesaver. I'll pay you back later.'

'Voddie Reds all round?' Flora said, and without waiting for anyone to reply, she scooped up the money and headed over to the bar.

'I'll help you,' said Sophie, following Flora.

As soon as they were out of earshot Milly leaned across the table and said to Izzy, 'Have you been with Jack?'

The two guys at the end of the table tilted their heads close together and, knees touching, started talking in voices so low that I couldn't hear anything they were saying. Meanwhile, Milly was hissing across the table at Izzy. 'I saw you leave with him last night. Tell me you didn't fuck him? Sophie will be devasted – she's convinced they're going to get back together.'

Izzy winked at me and I reached for my chin, patting it, simultaneously hideously embarrassed and completely fascinated. So *this* was what it was like to be an adult. Spending days in the pub, talking about *fucking*. I was confused, too – I thought Izzy hadn't known the name of the guy in her bed. Was he Sophie's *boyfriend*?

Millie was about to say something else, but Sophie arrived back at the table, plonking a vodka Red Bull in front of everyone including me.

'I was just telling Iz about the gig we're going to tonight,' Millie said.

'Oh, you should come,' Sophie said. 'You and …' She waved her hand at me.

'This is Grace, my super-smart cousin,' Izzy said, her tone suggesting everyone should have already known this. 'She knows almost as much about Mary Shelley and *Frankenstein* as I do – must run in the family, eh, Grace?'

I didn't know what to say. While we were walking towards the pub I had mumbled a few words about how I was rereading *Frankenstein* for school and how much I loved the book and empathised with the 'monster' as an outsider. If I had had any idea Izzy was an expert on Mary Shelley I would never have mentioned it. What must she think of me and my stupid teenage observations?

The miserable-looking guy at the end of the table – Will – said, 'I didn't know you were an expert on *Frankenstein*.'

'I'm not –' I began, but he cut me off. 'I didn't mean you. I meant her.' He nodded at Izzy.

'Sure,' she said. 'Last year Professor Mason asked me to run a seminar on it.'

Will frowned. 'You mean the module where everyone leads one of the seminar classes?'

Millie, who was about to have some of her drink, put her glass down and grabbed my hand. 'So, Grace, is it?' she said. 'You're Izzy's cousin?'

'Sort of,' I said. 'My grandfather recently married her grandmother.'

Flora nudged Izzy. 'You didn't mention anything about a wedding. When was it?'

I said, 'The twenty-second of October,' and at the same time Izzy said, 'Ages ago.'

Will leaned forward. 'That weekend?' he said. 'Really? Huh … that's interesting.'

Izzy looked at him blankly. 'I don't know what you mean.'

'Of course you don't.'

I decided I didn't like this Will person, with his buttons done up wrongly and his floppy blond hair which looked like it hadn't been combed for weeks, let alone washed. He had stubble along his jawline, but aside from that, his skin was blotchy, like he'd just got out of a really hot bath.

Flora turned to Will. 'You're not going on about Armgate again, are you?' she said. At least, that's what I thought she said.

'What's Armgate?' I asked.

'An arm disappeared from the med school morgue,' said Will. Paul reached for Will's leg and gave it a squeeze and I couldn't help noticing how he left his hand halfway up Will's thigh.

'An arm?' I said, embarrassed to hear my voice coming out in a squeal. 'What? Like an actual human *arm*?'

'Yep,' said Will. 'A good mate of mine, Noel, who's a med student, has been suspended and it looks like they're going to kick him out. The faculty got an anonymous tip-off that he was seen leaving the morgue on Saturday morning, when no one was supposed to be there. They checked the morgue, realised an arm was missing, checked his room and found the arm in the wardrobe.'

I couldn't believe what I was hearing. Alcohol suddenly seemed like quite a good idea and I took a proper swig of my drink, forcing it down, before asking, 'But why would anyone steal an arm?'

'What a very good question,' Will said. 'Why *would* anyone steal an arm? More specifically, why would *Noel* steal an arm? Why would he jeopardise his whole future for – what? Some sort of joke? It makes no sense.'

'But I don't understand … what has this got to do with my grandfather's wedding?'

'Nothing really,' Will said, his gaze flicking between me and Izzy. 'Except Noel says someone else put the arm in his wardrobe before the weekend.'

'Who?' I asked.

'I wonder,' Will said. 'Any thoughts, Izzy?'

'How should I know?' she said, without looking at him. 'I wasn't even here. We've already established I was at my grandmother's wedding.'

'No. You were here during the week and you knew Noel was away until the Friday because of his mum's operation and "someone",' Will did air quotes, 'could have put the arm in his wardrobe before he got back.'

'Wouldn't the arm have ... I dunno ... defrosted? Started rotting?' asked Sophie. 'Surely whoever found it could tell if it had been there for a while?'

I tried unsuccessfully to stop myself thinking about a defrosting, rotting arm. Vodka Red Bull rolled around my stomach.

'Med school cadavers are embalmed. It would have smelled of formalin, but it was wrapped in several plastic bags and shoved under Noel's clothes,' said Will.

'What exactly are you suggesting?' asked Sophie.

'Maybe you should leave it,' Paul said to Will.

'Why?' asked Will. 'We're only chatting, aren't we? Mates in a pub, few drinks. A friendly chat.'

Izzy said to Millie, 'So, this gig tonight, who's playing?' but before Millie could reply, Will said, 'So have I got it right, Izzy? You're still claiming you had absolutely nothing to do with Noel's suspension?'

Izzy sighed loudly. 'This is boring, Will. I was having a quiet drink with my cousin. No one invited you to join us.'

'That's not an answer,' he said, his voice sounding like he was forcing it through his teeth.

'Look,' Izzy said. She sounded like she was about to go to sleep. '*You* probably took the arm and hid it in his wardrobe.'

'Why the hell would I do that? Noel's my mate.'

Izzy laughed. 'We all know what type of mate you'd *like* him to be.'

'Just because we're gay doesn't mean we want to fuck every man we meet, Izzy,' said Paul. 'Unlike you. I mean, *you're* the one who fucked Noel.'

Flora muttered, 'Christ's sake, not this again.'

I had absolutely no idea what was going on. I glanced at Izzy, but she appeared completely unflustered by the conversation, sipping her drink and replacing the glass gently on the table. Although her head was turned in Will's direction, it appeared she was doing her best to look right through him to the bar at the back of the room.

As Will spoke, he jabbed the table with his middle finger. 'Everyone knows what Noel said about you after you fucked him, Izzy –'

She stood abruptly and tugged at my arm, so I had no choice but to stand up too. 'C'mon Grace,' she said, as calmly as if she was commenting on the weather. 'I'm bored. Let's go up to the campus and I'll show you around.'

We didn't go to the campus. Instead, we returned to Izzy's house via M&S where I spent the last but one of my emergency twenty-pound notes on an assortment of snacks. Back in her room (where, thankfully, there was no sign of Jack or whatever-his-name-was) we sat on Izzy's bed, her at the pillow end and me at the other, and

I asked what I'd been waiting to ask her ever since we had left the pub.

'Why was that guy so angry with you?'

'Poor Will,' she said. 'Such a fuck-up.'

I waited, hoping there was more to come.

'Right,' she said. 'Well, you realise he's gay, yes?'

I nodded.

'Well, Will liked Noel – I mean *like* liked him – and when I hooked up with him Will was really jealous so now he takes any opportunity to make up shit about me.'

'But if Noel went out with you,' I said, uncertainly, 'surely he wouldn't have been interested in Will?'

'Noel's bi.' Izzy shrugged. I tried to keep my expression as bland as hers, although inside I was thrilled to be having a conversation like this. To be talking about people being 'bi' as if it was the most normal thing in the world was like being granted entry to an exclusive club which I never even knew existed, let alone dared to imagine I'd have access to.

The trouble was, I had no idea what to say next and all I could come up with was '*Was* that Sophie's boyfriend in your bed this morning?'

Izzy got onto her knees on the bed then, scattering the biscuits we'd been eating, and leaned very close to me.

'Oh, Grace,' she said, her voice really quiet. 'You disappoint me. I thought you were different. I've been telling everyone about our special connection and how you're like a sister to me. I've been so excited for you to come and stay. And now what? You're chatting shit, just like Will?'

I instantly felt terrible. I'd blown it. I'd said the wrong thing and upset her.

'I'm sorry, I shouldn't have said anything,' I said. I thought I might cry.

Izzy retreated to her end of the bed and picked a biscuit off her pillow. 'It's OK.'

'Really?'

'Really. I forgive you. So anyway,' she said, 'I want to hear what been going on with you.'

'With me?' I asked, surprised by the abrupt change in both tone and topic.

'Of course. Tell me everything.'

I took a deep breath and, buoyed by the fading buzz of vodka Red Bull, I regaled her with stories of petty arguments among my friends and my suspicions that my mother was dating someone new and how I was steeling myself to go through the ritual of meeting him, having to answer whatever awkward questions he thought he should ask a sixteen-year-old girl, before pretending to like him.

Even as I was working myself up into a frenzy of self-pity, I was aware of how Izzy was giving me her whole attention, never taking her eyes off me, hardly ever blinking, listening without interrupting, apart from the occasional prompt for me to continue speaking. Being the sole focus of her attention was like wrapping myself in the soft, fleecy dressing gown that Mum had recently bought me. I felt safe, warm and like nothing bad could happen.

One of the main things I wanted to talk to Izzy about was how hurt I'd been when, in a recent phone call with my father, Dad had said Maddie and Tom had had really good school reports and he couldn't understand how he'd managed to produce two such intelligent kids. Although I knew he was making a sort of joke, because he had begun by saying 'They certainly don't get it from me', I couldn't help but wonder why he hadn't said he'd managed to produce *three* such intelligent kids. Didn't he think I was as bright as the other two? Or didn't he really count me as one of his kids? I was his daughter. I'd done really well in my GCSEs. Why was I any different from Maddie and Tom?

'My poor Grace,' Izzy said, when I finally stopped speaking. 'It's not fair, is it? It's like you're supposed to do all the work for them. Half the time they treat you like a kid but expect you to behave like an adult, and the other half they treat you like an adult and forget you're still a kid.'

'That's exactly it,' I said. 'Were your parents like that with you, too?'

'No,' she said. 'But they are with Danny.'

To be honest, I'd almost forgotten about Izzy's brother. I'd met him at the wedding, of course, but because he was a boy around my own age, actual conversation with him was impossible.

'Danny is really smart, of course,' Izzy was saying. 'My family are all members of Mensa – in fact we're the highest scoring family they've ever seen. But with Danny, my parents are, well … you know Danny's got his PPL?'

'What's a PPL?'

'Private pilot's licence.'

'Oh right, yes, Pops told me Danny wanted to be a pilot.'

'He doesn't *want* to be a pilot, he *is* a pilot,' she said. 'He's the youngest person ever to get his PPL.'

'Like *ever*?' I asked.

'Yes,' she replied.

All I could think of to say was 'Wow'.

What a family. Was my grandfather aware of what he'd married into? He had mentioned Danny's flying, but he hadn't said anything about him being the youngest ever person to get a licence or how their whole family were members of Mensa.

'So what were you saying about your parents and Danny?' I asked.

'Ah, nothing, really. He's more dependent on them than I am. It's their own fault, what with all the money they've poured into his flying training.'

'Is it expensive?' I asked. I couldn't imagine how much it would cost to learn to fly.

'It costs a fortune,' she said. 'And they've paid for it all. Not that I mind, of course, even though *I've* never had a penny from them.'

'What? Nothing?'

'Nope, nada, zip, zilch. Not a penny. They say I need to make my own way in the world. Which I am doing.'

'But don't you mind?' I asked – a bit nervously because it was a big question.

Izzy looked at me. 'What?'

'Well, it seems really unfair to give loads of money to Danny and nothing to you.'

Izzy went over to the window and stood with her back to me, looking out. I was worried I'd upset her all over again and tried to think of something else to talk about. I saw my bag lying on the heap of clothes where Izzy had thrown it when I had arrived and remembered the present I'd bought her. Despite all the time I'd spent choosing it, I was worried. What if she didn't like it? Was I was being too presumptuous giving her a 'friendship' bracelet? Did she even think of me as a friend?

I shouldn't have worried because when she saw it Izzy seemed genuinely thrilled and insisted on wearing it immediately. 'I adore it. I'll never take it off. But I need to give you a gift, too. Then we'll each have something to remind ourselves of the other.'

I didn't need anything to remind me of Izzy but she was already pulling open drawers. Finally, from inside a carrier bag, which was buried beneath yet more piles of clothes in her wardrobe, she produced a small box. It had the name of a very expensive jewellers on it, which I recognised only because it was where Pops had bought Clare's engagement ring and Mum had gone on and on about 'of course he'd had to buy her a ring from *there*'.

Izzy opened the box and turned it to face me.

On a satiny cushion was a pair of diamond earrings exactly like the ones she herself was wearing. 'Half a carat each,' she said.

I didn't know what that meant but I could tell they must have cost a fortune and said, 'You can't give me them, they're far too expensive.'

'But I want to,' Izzy said. She ran her finger down the back of my ear so lightly I shivered. 'Then we'll have the same earrings. I'd like to think of you wearing the same earrings as me.'

My ear tingled where she had touched it.

'Let's see how they look on you, OK?' She slipped the earrings out of the box and, taking my earlobe between her fingers, she gently pushed the earring through. I stood stock still, feeling her breath tickling my neck. She fixed the butterfly onto the back of the earring and gently turned me round so I was facing the other way. Then she did the same with my other ear. When she'd finished fixing the second one, she bent close and first kissed my cheek, then, to my utter surprise, she took my earlobe complete with its diamond earring into her mouth. Her tongue brushed my skin. Abruptly I pulled away.

Izzy laughed. 'They really suit you,' she said, and pulled me over to look in the mirror on the front of her wardrobe.

The diamonds caught the light from the naked bulb hanging from her ceiling. They were stunning.

'Izzy, really,' I said. 'I can't take them. They must have cost you a fortune.'

'But I want you to have them,' she insisted and kept insisting until I agreed to keep them.

We went to the cinema and watched *Harry Potter*, like Izzy had promised. We even had toffee popcorn. I spent the night on a futon, which we dragged in from one of her housemates' bedrooms, and we talked and talked until we fell asleep. It was brilliant.

The next day, Izzy made me a milky coffee, just how I liked it, we finished the snacks we'd picked up in M&S, then we caught a bus to the train station, sharing earbuds and listening to music (when I'd finally confessed to Izzy that I loved Joss Stone, she said she loved her too). We were there in plenty of time for the train, and Izzy called my mother to let her know I was at the station. 'Yes,' she told Mum, 'we've had a marvellous time together' – that was the word she used, 'marvellous'.

Halfway home, a lad about my own age got on the train and sat opposite me. At first, I studiously kept my eyes on my book but, curiosity getting the better of me, I glanced up and noticed two things. The first thing was, like me, he was reading *Frankenstein*. The second thing was, he was *really* good-looking. Much to my embarrassment, he looked up while I was staring at him, and he smiled at me. I automatically lifted my hand to pat my chin but, almost without realising, my fingers kept travelling, up past my jaw, coming to rest on my earlobe, where I touched my new earring. I smiled back at him and held my book up so he could see we were reading the same thing. He laughed, then I laughed and for the rest of my journey I kept touching the heavy diamonds, imagining them bright and twinkly beneath my fingers.

Notes

Interesting though Izzy and Grace's relationship was, Grace had hardly made any mention of Daniel. However, when I suggested that perhaps she tell me a little more about her husband, her reply was unequivocal. She *would* tell me about Danny, she said, she *wanted* to tell me about Danny, but if I didn't understand her relationship with Izzy then I would never understand what happened later. Those were her words: 'what happened later'.

What was it with these two women? Although they might hate each other, they certainly shared a determination to talk almost exclusively about themselves, rather than about Daniel. It was deeply frustrating. Even after several hours of interviews, I still knew hardly anything about him. Who was he, really? What was he like? What could possibly have made him fly that plane into a mountain? I was absolutely no closer to finding out.

My other lines of investigation had stalled – Goldfinch had refused point blank to let me interview anyone on their management team, just directing me towards their press releases – so, in the absence of anything else to do, I'd been immersing myself in flight statistics for my *Planet Home* articles.

The frequency of ghost flights was staggering. After the pandemic lockdowns were over, the reintroduction of the 'use it or lose it' policy for landing slots meant there were now around five hundred empty planes a month flying around the UK. And the pattern was repeated across Europe, where some estimates put the number of annual ghost flights at two hundred thousand, which was roughly equivalent to nearly three million additional cars on the road.

Shocking and important though these statistics were, regurgitating facts and figures was hardly going to reignite my stalled career, and once I'd completed the *Planet Home* series I'd officially be out of work. It seemed that my only option was to let Grace continue to tell me her story in the way she wanted and hope that, at some point, she would eventually start talking more directly about her husband.

Inevitably, though, she returned to the subject of Izzy. Their friendship had been so important to her, she explained, because she – Grace – had never had a close friend before. In primary school she had been bullied and although the teachers generally put a stop to the pushing, the ponytail-pulling and rib-elbowing, she had still had to navigate her way through other torments like name-calling and its big sister: the silent treatment.

When it came to secondary school, her grandfather had convinced her mother to let him pay for Grace's education, and she was enrolled in an all-girls school. My heart went out to Grace as she explained in detail the effort she made to remain invisible and thus deflect the attention of the bullies: wearing the uniform in exactly the right way (top of the skirt rolled over twice: less than that and you invited scorn, she said, more and you were labelled a slut) and only using plain logo-less bags, pencil cases and other paraphernalia.

I, too, had navigated my school years by trying not to draw any attention to myself and found Grace's memories – particularly when she talked about not showing any overt interest or intelligence in class, answering questions only when called upon to do so by the teacher – all too familiar.

I was bullied for the first three years of secondary school, crying myself to sleep every Sunday evening. My way of coping with those awful teenage years was to spend hours writing in my diary and still, today, if I'm worried or upset, I write everything down. Even as I'm doing it, I can feel the words themselves taking on my worries, and once it's all out, I'm able to sit back and look at what I've written, consider the words from all angles and rationalise the emotions I've poured into them.

For me, it's a form of alchemy and it's why I became a journalist.

Grace told me her school years weren't entirely friendless.

'Us invisible kids were visible to each other,' she said. 'There were four or five girls who I hung out with from time to time, although it did mean occasionally having to endure the whole sleepover ordeal.'

Her voice on the recording became so quiet at this point I had to strain to hear it.

'When the invisibles had sleepovers, it always felt, to me at least, that we were performing a sort of parody of what we thought a real sleepover should be like. My ideal night would have consisted of scoffing a family-sized pack of toffee popcorn while watching back-to-back *Harry Potter* films, which I secretly suspected was exactly what the popular girls did on their sleepovers. However, us invisibles spent our time doing what we imagined the other girls were doing. We had earnest conversations about make-up brands which none of us could afford, enthused about hot boys we knew, or more likely pretended we knew, and speculated on the best way to make our boobs look bigger and our thighs look smaller. These conversations were always conducted while pretending we were too full to eat whatever snacks had been provided. My heart was never in it and I seriously doubt if anyone else's was either, but no one wanted to be the person to say anything, because what if we were wrong? Being cast out from the invisibles could only lead to even more loneliness and misery, so we all continued to pretend we were enjoying ourselves.'

'Then you met Izzy ...' I prompted.

'Yes, then I met Izzy. And by the time I did I was obsessed with the idea that not a single person in my life knew the real me. Don't get me wrong, I loved my mum more than anyone, but once I hit puberty there were plenty of things I didn't want to talk to her about. When I met Izzy it felt like she saw through the walls I'd constructed around myself. She saw me. She not only saw me but she actually appeared to like what she saw. And I adored her for that.'

Grace's Story

2005–2006

1.

After I visited her at university, I didn't see Izzy again for almost eight months, by which time she'd taken her final degree exams and I'd finished my first year of A levels.

Mum wasn't happy when I told her I had spent all the emergency money in Reading (the fifth and final twenty-pound note had gone on the cinema tickets for Izzy and me). Although she'd promised to send me money, I presumed Izzy had forgotten, and after she'd told me about her parents never giving her any money, I didn't remind her. In any case, Mum didn't seem to mind too much because she said more than once that I had returned with a 'new confidence' and seemed 'happier in myself' and she thought Izzy had obviously been 'a good influence'.

I'd have loved to stay with Izzy again, but every time I suggested a potential date, something always seemed to come up. We texted a lot, though, and having Izzy at the end of the phone made coping with the day-to-day dramas at school so much easier.

Sadly, she was going skiing with friends over Christmas so I wouldn't see her, but when I came home from school on the last day of term, there was an envelope waiting for me. Inside were two tickets to see Joss Stone. That would have been exciting enough, but they were no ordinary tickets: they were special VIP ones. I would be going backstage for a 'meet and greet' with my musical idol.

There was no note or anything and at first I thought they must be a Christmas present from either Pops or my father, but they both said they didn't know anything about them. It remained a mystery until, two days after they'd arrived, Izzy texted me.

Get the tickets? Iz xx

I couldn't believe it. My text back to her was gushing, but her reply made it sound like it was no big deal.

No probs at all. I called in a favour from someone who owed me.

Will you come with me?

Course.

But then, on the day of the concert, as I was about to leave the house, Izzy texted to say she was having some 'personal issues' and she couldn't come. I was gutted. In the end, Mum came with me, although only after a lot of grumbling about why Izzy 'couldn't have given you more notice'.

The whole evening was amazing: Joss Stone was brilliant and backstage she gave me a hug and signed my T-shirt.

The only way it could have been any better was if Izzy had been with me.

Easter holidays arrived but with revision and exams looming I didn't see Izzy then either. My life was also busier because Mum and I had joined the local squash club (amazingly, a New Year's resolution we actually stuck to) and, as it turned out, I was quite good at it, better than Mum in fact, and I had begun to move up through the ranks. Because of the regular exercise, I was fitter, less obsessed with my weight (my chin no longer occupied my every waking thought) and thanks to the social side of the club I met my first proper boyfriend – Liam – although our relationship came to a premature end when his family moved to Singapore. After he left, I was surprised to realise that, although I missed him, what I missed most was no longer being able to casually insert the words *my boyfriend* into every other sentence.

A few weeks after Liam had left the UK, Pops arranged for us all (him, Clare, me, Mum, Mum's boyfriend Ian, Izzy, Danny and their parents) to spend the weekend at a country house hotel in the Cotswolds to celebrate Pops's seventieth birthday. There were only six bedrooms, so we would have the entire place to ourselves.

Thrilled that I was finally going to be seeing Izzy again, I immediately started writing a list of things to talk to her about.

When the day arrived, Mum, Ian and I left at lunchtime to drive to the hotel. Thanks to Ian, the journey seemed to go on forever. It wasn't that I didn't like him – he was fine and Mum was always happier when she was in a relationship. Ian hadn't tried to be a 'dad' to me, which gained him big brownie points, but unfortunately he was obsessed with Crystal Palace football club and on the way to the hotel he treated Mum and I to a lengthy, and exceedingly boring, diatribe about the club's various financial woes, which neither of us knew nor cared about.

When we finally arrived at the hotel, Clare and Pops were already there, and about half an hour later, we heard Roger and Sarah's car pull up outside. Everyone piled into the hallway, where I took the opportunity to check my reflection in the mirror. The sight of my own face no longer appalled me. Playing squash had definitely helped me lose my puppy fat and a healthier lifestyle had cleared up my greasy skin, but the one thing it had no discernible effect on was my limp hair, which I'd pulled it into a high ponytail, the better to show off my earrings. I was so scared of losing them that I had only worn them four times since Izzy had given them to me – Christmas Day, my first proper date with Liam, Mum's birthday afternoon tea at the Savoy in London and the last time I saw Liam. I wondered if Izzy would be wearing her friendship bracelet.

Sarah and Roger came in first, followed by Danny, who pushed the door shut behind him. I pulled it open again and looked outside for Izzy. There was no sign of her. Behind me everyone was taking off their coats and hugging each other, Ian was offering to help with luggage, Sarah was talking about traffic jams, Pops was talking about road closures, Roger was asking Danny to *please* put his bag somewhere it wasn't going to trip everyone up, and Clare was saying 'Drinks everyone?' It was so noisy no one heard me ask where Izzy was.

I repeated the question more loudly and it was Danny who replied. 'She was out last night and wasn't back by the time we left.'

I felt as if all my breath was rushing out of me and, stupidly, *embarrassingly*, for a moment I actually thought I might cry.

Pops was ushering everyone through to the lounge where bottles of champagne had been chilling in large ice buckets, but I pressed myself into the coats hanging from the wall and wondered if anyone would notice if I went up to my room. Danny was the last one in the hallway and

when he saw I wasn't following the others he said, 'Don't
worry, Izzy'll turn up. Well, as long as she doesn't get a
better offer.'

He laughed but I didn't join in. I was thinking *I don't
even want to be here if Izzy's not coming.*

'Nan told me you've started playing squash,' Danny
was saying. 'We should have a game sometime.'

He said something else, but I wasn't listening.

'Sorry, what did you say?' I said, dragging my attention
back onto him.

He was fiddling with the hair behind his ear and he
coughed a couple of times – a dry cough which sounded
like a small dog barking – before repeating what he'd said.
'How did your exams go?'

'They were OK. What about yours?'

'Same.' He shrugged. 'Waste of time, really.'

'Why d'you say that?'

'I don't need A levels to be a pilot, but Mum and Dad
said they'll only help pay for my commercial pilot's licence
if I continued with my education so I've got something to
fall back on.' He rolled his eyes when he said the last
words and his voice dripped with exaggerated boredom.

I laughed, forcing my thoughts away from his sister.
'Have you always wanted to be a pilot?' I asked.

'Ever since I can remember,' he said. He blushed and
looked down at his feet. This was Izzy's brother. Surely he
wasn't actually shy.

'Why a pilot?' I asked.

He didn't reply straight away and I liked how seriously
he was thinking about how to answer my question.

In the end he said, 'Mum calls me the family worrier
– but when I'm in a plane … it's like it's the only place

where I can really breathe. I imagine everyone on the ground, I think of all the buildings pressing in on them, and all the cars and lorries and roads and offices and ... I don't know ... it's like everything down here feels heavy and grey.' He caught my eye and grinned and this time it was me who looked away first.

'I'm not sure that even makes sense,' he continued. 'I look out of the plane and there's just sky and clouds. And even the clouds, they're so much lighter up there. And on the days when there are no clouds, everything is so bright and weightless.' Again, he coughed a dry barking cough. 'I know it sounds stupid. I can't really explain.'

'It doesn't sound stupid at all,' I said. 'It sounds cool. It must be amazing to feel like that.'

'I'll take you up sometime if you like,' Danny said. 'Flying in a small plane is so different to a jumbo jet. You know how on a big plane if you don't sit next to a window you can't see out? And even if you're next to a window, usually the wing's in the way or the windows are so tiny you can never really see much? It's completely different in a small plane. You can see everything.'

He was so unashamed of his enthusiasm, so different to everyone else my age who took pride in drenching every utterance with cynicism. He was different in other ways too. Compared to Liam, who had been positively skinny (I'd been mortified that my thighs were bigger than his) and not yet really shaving, at seventeen Danny looked like a fully formed man. He was tall, his back was broad, and his T-shirt showed off the muscles in his upper arms.

I smiled at him, and when he smiled back, I felt myself blushing and I turned away, fiddling with the pocket on one of the coats, saying the first thing that came into my head. 'Do you ever take Izzy flying?'

'She came up with me once, but she's not really interested. Mum's been a few times. Dad's scared of heights, though, so he's never let me take him flying.'

'What? Not ever?'

He laughed. 'Not ever. You'd have thought with all the money he's spent on the lessons he'd want to get some benefit out of it, but no.'

Almost as if he knew we were talking about him, Roger put his head around the door. 'What are you two doing still standing out here? Come and join us. Your mum's said you can have a glass of champagne, Grace. You too, Dan.'

He disappeared into the other room. Danny smiled at me again, and this time I returned his smile and didn't look away.

'I'd like to take you flying,' he said. 'Come with me sometime?'

'Sure,' I said. 'I'd love that.'

Pops poured me a glass of champagne. I kissed him on the cheek, he squeezed my arm and I went to join Mum and Sarah who were side by side on a sofa so deep that when I sat down my feet dangled in mid-air. I tucked my legs under me and listened to Sarah telling Mum about a holiday to Cuba which she and Roger had booked for the following spring.

'Changing the subject,' Mum said, 'how's Izzy? What are her plans now she's finished uni?'

Sarah sipped her champagne, then said, 'Your guess is as good as mine. She says she deserves a break. There's also some sort of issue with her degree classification.'

'Oh yes?' Mum asked, but then Ian called to Mum from the other side of the room.

'Laura. Come and listen to what Roger's been telling me about that golf club down the road ...'

Mum gave her an apologetic look, but Sarah said, 'It's fine. Besides, it'll give me a chance to catch up with Grace.' She smiled at me. 'I've been looking forward to hearing all your news.'

Once Mum and Ian were officially a couple, Mum had got back into the routine of having people over for dinner (she loved cooking but hated hosting dinner parties unless she had a 'wingman'). Because Mum and Sarah had got on so well at the wedding – it turned out they actually had friends in common – and as Izzy's parents lived less than a mile away from us, they were immediately included on Mum's list of regular dinner party guests. I'd grown very fond of them.

I could see quite a lot of Izzy in Roger, who was something of a raconteur. He loved good wine and good conversation, and even though most of his stories were about people I'd never met, that didn't stop them being interesting, and usually very funny.

Sarah was more reserved than Roger and seemed perfectly happy to let him take centre stage. She had gone back to nursing when Danny had started school and I imagined her as a sort of Florence Nightingale, floating soundlessly around her wards, pressing her cool hand to the hot foreheads of sick people and murmuring comforting thoughts. I realised being a nurse in a busy NHS hospital couldn't really be like that, but Sarah was so serene and caring that the image persisted.

'It's lovely to see you, Grace,' she said. 'You're looking

great. That dress is a wonderful colour on you, and I *love* your earrings.'

'Thank you.' I stroked the left one lightly with my forefinger.

'They really suit you.'

'That's exactly what Izzy said when she gave them to me.'

Sarah frowned. '*Izzy* gave them to you?'

I nodded. 'When I went to stay with her at uni. I know diamonds cost a lot and I'm paranoid about losing them so I don't often wear them.'

'Did Izzy happen to mention where she got them from?' Sarah asked.

I shook my head, immediately worrying I'd got Izzy into trouble. Maybe the earrings had been a present from her parents. Had she felt pressured into giving them to me because I'd given her the bracelet? Was Sarah annoyed with me? More importantly, was she annoyed with Izzy?

Sarah glanced across the room at Roger, but by the sounds of it he was still midway through his golf-club story. She turned back to me and said, 'Tell me about your plans for the summer holidays. Are you going to see your dad?'

I shook my head. Mum had stuck to her promise of not forcing me go to Canada, and I had told Dad I didn't want to miss out on the competitions taking place at the squash club over the holidays, which was only half a lie. He sounded really sad, and when he said 'OK, sweetheart, but we'll really miss you' I did feel guilty, but if he wanted to spend time with me that badly, he could always get on a plane and come to England.

Pops brought a newly opened bottle of champagne over to us.

Sarah drained her glass and held it out. 'Thank you so much, Jeff,' she said. 'This is so generous of you. Such a treat.'

Pops smiled and said, 'It's lovely to have everyone here,' then wandered off to pour champagne for the others.

'It can't be easy,' Sarah said, 'having your brother and sister so far away.'

'It's OK. They're quite a lot younger than me, so we're not really into the same things.'

'Still, I'd love to have siblings.'

'You're an only child?' I asked.

She hesitated for a moment, but then nodded. 'Me *and* Rog. We both hated it, which is why we were determined we wouldn't have only one.'

'Did you want any more children after Danny?' I asked, then blushed. 'Sorry, is that too personal? Mum's always telling me off for not thinking before I speak.'

She laughed and I realised her laugh was just like Danny's. They laughed like they meant it. Like they were laughing with their whole bodies.

'No, it's not too personal at all, sweetheart,' she said. 'And to be honest, before I had any children I always imagined having a whole tribe of them. Being like a sort of modern-day earth mother with an endless cycle of babies, toddlers and older ones running around, you know?'

She took a sip of her champagne, then another. I guessed she must have had quite a lot already to talk to me like this.

'But the truth is,' she continued, 'I had a completely unrealistic view of what being a parent would be like. Don't get me wrong. I love being a mum, I wouldn't change it for the world. But you soon realise every child has their own personality and their own view of how they want to make their way in the world. And their views aren't necessarily the same as your views, and that can be challenging. It's a good challenge, of course, the best. But it's like a mix of exhilarating and exhausting and as a parent you always feel you're not doing enough, or you're doing too much, or you've done the wrong thing.'

She looked at me and smiled. She had a dimple on her left cheek in exactly the same place as Izzy.

'I'm not putting you off having children, am I?' she asked.

I shook my head. On the other side of the room, everyone was laughing at something Roger had said.

'Good,' Sarah said. 'It's the best job in the world. But, well, our two were enough of a job for me.'

'But Izzy and Danny are so —' I hesitated, trying to find the right word '— brilliant,' I said, immediately appalled at how childish I sounded.

'My kids are great,' Sarah said. 'They are. But they aren't always easy.'

'Really?' I asked, genuinely surprised.

'Well, take Danny's obsession with flying,' she said. 'I mean, he's obviously got a real talent for it, which is great, but he's really reluctant to go university and get a degree. *You're* going to uni, aren't you, Grace?'

I nodded. 'I hope so.'

'Good. The thing about Dan is he's so focused on being a pilot he won't even consider whether there might be other things he'd enjoy doing.'

'He told me before that he can't remember when he didn't want to be a pilot,' I volunteered.

'I know. But Izzy took up most of our attention, so I worry we didn't do enough to help Danny broaden his horizons and see that there are other possibilities out there.'

Pops was circling back towards our sofa with yet another bottle of champagne in his hand, and as Sarah drained the rest of her glass I asked, 'Why did Izzy need so much attention?' But then Pops arrived in front of us, and when he poured the champagne, it fizzed up and over the top of Sarah's glass, dripping onto the rug. She hurried off in search of a cloth, Pops took her place next to me and that was the end of our conversation.

By the time we sat down for dinner, everyone had moved onto wine apart from Clare, who had insisted Pops make her something called a gin gimlet which, she said, 'took him a while, but he's finally mastered it'. When he put the glass in front of her, she put her hand behind his neck and pulled him down for a long kiss which made me blush and look at the table.

I was at the other end from them, opposite Danny and next to Roger, and we were in the middle of a conversation about how Gnarls Barkley's song 'Crazy' was inspired by spaghetti westerns, which it turned out Roger was obsessed with. I was saying I didn't think I'd ever seen a western, spaghetti or otherwise (it definitely wasn't the sort of thing Mum and I chose for our weekly film and popcorn nights), and Roger was telling me how I *had* to watch *A Fistful of Dollars* immediately, because 'You cannot possibly live a day longer without seeing one of the best films of all times, am I right or am I right, Danny?' and Danny was laughing and saying, '*Daaaad*, enough already, we were talking about *music*,' and Roger was saying, 'Well, you can't properly appreciate a song without understanding its influences,' then he started singing the intro to 'Crazy' really badly, and I was laughing and Danny was saying, '*Daaaaad*,' again and fake-stabbing him with his fork, when the dining-room door crashed open, almost knocking a picture off the wall. All conversation around the table stopped instantly.

'I see you've started without me,' said the figure in the doorway.

'Izzy! Darling girl. You've made it,' Clare bellowed as Izzy threw herself into the empty chair next to me.

'Course I did. Wouldn't miss this for the world,' she said, then leaned over and gave me a hug, pressing her lips to my hair. 'I only came so I could see you, Grace. I've really missed you.'

'How did you get here?' asked Sarah.

Izzy waved a hand in the air. 'Got a lift. Any food left? I'm starving.'

Clare said to Pops, 'Be a darling and go and ask them, will you?' and he was about to get to his feet but Mum said, 'You've done more than enough already today, Dad, I'll go,' then Sarah stood up and said to Mum, 'It's OK, *I'll* go.'

'Lovely to have you all fighting over me,' Izzy said. 'Just as long as someone gets me some food before I die of hunger.'

As she walked past us, I saw Sarah shoot an annoyed look at the back of her daughter's head.

'You look amazing, darling,' said Clare. 'Such a fabulous dress.'

Izzy looked down at herself for a moment, as if trying to remember what she was wearing, then she shrugged.

'Oh, this old thing. It's one of Roland Mouret's Galaxy dresses. Dita Von Teese wore it at some red-carpet event or other and I thought I might as well get one too.'

I'd never heard of Roland Mouret but the dress was like nothing I'd ever seen. It clung to Izzy, accentuating her curves in all the right places. I was sure no one, not even Dita Von Teese, would look as amazing wearing it as Izzy did. And, even while I was thinking how much I would love to own a dress like it, I also knew I would never have the confidence to wear something so figure-hugging.

Izzy pulled Roger's wine glass towards her and had a big swig. 'What have I missed? Apart from a rather decent Pinot Noir ...'

Roger reached for his glass and, when she handed it back to him, she let her hand drop casually onto mine. She wasn't wearing the friendship bracelet. Squeezing my fingers, she said, 'Look at you, my little chickling. You look beautiful. Like the ugly duckling who became a swan.'

I felt a momentary stab of hurt that Izzy had ever thought of me as an ugly duckling, but it was buried beneath the joy flooding through me that she'd called me a swan. A swan. *Me.*

She leaned close. Her hair, which was piled up on top of her head in an artfully messy bun that I could never achieve, brushed my face. 'We have *so* much catching up to do. I need to know all your news. Every little bit of it.' She laced her fingers through mine, but then Sarah came back in, followed by one of the hotel staff carrying a plate of food, and she pulled her hand away.

Izzy ate ravenously, as if she hadn't seen food for weeks, washing it down with gulps of wine. When she had finished, she pushed her plate away and hoisted her bag onto her lap, digging around inside it and pulling out a small package, which she passed to her dad to give to Pops. She raised her voice. 'Happy birthday, birthday boy!'

Roger handed the gift to Pops. It was a silk tie from Paul Smith, unwrapped save for the transparent plastic cover from the shop and a security tag which Pops wrestled with, finally slicing it off with his knife. He ran his fingertips over the flawless silk and the beautiful multicoloured swirls. 'You really shouldn't have, Izzy,' he said. 'It's lovely, thank you so much.'

'It's so generous of you,' Mum said. 'It's too much, really.'

'Yes, too generous,' Sarah said, so quietly I barely heard her.

'Nonsense,' Izzy said. 'It's the least I could do to thank you for inviting me to share your weekend. It's a privilege to be part of such a wonderful family.' She reached for my hand again.

Everyone was silent, as if no one quite knew how to respond, but then the waitress came in with dessert. She put a crème brûlée in front of Izzy, who said something to her I didn't catch. A few minutes later, the same waitress returned with a tray loaded with shot glasses, a bowl of lime quarters and three small pots of salt. Izzy dug around inside her bag again, this time producing a large bottle of Patrón Silver tequila.

'Shots time!' Izzy announced.

'That's my girl,' said Clare.

'Now you're talking ... I haven't done a tequila shot in years,' said Roger.

'Can you believe I've never had tequila?' said Mum.

'Count me out,' said Ian. 'Can't bear the stuff ever since it got me banned from the night bus. Funny story ...' but when he realised no one was listening, he stopped talking.

'I'm not sure it's a good idea,' said Sarah. 'We've already had so much to drink.'

'Rog. Tell your wife not to be such a spoilsport,' said Clare. 'One shot won't hurt.'

'There's plenty more wine,' said Pops, 'if anyone wants that instead.'

Izzy set about pouring the tequila into the shot glasses.

'Not for me, Iz,' said Sarah.

'Me neither,' said Ian, reaching for the wine.

I looked at Mum. 'Can I try it?' I asked. 'Please?'

Before Mum could say anything, Izzy said, 'Of course you can. Besides, tonight's a double celebration.'

'Why's that, love?' asked Roger.

'I've finally heard from uni,' said Izzy. 'Gave me a load of bullshit apologies, but the upshot is they've agreed the exam marking was wrong.'

'What does that mean?' asked Sarah.

'It means I've got what I should have got all along. A first-class honours degree.'

Roger leapt to his feet and gave Izzy a big hug. While Pops went off to hunt down more champagne, Clare hugged Izzy too, saying, 'I'm so proud of you, I knew you could do it.' Danny patted Izzy's arm, smiling broadly. Ian slapped the table by way of congratulations, knocking over an empty bottle of wine as he did so, which hit Mum's wine glass, which fell against the side of her dessert plate and smashed, so Mum and he started picking the pieces off the table. Sarah leaned close to Roger and said something. Until that moment, all the attention had had no noticeable effect on Izzy who, in between the hugs, continued pouring tequila into the shot glasses, but seeing her mother muttering to her father, she set the bottle on the table and said, very calmly, 'What is it, Mum? You don't think I'm intelligent enough to get a first in my degree?'

'Of course you're intelligent enough, darling,' Clare said. 'Hell, you know more than the lecturers.'

'Mum obviously doesn't think so.'

Sarah flushed. No one spoke.

'You know full well that's not what I think, Izzy,' Sarah said, and her voice was weirdly high-pitched. 'There's no doubt you're clever enough.'

Izzy kept her gaze fixed on her mum and said, 'So what's the problem, mother?' There was no emotion in her voice at all. She might as well have been asking about the time of a train.

The mottled red on Sarah's face had spread to her neck and she looked around the table. Still no one else said anything. Mum and Ian were staring intently at the table-cloth which they were dabbing with their napkins, trying to mop up the spilt wine. Clare was glaring at Sarah. Roger reached across me with one hand to pat Izzy's arm, reaching for Sarah's hand with the other.

I looked at Danny. He was staring at the table, his expression giving nothing away.

I had absolutely no idea what was going on but my heart ached for Izzy. Why wasn't Sarah delighted at Izzy's news? She should be thrilled. A first-class honours degree was amazing. I tried to catch Izzy's eye but she was still staring at her mother.

Sarah, whose face was now flaming red, looked down at her hands. 'It's nothing, darling. Nothing,' she said, and her voice caught a little.

'Mum was saying how proud we are of you,' said Roger. 'We should celebrate. Are you going to finish pouring the tequila or do I need to do it for you?'

As if his words had flicked a switch in Izzy's head, she laughed loudly and said, 'It's OK, Mum, I forgive you.'

She started handing shot glasses, limes and salt up the table. Suddenly we were all laughing, even Sarah, although her laugh was more restrained than usual, and everyone was talking at once, telling stupid stories and downing shots and asking for another tequila, or refusing to have another, and Pops was pouring yet more champagne and I didn't know what it was like for everyone else, and no doubt the drinks helped, but it was as if the evening was lit by a thousand crystal chandeliers, as if the carpet had turned lush and spongy beneath my feet. Even the air tasted sweet and everything sparkled, like the walls were papered in a shimmery gold. Inanimate objects shone. People sparkled. Conversation was wittier. Laughter was louder. And at the centre of it all was Izzy, because when she was around, nothing was dull or tarnished, and the whole world was brighter. With Izzy around, life was fun. Life was always fun.

2.

On 17 September 2006, two days before his eighteenth birthday, Danny took me flying for the first time.

When he suggested going up in a plane with him I had assumed it was one of those things people said but didn't really mean. However a couple of days after we got back from the Cotswolds he sent me a text message.

Let me know when you'd like to come flying D x

I knew what I was supposed to do when a boy – any boy – texted me. I was meant to play it cool, leave them hanging, wait a couple of days, which is exactly what I did when Liam had first asked me out. This was different. Danny was just a friend, and besides, I wanted to go flying with him, so I replied almost immediately.

Anytime G x

In the end it took almost two months to arrange a date because Mum really wasn't happy about it. 'He's so young to be a pilot,' she would say whenever I pointed out Danny had already flown more than a hundred hours since he had got his PPL. In the end, it was Sarah who persuaded Mum. 'You'd let him drive Grace in a car, wouldn't you?' she said, and as it happened, Mum had let Liam taken me out in his mother's car.

'Statistically there are so many more car accidents than plane crashes,' Sarah continued, although mentioning accidents and crashes didn't really seem like the best way of persuading Mum.

Since the weekend in the Cotswolds, Mum and Sarah had been seeing more of each other, meeting for coffee and going to the cinema, although I would most regularly find them sitting side by side on barstools in our kitchen, making their way through bottles of 'sauv blanc'. Annoyingly, since the weekend away and despite her growing friendship with Sarah, Mum had changed her mind about me spending time with Izzy.

'I'm not sure it's such a good idea, honey,' she said.

'You're the one who said she was a good influence on me.'

'I know, love, but that was before I got to know her a little better.'

'Why are you allowed to be friends with Sarah, but I'm not allowed to be friends with Izzy?' Even as I said the words I realised how childish they sounded.

'I'm not saying I won't *allow* it, Grace. I just think it's better to stick to friends your own age.'

'Why? I can make up my own mind about who my friends are. I'm not a kid.'

Mum sighed. 'I know you're not. But you're so trusting, which is lovely, darling, but it makes it easy for people to take advantage of you, and I just think there's something a bit off about her.'

'*What?* What's *off* about her? What does that even mean?'

'Do you really not have any idea what I'm talking about?' Mum asked.

'No.' I knew I sounded sulky, but she was really winding me up.

'Well,' Mum said, 'take our weekend away. She turned up hours late, brought Pops a present which was totally over the top, completely dominated the evening, kept you up all night, then on Saturday morning some man old enough to be her father turns up unannounced in a brand-new convertible Porsche and away she goes.'

It was true Izzy and I had been up all night – I'd nearly fallen asleep over lunch the next day in the award-winning restaurant Pops had booked for us all – but it was worth it because I'd had such a brilliant time catching up with her. In any case, it was a good job we had stayed up because, yes, she had left early Saturday morning, but she had her own life, didn't she? Rather than being pleased she had actually made the time to come for some of Pops's weekend, Mum seemed determined to think the worst of Izzy.

'The tie she bought him was lovely,' I said.

Mum shook her head. 'Oh, sweetheart. It was beautiful. But that's not my point.'

'So what *is* your point? I don't get what you're trying to say.'

'What I'm trying to say is we were all having a great time together, weren't we? Everyone chatting to everyone else, all of us getting on so well. Then Izzy turns up and immediately everything becomes all about her. Surely you can see that?'

I shrugged. It wasn't Izzy's fault she was so much more interesting than everyone else. Privately, I liked to imagine her as a firework in the first seconds after being lit, fizzing, sparking, barely keeping contact with the ground, desperate to light up the sky. I would have given a lot to be a little less damp squib and a little more brilliant firework.

'Look,' Mum said, 'I just think you'd be better off spending time with friends your own age.' I thought about pointing out that I didn't exactly have a lot of 'friends' my age to choose from, but Mum was still talking. 'Her behaviour can be inappropriate. You must have seen the way she was flirting with Ian ...'

'That's gross, Mum. Izzy does *not* fancy Ian.'

'I know that, darling, but she *is* a terrible flirt. And there's that odd way she's always staring at everyone ...'

'Now you're being rude, Mum. Have you told Sarah how you feel?'

'Obviously I haven't said any of this to her,' Mum said, looking embarrassed. 'And you mustn't either.'

I didn't say anything.

'Promise me, Grace.'

Eventually I said, 'I promise,' and when she smiled, I continued, 'as long as you let me go flying with Danny.'

It wasn't until we were in a plane heading towards the runway that I wondered why on earth I hadn't listened to Mum.

I say 'runway'.

We were rolling towards a strip of what looked like not particularly well-maintained tarmac which was surely far too short for anything to actually take off from. Danny and I were side by side – I hadn't expected to be quite so close to him in the plane, which he had told me was a Cessna ('fixed wing' he said, as if that was supposed to mean something to me) – and it was like sitting in a cupboard with windows. Windows and an extensive instrument panel. How on earth could he, or anyone else, understand all the switches and dials?

We came to a halt beside the runway. There was no sign of any other planes and I wondered what we were waiting for. It was uncomfortably stuffy and I momentarily considered unbuckling myself from the seat and jumping out.

'Foxtrot Echo Alpha, request enter and backtrack runway 28.' Danny's voice sounded tinny in the headphones he had given me to wear.

'Foxtrot Echo Alpha, cleared to enter and backtrack runway 28,' replied a disembodied voice, then Danny said, 'Cleared to enter and backtrack runway 28,' and as we turned right onto the runway and trundled – there was no other word for it – towards the far end, the time for escaping had passed.

Until then, I had assumed the 'Foxtrot Echo Alpha' thing was something they only said in films – I hadn't realised pilots said it in real life. Then I had a ridiculous thought: what if Danny was an actor? Did he even know how to fly?

We reached the end of the tarmac and turned so the plane was facing the length of the runway. Sweat trickled down my back.

'Foxtrot Echo Alpha, ready,' Danny said and I didn't catch the reply, but then he said, 'Clear for take-off runway 28, Foxtrot Echo Alpha,' and we were accelerating, jolting and bouncing over what felt like enormous craters in the ground. I wondered if the plane might actually break apart before we ever got anywhere near the sky and I gripped the sides of my seat, digging my fingers into the plastic covering. If I kept a tight hold then maybe, just maybe, the plane might stay in one piece. I stared straight ahead, watching the line of trees at the far end of the field rushing towards us. I didn't dare look at Danny because what if the movement of my head put him off? What if I distracted him at the wrong moment? What if he suddenly forgot how to fly this fixed-wing cupboard with windows?

The end of the runway was too close – we were going to shoot right off it and smash into the trees. We bounced sideways, ever so slightly, and my fingers started cramping with the effort of holding the plane together, then, without warning, the nose lifted and I felt the plane straining, like it couldn't decide whether to leave the ground or not, but suddenly we were rising, clearing the trees and carrying on up and up and up.

In the air, the plane no longer felt as if it would break apart, and it was immediately cooler and less stuffy. As we kept climbing, I remembered a documentary about penguins that Mum and I had watched. They were so awkward on land, but as soon as they slipped into the water, they transformed into something sleek and graceful – obviously where they were supposed to be. This plane was supposed to be in the sky, I thought, not bumping around on the ground, and I loosened my grip on the seat, stretching my fingers to rid them of the cramp, wriggling to try and itch my back where the sweat was prickling.

After a couple of minutes, while we were still climbing, Danny looked over at me, grinning broadly. In my headphones his voice cut out every few syllables. 'You OK, Grace?'

I nodded. 'It's like penguins.'

He looked confused. 'What?'

I explained about the programme. 'The plane's a penguin,' I said, and even distorted by the headphones, his laughter was infectious and I laughed too.

'You're funny,' he said. 'No one's ever said that before.'

The pitch of the engine dropped a little, and I realised we had levelled out.

'How high are we?' I asked.

He pointed at one of the instruments in front of us. 'This is the altimeter. You'll be able to work out our height.'

The altimeter had a short hand and a long hand and looked like a clock except, instead of 1 to 12, the numbers around the face of it went from 0 to 9.

'The short hand indicates thousands of feet and the other one shows the hundreds,' he said.

We were at 6,500 feet.

'Roughly one and a half times the height of Ben Nevis,' Danny said. I'd never seen Ben Nevis and had no idea how big it was.

'Fourteen times as high as the London Eye,' he said. 'Six and a half Eiffel Towers. Four and a half Empire State Buildings.'

I grinned at him. 'You've done the maths before.'

He smiled and said, 'Ready?' and without waiting for a reply he turned the handles towards me. The plane banked, not sharply, but enough that I felt my weight shifting. My breath caught, and I hooked my fingers around the seat again, but then I took a deep breath, forced myself to relax and looked out of the window beside me. Save for a few scratches and two small milky patches near the bottom of the window, my view was unobstructed.

'Isn't it incredible?' Danny said. 'Being up here. Away from everything. No parents or teachers. No homework. No exams. No worrying about what anyone is saying about anything. Just us, the plane, the sky and the view.'

What Danny had said was right: it *was* completely different from being in a big passenger plane. I leaned close to the window, wanting to see everything. Below me, a river stretched into the distance, carving lazy bends. I was amazed at quite how much of the land was fields, patchworks of greens and yellows, dotted with darker, almost black, clumps of woodland. The roads which bisected them looked like slug trails. It was as if Danny and I were the only two people in the world. I felt my chest expand, like the air I was breathing was lighter, which it was, of course, but it was as if *I* was lighter, as if I was shedding my fears and anxieties as we flew, speed-ing away from them.

Tears prickled my eyes and I rubbed them away.

'You OK?' Danny asked, but I couldn't speak. 'Grace? OK?'

I nodded, swallowing my tears past the lump in my throat. 'Can we stay up here forever?' I said, my voice barely above a whisper, but he heard me because he reached over and put his hand on mine.

When he took it away the warmth of his skin remained.

'That's how I feel,' he said. 'I want to stay up here forever, too.'

At the flying-club café, Danny bought us both a hot chocolate, complete with a huge cream hat with a chocolate Flake sticking out of it at a jaunty angle. When he set the mug down in front of me I wrapped my hands around it, welcoming the warmth against my chilly fingers. It didn't seem possible that it was less than an hour since we'd been trundling towards the runway.

'You enjoyed it then?' Danny asked and I was surprised to hear him sound almost worried, as if I might say I had hated it.

'It was –' I tried to find the right word '– incredible.'

His smile then was so wide, so unguarded, so different from anyone my age. Everyone was always worrying about what everyone else thought about them, always putting up a front, never showing any genuine emotion.

'So you get why I want to be a pilot?' he asked.

I nodded. And it was true. I tried to imagine an older version of Danny working in an office each day, sitting at a desk, shuffling paperwork, tapping at a computer, enduring endless meetings, but now, having seen him up in the vast open expanse of sky, I understood he belonged there and I honestly couldn't imagine him doing anything else.

I took a sip of my drink. It was properly chocolatey, sickly sweet, and it tasted great. I wiped some cream from above my top lip and, feeling myself blushing, I looked down at my mug and tried to think of something to say.

'How's Izzy?' I asked, reverting to my favourite subject. 'I texted her last week, but she hasn't replied.'

'She had a big argument with Mum a couple of weeks ago,' Danny said. 'She's been staying with a friend, I think. Or maybe a boyfriend. I don't really know.' He fished his chocolate Flake out of the whipped cream and bit it in half.

'What were they arguing about?'

'Same thing as always,' he said, popping the rest of the Flake into his mouth.

'What's that?' I asked, but Danny didn't say anything; he concentrated on running his thumb along a fine crack in the handle of his mug.

'Your mum's really lovely,' I said. 'But I don't get why she's so hard on Izzy.'

'Mum's great,' he agreed. 'I've got so many friends who moan about their parents, and I never do. I mean, they're obviously not perfect, but they're massively supportive of both me and Izzy, it's ...'

'What?' I said.

'Nothing,' he said. 'It's probably just mother–daughter stuff.'

'Does it bother Izzy?'

'Izzy's never really bothered by anything. Like, she doesn't really get angry or upset. She always does this walking out thing which Mum hates because it means they never really resolve anything.'

'Do you think it might have something to do with all the money they spend on your flying lessons?'

'What do you mean? Why would that have anything to do with Izzy?' He sounded irritated and I wished I hadn't mentioned it.

'Nothing,' I said, drinking some more of my chocolate.

'No. Come on. You obviously meant something. You don't think my mum and dad should have paid for me to get my PPL? I thought you got why I wanted to be a pilot.'

'God no,' I said. 'I do. Get it, I mean. I totally get it. No. That's not what I meant at all.'

'So what *did* you mean?' he asked.

'When I went to see Izzy at university she told me about how your parents paid for all your flying lessons and everything, but they'd never given her anything. It seemed a bit, well, unfair, I suppose.'

'Izzy's had loads off them,' he said. 'They've paid her university tuition fees and given her a big allowance for the last three years. Plus, they bought her a car.'

'How weird,' I said. I was sure Izzy had said her parents didn't give her anything. We'd had a whole conversation about it.

'Mum and Dad have always made a big deal out of how important they think it is to treat us equally. I know my flying lessons and everything have cost them a fortune, but so has Izzy's degree. Plus her car, and all her skiing holidays, and loads of other stuff.'

'But she doesn't have a car, does she?' I said.

'Not any more. But you do know why not?'

I shook my head.

'She was caught drink driving a few weeks before the wedding last year. She lost her licence, obviously, so she sold her car. She'll be getting her licence back soon and she wants Mum and Dad to buy her another car, but they've refused. Mum was really angry with Izzy when it happened. She was really unlucky because she got caught the morning after a party and she hadn't had any alcohol for hours and hours. She said drinks were spiked the night before, but Mum didn't believe her.'

'Why not?'

'Probably because Izzy's always pushed her luck – she doesn't like being told what to do. Not like me. I prefer to stick to the rules. Have to, really, if I want to be a pilot. What about you?' He was smiling at me, waiting for an answer.

'What about me what?' I asked.

'Where do you come on the "obey the rules" scale?'

'I feel guilty if I even *think* about not doing what I'm supposed to do,' I said, adding, 'I'm really boring.'

'Not you're not,' Danny said, smiling that generous smile of his. 'Not boring at all.'

I grinned back at him so much my cheeks hurt, and I hoped they weren't as red as they felt.

Danny drained the rest of his chocolate and I did the same, running my finger around the inside of the cup to get the last bit of cream. He had a smudge of chocolate on his cheek and I had to fight the urge to reach over and wipe it off.

'Would you like to do something next week?' he asked.

'Go up in the plane again, you mean?'

'I was thinking more along the lines of the cinema. I'd love to take you flying again, but I can't really afford to hire a plane for every date.'

I blinked. This was a date?

Of course.

This was a date.

It was as if part of my brain suddenly fell into place.

This was a date. I was on a date with Danny and he was lovely and clever and handsome. He was a pilot, for goodness' sake. And he liked me. And he wanted to go on a date with me. *Another* date.

I didn't need to think about it.

I said, 'I'd love to.'

He grinned at me and I grinned right back.

Notes

The Guardian
Live news feed
17 July 2021
10:55 BST

Although the final results of their investigation into the cause of the crash of flight GFA578 have yet to be released, the UK's Air Accidents Investigation Branch (AAIB) has revealed data showing that in the final minutes the aeroplane undertook a controlled descent from its cruising altitude of 32,000 feet to ground level. During that time the speed was increased on three separate occasions.

The AAIB has also confirmed reports that for almost forty minutes prior to the crash the two pilots on board the doomed aeroplane failed to respond to repeated requests for contact from both civilian air traffic control and from the RAF, which scrambled two Typhoon jets from its airbase at RAF Coningsby to intercept the Airbus A320. Both RAF pilots witnessed the plane crash into the south-eastern slope of Big Crag mountain on the northern edge of the Lake District.

Although no date had been set for the inquest to reopen, reports had begun emerging which suggested mechanical failure may not have been responsible for the plane crash. The AAIB wasn't saying so publicly, but the apparently intentional increases in speed during the descent were adding weight to the rumours that the plane had been deliberately flown into the mountain. Why else would a pilot increase speed as a plane headed towards the ground?

I was still no closer to understanding what had happened on board flight GFA578 and the last thing I needed was other journalists poking around in Daniel's life, stealing my story. I'd already accumulated hours of recordings with Izzy and Grace and I was relieved that Grace had finally started opening up to me about Daniel.

Unlike with Izzy, checking what Grace had told me was relatively straightforward. For example, although I have never been able to verify Izzy's degree classification, Grace was tagged by the official Portsmouth University social media account on the day of her graduation: 'Grace Lawrence 2:1 BA (Hons) Primary Education with Qualified Teacher Status'. She had also been active on Facebook for years, her feed full of photos of her and Daniel, almost always with wide smiles, cheeks pressed together.

I scrolled through endless pictures of exotic holidays, other people's weddings, Grace's engagement ring, dress fittings and countless photos from their own wedding and honeymoon. There was even a picture of a light box on a mantelpiece proclaiming in blocky black letters: 'Mr and Mrs Taylor. Founded 2017'.

Her posts slowed after that, but a renewed devotion to Facebook began when they brought Beth home, with updates almost daily, then her first smile, her first steps, her first word, page after page of it until the timeline arrived at the end of April 2020 when it stopped abruptly. Grace had posted nothing since.

There was no indication of the controlling dynamic that Izzy had mentioned or anything to suggest that Grace and Daniel had had anything other than a happy marriage, and certainly no clues as to why the pleasant-looking young man grinning out of all those photographs would decide to get into a plane one afternoon and fly it into a mountain.

Perhaps my instincts were wrong. Perhaps there was no story.

But the news reports were beginning to suggest otherwise and I'd nearly finished my work on the *Planet Home* articles. I'd already invested so much time and I had nothing else. It was this story or nothing. I had to keep digging.

Trying to find a new angle, I contacted Grace's mother and grandfather and asked if they would be willing to be interviewed, but they both refused. Before she hung up on me, Grace's mother accused me of taking advantage of her daughter's grief. I didn't agree. A couple of other journalists approached Grace after the AAIB had started releasing information, but I was the only one Grace ever spoke to. She may have been reluctant to talk to me in the first place but, despite her initial hostility, I know she felt some affinity with me: we were a similar age, she knew my brother flew for Goldfinch, and I had the impression that maybe, in some small way, she found our conversations cathartic.

Going back over those first interviews with Grace, trying to find something worth pursuing, it struck me as strange that Izzy had never mentioned that her grandmother had married Grace's grandfather. It was probably irrelevant, but in light of the friction between the two women, and in the absence of anything else to follow up, I contacted Izzy to arrange another meeting.

At first she claimed to be too busy but eventually she agreed to meet me at eleven on a Tuesday morning at the same coffee shop where we'd met every other time. I got there early and settled myself at a table at the back where it was quiet. When she hadn't turned up by 11.30 I tried calling her, but it went straight to voicemail. It wasn't the first time she'd been late, in fact she was rarely ever on time, and I called a couple more times until, at 12.45, I finally gave up and left.

Three days later I received a text from her. *Got caught up. Tomorrow?* I replied immediately, suggesting the same café. She replied *Place is a dump* and sent the address of an alternative coffee shop.

I half-expected her not to turn up this time either, but when I arrived she was already waiting. At her request, I bought her a coffee and a sandwich then began by telling her I'd been talking to Grace.

'Dad told me,' she said, between bites of the sandwich. 'And I'm disappointed, Carly. I told you what that woman was like. Didn't you believe me?'

'I'm just trying to gather as much –'

'I heard you were the other pilot's girlfriend,' she said, interrupting me.

'Where did you hear that?' I asked.

'Were you his girlfriend?'

'No,' I said, struggling to keep my voice level. Strictly speaking, it was the truth – when Luke died I wasn't his girlfriend – but still, I felt like I was disowning him in some way.

'But you knew him, right?' She pushed her plate away and picked up her coffee.

'I did.'

'You were in love with him, weren't you?'

I shook my head.

'C'mon, you can tell me. You were, weren't you?'

I didn't reply. I wasn't going to have this conversation with her.

'No? Are you sure?' Izzy wiped her hands on a napkin. She took a sip of coffee. 'You're not lying to me are you, Carly?'

'What? No.'

'Because I'd be really disappointed if you weren't being truthful.'

'I knew Luke,' I said. 'But I wasn't his girlfriend.'

'If you say so,' she said. 'Are you interrogating his family as well?'

'Is that how it feels? Like I'm interrogating you?'

'Aren't you?'

'I'm just trying to understand what happened on that plane,' I said.

'Maybe,' she said. 'But what you need to understand before anything else is that *I'm* the only person who really knew my brother. Not Grace. Me. I was the one person that was always there for him. *Always.* Dan wasn't Dan without me. Understand?'

She gazed at me, unblinking, until I nodded my head, then moved her chair so she was facing away from me.

This was a side of Izzy I'd never seen before. She'd always been so friendly. Supportive. Understanding. I thought we had a real connection. I mean, sure, she'd told me some very questionable stories, but she was chatty and warm and always seemed genuinely interested in me. I'd been looking forward to seeing her. But now she was behaving as if I'd let her down in some way that I didn't understand.

I was suddenly very hot, my mouth completely dry, beginning to feel really panicky. Without Izzy, I had no story.

I stood up. 'I'm going to get to some water.'

I went to the back of the café where they kept jugs of iced water and poured us both a glass, trying to understand what was happening.

Was it because of Luke? I hadn't told Izzy I knew him, but plenty of our friends had shared pictures of us on social media over the years, so it would have been simple enough for her to work out that we knew each other.

Maybe I should have been more upfront about knowing Luke and my belief that her brother was responsible for his death. But I'd given Anthony my word that until the results of the investigation were made public I wouldn't tell anyone what he'd told me. Besides, I'd given Izzy no reason to think that I knew anything more than she did about what had happened.

No. It must be because I'd been speaking to Grace. Could the antagonism between them really be so all-consuming that Izzy couldn't bear the idea of me talking to her? Surely she could understand why I would want to interview Daniel's wife.

I carried the glasses of water back to the table. Izzy was still facing away from me, scrolling through something on her mobile. As I sat down I accidently banged the table leg with my foot. Water slopped out of the glasses and a pepper grinder that had been precariously near the edge of the table fell onto the floor. Izzy didn't react. She didn't even glance up from her phone.

I picked up the pepper grinder, mopped up the spilled water, drank what little remained in my glass and, with my mouth still dry, broke the silence between us.

'I understand that you're unhappy I spoke to Grace,' I said, picking my words carefully. 'But what sort of journalist would I be if I didn't?'

She put her phone on the table and scraped her chair back round to face the table. 'Are you still writing about ghost flights?'

'I am. Look …'

Relieved she was at least talking, I opened the *Planet Home* website on my phone and clicked on the most recent article, holding it up for her to see.

'I know, I know. I read it.'

In which case, I wondered, why had she asked the question?

She crossed her arms. 'Why am I here, Carly?'

'As I've said all along, I'm just trying to find out what happened on that plane. I apologise if you're finding it upsetting.'

'I'm not upset.' She shrugged. 'What is it you want to ask me about this time?'

'Well,' I said, 'I hoped you might tell me a little more about your family's connection with Grace's family. I know your grandmother married her grandfather and I was curious that you hadn't mentioned it. I gather they weren't married for very long. Is that right?'

Izzy reached across the table, putting her hand on top of mine. As the weight of her fingers settled on mine, she smiled. 'See?' she said. 'How difficult is that? You ask me questions and I'll tell you everything you need to know.'

Izzy's Story

2008

1.

I was twenty-three when Nan had a stroke. I went to the hospital to ask her to give me her car. My parents were refusing to buy me one and Nan obviously had no need of hers. She'd be lucky to ever walk again, let alone drive.

She didn't wake up while I was there. Instead, she died. They said afterwards that it was another massive stroke, but all that happened was one of the machines started beeping and she stopped breathing. One moment, my grandmother was there in the room, and the next, she wasn't. I'd handled an embalmed arm at university but this was the first time I'd seen an entire dead body. I pressed a finger into her pale cheek – she always hated to be seen without make-up – and tried to work out exactly what had changed in the moment when she went from being alive to being dead. From being a person to being a corpse. Her heart had stopped beating, and she had stopped breathing, but it seemed like there was something else, although what it was eluded me. It was annoying, but not nearly as annoying as the fact she had died before I had had a chance to resolve the car situation.

I understood how I'd be expected to behave after Nan died, which is why, when I left the hospital, I considered heading straight for the train station. The problem was I didn't have anywhere to go. The guy I'd been living with had lost his job so the meals out and weekends away had come to an abrupt halt. Returning to his flat was a non-starter. Besides, if I didn't go to my parents, I wouldn't have a chance to speak to Jeff about Nan's car. Reluctantly, I went home.

I'd been back for less than a day when I found Dad crying in the living room. I didn't understand the purpose of his tears (after all, Nan was dead, and sitting in an armchair sobbing wasn't going to change that) and I had no idea how to interact with him when he was like that.

Mum tried to talk to me. 'It's OK to be angry,' she said. 'It's understandable. But it's not Dad you're angry with. You shouldn't take it out on him.'

Actually, it *was* Dad I was angry with, but there was nothing to be gained by telling her that.

Mum continued to drone on about how 'close you were to your Nan', and did I want to talk about 'how you're feeling'.

I explained how interesting I had found it, watching someone go from being alive to being dead, but how I hadn't been able to identify what exactly had changed. As usual Mum completely misunderstood what I was saying and said, 'Don't feel guilty about not visiting her for a few months. Nan knew you loved her.'

The truth is, I don't think I did *love* Nan. I mean, I *liked* her. I liked her a lot. She had been one of my favourite people. She could be very funny, and she was one of the least dull people I knew. I liked the money she gave me, and I liked how she had let me drink alcohol with her when I was a child. I liked how she preferred me to Danny, and I liked how she didn't give a shit about anything or anyone, but *love*?

What I can say is that I *respected* my grandmother.

I respected how she relentlessly pursued what she wanted. She was single-minded and driven and eventually she bagged herself a rich man. She could finally put her bridge cards down on the table with a flourish, knowing her fingers were littered with rings which were bigger than anyone else's. She wore expensive clothes, she lived in a large house, she went on extravagant holidays, she flew first class. She drank champagne not Prosecco, exactly as she had wanted, and I respected that.

It was just a shame she only managed to get three years of marriage out of Jeff before she died.

There was to be a service at the crematorium, followed by drinks and sandwiches at Jeff's golf club. I offered to give a speech – there were any number of amusing anecdotes I could relate about my grandmother – but Dad said, although it was lovely of me to offer, there would only be enough time for him and Jeff to speak.

As chief mourners, we travelled in a car behind the hearse and everyone else was already there when we arrived at the crematorium, which meant I could show off my outfit. I felt as if I'd been in training for this day for most of my life. I'd really enjoyed assembling my grand-daughter-in-mourning look, and in the end I paired a vintage Jean Muir little black dress with some Maud Frizon purple pumps (which I'd had to get shipped from America), a Chanel pill-charm double-chain necklace and a vintage pillbox with a spotty gauze veil. As we followed the coffin through the hall, everyone was looking at me.

When we reached the front, Grace, her mum and her mum's deadbeat boyfriend were already occupying three of the seats. Of course they were. They were such a pathetic little family that they had adopted ours. Or got themselves adopted by us. That was more like it. How thrilled they must have been when Jeff met Nan and they had an opportunity to become part of our family. How shamelessly they had wormed their way into our lives. My mum and Grace's mum had even been on a 'girls holiday' to Majorca together.

But that was *nothing* compared to the Danny and Grace 'relationship' which, by the time of Nan's funeral, had been going on for nearly two years. It was impossible to imagine anyone good enough for my brother, but *she* really could not have been less suitable. I had no idea what Danny saw in her.

But before I could turn my attention to the Grace problem, I had a funeral service to get through. The crematorium was almost full, which wasn't really a surprise as Nan had been considered something of a 'character' in the various clubs to which she belonged, and although in the last few years she had spent a lot of time away on holiday with Jeff, she had nevertheless kept up her attendance when she was at home. After all, she wanted as many people as possible to hear her say such things as 'Yes, we're off to the Seychelles next week' and 'So important to get some winter sun, don't you think?' There was a good turnout from the bridge club, the bowling club, their local pub and Jeff's golf club. I guess the promise of free wine after the service was a draw as well.

Jeff, dressed in a very dull black suit and tie, stood at the lectern and began to talk about Nan.

'At our wedding, only three years ago, I called my Clare a bird of paradise,' he said and I hoped he wasn't planning to regurgitate the whole of what had been a particularly nauseating speech.

He wasn't, as it turned out, and in fact he didn't get much further before he began to cry. I don't know what my grandmother would have made of this – I never saw her cry and I personally haven't cried since I was a baby – but when Jeff began to cry, it started Mum off. Grace's mum, Laura, reached over to hold Mum's hand, then Laura was crying, too. Next to me, Dad's cheeks were wet and even Danny was sniffling, rubbing his sleeve across his face.

Selfishly, absolutely nobody was giving any thought to how this made me feel because, while Jeff was struggling to speak through his tears, droning on about how unbelievably happy Nan had made him in their short marriage and how it was a miracle to have another chance at love, the weight of their wanton, uncontrolled, incontinent emotions buffeted me from all sides. I began to feel sick. It was impossible to sit still. I shifted in my seat, crossed and uncrossed my legs, pressed my thighs tightly together. I rolled my head from side to side. I folded and unfolded my arms. Folded them again. Crossed my legs again. Jeff went on and on. Tears splashed onto Mum's hand, Dad gulped into a handkerchief, Danny wiped his nose on the back of his hand. For god's sake, why wouldn't they stop? Their emotions pounded me relentlessly and I could feel my skin tightening, smothering me, clogged and filthy with their grief. I considered whether it was possible to rip out their stupid fucking tear ducts. I glared at Jeff and mouthed 'Shut up'. Shut UP. Shut the fuck up. Shut up. Shut up. SHUT THE FUCK UP.

I stood. Mum tried to pull me back down.

'Where are you going?' she hissed through her tears.

'Toilet,' I hissed back.

I'm very proud of walking away that day rather than 'making a scene' as Mum would have called it. I like to think my grandmother would have been proud of me too. I took step after step away from them all. Step after step towards the back of the room, and with each one I felt a little looser, breathed a little easier until, eventually, I reached the exit. People were looking at me but whatever they were thinking was their problem, not mine. I made a particular point of leaving quietly, shutting the door behind me without a sound, before crossing the foyer and stepping outside.

The four undertakers were leaning against the cars. When they saw me they stood up straight and fussed with their black coats, doing up the buttons, but when they realised no one was following me they relaxed.

'Anyone got a cigarette?' I asked.

Three of them shook their heads, but the youngest one, not much older than me, reached inside his coat and pulled out a pack.

'Not on the job, John,' said one of the others.

'I'm not,' he replied, holding the packet out towards me.

I never buy cigarettes myself, but bumming a smoke is the most effective shortcut to striking up a conversation so I took one and leaned in so John could light it for me.

'Did it get too much for you in there? It happens a lot,' he said, tucking the cigarettes and lighter back inside his coat. His biceps strained against the material; he obviously worked out.

'Got a bit hot.' I winked at him. 'You know how it is.'

He glanced at the other three men and I looked at them too, but they weren't paying us any attention.

'Your grandmother's funeral, isn't it?' he said.

I nodded.

'I'm sorry for your loss.'

I didn't say anything, instead I considered how elegant my hand looked, holding the cigarette between my thumb and my first finger. Perhaps I should start carrying around one of those long cigarette holders. I'd seen a picture of an old actress with one and it looked really sexy.

'Were you close to her?' John asked.

'Who?'

'Your grandmother. Were you close?'

'Oh. Yeah. She brought me up when my parents were in Ulan Bator.'

He looked at me, blankly.

'In Mongolia. They were Christian missionaries. I lived with Nan while they were there.'

'Wow,' he said. 'So how come the funeral isn't at a church?'

'What do you mean?' I asked.

'I mean, with your parents being missionaries.'

'They lost their faith. Came home. I went back to live with them and that's when Nan took up skydiving.'

John frowned, looking past me towards the other undertakers. For a young guy, he was very serious, but at least talking to him was more fun than listening to Jeff drone on about his dead wife.

'It's how Nan died,' I said. 'Jumped out of the plane. Parachute didn't open.'

John felt around inside his coat, half pulling out the pack of cigarettes before presumably remembering he wasn't allowed to smoke on the job. He pushed them back into his pocket and I offered him a drag of mine, but he shook his head. 'Is that *really* how she died?'

'What?' I said. 'Don't you believe me? It was all over the news. High-flying supergran dies in terrifying plunge … that sort of thing.'

He looked at me for a moment before saying, 'That's awful.'

'Mmm,' I replied. Then I said, 'Funny job to have. Shifting dead people around.'

'It's my father's company.' He nodded at one of the other men. 'That's him there. I'm actually training to be an architect, but Dad asked me to help out because his usual fourth man has broken his leg. Bit difficult to carry the coffin with your leg in a cast.' He laughed, but he hadn't said anything funny, so I didn't.

I nodded at the car. 'Ever done it in the back of the hearse?'

'What? No!' He looked shocked.

'Never?' I asked.

'No.'

'Shame,' I said. I'd reached terminal boredom with John so it was a relief to hear the opening chords of 'Wind Beneath My Wings' inside the crematorium, which Jeff had chosen to mark the moment the service ended and the coffin rolled out of sight.

I threw the cigarette onto the ground, took a few steps away from John, buttoned up my blouse, arranged my face into a sad expression and turned to face the door.

At the golf club, people I didn't know kept coming up to me to tell me how proud of me Nan was, how like her I looked, how she had always said I took after her. I was tempted to get drunk, but the wine tasted like shit, so instead I occupied myself by working on a plan to get Grace out of Danny's life.

Obviously she had made a beeline for me. She never changed, always so timid and needy. I couldn't remember why on earth I had let her hang around with me, beyond the fact it was always useful to have an acolyte or two. It was pleasant to be adored, but people had to have something more about them for me to stay interested, and Grace was completely pathetic. Toying with her had stopped being fun long ago, but she never gave up: always coming back for more, trying to pretend we were best friends.

Right on cue, she came bounding up to me like a baby goat. She flung her arms around me and, in that irritatingly breathless way she had, she said, 'I'm so sorry about your nan, Izzy.'

'Hello, Grace,' I replied, pushing her away.

She was wearing the earrings I'd given her. It was funny, really, how she was always wearing them whenever I saw her. I wondered if she would be quite so keen on flaunting them if she knew where they had come from. Having said that, they *were* lovely, not like that horrible bracelet she'd given me which I got rid of the first chance I could – in a bin outside Reading train station.

'I've missed you,' she said. 'How are you?'

I shrugged. 'OK.'

'Are you going to be staying at your parents for a while?' she asked. 'We must have a proper catch-up.'

I shrugged again. 'Dunno.'

She tried to hold my hand, but I shoved it in my pocket, leaving her arm hanging in mid-air, so instead she reached for the underneath of her chin, stroking it with her knuckles. She was always doing that.

'It must be really hard for you today,' she said. 'Danny's really upset.'

As if she had summoned him, my brother appeared in front of us, putting an arm around Grace, pulling her close and touching his lips briefly to her head. 'Hey, gorgeous,' he said. Grace closed her eyes for a moment and slipped her arm around his waist. I almost spat out my wine.

Why was he so concerned about *her*? His first thought should have been for *me*. I always, *always* put Danny first, above all others. I always had. But this limp-haired little mouse-baby had inveigled her way into his affections and stayed there. Somehow she had charmed Danny with her blandness. God knows I'd tried telling him that she didn't deserve him, but whenever I said that to him he'd just laugh, as if I was making a joke. Occasionally he'd say, 'She'll never stop being your friend, Iz,' as if I was somehow concerned that she liked him more than she liked me, and other times he'd say, 'You'll find someone soon, Iz,' like *that* was my concern. Poor deluded Danny. As usual it would fall to me to do what was best for him.

Later, our families went back to Jeff's house, and while everyone else was eating a takeaway and gossiping about the people who had come to the funeral, I waited for Jeff outside the bathroom. I could hear him splashing water on his face, blowing his nose, then splashing water on his face again. Eventually he unlocked the door.

'Oh, hello, Izzy love,' he said. His face was pink and blotchy and his forehead shone with drops of water. 'What a day it's been. Are you doing OK? I know how close you were to your nan. I still can't really believe she's gone –'

'It was a lovely service,' I said, cutting him off before he could work himself up into yet more tears. 'You did her proud. You did us all proud.' I'd heard Mum say the exact same thing to him earlier.

'Thank you, love,' he said. 'That's so kind of you. Clare deserved the very best. She made me so happy.'

His face contorted and he looked like he might be about to rush back into the bathroom for another round of tears, nose-blowing and face-splashing, so I said, 'I wondered if I could ask you a favour?'

He nodded and put his hand on my arm. 'You ask away, love. Anything for Clare's little Izzy.'

'I wondered if I might borrow Nan's car for a while. I'd like to feel close to her. You know, have something that belonged to her. I think it'll help.'

I pulled my face into what I hoped was an approximation of a grief-stricken expression. He held his arms wide and I stepped into his embrace, letting him hug me tightly. When he finally let go he said, 'You take the car, love. I know that would make Clare happy.'

As I accelerated away from Jeff's house in the convertible BMW, I was annoyed to see there was less than half a tank of petrol, but I consoled myself that at least something positive had come out of a long and tedious day.

Notes

I asked Izzy why she had told the undertaker that her grandmother had died in a skydiving accident, but she just laughed. When I repeated the question she sighed loudly, as if I had asked her something really stupid. 'Why not? It was a boring day – I had to do something to liven things up.'

Then she shrugged and changed the subject, saying she'd read another of my *Planet Home* articles and that it was 'Brilliantly articulate. Forensically researched. Compelling reading.'

I was, and remain, really proud of that series of articles, which ended with a clarion call to arms:

> *When future generations look back on the failure to halt the climate catastrophe, who will they hold to account? As we have revealed in this series, the aviation industry, governments and the EU are all complicit. And today, with the publication of our Clean Sky Manifesto, we at* Planet Home *are demanding the immediate cessation of all ghost flights and an end to this entirely avoidable scandal in our skies.*

However, no matter how urgent the subject matter and as much as the *Planet Home* team and I hoped to raise awareness of the ghost-flight scandal, the articles appeared to have sunk without trace. Other than my family, who loyally read everything I wrote, nobody else apart from Izzy had mentioned them to me.

Not for the first time, I allowed Izzy's praise and her apparent interest in my career to cloud my judgement.

I should have been pressing her harder. I should have done more to understand what was true and what wasn't. I shouldn't have accepted her increasingly outlandish stories. Was she telling the truth about lying or was she lying about lying? When I listen to recordings of my conversations with her, I'm embarrassed and I accept that I was unprofessional.

Frequently, Izzy would go off on completely random tangents and I'd struggle to bring the conversation back to what I wanted to talk about. For example, I asked Izzy why she was angry with her father after her grandmother died, and in response she launched into a rambling speech about how almost everyone except her spends their lives entirely at the mercy of their emotions, over which they have little or no control, never sure when an unwanted or unneeded feeling is suddenly going to overtake them and throw them off course. After several minutes of this, she said, 'Some emotions, like fear, insecurity or shame, are really useful to work with. But for me, people in the grip of grief or rage, say, are chaotic and baffling because they're unpredictable. It's exhausting for me to act how they expect me to act.'

I had no idea how to respond to that, and on the recording there is a long pause while I tried to think of something to say.

She also liked to talk about her business and its roster of wealthy, high-profile clients, making it very clear how much she respected money. 'Rich people can indulge their whims. They can be spontaneous and reckless. Rich people can afford to act without worrying about consequences. Money solves all problems.'

Another time she told me, 'There's plenty of money out there. All you have to do is work out how to get it. Poor people are usually poor because they are either stupid or lazy.'

But I'm *poor*, I thought. My card had just been declined when I tried to buy her a second cup of coffee.

Almost as if she could read my thoughts, Izzy said, 'You're different, Carly. I can tell. You're neither stupid nor lazy. It's just a temporary situation. Once I introduce you to my contacts you'll be rolling in it.'

The thing about Izzy was that, no matter how unlikely her claims, her absolute confidence in her own abilities made them seem so plausible.

It's only with the benefit of time and distance that I can see how obviously she manipulated me. It's deeply embarrassing and all I can offer in my defence is I was lonely, grieving and desperate to uncover a story.

However, it is also true that had I refused to indulge her and listen to her outlandish tales, then I would never have got to the bottom of why Daniel did what he did.

Izzy's Story

2009–2010

1.

I started my first business when I was at university. The idea came to me when I was trying to find someone to write an essay for me or, failing that, trying to find an essay which I could copy. It was clear there was a demand among university students for pre-written, high-quality, grade-guaranteed essays. At the time, I had had a brief relationship with a postgraduate student, and when I realised what a hand-to-mouth existence most postgrads had I was certain some of them would be happy to churn out words for money. I'd identified a demand and found a supply. All I needed to do was bring the two together. Simple.

By the time of Nan's funeral, I had built up a network of postgraduates across multiple universities who kept me supplied with essays. Once a student bought an essay, they would often recommend my services to their friends and all I had to do was collect money from the under-grads, pay the postgrads their share and make sure students on the same course weren't submitting the same essay (not that I cared if they were caught – which happened more than once in the early days – but if they were caught they were less likely to recommend me to their friends).

The issue was that a client base made up entirely of students was never going to generate sufficient income for my needs, so from time to time I had to resort to getting what my parents insisted on calling a 'proper job'.

The way they threw the phrase 'proper job' around all the time was so boring. They said things like unless I had a 'proper job' I wasn't allowed to treat our home 'like a hotel'. I frequently pointed out how unreasonable they were being. They were the ones who wanted to have children and they couldn't simply abandon their parental responsibilities as and when they chose. Their home was my home and always would be. Besides, I didn't see them telling Danny to get a 'proper job' and all he did was work at the flying club while he studied for his commercial pilot's licence (which *they* were paying for).

But once I left university Mum and Dad were adamant that they would only let me live at home if I had one of these so-called 'proper jobs'. It was handy to be able to go back there when I wanted – it was rent free, with a well-stocked fridge – so it was in my interests to keep them happy. I had a variety of roles but either the hours were too much of a drag (evening bar work and early morning barista) or a waste of my abilities (receptionist and data-entry clerk). On the occasions I secured a position that was more appropriate for someone with my talents, I was never kept on beyond the probation period, which was no surprise. No one would say it out loud, but it was obvious that senior management were intimidated by my intellect and scared for their own jobs.

Employment opportunities came and went in rapid succession until I saw an advert for a role at a charity.

I updated my CV to add my recent experience. 'Deputy head of marketing' at the insurance company where I had worked most recently was going to have more impact than 'customer services assistant', I thought, typing it in immediately below 'first-class honours degree'. As it turned out, it was the deputy head of marketing job that convinced Flora's mother to employ me.

Flora and I had been friends at university. She knew how to have fun and I enjoyed having her around. That is, until part way through our final year when her brother Christopher, a professional footballer, died of hypertrophic cardiomyopathy, which basically meant his heart stopped. After that, Flora changed. Instead of partying, all she did was mope around, and when I did make the effort (and it really was an *effort*) to spend time with her, she expected me to listen to her whine on about how much she missed dead Christopher, and how *unfair* life was, and how, even though she was on antidepressants, just getting out of bed felt impossible and no *of course* she didn't want to come to a party with me and please could I sit with her and listen to her while she went on and on about how completely and utterly tedious she had become.

The burden on me was enormous, so I cut off all contact, stopped responding to her texts and messages, ignored her phone calls and found other people to spend my time with.

But after leaving the insurance company, when I saw the marketing and communications manager role advertised at HCAssist – the charity her mother had set up to support families of people affected by hypertrophic cardiomyopathy – I decided it was time to get back in touch with Flora.

She wasn't as enthusiastic to see me as I had expected and we hadn't even finished our first drinks when she said, 'I nearly didn't come this evening. You dumped me as a mate, Izzy.'

I didn't reply. I mean, obviously she was right.

'I was going through a really shit time,' she continued. 'The worst time of my life, and you ghosted me.'

'I had shit of my own to deal with,' I said.

'Really? Like what? What can be as bad as my brother dying?'

I shrugged.

'You really hurt me, Iz. I thought we were best mates but when I needed you, I mean, when I *really* needed you, you cut me off without a word. What sort of friend does that?'

'My sister died,' I said, forcing myself to speak quietly, which people do when revealing something they find difficult to talk about.

Flora sat back in her chair, not noticing the wine she was spilling onto her dress. 'What? What the actual fuck, Iz?'

'My sister died,' I said. 'And when your brother died, it brought back memories. Really traumatic memories. It made me feel –' I cast around for appropriate feelings '– sad ... and depressed. I was sad and depressed.' Then I threw in, 'And anxious,' for good measure.

'Fucking hell, Iz. I knew you had a brother, but I had no idea you had a sister. That's awful. When did she die?'

I thought about it for a moment. *Before I was born* did not seem likely to elicit the appropriate response, and before I could reply, Flora said, 'Can you talk about it? I mean, do you *want* to talk about it?'

I shook my head. I did not want to talk about it.

Flora got up from her chair, put her arms around me and pulled me close. She buried her face in my neck and said, 'Oh my god, Iz. I had no idea. Why didn't you ever tell me?'

When she sat back down, her eyes were wet and I wondered if it might be a good time to mention the job at her mother's charity, but then she said, 'What was her name?'

'Daisy,' I said, which was an easy one since my dead sister really *had* been called Daisy.

Flora leaned forward. 'How old were you when she died?' she asked.

'Ten?' I offered, which was probably old enough to have been terribly traumatised by the death of a sister.

'And how old was Daisy?'

'Twelve.'

'Shit. So young. How did she die?'

'Car crash. Me and Danny were both OK,' I said, warming up a little to the idea of my sister's death. 'But Daisy was between us on the back seat and she wasn't wearing a seat belt and she broke her neck. I watched her die.'

Flora wiped her eyes. 'Christ, Izzy. I can't believe it. That's horrendous. I'm so sorry.'

'It's OK,' I said.

'No,' she said. 'No, it's not OK. I wish you'd told me. I wish I'd known you were carrying such an awful thing around with you.'

'I don't like talking about it.'

'Of course not, no, I can understand that. It must be so difficult. And that's why you were so off with me after

Chris died? I mean, of *course* you were. It's completely understandable. The whole thing must have brought back such awful memories. God, I feel terrible that I didn't realise something was up with you. I should have known because it was so weird, the way you disappeared, but I get it. I get you were protecting yourself, but I wish you'd told me.'

'I don't like talking about it.'

'God, no, I know. I'm so sorry. I feel terrible. Forgive me?'

I smiled. 'Of course. Another bottle?'

'This one's on me,' she said.

Later that evening, when I happened to mention how I had recently resigned as deputy head of marketing at an insurance company and wasn't sure whether to take some time off or start looking for another job, Flora said, 'Oh my god, the charity my mother set up is looking for a marketing person. You'd be perfect for it, Iz. Shall I put you in touch with Mum? She'll totally love you.'

I got the job. Of course I did. There really was no doubt after Flora gave her mother a copy of my CV and explained that I too had suffered a sibling bereavement. 'Impressive,' her mother said, about my accomplishments. 'You've done so well since leaving university.'

She nevertheless insisted on getting a reference, so I gave her the name of one of my old colleagues at the insurance company, someone I'd helped out. When the switchboard put Flora's mother through to him, he gave me a glowing reference, and a few hours later, I signed my new job contract.

Notes

In February 2022 it was announced that the inquest into the death of Daniel Taylor and Luke Emery would be reopened at the end of April. Because of the large number of people who would be giving evidence and the media attention it was expected to receive, the venue had been moved to London. Grace had previously mentioned that she was planning to take Beth to stay with her father in Canada after it was over so, acutely aware that other journalists would be crawling all over this story once the inquest began, I arranged to meet her again.

It was a cold day but, although there was a seating area inside the garden centre, Grace insisted on sitting outdoors. Both she and Beth were wearing several layers of clothing and hats, scarves and gloves. It was the only occasion when Beth stayed on her mother's lap, sucking her thumb and snuggling her face into Grace's scarf.

'She's been poorly,' Grace told me as I set the cups down – herbal tea for her, coffee for me. 'We both have. We went to stay with Mum for a few days, so she could help me with Beth.'

I said something about imagining how difficult it must be, looking after a sick child by yourself. It was one of those thoughtless throwaway comments you make when you're not sure what else to say and it deserved the response it got.

'Of course it's bloody difficult. It's beyond difficult. It wasn't meant to be like this. The only reason I get up every morning is because of Beth. Getting through the day is like climbing a gigantic mountain, except every single day I begin right back at the bottom, staring up and wondering how I'm supposed to put one foot in front of the other. I trudge along waiting until I can go to bed only to lie there wondering how on earth I'm going to do it all over again the next day. Nothing, and I mean *nothing*, prepared me for this. Until Danny died, the worst thing that had ever happened to me was when we split up.'

'I hadn't realised,' I said, surprised. There had never been any mention of a break-up before. 'What happened?'

Beth was sniffling and as Grace dug around in her bag for some tissues I thought she wasn't going to reply, but after she'd wiped Beth's nose, she said, 'Has anyone ever cheated on you?'

I wondered what she say if I said *No, but I cheated on the man your husband murdered.*

I shook my head.

'Lucky you. You won't know how terrible it makes you feel about yourself.'

I do know, I thought. *I know because Luke made sure I knew.* It was a stupid, meaningless one-off thing. Drinks at work. A colleague. I felt guilty even while I was doing it and was naïve enough to believe if I confessed my 'mistake' to Luke he'd understand it meant nothing. We'd both done similar during our 'off-again' periods. But he didn't see it as nothing. In his eyes, it wasn't like before, because this time we were together properly. He couldn't forgive me. Not then, anyway, but I knew he would. He just needed time. But that, as it turned out, was what we didn't have.

I tried to focus on what Grace was saying.

'I always swore that I'd never ever forgive anyone who cheated on me. Not after what Mum went through after Dad did it to her. Danny knew all of that, but he did it anyway.'

I coughed, then sipped my coffee, still trying to clear my mind of Luke. 'When was this?'

'It was in 2012. I was twenty-four,' she said.

'But even though you said you'd never forgive him, you obviously did?'

'Not at first. In fact I didn't forgive him for a long time, but in the end, yes, I did.'

Grace's Story

2012–2013

1.

I found out Danny had cheated on me because the girl he slept with sent me photos of them together. And when I say together, I mean *together*. She sent me naked photos. At first I thought it was a joke, that they'd been photoshopped or something, although I couldn't understand why anyone would think that was funny. But it was definitely Danny and he was definitely with someone who wasn't me and when I showed him the photos and saw all the colour draining from his face I knew, absolutely, that it was not a joke.

I walked away from him then. Just like I had always said I would. And I stayed away for months. The thing was, even though he deserved everything he got, what Danny went through afterwards was just as bad, if not worse, than what I went through.

For starters, a few days after I split up with him he failed a really important flying exam. It was the final one before he would have got his commercial pilot's licence, and up until then, Danny had never failed a single exam. He thought his dreams of being a pilot were over. All because of this stupid thing he'd done.

Because his mum and mine were close, I knew that he wasn't flying or working – he was barely even getting out of bed. Eventually Sarah took him to a doctor and he was put on antidepressants, but even then he didn't really do anything apart from call and text me over and over again – hundreds of times – saying how much he loved me and missed me and how he'd been so drunk that he couldn't remember anything about the night it had happened.

Obviously I didn't believe him. I mean, why would I? Who cheats on their girlfriend and doesn't remember anything about it?

But even though I was sure he was lying and despite my vow never to forgive him if he cheated on me, the truth was that not being with him was awful. I missed him so much. Some days when I woke up, the pain of remembering that he wasn't my boyfriend any more was so heavy it pinned me to the bed.

It went on like that for months, both of us utterly miserable, until, in the end, I agreed to see him.

He came round to my mum's house. I was horrified when I saw him – he'd lost loads of weight and his clothes were hanging off him. He had these bags under his eyes that were so dark they looked like bruises. And he'd developed these tics, tapping his fingers, tugging his hair, and the dry barking cough he'd always had had got so much worse – he was coughing two or three times a minute.

He started saying over and over again how the only thing he remembered was waking up alone in the room in the photos. He told me how he'd been scared, that he didn't know where he was, that he hadn't even realised he was in a hotel at first. He swore he had no idea how he got there and absolutely no memory of the girl.

If this was true, I said, why hadn't he told me about it.

'I wanted to. I should have done. I wish I had. But the miniatures from the minibar were all over the floor and they were empty. I was ashamed. I'd checked into the hotel so I could get drunk. But why would I do that? I've gone over it and over it. I've driven myself mad trying to remember. But I can't remember anything. I still can't.'

He reached into his bag and pulled out a folder containing research he'd been doing into alcohol amnesia and blackouts and memory loss. He insisted on going through it all, pleading with me to believe that he remembered nothing. It was clear how terrified he was about it happening again.

The thing was, I loved him. I'd never stopped loving him. I had only ever wanted to be with Danny and that hadn't changed, but if I was going to take him back there were two conditions.

The first was that he would never contact the girl in the photos.

'I don't even know her name,' he said. He thumbed through his phone, insisting on showing me every single contact. 'I don't know who she is or how to get hold of her. Not that I want to. Honestly, you've got to believe me.'

'So how did she get my number?'

'You called me a lot that night, Grace. I had something like thirty missed calls from you the next morning. And loads of texts. She must have seen them, got your number off my phone.'

He was right about me bombarding him with calls and texts. It had caused problems between us before. If Danny didn't answer the phone, I'd immediately start catastrophising. Why was he ignoring me? Had he been in an accident? Was he with someone else? Turned out the answer to *that* particular question was 'yes'.

He was quite right that his phone would have been full of missed calls and messages so I suppose it would have been simple enough to copy my number and send me those awful photos.

But why? Why did she do it? For months, every single time I closed my eyes, I saw Danny with her. The pair of them together. And every time, I felt sick.

'Honestly, Grace, you have to believe me,' he said. 'I wish I could give you an answer, but I don't know why she did it.'

I had to accept I'd never find out.

My second condition for getting back together was that he had to give up alcohol completely. If he loved me as much as he said he did, and if he'd only cheated on me because of alcohol, then he should have no problem giving it up. He said he'd already made that decision; he hadn't drunk any alcohol in the months we'd been apart. He said even if I wouldn't have him back, what he'd been through was so terrible, he would never drink again.

And he never did.

We got back together, but we were both changed by what had happened and our relationship never entirely returned to how it had been before. For one thing, I was even less trusting, even quicker to question where he was and what he was doing. I found it difficult to control my jealousy when I thought of the women he worked with, particularly on the nights he spent away from home. He never mentioned who he was with on those overnight trips, yet I still lay awake imagining all the things he could be getting up to in Prague, say, or Budapest.

For Danny, though, the after-effects of his cheating were more insidious. He retook the flying exam that he'd failed, and this time he easily passed. Flying was always something he excelled at and he had no concerns with his abilities in a cockpit, but in so many other ways his confidence in himself was permanently shattered. He would always second-guess the smallest decisions and spend far too much time worrying about the consequences of insignificant things he'd said or done. Silly things for the most part, and I hated to see how he tied himself up in knots about them.

In time, I forgave Danny for what he had done, but he never forgave himself. From then on, although the severity of his stress habits came and went, they never left him. Every day of his life I would hear that dry cough, watch him tugging his hair, see him suffer through another awful headache – all of it an indelible reminder to us both of what he'd done. One stupid mistake.

Notes

This was the first time either Grace or Izzy had mentioned that Danny had been on antidepressants. Depression does not make someone fly a plane into a mountain and it certainly doesn't make someone murder someone else, but Daniel's state of mind had to be relevant. How could it not be? It felt like a breakthrough.

After that particular meeting with Grace, I asked my brother to talk me through the checks in place at Goldfinch to ensure that pilots were emotionally and mentally fit to fly planes. I was shocked when he told me that the airline didn't really do anything to ensure their pilots weren't suffering with any mental-health issues.

Each pilot had an annual medical with a Civil Aviation Authority appointed doctor, which I already knew because every year my brother and Luke would go on intensive health kicks in the weeks leading up to their medicals, but they were focused entirely on the physical side of things – eyes, heart, cholesterol levels – and almost no attention was paid to mental health. In fact, Jamie said there was really only one question: 'Do you ever feel depressed?'

That was it. As long as a pilot appeared to be fine, they'd be allowed to fly.

Grace was adamant that she never had any concerns about Daniel's abilities as a pilot. The same couldn't be said for other areas of his life.

Grace's Story

2016

1.

Pops gave Danny and me the deposit to buy a house. At first we refused. We didn't know anyone else our age who could afford to buy a house and accepting his help felt like cheating.

He wouldn't let it drop, though. *There's no sense you both struggling for years to save a deposit*, he wrote in a long email. *The money will be yours and your mum's soon enough anyway.*

It was Mum who eventually convinced me to say yes.

'Pops loves you to bits,' she told me. 'Think how thrilled he'll be if you let him help you buy somewhere of your own. I'm proud of you, darling, of both of you, for not wanting to take the money, but this is something that will make Pops really happy *and* make your lives so much easier.'

'We'll pay you back,' I promised him.

'No, you won't,' he said. 'This is a gift, not a loan. You'll still have a mortgage and all your bills and car expenses and what not. Spend your money on building your life together. Do it for me. And do it for Clare, too.'

In 2016, we moved to a village close to Stansted Airport because Danny had been offered a job at Goldfinch Airlines flying Airbus A320s to destinations all over Europe. I was so proud of him.

With Pops's help, we found a lovely little Victorian terrace with two bedrooms and a bathroom, kitchen, dining room and living room, complete with a basement which was ideal for my books and Danny's model aeroplanes. It was perfect.

I had a job in a nearby town. I had surprised everyone, including myself, when I announced I wanted to become a primary school teacher. After all, I hadn't had a great experience at school, but it wasn't the teachers or the studying which had made things difficult for me: it was the other students, their bullying, the way they pretended I didn't exist, the constant pressure to make myself invisible. But the way I saw it, everything that had happened to me would make me a better teacher, make me more alert to bullying, help me to make sure no one else went through what I had. That was my reasoning, anyway. Besides, I couldn't think of anything else I wanted to do.

The day we got the keys to our house, Mum, Pops, Roger and Sarah came over to help us move in – all the most important people in our lives, except Izzy, who had an emergency at work so couldn't make it. Sarah was feeling poorly and looked as if she probably should have been at home in bed but insisted there was no way she was going to miss such a special day.

Mum gave us six antique art deco champagne saucers as a house-warming present. They had belonged to her grandmother and I'd always loved them. And, ever generous, Pops brought a jeroboam of champagne. When we had all crowded into the narrow galley kitchen, he held the bottle out to Danny, saying, 'You do the honours, son.'

Danny glanced at me, then said to Pops, 'It's OK, you open it.'

'I wouldn't dream of it. Go on, take it.' Pops thrust the bottle into Danny's hands, oblivious to his discomfort as he eased the cork out of the bottle and poured generous measures into five of the glasses, handing them round to each of us.

'You've forgotten yours,' said Pops.

'It's fine, I'll pass,' replied Danny. 'It's not really my thing.'

'Come on, a little won't hurt you,' Pops said, tilting the sixth glass towards Danny, who obediently took it and poured a dribble into the bottom.

'Cheers,' Pops said holding his glass out.

'To Grace and Danny,' said Roger.

Everyone else said, 'Grace and Danny,' and we all carefully clinked the delicate crystal saucers.

Danny said, 'To us,' and leaned over to give me a kiss.

While the rest of us sipped our drinks, Danny set his glass down on the counter with the champagne untouched and started drumming his fingers.

Finger-drumming was one of his most common habits – if anyone even suggested he have a drink his fingers would start to move of their own volition, like a tiny cavalry rushing to support him. Most of the time he wasn't even aware he was doing it until I covered his hand with my own.

As well as the barking cough, the sporadic stomach pain, the acute headaches, the growing bald patch behind his left ear where he tugged out his hair, there was another new habit which I found really upsetting. When he was stressed, he had started raking his upper right canine tooth – which was longer than his other teeth and looked slightly vampiric – over his bottom lip, only stopping when it started bleeding. Compared to the skin-gouging, the finger-drumming was pretty innocuous.

Everyone except Danny sipped the champagne and Pops said, 'Unaccustomed as I am ...' and all of us laughed, except Mum who groaned and said, 'Please, Dad, no speeches,' but he pretended he hadn't heard her.

'I want to say how happy this makes me,' he continued. 'Seeing the two of you, Grace and Danny, beginning your lives together in your new house. I only wish my Clare was here too.'

I put my glass down and threw my arms around Pops, hugging him hard, hoping he could feel my gratitude. Hoping he understood that moving with Danny into this house – our home – was the best moment of my entire life, and that I wasn't taking any of it for granted, hoping Pops knew how much I loved him.

'Thank you,' I whispered. 'Thank you, from the bottom of my heart.'

It was almost two months before Izzy found time to come and visit, turning up one evening as I was preparing a lesson for the following day, looking forward to a long bath and an early night.

'I'm dying for a drink,' she said when I opened the door, as if she'd just popped in from the next room.

'Izzy,' I said, ushering her in. 'It's lovely to see you.'

I led her into the kitchen and flicked on the kettle. 'Tea? Coffee? Or I've got some peppermint tea somewhere?'

'Not that sort of drink, you idiot,' she said. '*Drink* drink. Gin. Wine. Preferably both.'

I peered into a cupboard in the corner of the kitchen where we shoved things we rarely used. Behind a stack of

plastic takeaway boxes, a juicer we'd been given as a
house-warming present and a rice cooker with a broken
plug, there was a bottle of red wine. I fished it out and
searched for a corkscrew. Izzy took two of my grandmother's champagne saucers out of the cupboard and put
them on the countertop.

'Not those,' I said.

'But they're so pretty.'

'I know, but they're really old – they were my
great-grandmother's.'

Reaching past her I found two ordinary wine glasses,
uncorked the bottle, poured us both some wine and
handed Izzy a glass.

'It's so lovely to see you,' I said.

'Likewise. And where is that little brother of mine?'
she asked.

'Stuck in Prague overnight because of fog.'

'Are you sure about that? Cheers, by the way,' she said,
holding her glass out towards me.

'Cheers,' I said, touching my glass to hers. 'What do
you mean, am I sure?'

I hoped Izzy wouldn't want to drink *too* much or stay
up *too* late. One of the first lessons I had learned about my
job was that, although teaching a class of eight-year-olds
was hard work, teaching a class of eight-year-olds while I
was tired and hungover was a special form of torture.

'Are you sure Danny is in Prague because of *fog*?' Izzy
said.

'It happens quite frequently this time of year, apparently. Flights get cancelled, and the air crew are put up in
a hotel overnight. Did you tell him you were coming?
He'll be gutted to have missed you.'

I was already heading into the living room when she said, 'Right,' and something in her voice made me turn back to face her.

'What?' I said.

'Fog? Really? I thought planes landed themselves nowadays.'

'It's not uncommon. He was stuck in Malmo last week.'

'I see,' she said.

'What?' I said again.

She shrugged. 'Just looking out for you. Like I always do.'

'I know,' I said. 'But …' I stopped. What could I say? I didn't want to sound ungrateful; however, in the space of five minutes I'd gone from being fine about Danny being in Prague – my jealousy under control – to feeling concerned for absolutely no reason. I put my glass down, pulled out my phone and opened the flight tracker website.

'There's a copy of his roster on the fridge,' I said, pointing at Danny's schedule for the day. 'He flew out to Prague on flight GFA2071 this morning and he's supposed to have been coming back on flight GFA2072 this evening.'

I showed her the flight tracker website on my phone. 'But here, flight GFA2072 was cancelled. See?'

'I'm sure he'd rather be here,' she said. 'Now, let's drink. It's been ages. We've so much to catch up on.'

She followed me into the front room, which was my favourite room with its wooden floors, bay window, original fireplace (which I had draped with fairy lights) and a squidgy sofa. I smiled at the memory of what Danny and I had done on the sofa the previous evening.

I busied myself lighting candles, making everything

look lovely, before going to sit next to Izzy. I tucked my legs under me and watched her look around the room.

'Nice,' she said. 'Very nice. You've got a real eye for domesticity.'

'Thank you,' I said. 'I love this room. Well ... I love the house, but I really love this room in particular.'

She had a gulp of her wine. 'You're so lucky,' she said, smoothing the velvet arm of the sofa.

'God, I know, *so* lucky,' I said.

'Do you know, though? Do you really understand how lucky you are?' she asked. 'Rich grandfather, money on tap. Everything you want always dropped into your lap.'

'It's not quite like that,' I said.

'It's funny, working in the charity sector,' she continued, as if I hadn't spoken. 'You get a real insight into how unequal the division of money is in this country.'

'I'm sure you do,' I said, although I wasn't really listening. Instead, I was thinking about everything I still had to do before tomorrow.

When I turned my attention back to Izzy, she was saying, 'Working for a charity has really opened my eyes. If only the people *with* money were prepared to share their good luck because, let's be fair, the only reason they have money is luck, because they come from a wealthy family or whatever. If only those people who, purely through the circumstances of their birth, were prepared to share just a little of their money with people who didn't have the same good fortune, the world would be so much better. Don't you think?'

I nodded and sipped my wine, really not in the mood for a deep and meaningful conversation about the unequal distribution of wealth in the world.

'For example,' Izzy said, 'think how different things would have been for Flora's family if money in this country was shared more equally.'

'You mean if more money was made available for medical research?' I asked, trying to work out exactly how money would have prevented Flora's brother dying from a heart condition.

'Well, yes, obviously that,' Izzy said. 'But there should be a more equal distribution of wealth among us all.'

'Right,' I said, at a loss to know what I could possibly add. I was tired. Was Izzy staying? Would she think I was being rude if I said I was going to bed even though she'd only been here for half an hour?

'I *knew* you'd agree,' she was saying and I realised I'd been nodding my head.

'Sorry, what was that?' I asked.

'To lend me some money,' she said.

'What?'

'You'll distribute some of your wealth to me.' She laughed. 'Only temporarily.'

'But I don't –'

She interrupted, saying, 'You know I'm good for it, right? I mean, you know I'll pay it back?'

'Of course,' I said.

'Great, so …?'

'But I don't really have anything I can give you,' I said, which was true. Danny and I had spent our savings and a lot more besides on furnishing the house, not to mention tanking and redecorating the basement and ripping out the old bathroom to install a wet room. We had our credit-card bills plus, of course, the mortgage to pay every month and the cost of running two cars. I knew how fortunate I was – I had absolutely nothing to complain about – but that didn't mean I had spare money lying around.

'I don't need much,' Izzy said. 'Just to cover a temporary cash-flow issue until I get paid. Two weeks, tops.'

'How much do you need?' I asked.

'A thousand.'

'A thousand pounds?' I said, appalled. 'I don't have a thousand pounds, Iz.'

'Really? You sure about that?'

'I don't know what you mean ...' but then I realised I *did* know.

It was a couple of years since I'd been to Canada to see Dad. It wasn't that I didn't want to go but other things always seemed to come up. Dad kept asking, and I continued to put him off, until the day that he called me and said he had news.

He was going to be fine, he insisted. It was one of the 'better' cancers. Survival rates were excellent. They'd caught it early; he wouldn't be in hospital long. There might be some follow-up treatment, but I wasn't to worry. I wasn't to worry at all, but if I *did* have time in the school holidays to fly out to Vancouver, then they would all be so happy to see me.

I had wanted to get on the first plane to Canada, but Dad talked me out of it. 'I'm not at death's door, Grace. You've got your job to think about and the school holidays are, what? Only five weeks away? Come then.'

Dad had transferred a thousand pounds to my bank account so I could buy plane tickets for Danny and me and now, less than twenty-four hours later, Izzy was sitting opposite me, sipping wine.

'You're talking about the money from my dad?' I asked.

'You're so lucky to be going on holiday to Canada.'

'It's not really a holi–'

'Dan told me how your dad sent money for the flights. I wish someone would send *me* a plane fare.'

'It's not my money, though,' I said. 'It's Dad's money. He only transferred it to me so I could buy our tickets. Did Danny also tell you about the cancer?' Even just saying the word was upsetting and I took a big gulp of wine.

'Yes.' Izzy moved closer to me and took my hand in hers. 'I'm so sorry. You must be feeling very … well, you know I'm not good with feelings. But I know you're upset. Sad and upset.' She squeezed my hand. 'As I always say, sadness is the price we pay for love.'

I'd never heard her say that before and it sounded like something she'd read on a poster but I immediately felt guilty – she was only trying to comfort me.

Meanwhile, she was still holding my hand. 'The thing is, I only need the money for one week. Two, tops. You know I'll pay you back, then you can book your tickets. Where's the harm in that?'

'I don't know …' I said.

'It's not like you need it all, anyway,' she said. 'Danny gets cheap flights.'

'Only with Goldfinch and they don't fly to Canada.'

Izzy put her glass down on the table beside the sofa. 'I get it,' she said. 'You don't trust me. All this talk of being like sisters. It's just words for you, isn't it?'

'You know that's not true,' I said.

'I get it,' Izzy said again. 'Time passes. Things change. It was stupid of me to think our friendship still means as much to you as it used to.'

'It does. Honestly it does, I just –'

'You don't need to explain. I was there for you when you needed me. We used to be close. But now you've moved on.' She gestured around the living room. 'You've got all this. I'm not a part of your life like I used to be. It's fine if you don't want to help me out. I understand.'

'Please, Izzy …'

'Don't worry. I know when I'm not wanted. Sorry for interrupting your evening.' She stood up. 'Thank you for the wine. I'll leave you alone.'

'Izzy, wait.' I said. 'It's no problem – I'll lend you the money. You took me by surprise, that's all. It's been a horrible few days, finding out about my dad and everything. I'm not thinking straight.'

She didn't say anything.

'I'm really sorry, Izzy. The last thing I want to do is hurt your feelings. Honestly. I feel terrible. Look, I'll transfer the money now. Shall I do that, Iz? I'll transfer the money … then we'll finish the wine. Shall we do that?'

I hoped she could hear the sincerity in my voice. It didn't happen very often, but on the occasions when I said something to upset her, she would become really cold and ignore me, which always made me feel panicky for reasons I hadn't ever quite understood. No one else made me feel like that.

Izzy looked down at me, unsmiling, and I shifted further back, wedging myself into the corner of the sofa.

I didn't know what else to say. There was a thickening behind my nose and eyes and I realised I was on the brink of tears. I pressed my lips together firmly and concentrated on the shadows cast by candles onto the wall that I had only recently painted myself.

Eventually, Izzy opened her arms wide. 'Come here.'

I immediately stood and we hugged each other tightly.

'I knew you'd help,' she said. 'You're always here for me, Grace. My little almost-sister. You really are the best.'

The panic began to ebb away and the unshed tears dried up. I took a shaky breath and went to fetch my laptop from the kitchen.

With my finger poised over the keys, ready to authorise the bank transfer, I hesitated. 'You'll definitely be able to pay me back in two weeks, won't you?' I asked. 'I'll have to book the flights then. The prices are already going up. It's always so busy in the school holidays …'

'Two weeks, max,' she said. 'You know you can trust me.'

2.

Because the holiday season was starting, Goldfinch Airlines was operating at full capacity and Danny was away all the time. I was really busy at work too, finishing up the school term, and before I knew it, a fortnight had gone by and it was less than a month before we were due to leave. Dad sent me an email saying how much they were all looking forward to seeing us and to let him have our flight details.

I checked my bank account, but there was no money from Izzy. I tried calling her, but it rang and rang and eventually went through to voicemail. I tried again five minutes later and this time I left her a message. I looked up flights to Vancouver and was alarmed to see the prices had already gone up significantly. I rang Izzy again and the next day I rang her half a dozen times. On one occasion, she did pick up, but before I could even say hello, we were cut off.

My car was due for its MOT and the garage said all the tyres needed replacing and, even worse, it had to have a new exhaust. Paying for it maxed out my overdraft. If I had had any idea where Izzy was living, I would have gone to see her, but she'd moved again. I didn't have her current address, and when I asked Sarah, all she knew was that Izzy was living with a friend somewhere in south London.

Dad was emailing frequently, saying things like *Is everything OK, sweetheart? It's not like you not to respond* and *I hope you're not worrying about me* and *I can't tell you how much better I feel, knowing I'll be seeing you soon* and *Ping me your flight details, Grace, so we can make plans at this end.*

With our supposed departure date less than a fortnight away, I walked through the door after work one evening to find Danny at home and awake for the first time in ages. He gave me a massive hug and I promptly burst into tears.

He shepherded me into the kitchen, where I sat on one of our breakfast-bar stools while he flicked the kettle on. Then he leaned against the countertop and said, 'Is it your dad? Is he worse?'

I shook my head.

'So what *is* the matter? Oh god, are *you* ill?'

I pulled myself together enough to say, 'No, no. I'm fine. And Dad's no worse, as far as I know.' At the thought of my father, and how excited he was to see us, the tears came again, 'But I haven't booked our flights.'

'What? Is that all? Let's do it now,' he said.

'I lent the flight money to Izzy.'

At first Danny didn't say anything. He busied himself making us both a cup of tea, although what I *really* wanted was a glass of wine or a large vodka – frankly, any alcohol would have done at that point.

He put the mugs down, sat on the other stool and only then said, 'I don't understand. What are you saying?'

I took a sip of the still-scalding tea, then a deep breath, and said, 'When Izzy came here – the night you were stuck in Prague – she asked me to lend her the money Dad had given me for the flights. She said she really needed to borrow it for a few days, two weeks tops, but she hasn't paid me back, and what with the problems with the car and my credit cards being maxed out, I haven't got enough to pay for our flights. I've been chasing and chasing Izzy but she hasn't replied to *any* of my calls so I haven't booked the flights and now there's hardly any seats left and they're all really expensive.'

Danny frowned, staring into his mug of tea and raking his bottom lip with his incisor. 'So you gave Izzy the money your dad sent you?' he said.

'Not *gave*, lent. She said she'd pay me back within two weeks.'

'And she hasn't?'

'Obviously she hasn't. Otherwise I would have booked the flights, wouldn't I?'

'Don't get annoyed with me,' he said. 'I'm not the one who's been pretending everything's sorted for our trip.'

'I haven't been pretending,' I said. 'You said yourself, we've hardly seen each other. I've tried calling Izzy about a million times but she never answers.'

'There'll be a good reason – I know she's been really busy at work,' he said. He sipped his tea, flinching when the mug touched his lip.

I kept my voice level and my words as reasonable as I could manage, in the circumstances. 'But she hasn't replied to *any* of my messages. She promised she'd give me my money back.'

'OK, OK,' Danny said, a drop of blood blooming on his lip.

Usually, I would do my best to try and stop him worrying, but this was too important. 'It's not OK, is it? What if Dad's worse than he's telling me? What if I don't see him and something happens to him?'

'I'm sure he'll be fine.'

'Really? How can you be sure? You're an oncologist now?'

Danny put his tea down and blotted the blood on his lip with his finger, then he said, 'Can't you just ask your grandfather for it?'

'Is that your solution? Ask Pops for yet more money? Like he hasn't already given us so much.'

'I only meant –'

'I know what you meant. You're saying we should completely ignore the fact that it's a member of *your* family who owes *me* money because I can just go and ask my family for even more. My grandfather paying the deposit on our house wasn't enough for you so he should cough up for our flights, even though my dad has already given us money for them.'

'That's not fair – it's not what I meant.'

'It's what you said.'

We glared at each other for a few moments – we argued so rarely that we didn't really know how to do it.

Eventually he broke the silence. 'All I meant was the priority is booking flights, so we should ask your grandfather if he could lend us the money and at least get them sorted.'

'But why should we? If Izzy gave me back my money then I wouldn't need to ask Pops.'

'Look, I'll call her and see what's going on.'

'She won't answer,' I said.

Danny reached for his mobile. She answered immediately.

'Hi, Iz,' he said. 'How's things?'

He was silent for a long time. I couldn't hear what she was saying, but I watched his face switch from a smile to a frown to a look of serious concern. His fingers crept up to the patch behind his left ear and he started tugging his hair. Every now and again he'd say something: 'Oh, Iz' or 'Shit' or 'I can't believe it'. Eventually he said, 'Yes, yes, of course, but don't you think you should tell them?' He looked at me and nodded, but when I mouthed 'What?' he shook his head and turned away.

'No, of course I won't tell them,' he said. 'Look, if there's anything I can do, anything at all, you know where I am.' He paused, listening again. 'Yes, that's a great idea. Yes, let's do that. You'll be OK? Fine, yes. I'll let you know. See you soon.'

He put his phone down.

'What's going on?' I said. 'Did she say when she's going to give my money back?'

'God, Grace. Some things are more important than money.'

'But that's why you were ringing her.'

'She's going through a rough time at the moment,' he said.

'So am I! My dad has *cancer*, Danny. I have to go and see him.'

'Look, I don't want to argue, but can you ask your grandfather? Just this once?'

'He's already done so much for us. Izzy owes me that money and she should give it to me.'

'She can't pay you back right now.'

'Why not?'

'Will you just trust me?'

'Why can't she pay me back, Danny?'

'She's moved out of her flat,' he said. 'She's staying on a friend's sofa but she didn't want to tell us or my parents because she knew we'd be worried.'

'If she's not paying rent she can give me my money.' I reached for a paper towel and handed it to him. 'Use this. Your lip is really bleeding.'

He pressed it against his mouth for a few seconds, wincing. 'Her landlord came round one evening, to look at a broken boiler or something. Apparently she offered him a glass of wine, and he tried it on with her and when she said no, he assaulted her ...'

'*Assaulted* her? What happened?'

'She didn't tell me the details, only that she managed to get him out of the flat, but she was scared he'd come back so she moved her stuff out the same night and now the agent's saying she broke the terms of the lease and the landlord is refusing to give her the deposit back. That's why she hasn't got any money at the moment.'

'Has she been to the police?'

'She doesn't want to involve them.'

'But she can't let him get away with it.'

'It's her decision, Grace.'

'But the guy assaulted her. She *has* to tell the police.'

He shook his head.

'You've got to persuade her to report him.' I pushed his phone towards him. 'Seriously, Danny, call her back.'

He didn't pick up his phone. He didn't even look at me, just stared out of the window at the narrow passage that ran alongside our kitchen. 'The thing is ...' he began, then hesitated. 'The thing is, it's ... complicated.'

I didn't understand. How complicated could it be? She

had been assaulted. She should tell the police. What was complicated about that?

I reached for his arm, pulling his hand away from tugging his hair and lacing my fingers through his. 'Complicated *how*?'

'Look, I don't know exactly what happened,' he said, staring straight ahead, out of the window. 'I was really young and, to be honest, I don't *want* to know. We never talk about it and I always promised her I'd never tell *anyone*. Not even you.'

He fell silent and I waited. I had absolutely no idea what he was going to say.

Eventually he said, 'It was my uncle William.'

'Which uncle? I thought your mum and dad were only children.'

'Mum always says that. I guess it makes it easier.'

'Makes what easier?' He wasn't making any sense.

'When Izzy was quite young, nine or ten, William molested her.'

Whatever I'd been expecting him to say, it wasn't that.

'She told Nan,' Dan said. 'Nan told Mum and Dad and they confronted William but he denied everything. Dad wanted to go to the police, but Mum begged him not to. In the end, my uncle agreed to move to Australia – the company he worked for had offices out there and they offered him a job – and he left straight away. No one in my family has spoken to him since.'

'You have an uncle living in Australia?' I said, scarcely able to believe what I was hearing.

'Yes.'

'And he sexually abused your sister but your parents didn't tell the police?'

He nodded, wincing at my blunt words. 'Like I said, I wasn't really told much about what went on. I only know the bits and pieces Iz told me, which is not much. She hasn't talked about it since we were teenagers.'

I'd always known there was something a bit off between Izzy and her mother, but I could never have imagined it was *this*. 'I can't believe your mum let her brother swan off to Australia.'

Danny finally dragged his gaze away from the window and looked at me. 'She didn't want him to go to jail. I was only ... what? Five? Anyway, I don't remember anything about it but Iz told me there were huge arguments because Nan was all set to go to the police. I always assumed that's why Nan and Mum never really got on.'

'Jesus,' I said. How would anyone even begin to deal with something so appalling? 'Did Izzy get counselling?' I asked. 'She must have needed it.'

'Not as far as I know. She told me she wanted to forget about it. I don't think she even told Mum all the details of what he did. Only Nan. Around the time of her A Levels she started having flashbacks and had to tell the university, so they'd understand about her grades. That's when she told me, too. But she's never mentioned it since. Not until today, anyway. She said when this bastard of a landlord tried to force himself on her, it brought it all back. She doesn't want to have anything to do with him again so she's going to let him keep the deposit, which is why she's totally broke.'

'Poor Izzy,' I said. 'I'll call her. Let her know I'm here for her.'

'No, Grace. I told you, she doesn't want anyone to know, not even you. When she first told me about it, she said even thinking about it makes her feel ashamed.'

SCENES FROM A TRAGEDY

'That's the last thing she should be feeling. It's not her fault – she was a child. The school sometimes gets involved in these sorts of things so I could get the details of a therapist for her to talk to.'

'Absolutely not. Izzy's adamant that she doesn't want to rake it up all over again.'

'But a therapist would help.'

'No, Grace. I'm serious,' he said. 'The *only* thing that matters is what Izzy wants. You can't mention this to anyone, ever.' He caught hold of my hand and squeezed it. 'Promise you won't ever talk to anyone about this. Not Izzy, not my parents, not your mum. Promise?'

'OK, OK,' I said.

But even though the conversation was over, I couldn't stop thinking about it. How could I not have realised something so terrible had happened to her? What sort of terrible friend was I? And it wasn't just Izzy, it was all of them, their whole family. All that time I'd spent with them and I hadn't had the slightest inkling they'd been through something so devastating. I liked to think of myself as empathetic and sensitive to people's emotions. Obviously I wasn't nearly as empathetic as I thought I was.

In the end, I did ask Pops and he gave me the money to go and see my father in Canada, but because we had left it so late and it was the school holidays there were hardly any flights left so we ended up having to go for a week, rather than the ten days we had originally planned, and we had to fly via Frankfurt, with an eight-hour layover each way.

At least I got to see my dad.

Notes

There was a lot to process.

For a start, the appalling thing that had happened to Izzy cast my conversations with her in a completely different light. No wonder she was so reluctant to talk about her feelings. I couldn't imagine how difficult it would be for her to open up to anyone after experiencing something like that. It couldn't have been easy for Daniel, either, knowing what had happened to his sister, and surely explained some of his own anxieties.

It just showed how you never knew what was going on behind closed doors. At first glance, it appeared both Daniel and Izzy had had a pretty idyllic childhood: supportive parents, comfortable upbringing, never wanting for anything. Yet Izzy had apparently been through something absolutely shattering when she was a child and her parents had just swept it under the carpet while they all pretended it had never happened.

I tried to arrange another meeting with Izzy, but I couldn't get hold of her. For reasons that were never entirely clear, she changed her mobile phone number frequently, and although I had an email address for her, it could take days, sometimes longer, for her to respond.

In the end, I met up with Grace before I saw Izzy again. She and Beth had recovered from their illness and while she kept a close eye on her daughter as she pottered around the outdoor seating area, Grace told me about the Taylors' anniversary party.

Grace's Story

2016

1.

A few weeks after we'd returned from Canada, we arranged to see Izzy.

Sarah and Roger's fortieth wedding anniversary was later in the year and Danny had decided to throw them a surprise party.

'Why couldn't Izzy come and stay with us?' I asked. It was a Friday evening and we were on a train to London to meet Izzy to discuss plans for the party. Work had been really tiring that week – one of the pupils in my form kept turning up hungry and in dirty clothes, which had necessitated several internal welfare and safeguarding meetings, on top of which I'd had parents' evening the previous night – and I was exhausted.

'You did tell her you've got to get up for work at four o'clock tomorrow morning?' I asked.

'I don't mind going to London,' Danny replied.

But what if I *mind?* I thought, although what I said was, 'But we've got a spare room she could stay in. We could have had a meal, discussed the party and you could still have been in bed by ten. You know I hate the thought of you flying when you're tired.'

'It's *fine*, Grace. Really. Don't make this into a thing.' He drummed his fingers on the table between our seats.

'I'm not,' I said, covering his hand with mine. 'I just don't understand why we have to go into London.'

He shrugged. 'It's what Iz wanted.'

I let it drop and instead watched the houses on the outer reaches of London flick past the train. I knew why Danny had agreed – for the same reason he always agreed to everything Izzy wanted him to do. Since we'd got back from Canada I'd tried to talk to Danny about persuading Izzy to see a counsellor or therapist – someone specialising in helping survivors of sexual abuse – but he refused to discuss it.

'I shouldn't have told you about it,' he would say. 'Izzy would hate you knowing.'

That hurt. Why wouldn't she want me to know? But then I'd remind myself that this wasn't about me, or my feelings – it was about Izzy and I had to respect her decision not to talk about it. In any case, she always seemed so sure of herself, so certain of everything, so unencumbered by any anxiety. Perhaps ignoring everything really was the best way for her to deal with it.

No matter how much we might put ourselves out for her, it was nothing compared to everything she had been through.

Izzy was near the back of a crowded bar, sitting with a woman I didn't recognise. There was a laptop, papers and a couple of notebooks on the table in front of them. And two bottles of wine. One empty, one almost full.

'Here they are,' she said when she saw us, as if we had kept them waiting, although we were fifteen minutes early. 'Louise, this is Dan, my insanely talented brother,' she said, standing to give him a kiss on the cheek. 'And his devoted girlfriend, Grace,' she added, brushing my fringe away from my forehead.

I looked around for a spare chair. There was one at a neighbouring table, and I brought it over. Louise shuffled her chair to the side to make room for me while Dan went to look for another.

'Do you work together?' I asked.

'Well –' Louise began.

'No,' said Izzy.

Danny had located a stool and was holding it over his head, manoeuvring his way back to us. When he reached us, he carefully lowered the stool to the floor between Izzy and Louise.

'So, if you guys don't work together, how d'you know each other?' I asked.

'We're talking about going into business,' Izzy said.

I was surprised. As far as I was aware, her job at the charity had been going well and I hadn't realised she was looking around for something else. I wondered if Louise knew about Izzy's less-than-glowing employment history – all the jobs she left after only a few days or weeks, how it wasn't quite clear if she'd quit or been asked to leave. Like the insurance company where she'd worked before the charity. She had told us that she'd resigned, but a friend of a friend who'd worked at the same place had told me there was a rumour that Izzy had been fired for running a scam extorting money from colleagues after illegally authorising them to use loan cars. I wasn't sure if I really believed that, but it was certainly the case that the job at the charity was the first one Izzy had stayed at for any length of time.

Louise was saying, 'I run a start-up and I'm looking for a couple of angels. I'm hoping Izzy might be able to help.'

'Angels?' I said, thinking perhaps I'd misheard her.

'Angel investors. I'm looking for seed funding.'

I nodded, although I had no idea what she was talking about.

'Are you going to be an angel?' Danny asked Izzy.

'It's not out of the question. But first, Louise wants me to shake the tree, see what falls out.'

My confusion must have been obvious because Louise laughed, although not unkindly. 'I'm trying to persuade Izzy to consider leveraging her contacts for my business.'

I was still none the wiser, but before I could ask anything else, Izzy slapped her palms on the table and said, 'No more business talk. These two are here to discuss a party.'

'Of course,' Louise said. 'I've taken up enough of your time.' She gathered her belongings, stowing them in a very expensive-looking leather satchel.

'Lovely to meet you,' she said to Danny and me, then turned to Izzy. 'I hope you'll seriously consider coming on board,' she said. 'With you and your contacts, I think we could really ratchet our PE ratio, get on the radar of the private-equity boys.'

With that frankly incomprehensible parting shot, she left.

'What was that all about?' I asked.

Izzy shrugged. 'Exploring options.'

'It sounds exciting, Iz,' Danny said. 'Are you leaving your job at the charity?'

'Maybe.' She had some wine and shrugged again. 'It's boring.'

'I thought you liked your job?' I asked.

'Oh my god, what is this? I haven't seen either of you for ages and now you're interrogating me. Aren't you happy to see me?'

'Of course we are,' Danny said, shooting me a warning look. 'Aren't we, Grace?'

I nodded. 'Of course.'

I poured myself some wine. I'd regret it on the way home, but it felt necessary.

'We've missed you, haven't we, Grace?' Danny said.

'Yes, we have,' I replied, but even as I spoke I wondered if perhaps I hadn't actually *missed* Izzy. I had certainly *worried* about her, after what Danny had told me. I'd been concerned for her, wanted to help her, but had I actually *missed* her?

Suddenly, I wasn't so sure.

Everything about her was always so chaotic: plans changed at the last minute, and she could never be relied on to do what she'd said she was going to do. To be fair, she'd always been unreliable but, more recently, whenever I saw Izzy I'd been aware of an uneasy feeling that I had somehow let her down, although I was never sure quite how or why.

For years I had told myself being around Izzy was exciting and fun, but that evening, I wasn't having fun. It wasn't exciting. Annoying and exhausting would be closer to the truth.

I was desperately upset about what she'd been through – I felt sick even thinking about it – and I couldn't imagine how, if it were me, I would live a normal life or be happy ever again. But in that bar, as I listened to her telling Danny about some hugely expensive Michelin-starred restaurant she thought we should hire for their parents' anniversary,

I realised that Izzy always, without exception, gave every impression that the terrible trauma in her childhood had had absolutely no effect on her whatsoever.

Almost as if it had never happened.

2.

It was typical of Danny to want to do something lovely for his parents and I couldn't fault him for it. But the difference between having an idea for a surprise party and doing all the planning for a surprise party, with a limited budget, while also working full-time (and, in Danny's case, being out of the country most of the week) was enormous.

Danny wanted to invite about sixty people, which would have made it far too expensive for us to afford a sit-down catered meal. Instead, we spoke to a pub near his parents in Richmond which had recently closed for a refit. They offered to let us hire the whole place before their official reopening: they wouldn't charge us for the venue, as long as we spent a minimum amount on food. It would cost a little more than we had hoped, but we figured everyone could pay for their own drinks.

We went to see the pub and it was perfect: sanded floorboards and walls freshly painted in moody atmospheric colours covered with dozens of colourfully ornate masquerade-type masks. The owners were great too, even letting us try some of the tapas-style dishes from their buffet menu for free.

Next on the to-do list was contacting the guests – Danny took charge of that, calling the people whose contact details he had and asking them to pass on the invitation to other friends. Almost everyone who was asked said they would come. It was shaping up to be a wonderful evening for Sarah and Roger.

Despite Izzy saying she would meet us at the venue when we'd gone to check it out, she hadn't turned up – apparently she had had an emergency to sort out with her 'business plans' – and in fact neither of us saw her until several weeks later, on the screen of Danny's laptop, on a Skype video call at about 9.30 one Sunday evening.

'Hi, you crazy kids,' she said, her voice booming around the kitchen where Danny and I were sitting side by side on our barstools. I reached over to turn the volume down a little. She'd cut her hair since we'd last seen her and her curls, which had previously reached halfway down her back, now ended at her jawline. She looked even more gorgeous than before.

Behind her was a vast floor-to-ceiling window stretching along an entire wall, and beyond that was the London skyline.

'Wow, what a view,' said Danny. 'Where are you, Iz? It's amazing.'

She glanced over her shoulder, then back at the screen. 'Thirty-eighth floor of Strata.'

I looked at Danny, but he was clearly as confused as me. 'What's that?' I asked.

'Strata,' she said again, but when neither of us responded, she sighed. 'Oh, you two, tucked away in your cosy village life. Strata's a high-end development in Elephant and Castle.'

'How come you're there?' said Danny.

'Crashing here for a while. Mate of a mate. You know how it is.'

I most definitely did not know how it was. I didn't know anyone who lived on the thirty-eighth floor of anywhere, let alone in a place with a vast picture window and a leather sofa that could comfortably seat twenty. She had certainly moved up in the world since she'd left her previous apartment. Quite literally.

Izzy reached for a bottle of wine and poured some into a champagne saucer. It was beautiful, art deco, exactly like the glasses Mum had given me. She sipped the wine, then put the glass down, out of view of her camera.

I slipped off my stool and crossed the kitchen.

'So, you crazy kids,' Izzy said, and I wondered quite how much wine she'd had before Skyping us.

We kept my great-grandmother's glasses lined up in pairs in the narrow cupboard and they hadn't been used since the day we'd moved in. I lifted the first pair down onto the countertop.

'I've been doing some thinking,' Izzy was saying. 'And I've had an amazing idea ...'

'Great,' said Danny. 'What is it?'

I reached for the second pair of glasses.

'We should hire Hysteria,' Izzy said.

I reached into the depths of the cupboard for the third pair of glasses, but where there should have been two, there was only one.

'Who's Hysteria?' said Danny.

Izzy laughed. 'You're funny. Not *who*. *Where*. Hysteria. It's a bar in Shoreditch with the most incredible cocktails and a totally cool hip-hop vibe. It's perfect.'

I sat back down and waited for Izzy to have more wine. When she did, there was no doubt about it. The sixth of my great-grandmother's champagne saucers was not in our kitchen cupboard. It was in Izzy's hand.

'Is that my glass?' I asked.

'Sorry. What?' she said.

'One of my glasses, Izzy. Is that one of my special glasses you've got there?'

She looked down at the champagne saucer as if she'd never seen it before and shrugged. 'I don't know. Maybe.'

'You took one of my great-grandmother's glasses.' I turned to Danny. 'Can you believe it?'

He looked at Izzy who, as far as I could tell through a screen, looked supremely unconcerned.

'You gave it to me, Grace,' she said. 'Remember? We'd had some wine, I said how much I liked the glasses. You said I could have one.'

'No, I didn't.'

Under the breakfast bar, Danny put a hand on my thigh and squeezed. Not painfully, but hard enough to let me know he didn't want me to create a scene.

'Can I have it back?' I said.

'Sure. You only had to ask, Grace. Next time I see you I'll bring it with me. Now, back to Hysteria. It's absolutely perfect.'

'Perfect for what?' Danny said.

'For the party. For Mum and Dad's party. The part*ay* of the centur*ay*.'

Next to the screen, Danny's fingers started tap, tap, tapping.

'But Iz,' he said, 'the party's only a few weeks away and we've sorted pretty much everything. I've texted and emailed you the details. Venue. Food. It's all arranged.'

Izzy reached for my great-grandmother's glass and

tilted her head back, draining the rest of it. From behind the screen she produced the bottle, banging the neck onto the glass as she topped it up.

'But Danny,' she said, 'what you've *sorted* is a local pub with stale crisps and dried-up sausage rolls. You need to have *vision*. What you need is Hysteria.'

Danny frowned and his hand snaked up to worry the patch of hair behind his ear.

'How much it is to rent this bar?' he said. 'This Hysteria. I mean, Shoreditch – it's going to be pricey, right?'

'But you two crazy kids can afford it. Look at you both … your own house, nice safe jobs. This is for Mum and Dad. Aren't they worth it?'

'Yes –' he began, but I cut him off.

'Izzy,' I said.

'Yes, darling Grace? You're looking wonderful by the way. So unusual to see someone let their hair be au naturel these days while the rest of us labour under the tyranny of regular trips to the hairdressers.'

I ignored what she'd said, determined to make my point. 'We've worked really hard on the arrangements for the party. We're not changing everything now to move it to some random bar in Shoreditch that probably costs a fortune that, by the way, we *can't* afford because we're up to our neck in credit-card bills, but even if we *could* afford, is nowhere near where your parents and most of their friends live.'

I could feel my heart racing – it was the first time I had ever disagreed with Izzy so forcefully, and even through the laptop screen I saw the precise moment her gaze hardened into a blank, expressionless stare. I reached for Danny's hand.

'Danny,' Izzy said, 'do you agree with your girlfriend?'

He stopped raking his lip with his tooth long enough to say, 'Iz, I'm sorry. Maybe if you'd suggested it sooner? Everyone's already been told the details. I'm not sure we *can* change it –'

'I'm the one that's sorry,' she said, interrupting him. 'Sorry that my job got in the way of you consulting with me about my own parents' party. Not all of us are so lucky as to be able to take a break whenever we feel like it. Some of us have to work 24/7 just to pay the bills, you know? Some of us are struggling to get by. But I get it. It's fine. I know when I'm not wanted – I've got the message. You both have a nice evening.'

'Iz. Wait,' Danny said. 'Don't say that. We didn't mean to upset you.'

'I'm not upset. In fact, I couldn't be less upset, but I *can* take a hint. You got everything sorted without involving me. You ridiculed my suggestion. That's fine. As I said, far be it for me to interfere where I'm not wanted. I guess I'll see you both at the party at the venue you chose *without me*.'

'Iz –' Danny said, but it was too late, she'd ended the call.

'Well,' I said, 'can you believe that? She makes zero effort to help then demands we book some bar in the centre of London. What was she thinking? And she was lying about that champagne glass. I absolutely did *not* give it to her.'

'Grace, don't,' Danny said, fingers creeping up behind his ear once again. 'I feel dreadful. We've really hurt her feelings.' He pinched strands of hair and started tugging.

'No, we haven't,' I said. 'She's just annoyed because she didn't get her own way.'

There was more I wanted to say. Even speaking those words out loud felt … liberating. Yes, that was the word, *liberating.* How had I never seen it before? Years of hanging off her every word. Waiting for her to throw me a crumb of affection. All those back-handed compliments. Hair au naturel, for fuck's sake.

Meanwhile, little strands of Danny's hair floated onto the countertop. At this rate, he would be lucky to avoid one of his headaches.

'I know she doesn't often show it,' he was saying, 'but underneath everything, she's really sensitive.'

Bullshit, I thought, but did not say.

I'm not proud of myself for what I'm about to admit. It doesn't put me in a good light. On the contrary, it makes me sound like a terrible person – and maybe I am – but the truth is that finding out what had happened to Izzy, the appalling, shattering thing her uncle had done, was what helped me finally see her for what she was.

Yes, what had happened was horrific. It was something no one should have to experience, least of all a child. And, *yes*, it would have had a profound effect on her. But, surely, at some point, Izzy had to start taking responsibility for her behaviour?

Izzy wasn't the sensitive one. It was my lovely, thoughtful, caring boyfriend who was sensitive. *Too* sensitive. I could see it now. How Danny adored his sister, even while she was towering above him on some elevated, gold-plated pedestal, wielding this terrible experience she had had to make sure he never challenged her, never questioned her behaviour, let her get away with whatever she wanted to do.

Yes, Izzy was damaged. Yes, she was hurt. But she was also a complete bitch.

3.

When Danny and I arrived one Saturday evening to collect his parents for what we had told them was going to be a quiet meal, they had absolutely no idea that twenty minutes later they would be walking into a room full of friends, all there to wish them a very happy fortieth wedding anniversary.

As we ushered them into the pub amid a huge cheer from the assembled guests, Roger and Sarah looked stunned. Roger laughed and flung an arm around Danny's shoulders, pulling him in for a hug, but Sarah's face was pale and she kept looking around, like she was searching for an escape route. I hadn't thought to check with Danny if either of his parents hated surprises.

'Did you *really* not have a clue?' Danny said, raising his voice over the synth-pop sound of New Order's 'Blue Monday', the first track on a huge seventies and eighties playlist we'd spent hours compiling.

'No!' Roger bellowed. 'This is incredible.'

We moved away to let the guests begin all their *hello*s and *how are you*s, *lovely to see you*s and *Happy Anniversary*s.

'Job done,' Danny said, giving me a kiss, then looking round the room.

I knew what he was looking for – or rather *who*.

He had met up with Izzy twice since our Skype call and on both occasions I'd found work-related excuses not to go with him. He had felt dreadful about the supposed 'hurt' and 'upset' we had 'caused her' on our call, but it transpired that by the time there was an 'opening' in her busy schedule to meet him for a coffee, she had forgotten all about it. She also forgot to return my great-grand-mother's champagne saucer.

In the end, she didn't arrive until the party was in full swing. Canapés were being handed round, people were already on their second or third drinks, Tears for Fears were 'Shout, shout'-ing and I was at the bar, chatting to Mum and Pops while Ian was buying drinks. The door was right in my eyeline, so I saw Izzy the moment she arrived.

She looked stunning as always and, for once, I actually recognised her outfit because one of my favourite celebrities – Cara Delevingne – had recently worn the same YSL tuxedo. Just like Cara, Izzy wore nothing underneath.

Our eyes met, and while I, reflexively, without really meaning to, half-raised my hand in greeting, she completely ignored me, her gaze continuing to move around the room as if she hadn't seen me.

Izzy stepped further into the bar and was followed through the doorway by someone holding her hand. He stood out almost as much as Izzy, not only for his good looks but also because he was dressed in jeans ripped at the knees and a Castrol T-shirt with what looked like an authentic oil stain on it. Izzy dropped the guy's hand and made her way over to where her parents were standing with a group of their friends. Roger saw her first and turned to give her a hug, followed by Sarah.

'Oooh,' said my mum. 'Who's the hunky chap with Izzy?'

'I've no idea. She told Danny she wasn't bringing anyone.'

'Ah, well, it's good to see,' Mum said, as Ian handed her a large glass of white wine, then passed over a G&T for me and a Coke for Danny, who was on the other side of the room, talking to an older couple I didn't recognise.

'Thanks, Ian,' I said, then, 'What were you saying, Mum?'

'It's good to see Izzy with someone. It can't be easy being the singleton in the family.'

I gave a sort of snorting laugh. 'Doubt she cares.'

Mum looked at me curiously, then continued, 'He must be important to her, though, to bring him along to a family party like this. Why don't you go and say hello? He's going to be feeling awkward if he doesn't know anyone. Look, he's standing by himself, poor chap.'

Leaving Danny's Coke with Ian, and more out of curiosity than anything else, I carried my drink over to the guy. He was staring at Izzy – she had been absorbed into a circle of her parents' friends – and as I passed behind them, I paused long enough to hear her saying, 'Us millennials are reinventing the concept of angel investing. I'm looking into patenting my crowdfunding concept. The PE ratio of the target co is in my wheelhouse.'

The people listening looked politely bored, although maybe that was just wishful thinking on my part.

Meanwhile, her date was standing off to one side, wedged between an old fireplace with fairy lights strung along the top and a knee-high glass table with two bottles of red wine on it. Izzy obviously hadn't bothered to tell him everyone was supposed to buy their own drinks because he was helping himself to the wine.

'Hi,' I said, raising my voice to make myself heard over Spandau Ballet insisting I was indestructible.

The guy looked at me briefly. 'Hi.' He let his gaze slide right back to Izzy.

'I'm Grace,' I said, wondering if he was always so rude. He looked blank.

'Danny's girlfriend?'

He shook his head.

'Izzy's brother Danny?'

'Oh, right. Sure. Hello.' He was slurring his words – the wine obviously wasn't his first drink of the evening.

'How long have you known Izzy?' I asked.

'What?'

'How long have you two been together?'

'We hooked up this afternoon,' he said.

Jesus.

Previously, I would probably have convinced myself her behaviour was entirely reasonable. But in no way was this reasonable behaviour. Who came to a long-planned party to celebrate something so meaningful as your own parents' wedding anniversary dragging along a bloke, wearing an oil-covered T-shirt, you'd only met (hooked up with!) that afternoon?

Before I could tell the guy to buy his own drinks or, better yet, stop drinking, the music faded out and Danny's voice boomed around the room, amplified by the microphone he was clutching in his right hand.

'Hello, everyone,' he said, and waited for quiet before continuing. 'I want to thank you so much for being here this evening to celebrate my parents' wedding anniversary.'

Next to him, Roger was beaming broadly, his gaze darting around the room as if he didn't want to miss a moment. Sarah was on Danny's other side, sitting on a barstool someone had brought over for her.

Beside me, Izzy's 'date' stumbled, falling against the side of the fireplace. He propped his arm on the mantelpiece to steady himself, tangling it in the string of fairy lights. I turned my back to him.

Danny's speech was short and heartfelt. He told a story everyone already knew (because it was one of Roger's favourites) about how his parents had met on a blind date but Roger had thought he was meeting the girl on the table next to Sarah and almost left without ever speaking to the woman who would become his wife. Danny talked about how his parents had set the bar high for him and Izzy because they'd shown him what a 'loving, supportive, wonderful marriage should be like', which made everyone in the room go 'ahhhh' and look a bit teary. He ended by thanking his parents for all the 'support they've always given my sister and me, no matter what', and saying, 'Mum and Dad, we love you.'

Then he said, 'Iz, do you want to come and say a few words?'

His sister made her way towards the front. When she got there, she slipped her right arm around Roger's waist and her left around Danny's, pulling them both close. Danny looked at his sister, smiling, and a moment later she lifted her mouth into the same shape so their expressions were identical.

Izzy tucked the fingers of her left hand into the back pocket of Danny's jeans. I shivered, even though it was stifling in the pub.

'Mum, Dad,' Izzy said into the microphone which Danny was holding for her, 'I hope you're enjoying the evening Danny and I worked so hard to put together.' There was a ripple of applause while I marvelled at her barefaced cheek. Why did no one ever say anything? Why didn't Danny? He – *we* – had spent ages organising everything, whereas *she* had done absolutely nothing. And yet she always, *always* got away with it.

Izzy was saying, 'I know it can't always have been easy, bringing up two gifted children, and they say the best way to know if parents have done a good job is if their children are more successful than themselves. Well, Mum and Dad ... you've done an excellent job!'

Roger and Danny joined in the laughter, but Sarah did not. In a room full of people, she looked strangely alone, separated from her family who were embracing each other. From where I was standing, she appeared to have her eyes closed.

'Mum, Dad,' Izzy said, turning to smile at her father, 'I'm sure everyone here would agree that you've been the best parents to me and Danny.'

She paused to allow everyone to 'aww' and 'ahh' before continuing, 'Just look how brilliantly we turned out.'

Before she could say anything else, there was a deafening crash behind me. I turned to see Izzy's 'date' had fallen right through the table. He was lying on the floor, surrounded by thick shards of glass. For a moment, the only thing I could hear was the sound of Izzy laughing.

Then the bar manager – Scott – was saying, 'Stand back, stand back,' and we shuffled into a semicircle around the man on the floor.

Scott leaned over him. 'Can you stand?'

The guy nodded.

'Easy now,' said Scott, helping him to his feet as he swayed.

One of the guests – a woman I hadn't met – came forward. 'Have you hit your head?' she asked, then turning to Scott said, 'I'm a doctor. Let's help him into a chair.' She turned back to the guy. 'What's your name?'

'Spencer.'

'Let's get you into a chair, Spencer,' she said. 'Then I can check you over.'

To the unmistakeable opening strains of Madonna's 'Holiday' – someone had turned the music back on – Scott and the doctor led Spencer over to a little alcove by the door, one of the members of staff appeared with a large broom and started sweeping up the glass, and gradually everyone else began drifting back to the other end of the room.

I made my way over to Danny and linked my fingers through his. 'Your speech was great,' I said.

He kissed me.

'Danny, mate, we've got a bit of an issue.' It was Scott. 'D'you think you could come and –?' He waved towards the doctor who was kneeling on the floor beside Spencer.

When she saw us approaching, she got to her feet. 'I'm Lauren,' she said to Danny shaking his hand, then mine. 'Friend of your mum's.'

'Thanks so much for helping him,' Danny said.

'Of course, no problem, but –' She looked down at the guy in the chair. 'I'm concerned he might be concussed. He needs to be checked out but he's refusing to go to hospital. Can you try and persuade him? He'll probably respond better to a friend than a complete stranger.'

'I can try,' Danny said. 'But I don't know who he is. I've never seen him before.'

'He came with Izzy,' I said. 'I'll go and get her.'

She was at the bar, where one of Roger's friends was handing her a large glass of wine.

I nudged her arm. 'You need to come.'

She ignored me.

'Izzy, you need to come.'

She sighed heavily. 'I do apologise,' she said to the man next to her, before turning to me. 'What is it?'

'You need to help Spencer.'

'Who?'

'The guy you brought with you. The doctor thinks he's concussed. He needs to go to hospital.'

'He'll be fine.'

'Izzy,' I said, more forcefully. 'You're the only person he knows in this entire place.'

She looked across at the little group standing around Spencer. 'Danny's over there.'

'So?'

She shrugged and knocked back half the wine in one go. 'He can sort it out.'

'It's not Danny's problem. You should be with him.'

She shrugged again and turned back to the man beside her. Wrapping a strand of her hair around her finger she tugged it so the curls flattened. Then she let them spring back. 'Buy me another?'

The man's reply was drowned out by the opening bars of 'Endless Love' by Diana Ross and Lionel Richie, which had been Roger and Sarah's first dance at their wedding. At the far end of the room, Roger was pulling Sarah into the centre of a circle of their friends.

Leaving Izzy at the bar, I went back to Danny. He was apologising profusely to Scott, who was mopping the floor.

'The poor guy's been sick,' said Danny.

'I'm going to drive Spencer to the hospital myself,' said Lauren. 'If I bring my car round to the front door, will you help me get him into it?'

'Of course,' Danny said, picking up her bag and handing it to her. She rummaged around for her keys. 'About five minutes, OK?'

'I'm going to put this away,' said Scott, giving the bucket and mop a nudge with his foot. 'You OK to watch him?'

'No problem,' said Danny.

'I asked Izzy to come and help, but she wouldn't,' I said.

'It's fine. There's nothing she could really do anyway – Lauren's got it all under control.'

'But she's the one who knows him ...'

'He's had too much to drink,' Danny said. 'And I'm hardly in a position to judge someone for that, now, am I?'

He was missing the point.

Mumbling something about getting some water, I marched back over to Izzy as the opening of Queen's 'Who Wants to Live Forever' boomed around the room. As a kid, I'd always thought it was a morbid song, but on the first Valentine's Day Danny and I were together he had given me a card and inside he'd written out the lyrics in full. He'd blushed as he explained how he'd never thought he'd want to be with anyone forever until he met me. From then on, it became our song.

'Izzy,' I began, raising my voice to be heard over Freddie Mercury, 'Spencer's got to go to hospital.'

'So?'

'You need to go with him.'

'Why?'

'The guy's in a hell of a state.'

'If you're so concerned about him, *you* go with him,' she said.

'*You're* the one who knows him –'

'Jesus Christ, Grace,' she said. 'Stop whining on. Whine, whine, whine. I don't know how my brother stands it.'

I'd had enough. Someone had to confront her about her behaviour, and if no one else was prepared to do it, then it would have to be me.

'Look, Izzy,' I said, putting my hand on her arm, 'I know what happened to you.'

She shook my hand off her tuxedo. 'Don't touch the Saint Laurent.'

'Danny told me about your uncle.'

She folded her arms. 'Well, this will be entertaining. Go on ...'

'I understand, I really do. Something like that is going to have a massive effect on you. It must constantly be there in the background, and sometimes in the foreground.' I was making a complete mess of this. I took a deep breath and tried again, raising my voice to be heard over the music. 'What I'm trying to say, is –'

'Oh, you're actually trying to say something, are you?' she said. 'Because so far all I'm hearing is blah blah boring noise blah blah.'

'You need to get help. You need counselling. I'm sure you don't realise but all the trauma you're carrying is making you hurt the people around you.'

There. I'd said it.

Izzy shrugged. Meanwhile, Freddie Mercury was asking if anyone wanted to live forever.

I tried again. 'Anyone that's been through what you went through, it's going to have a profound impact on your life, your relationships, everything.'

'Not me,' she said.

I was completely out of my depth; what she needed was professional help.

'If anyone here needs counselling,' Izzy said, as if she could hear my thoughts, 'it's you. You're insane if you think your cutesy little life with Danny is going to last. He's only stayed with you this long because your grandfather bought you a house.'

She leaned in close, but I still had to strain to hear. 'What do you honestly think my brother sees in you? Boring little Grace. Safe little Grace. Twenty-eight going on seventy-eight. Not even that. I mean, even in her seventies my grandmother had more excitement in her little finger than you've got in your entire body. And look at the state of you. Frumpy little Grace. Dressed in your frumpy shift dress, covering your frumpy body. If you didn't have a rich grandfather, Danny would have left you years ago.'

I couldn't help it. Her words needled their way through my gossamer-thin layer of confidence, stabbing deep inside me, all my insecurities rising instantly to the surface.

'It's no wonder he cheated on you,' she was saying, her lips touching my ear. I jerked my head away, but she hadn't finished. 'Haven't you got it yet, Grace? This so-called relationship you think you have with my brother? It's over. You might as well give up now. Do the right thing. Walk away. At least that way you might keep a shred of dignity.'

'Danny loves me,' I managed to say. All round us, the party guests were showing their very vocal appreciation for the next song on the playlist, which was 'Thriller'.

'No, he doesn't. How could he? You must realise he deserves someone better than you. Brighter, prettier, *better* than you. Someone he *actually* wants to be with. If you really loved him as much as you say you do, you'd do the right thing and leave him.'

There was a pressure at the back of my nose and eyes. I really didn't want to cry. I looked over to where Danny had been, but he wasn't there. I told myself *no*, she wasn't right. Danny *loved* me. I *knew* he did.

'Walk away, Grace,' Izzy murmured.

'And if I don't?' I asked, turning to face her, bracing myself for her strange blank-eyed stare. I watched her pull her mouth into the same smile she'd worn beside Danny earlier.

'If you don't, then you'll find out what happens to people who don't do what I want them to do.'

She turned away from me, as calmly as if she'd asked me the time, walked over to her mother and gave her a kiss on the cheek. Looking over Sarah's shoulder, Izzy smiled at me and mouthed *goodbye*.

I pushed my way through the crowd and into the ladies. In the cubicle, I took deep breaths, willing myself to calm down. I wasn't only upset because of the horrible things Izzy had said. What I felt was something altogether different. Something much worse.

The alarm which had been clanging in my head had become deafening.

Izzy was not only a selfish, self-absorbed bitch. She was dangerous. Very, very dangerous.

By the time I emerged from the ladies, Danny was back in the pub and Izzy's date was on his way to hospital. Danny gave me a kiss, said he was going to get himself a Coke and slipped away from my side.

A few moments later, the music faded out for the second time that evening and Danny's voice came over the microphone.

'Sorry everyone,' he said. 'Sorry. One more thing ...'

He waited until the room had quietened down. I had no idea what he was doing, and it appeared nobody else did either.

'It's been an eventful evening so far,' he said, and everyone laughed. 'And I know this is Mum and Dad's evening, but as it's a celebration of a very long and happy marriage, I thought ... well ... I thought perhaps this might be an appropriate time ... in front of our families and, well, I figured there wouldn't be a better time ...'

Mum and Pops turned to look at me, smiling broadly, and lots of other people were turning to look at me, too.

Danny held his hand out. 'Grace, can you come here?'

A path cleared in front of me and there was silence as I walked the few steps to where he was standing. Then he was no longer standing. He was down on one knee. There was a stain on his trouser leg – presumably from helping Spencer. The hairless patch behind his ear shone beneath the lights from the bar. But then I couldn't see anything else except the little box he was holding in his left hand. He put the microphone on the floor and, with his right hand, he lifted the lid. Inside was a ring, a sapphire surrounded by diamonds, catching the light, dazzling. He reached for my hand. Nobody was making a sound. I wondered if I was going to faint.

'Grace,' he said, 'I love you with all my heart. Will you marry me?'

Notes

After Grace told me about Daniel's proposal she lifted Beth, who had finally worn herself out, into a high chair, handing her a Tupperware container of chopped banana and kiwi fruit.

'How can I miss him so much and be so angry with him at the same time?'

I asked her why she was angry.

'Because we weren't enough for him. He had me, Beth, our house ... it should have been enough. But it wasn't. He always needed Izzy, too.'

Grace loved Daniel, I am sure of that, but occasionally I did get the impression she was guilty of confusing *things* with *love*. Despite her protestations about lack of money – not being able to afford the repairs to her car, for example – our conversations were always littered with mentions of what her family had given her and Daniel: the deposit to buy a house, for one thing, jeroboams of champagne (who's even seen a jeroboam of champagne?), money for the Canadian flights that both her dad and then her grandfather gave her, and of course the antique glasses casually passed down from her great-grandmother.

Izzy had referred to Grace as a 'control freak', always keeping tabs on Daniel, insisting on timetables and lists for everything they did together, making out her sister-in-law was overbearing and domineering. That wasn't my impression of Grace. Nevertheless, I couldn't help wondering if Daniel *had* felt suffocated by quite how much he was obliged to Grace and her family? Perhaps Grace *was* controlling. Maybe she *was* the reason Daniel seemed to have had no real friends?

Whatever the truth, there was no doubt that Daniel's state of mind was significant, and on this occasion, I asked Grace directly. 'Do you think Daniel's mental health ever caused issues at work?'

'Absolutely not. No way. Danny's record as a pilot was exemplary. He always passed the mandatory flight checks. I can show you his flying log if you like.'

'I'm not talking about his ability as a pilot,' I said. 'I mean his emotional wellbeing. After that time when he was on antidepressants, did he ever see a doctor about his anxiety?'

She shook her head. 'No.'

'Was he ever prescribed antidepressants again?'

'No.'

'Could he have been taking them without you knowing?'

'No. He'd have told me. I knew my own husband.'

She got to her feet, saying she had somewhere else to be, scooped her daughter up and strapped her into her buggy, much to Beth's very vocal disapproval. And then, with only the most cursory of goodbyes, Grace turned and wheeled Beth out of the garden centre.

I wasn't sure what to make of our exchange. Was it really the case that, despite all the talk of her husband's so-called 'stress habits', she'd really had absolutely no concerns about him being at the controls of a plane? Or was it that she didn't want to admit to them out of loyalty to Daniel?

I went to visit my parents, who were becoming insistent that I 'put everything behind' me and leave London. They couldn't be expected to help with my rent forever and they wanted me to come home and 'give yourself a chance to get back on your feet'.

In my childhood bedroom, I read and reread the notes from my interviews with Izzy and Grace. Looking at them scattered around me, they seemed to amount to almost nothing. Where was the story? Had this all been a colossal waste of time?

With less than two months to go until the inquest, when all of the available information about flight GFA578 would enter the public domain and any head start I had over other journalists would be well and truly over, I still needed to understand more about Daniel. I knew he loved flying, loved his wife and adored his sister, with whom he appeared to have had an unusually close relationship. He had no close friends, suffered with stress, anxiety and quite possibly depression, too. He had a problematic relationship with alcohol and his lifestyle was funded largely by his wife's family. His sister and his wife both considered themselves to be his best friend, and they had come to loathe each other.

Daniel had spent his entire adult life caught between these two women and it was obvious that jealousy lay at the heart of their antagonism. Izzy was jealous of the material possessions Grace accepted as her due, whereas Grace was jealous of how close Daniel was to Izzy, convinced it undermined her own relationship with him. But I still couldn't piece everything together. What was I missing?

Promising my parents that I would seriously consider coming home permanently, I got a coach back to London and returned to my lonely bedsit. Finally, after several weeks of silence, Izzy got in touch. We arranged to meet at the usual coffee shop, and when I mentioned that Grace had told me about Daniel's proposal at the anniversary party, it turned out that Izzy had quite a lot to say on the matter.

Izzy's Story

2017

1.

Grace didn't want me at her hen do and I didn't want to be there.

There were nine of us – me, her, six of her work colleagues, plus a school friend she hadn't seen for years but who she'd persuaded to come along to make up the numbers – and we were staying at a country house hotel in the middle of nowhere. Grace only invited me because she was worried about what people would think if she didn't, and I only went because I had nothing else on that weekend and it meant free food and booze (her grandfather paid for everything, of course).

The whole thing was intensely boring, exactly like Grace herself. The woman who organised it – Denise or Deirdre, something beginning with 'D' – had no imagination. None at all. There were no strippers, no tying Grace to a lamp post, no cocktails until we puked. There weren't even any Jagerbombs.

We were all corralled into a large drawing room which looked like something out of a period drama. There were heavy drapes on the windows and far too many pieces of oversized brown furniture. Nobody but me had made any effort with their outfit. I'd assumed it was a spa weekend,

so of course I was wearing my Vetements Juicy Couture
tracksuit – channelling my inner Kylie Jenner – but it
turned out that, no, there were no spa facilities and instead
Denise or Deirdre said we were going to play 'games'.
While she handed round paper and pens, I took the seat
closest to the large ice bucket loaded with bottles of
Prosecco, filled my glass to the brim and tried not to feel
nauseous at the thought of so many Next and Debenhams
labels gathered together in one room.

'I'm going to say half a sentence about Grace,' Deirdre
or Denise announced. 'And you need to write down the
rest of it. When we're done, I'll read them out.'

While the others squealed with excitement, I knocked
back the Prosecco. It was going to be a long weekend.

'We'll kick off with an easy one,' Denise or Deirdre
said. 'Complete this sentence, ladies. Grace's best quality
is …'

An easy one? Grace didn't have a single good quality,
let alone a best one.

In the end I wrote down: Grace's best quality is *that
she makes everyone around her look good.*

The next one was even trickier. The sentence began
'Grace's most annoying habit is …' and I was overwhelmed
with choice. In the end I wrote Grace's most annoying
habit is *having too many annoying habits to choose from*,
which was the best I could do in the circumstances.

The following one was easier. 'I'm glad Grace is my
friend because …'

'This is so embarrassing,' said Grace, clearly loving
every second. Her face was flushed, and even from the
opposite side of the room I could see the sweat patches on
her viscose dress. *Poor Dan*, I thought and wondered,

not for the first time, who he thought of when they were doing it.

I'm glad Grace is my 'friend', I wrote, *because I can keep an eye on her.*

Denise or Deirdre said, 'Two more to go, ladies. The three words I'd use to describe Grace are ...'

Three words to sum up a person – the game I used to play with Nan.

I topped up my glass and considered the words I could choose. My inclination, always, is to be honest, although very often my honesty is mistaken as humour. For example, when we first arrived and were milling around the entrance hall, one of Grace's identikit friends said to me, 'Are you admiring the staircase? Apparently it's 350 years old,' but when I replied, 'I was wondering if anyone had ever been thrown off the top of it,' her friend just laughed.

Three words to describe Grace? I settled on *timid*, *predictable* and *persistent*.

'And finally,' Denise or Deirdre said, 'Grace is perfect for Danny because ...'

This was the worst question of the lot. Grace wasn't perfect for my brother. She was the opposite of perfect. She wasn't worthy to kiss his shoelaces. I should never have allowed her within a thousand miles of him.

At first I thought about leaving this sentence blank, but in the end I scrawled something down.

We folded our papers then Deirdre or Denise gathered them up and put them inside a tote bag she'd brought for the purpose. The bag was pink with 'Team Bride' printed on it in large silver letters.

'Time to refill your glasses, ladies,' Denise or Deirdre trilled.

After the Prosecco had been passed around she said, 'Remember, poker faces, ladies. This is meant to be anonymous.' She waggled the revolting bag back and forth. 'What goes in the Team Bride bag, stays in the Team Bride bag.' This was clearly untrue, since she immediately plunged her hand inside and withdrew the first slip of paper.

'My favourite thing about Grace,' she said, 'is that she always puts other people first.'

Everyone in the room went 'awww', and Grace blushed an even deeper shade of crimson. I rolled my eyes. I have never understood other people's predisposition to sentimentality. It's one of those self-indulgent, annoying, pointless *feelings* involving a state of exaggerated warmth towards something or someone. I don't know if there's a specific trigger. I don't know how people know when it's appropriate to enter a state of sentimentality. But what I do know is once they are under the influence, I can spot them a mile off: their dopey half-smiles, their eyelids drooping over eyes which often, but not always, fill with tears. A person in the grip of sentimentality will often touch the subject of their emotion, stroking their arm, resting a hand on their shoulder or pulling them into a hug. There will be a lot of little half-laughs, meaningless words and incomplete sentences exchanged: 'lovely', 'ahhh', 'd'you remember …?', 'I know', 'mmm' or, in this case, 'awww'. It's nauseating.

Denise or Deirdre finished reading out the first piece of paper and reached in for another. It was filled with the same sort of saccharine guff. 'I'm glad Grace is my friend because I know she will always be there for me', which triggered another round of 'awww's and a couple of 'so lovely's.

The fourth set of answers were the ones I'd written.

Deirdre or Denise unfolded the paper and said, 'Grace's best quality is that she always makes everyone around her look good.'

Grace's gaze slid towards me and flicked away again. She probably hoped I hadn't noticed, but of course I had. She knew this was my paper. And she knew I knew.

'Grace's most annoying habit is having too many annoying habits to choose from,' announced Deirdre or Denise.

Everyone laughed, and I laughed along with them, although I hadn't intended it to be a joke.

Denise or Deirdre sipped her Prosecco while she scanned the rest of my answers. Then she opened her thumb and forefinger and dropped the piece of paper back into the bag. 'Oops, silly me.' She stuck her hand in and withdrew a different piece of paper. 'Here we are,' she said. 'I'll do this one.'

No one commented when my answers failed to reemerge but afterwards, as everyone was heading off to get changed for dinner, I saw Grace pull my piece of paper out of the bag. She had her back to me, so I couldn't see her reaction when she read what I'd written for the final sentence.

Grace is perfect for Danny because *she won't make a fuss when they get divorced.*

During the evening meal Deirdre or Denise instigated more of the same saccharine rubbish. This time we had to go round the table and tell everyone about our favourite memory of Grace and she had to do the same for each of us.

Dear god, I thought, *kill me now.*

Or instead, I considered, eyeing my knife, kill this woman instead. Kill this Deirdre or Denise, whatever her name is. Shove the knife into her neck. Right into her jugular. No. Her carotid artery would be preferable because there's more pressure in the arteries than the veins. Blood with your salmon, ladies?

But I fixed a grin on my face and dutifully listened as everyone droned on.

As it happened, I was last, so I'd had a chance to think about what I was going to say.

'My favourite memory of Grace,' I said, 'is when she came to visit me while I was at university in Reading.' I pulled my face into a smile and beamed along the table in her direction. 'You were – what, Grace? Eighteen? Nineteen?'

'I was sixteen.'

'Sixteen, then. And you were so innocent and naïve, so eager to please, so grateful for every scrap of attention. I liked that about you.'

Everyone other than Grace went 'ahhh', and assumed halfwitted expressions, turning towards me as if they expected me to say something else.

After a short period of silence, Deirdre or Denise turned to Grace. 'Your turn, Grace,' she said. 'Favourite memory of your soon-to-be sister-in-law.'

Grace looked at a point over my shoulder. 'I have many memories of Izzy,' she began. 'And my favourite one is probably also from when I went to see her in Reading.'

She touched her earlobes. 'She gave me these earrings. I had saved up my pocket money and bought her a brace-let. Mum wasn't very happy that I'd spent all my money, but I wanted to give Izzy something special, so she'd think of me every time she wore it. I was *so* embarrassed giving her the bracelet, but she said she loved it and she gave me these earrings.'

She turned her head from side to side, so the diamonds caught the light, and everyone went 'wow' and 'gorgeous'.

'Anyway,' Grace said, 'I was scared I'd lose them so I didn't wear them very often, but when I did wear them, I felt really special.'

Her eyes were glistening with actual tears. Pathetic.

The woman next to me, a deeply unattractive colleague of Grace's whose name I hadn't bothered to learn, patted my hand with her damp paw. 'So generous,' she said. 'They must be at least half a carat each. Where did you get them?'

I pulled my arm away. 'Funny story,' I said. 'I was in a jewellery shop. Someone asked to see the earrings but then didn't want them. The phone rang before the shop assistant could put them back in the cabinet, so while she was on the phone I put them in my pocket and walked out.'

There was a moment's silence then everyone but Grace started laughing.

'You're so funny,' the woman next to me said. Then, turning to Grace, she gave her a mock punch on the arm and said, 'She's hilarious. Pretending she stole your earrings. I love this woman. Where have you been hiding her?'

As I said, it's quite remarkable how many times people simply don't believe I'm telling the truth.

Grace was looking at me directly. I stared back. Unusually, she didn't flinch. She downed the rest of her Prosecco then, letting her gaze slide away, she refilled her glass.

'Oh, she's hilarious all right,' she said, removing first one earring then the other and putting them next to her plate. 'One big bundle of laughs.'

When it came to the wedding itself, Grace didn't ask me to be a bridesmaid. She made up some rubbish about how she wasn't going to have any bridesmaids because they had decided to keep it really low-key. But that was Grace all over – selfish and self-centred. No consideration for anyone but herself.

I put even more thought than usual into my outfit. I wanted to make it absolutely clear to everyone that, although Danny might be marrying trash, he came from class. I borrowed Dad's credit card – he would want me to look my best – and took myself off to London. In Selfridges I bought a silk-blend Falconetti midi dress in emerald green from The Vampire's Wife, which I'd had my eye on for a while. The dress was crying out to be paired with Manolo Blahniks and I found the perfect pair at a boutique in Burlington Arcade – 105mm stilettos, black calf leather with chain-link detailing. The assistant recommended I carry flats too, in case I needed to walk anywhere.

I went over to Bond Street to find a bag and, after some consideration, decided on a Bottega Veneta Padded Cassette in black. It was only big enough to carry my keys, phone and Dad's credit card, so I popped back to Selfridges and picked up a Balenciaga tote bag large enough to carry an alternate pair of shoes. I hesitated for ages over the lipstick: Lady Danger by MAC or Invincible by Chanel. I loved them both, but in the end I plumped for the Chanel (although obviously I bought the MAC too).

I looked great. It was just a shame no one else made the same sort of effort.

The wedding may have been low-key, but the party afterwards was the dullest event I'd ever attended – duller even than the hen do. If I heard the words 'lovely couple' and 'made for each other' once, I heard them a hundred times. It was nauseating. As was the endless droning on about their imminent honeymoon in the Maldives – paid for by her grandfather, obviously. I hung around for a while – there was a free bar – but in the end I couldn't bear the tedium any longer. I changed into my flats and headed to the nearest pub, ordered a triple vodka on the rocks then another. When Dad's credit card stopped working, I opened up Tinder, swiped right on the first hot guy I saw and arranged to meet him in a cocktail bar down the road.

Notes

On several occasions I asked Izzy what had happened to make her change her mind about Grace. After all, she had initially been very friendly towards her. But every time I asked her, she gave me a different answer, saying things like 'I liked Grace but she changed', and 'It amused me to have her around until I realised how boring she was', and 'I only liked her while she liked me', and, on several occasions, 'I never said I liked her'.

When I pointed out that I had her on record saying she *had* liked Grace, Izzy was adamant that I had misunderstood her, but I persisted. If she had never liked Grace why had she given her the earrings?

'Look,' she replied, 'you're making something out of nothing. I had a load of stuff in my room, and I gave her the first thing I put my hands on. I didn't even know what was in the box.'

'You didn't know you were giving her really expensive diamond earrings?'

'No.' She shrugged. 'Anyway, so what if they were?'

'And the Joss Stone tickets?' I asked.

'Someone gave me those. Grace was the only person I knew who liked Joss Stone. She's never had any taste.'

I tried a different tack. 'Grace was genuinely fond of

you when you first met. She told me she loved you. And, as far as I can tell, your parents were delighted to welcome her to your family. What exactly is it about her you don't like?'

'Everything.'

'Can you give me some examples?'

'I can give you some words. How about: dull, sanctimonious, nosy, entitled and always fucking there. Always around. All the time. Glued to my brother's side like an extra limb. Splashing her grandfather's money around. Never had the brains to make any of her own. Not like me. I was a natural when it came to business.'

Izzy's Story

2018–2019

1.

In 2018 my mother was diagnosed with myeloma, a type of bone marrow cancer. At the time she found out, I was between places to stay, so I moved back in with my parents. It was really challenging for me because every conversation revolved around Mum's cancer, her hospital appointments, scans, consultant's appointments, chemotherapy, radiotherapy. On and on and on. Not only that, but nobody was bothering to do any shopping so there was never anything to eat in the house and the instant I put on the television Dad would turn the volume down. It was like living in a morgue.

Before then, I'd been in an apartment in the centre of London with floor-to-ceiling windows and panoramic views. It was exactly the sort of place I *should* be living in. The guy who owned it was called James and he was a City trader who earned a fortune and was pathetically grateful for any scrap of attention I gave him. He couldn't believe his luck when I moved in. I didn't have to fuck him very often (he was very sympathetic when I told him I had problems *down there*) and the arrangement might have gone on indefinitely if he hadn't come home early from a stag do because he had tonsilitis to find some guy I'd picked up in a bar tied up and spreadeagled on his bed.

It was unfortunate timing, in no small part because James and I had been due to go to the Maldives the following week. Danny and Grace had gone there on their grandfather-funded honeymoon but James and I had been supposed to stay in a far-more-exclusive resort so it was really aggravating when it didn't happen. I did suggest we could go anyway, but he told me, through tears which turned his usually pasty face into a mottled aubergine colour, that he was giving me an hour to pack my things then he'd be changing the locks.

Anyway, I found myself back at my parents', an arrangement that quickly proved to be intolerable, which was why I decided it was time to make some serious money of my own.

I'd previously met a woman called Louise who was developing an app. I've always had an unerring eye for success and it was immediately obvious that the idea had promise. The app – which was named Astatine, after the rarest element found on Earth – would be *the* go-to membership app for anyone looking to book a last-minute table at a Michelin-starred restaurant, opening-night tickets to the hottest shows or a seat at the finest bar in town. Louise had plans to take this exclusive virtual members club global and she was looking for early-stage investors. I told her I could help, that I knew some people, could make some introductions. The charity where I worked had a lot of rich donors – plenty of famous sportspeople, for example – and as head of communications and marketing I had access to their contact details.

But, when I thought about it some more, it was apparent there was very little in it for me. I would make introductions but the most I would get out of it was an 'advisory role' on the Astatine board and some stock options.

So, instead, I bought the astatine.org domain name (Louise only had the .com one – goodness knows why she hadn't bought the .org one; some people are basically begging to be screwed over), copied all the documentation and presentations she had shared with me, replaced her name with mine and replicated her website (which, like hers, I password restricted). Then I got in touch with my contacts, convinced them they had the chance to invest in the opportunity of a lifetime, made everyone sign a non-disclosure agreement and promised if they invested at least £20,000 they would get free platinum life member-ship of Astatine, which I happened to know was what Louise was promising to *her* investors.

The money would go into a bank account I repurposed from one of my previous ventures and my investors received a share certificate from a pack I'd bought online. Obviously that wasn't all they got. I was on Louise's mailing list and every time I received progress updates from *her* Astatine I copied the contents, changed her name for mine and her website address for mine and forwarded the updates on to the investors in *my* Astatine.

It took a while, but once the business was up and running and money started coming in, I moved out of my parents' house, rented a twenty-first-floor apartment and left my job at HCAssist. Things were back on track.

I hadn't seen Grace for ages when she turned up at my apartment without warning. Because I was expecting a delivery I buzzed her up without bothering to check who it was and opened the door to find *her* standing outside.

'What are you doing here?' I asked, calmly and politely.

'I was just passing,' she said. 'Thought I'd pop up to say hello.'

She was such a bad liar and when she said, 'Can I come in?' I seriously considered slamming the door in her face or, preferably, *into* her face. However, I knew how much I would enjoy her envy when she saw my award-winning interior-designer-decorated apartment, so I let her in.

'Wow,' she said, walking straight out onto the wrap-around balcony. 'What an amazing view.'

'You can see every major London landmark,' I said, pointing out the Anish Kapoor sculpture at the Olympic Park, One Canada Square at Canary Wharf, The Shard at London Bridge and St Paul's Cathedral.

Back inside, I waved her towards the full-grain aniline leather sofa. She sat down and ran her hand over the burnt-orange silk cushions, no doubt appreciating the cool, sleek, sharp vibe of my home, which couldn't have been more different from her cutesy, chintzy, old-fashioned taste.

'How can you afford this?' she asked.

'I'm an entrepreneur,' I said.

'But doing what? *How* are you making this sort of money?'

I shrugged. 'Early-stage investment. You wouldn't understand.'

'I guess not,' she said.

'Wine?' I asked.

She looked at her watch. 'It's only half-past two.'

'Suit yourself.'

I took a bottle of wine out of the SMEG fridge and poured myself a large glass. It was the least I'd need to endure her presence.

'Maybe a small one,' she said, as I was replacing the bottle.

I took another glass from the cupboard and poured her some wine. I held it out to her, but she didn't take it – she stared at my hand, seemingly transfixed.

I waggled the glass in her face, saying, 'D'you want it or not?' until in the end she reached for it.

I brought the bottle with me and sat at the opposite end of the sofa. Grace lifted the wine to her lips but didn't drink anything, putting the glass down on one of the quartz coasters scattered across the coffee table. She'd had colour put in her hair at some point, but her roots had grown out and were uneven and greasy looking. She'd put on some weight and her face was doughy. She was wearing a sort of shapeless denim pinafore dress, with what looked like a fleecy hiking top underneath. Yet again I wondered what on earth Dan saw in her.

'I wanted to have a word,' she said.

I didn't say anything. Although remaining quiet does not come naturally, I have found silence is a useful weapon when deployed sparingly. Most people consider conversation to be a two-way thing, back and forth, back and forth, and if that doesn't happen, they become unnerved. And when they're unnerved they're not careful about what they say, which often proves illuminating. Strategies like this help me get through what would otherwise be intolerably dull interactions.

Grace cleared her throat, picked up her glass, but again put it down without having any of the wine. She straightened the coaster, first one way, then the other.

'Yes, so ...' she said. 'I wanted to have a word about your mum. Well, really about *you* and your mum, I suppose.'

I sighed, which is another way of unsettling people. Hardly anyone sighs during conversations, but I find audible sighing to be an effective way of expressing complete indifference. I sighed again, for good measure.

'I know how difficult it is to talk about,' Grace said. 'I get it, I really do. When my dad was diagnosed, I was the same.'

'We're not the same,' I said.

'No, well, Dad's cancer was less advanced than your mum's. But that's even more reason why you should be spending time with her, Iz. You'll regret it if you don't.'

'No, I won't.'

'How can you be so sure?'

'The only decisions worth regretting are bad decisions,' I said. She looked baffled so I spelled it out for her. 'I don't make bad decisions.'

I topped up my wine, and although I had no intention of offering her any more, she nevertheless put a hand over the top of her glass.

'When my dad had cancer,' she said, 'I realised all the resentment I'd been feeling about him moving to Canada was ridiculous. He was my dad and I loved him and that was what mattered.'

'My mother isn't in Canada.'

'C'mon, Iz. Don't do that thing.'

'What thing?'

'That thing you always do. Avoiding the subject. Not talking about stuff. Have you thought about how you're going to feel if she … well … you know …?'

'If she dies?'

Grace gave a weirdly contorted half-nod. People are ridiculously squeamish talking about death. Most of them can't even bring themselves to use the word *dead*, they use *pass* instead, as though their dead relative or friend is in an overtaking car. I can't bear euphemisms. If everyone said what they meant, if they were precise in their use of language, rather than using all these meaningless alternatives, expecting other people to interpret the imprecise way they talk about all their ridiculous *feelings* and *emotions*, the world would be a significantly better place.

Grace was still droning on. 'All I'm trying to say is I think you should spend a bit more time with your mum. If not for her, then do it for Danny. You must have noticed he's not coping well?'

I hadn't noticed because it wasn't true.

'Didn't he say anything when you saw him last week?'

'No,' I said.

'He's finding your mum's illness really difficult. He's spending every free minute at your parents' place and I know it would really help him if you could be around more. Maybe then he wouldn't feel so bad about spending a bit of time at home.'

'So *that's* what this is about,' I said. 'You're jealous. You've always been jealous of how close we are. And now you're jealous of the time he's spending with our mother – who, by the way, has advanced myeloma. Really, Grace, why don't you just admit your true feelings rather than pretending to be worried about whether Danny is *coping*.'

'That's not fair, Izzy. I'm at your mum and dad's almost every weekend. Danny's spending pretty much every minute there when he's not working. Your dad's taken a sabbatical. We're all trying to help. All of us. Except you.

You're hardly ever around. You're always saying there's a work thing or –'

'It's not *my* fault I've got a successful business to run. Not all of us have a rich grandfather to slip us money every time we need it.'

'Not this *again*. This isn't about money. This is about your mum, who is really poorly, and it's about your brother, who is struggling at the moment. They need you.'

I shrugged, drained my glass, then refilled it. 'Danny's fine.'

'That's what he *wants* you to think. On top of everything else, he's worried about letting you down. He's got you on this massive pedestal, Izzy, he always has had. He'll do anything to make sure you don't think less of him, but take it from me, Danny's not in a good place. He's desperately worried about your mum. His anxiety is through the roof – all his habits have got worse.'

'You should go,' I said, calmly and politely. 'Thank you for stopping by. It's been lovely to see you.'

'Come on, Izzy,' she said loudly. 'You can't ignore what's happening in your family.'

'Keep your voice down,' I said. 'I don't want the neighbours complaining.'

I couldn't care less about the neighbours, but Grace was always so uptight about what people thought of her I hoped it might shut her up.

Unfortunately, it didn't and she continued speaking at the same volume. 'This isn't normal behaviour. You do realise that, don't you?'

'Bye-bye, Grace.'

'Izzy. Please.'

'The door is over there,' I said, still calmly, still politely.

Unlike her, I wasn't shouting. 'You can see yourself out. Or if you'd prefer to take a shortcut, I could throw you over the balcony.'

Her mouth dropped open, hanging so low I could have lobbed one of the quartz coasters into it, but before I had a chance, she stood up, took the glass of wine over to the sink, poured away the contents – which she hadn't had so much as a sip of – rinsed the glass out and tucked it into her bag.

'This is my great-grandmother's glass,' she said. 'I'm taking it with me.'

She slammed the door behind her.

What a complete bitch, I thought, knocking back the rest of my wine.

And yet, as I stared from my balcony at my amazing view, I suddenly found myself laughing. It had been a *very* interesting interlude because, completely unexpectedly and seemingly out of nowhere, my sad, pathetic sister-in-law appeared to have developed a backbone. Which suddenly made everything much more interesting.

I raised my glass in a toast to the recently departed Grace, downed the wine, then hurled it over the balcony. A moment later I could make out the sound of breaking glass twenty-one floors below.

Game on.

2.

I found ways to distract myself from all the talking my family wanted to do about my mother's illness. There were the two nights I spent with a guy I met at the American Bar in the Savoy. That was fun. I'm not often surprised by someone's sexual kinks and I might have seen more of him but he created an almighty fuss about how I had known all along he was married and to please, *please* not contact his wife. 'Blackmailing bitch' was harsh, but I've been called a lot worse.

Not long after that, I had a lovely spa break (using Mum's credit card – it's not like she was getting any benefit from it) and stayed longer than planned when a woman twice my age offered to pay for me to stay an extra three nights if I agreed to share her bed. No kinks there, but she kept the champagne flowing, so it wasn't all bad.

And, of course, I had to find ways to spend my Astatine money, which wasn't difficult. For a start, I traded in my old BMW for a newer model and replaced my entire wardrobe with clothes appropriate to my status as a successful entrepreneur, buying pieces from Chanel, Bottega Veneta, Dior, Valentino, Sonia Rykiel (knitwear only, of course), Gucci, Prada, YSL (another tuxedo) and Balenciaga. There were others. And, of course, the new outfits necessitated an upgrade to my jewellery, shoes and bags (I even managed, finally, to get hold of an Hermès Kelly bag).

I avoided going to see my parents very often because their only topics of conversation were cancer and Grace. They *were* strangely similar, I suppose – both were unwanted malignancies you'd do anything to get rid of – but I lost count of how many times I had to hear how amazing Grace was. As far as I could tell, all she actually did was produce lasagnes and cottage pies and other carb-heavy meals that 'only need heating up', make endless cups of tea, chat to Dad and read to Mum.

My poor mother had to endure hours and hours of Elizabeth Jane Howard's *Cazalet Chronicles*, which Grace had deemed appropriate sick-bed literature, narrating it in that dull, monotonous voice of hers. Honestly, if I had been Mum, I'd have been begging the cancer to finish me off.

Then, one Sunday afternoon, Dad said there was something he needed to tell me. 'It's about Mum's cancer.'

Well, of course it was about her cancer – wasn't every bloody conversation about her cancer?

'They've moved her on to palliative care.'

Dad was hoping I would understand what he was talking about without him having to say it directly, but when I didn't say anything he eventually said, 'That means they're managing her pain, but they're no longer trying to treat the cancer.'

It's fun watching people become really uncomfortable when they're forced to say whatever they're doing their best to avoid saying. However, on this occasion I let my father off the hook. 'You mean Mum's going to die.'

He winced a little, then nodded and continued. 'We found out last week, but we didn't want to tell you over the phone. Danny and Grace were here yesterday, so they know. Thank goodness Danny's got Grace. She's such a great support. Not only for Danny but for your mum, too.' He paused as though he expected me to say something, but since he hadn't asked a question, I remained silent.

After a moment, he said, 'I'm so sorry, darling.'

I shrugged. 'It's OK.'

'You can talk to me. About how you're feeling, I mean. You can always talk to me.'

At least after Nan died all the *do you want to talk?* and *you should talk* stuff only went on for a little while. But with mum's cancer, the talking about talking had already gone on for months and showed no signs of slowing down.

Dad looked around the room as if he was seeing it for the first time. 'What am I going to do, Iz?'

I had no idea why he was asking me, so I didn't say anything.

It was an enormous relief to get back to my lovely airy apartment with its designer furniture and the twenty-four-hour concierge service. I poured myself some champagne and raised my glass to toast the London skyline, which was looking magnificent in the afternoon sunlight. I checked my bank account and found another investor had paid me some money, so I toasted myself, too. Astatine was a resounding success. My most lucrative business so far.

Not long after that, Dan and Grace FaceTimed me. They were sitting in their chintzy kitchen with stupid grins on their faces.

'We've been to see Mum and Dad,' Dan said. 'And obviously we wanted you to be the next to know …'

'Know what?' I said. I had no time for guessing games – I had people to see, places to be.

'Grace's pregnant,' said Dan.

My brother put his arm around his wife's shoulder, pulling her close and kissing her blotchy, chubby cheek.

'I thought there were issues,' I said. 'You told me she had an incompetent cervix.'

Grace turned to Dan. 'You told her that?'

I smiled. 'You know he tells me everything.'

'I can't believe you told her,' Grace said, still looking at Dan.

'I'm sorry,' said Dan. 'I only told Iz. I honestly didn't think you'd mind.'

'Hello,' I said. 'I'm still here.'

'Sorry, Iz,' said Dan. 'Look, all that matters is Grace is pregnant again and this time everything should be fine cervix-wise.'

'Can you please stop talking about my cervix?' Grace said.

'Sorry,' Dan said. 'Sorry, darling. Yes, of course.'

'I've always fancied being an aunt,' I said.

'You're going to be the best aunt in the world,' Dan said. 'Isn't she, Grace?'

The corners of Grace's mouth moved slightly but didn't manage to drag themselves up enough to form a smile. She picked up her mug. 'I'm going for a lie-down.'

'Good idea. You do look a bit rough,' I said.

She lifted a hand and gave me a limp wave.

Dan watched her leave the kitchen before turning back to the screen. 'Sorry,' he said, in a stagey whisper. 'It's been a really difficult few weeks. The news about Mum, you know … and Grace has had bad morning sickness, plus we were really worried about another miscarriage. But now they've done this procedure on her cervix, hopefully she'll start to feel better.'

'I completely understand,' I said. 'You don't need to explain. We both know how bad poor little Grace is at dealing with pressure.'

'I'm not sure that's –'

'I can't believe my little brother is all grown up and going to have a baby of his own. I'm really proud of you, Dan.' I mirrored his smile.

'It's given Mum something positive to focus on,' he said. 'She's already started knitting baby clothes. I hope ...' He paused for a few seconds. 'I just hope she gets to meet her grandchild.' He lowered his gaze and pushed his lips together, like he wanted to prevent any more words coming out.

I did the same thing with my mouth, looked down at my hands and scrolled through Instagram on my phone.

'Iz? Izzy?' Dan said.

I looked up.

'I'm sorry,' he said. 'I didn't mean to make you sad. This is supposed to be a happy day.'

'I *am* happy. I'll be the best aunt.'

'I know, you'll be brill–'

'As long as Grace gets over her problem with me before the baby comes.'

'Honestly, you don't need to worry. She's been under so much stress, not to mention her hormones are all over the place.'

'I'm sure you're right,' I said doubtfully. 'Do you think that's why she was so horrible to me when she came to my apartment?'

'Why, what happened? She didn't tell me she'd been to see you.'

'She turned up out of the blue, accused me of all sorts of things, including telling me it was my fault Mum got cancer.'

I dropped my gaze again, but this time I pushed my bottom lip ever so slightly over my top lip, then closed my eyes and gently ran the back of my right hand over first one eye then the other.

'That's awful. I'm so sorry. I can't believe she said that. You must have misunderstood, but I'll speak to her, I'll tell –'

'No, don't, Dan. Really, you mustn't say anything. Poor little Grace has enough to cope with already. You don't want to add anything else to her plate. As long as I've got you to fight my corner, Dan. Just promise me you won't let her cut me out of things when the baby is born.'

'There's no way that'll happen.'

'Promise?'

'Promise. You're going to be a huge part of our baby's life.'

I let out a big rush of air, so it sounded like I was letting go of a lot of pent-up worry. 'Thanks, Dan,' I said, then paused and sniffed a little, and swiped at my nose with the back of my hand. 'I hope I didn't do the wrong thing by telling you. It's just ... you and Grace are the most important people in my life. The thought of either of you being upset or angry with me is unbearable ...'

'You've got nothing to worry about,' he said. 'We both love you.'

'As long as you've got my back I can put up with pretty much anything.'

'Same here. But you won't need to *put up* with anyth–'

'Sorry, Dan, I need to rush off. Get together next week?'

'That'd be great. I'll check my work roster.'

I ended the call.

I couldn't fucking believe it.

When Dan had first told me about Grace's dodgy cervix, I was thrilled, naturally. If he wanted a child and she couldn't give him one, it would speed up the day when they split up. What I didn't expect was a medical solution to her problem. Of course, the only reason she wanted a baby was to embed her even more firmly in my family.

However, I'm nothing if not pragmatic, and while Grace was pregnant with my niece or nephew it was not in my interests to oust her from Danny's life. I would have to postpone that particular pleasure until after the baby was born.

It would make severing her from our lives all the more satisfying.

3.

Thankfully I didn't see much of Grace during her pregnancy. I was busy managing my business interests, which weren't all plain sailing. Rich De'Ath was the son of a very wealthy IT entrepreneur and had been a professional rugby player until he'd had a heart attack on the pitch in the middle of a game. After he retired he had subsequently become one of the biggest donors to Flora's mum's charity.

Not only was Rich De'Ath rich by name and rich by nature, but he was also extremely fit and, if viewed from the right-hand side, eminently fuckable. Sadly, when viewed from the left-hand side, his cauliflower ear was disgusting. While I was living in James's apartment I had spent a few nights with Rich but I always made sure I slept on his right side.

He was my first investor in Astatine and it was thanks to him (or his millionaire father) that I was able to put down the deposit on my flat and pay six months' rent in advance. Not long after that, he decided to go back to his wife, who was pregnant with their third child. At some point, at his father's insistence, Rich started using the services of his father's 'wealth manager'. Despite it being strictly against the terms of our non-disclosure agreement, Rich had told him about his investment in

Astatine. This wealth manager sent an email asking to 'have sight' of Astatine's 'memorandum and articles of association' and the 'most recent version of the business plan'.

I replied pointing out that the Astatine board of directors took any breach of the non-disclosure agreement extremely seriously but nevertheless forwarding on the most recent documents I'd received from Louise, which included business development updates, details of strategic partnership agreements and revised revenue projections for the actual Astatine. At that point both Rich and his wealth manager went quiet.

My niece was born on 16 July 2019 and, despite all indications to the contrary, Mum survived long enough to meet her.

I spent some time deciding on an appropriate hospital outfit – eventually settling on shredded jeans, a vintage spiked leather jacket I'd only recently come into possession of and my Jimmy Choo biker boots – so by the time I got there, it was nearly at the end of visiting hours. I breezed over to Grace's bed, but despite making a real effort to be full of cheer and happiness, the very first thing Grace said to me, looking at a point somewhere over my left shoulder, was, 'Are you pissed?'

'Are you drunk?' she repeated, before turning her head towards Dan. 'Is she drunk?'

He reached for her hand. She let him take it, her fingers flopping limply against his.

Again she asked, 'Is she drunk, Dan? Is she?'

Dan looked down at her. 'I'm guessing she's had a celebratory drink,' he said, grinning at me.

I lifted my mouth into the same shape as his and turned my face towards Grace. She didn't smile back.

'You can't blame her,' Dan was saying. 'Izzy's excited. *Everyone's* so excited Beth's finally here.'

'Maybe so,' Grace said, 'but no one else has turned up drunk.'

God she was always *so* dull.

'So where *is* my niece?' I asked, looking around the ward. Most of the other beds had cots next to them.

'They've taken her off for a couple of tests,' Dan said. 'Nothing to worry about, though, is there?' He bounced Grace's hand up and down on the bed a couple of times before she pulled it away, tucking it under the sheets. 'Beth's a little bit jaundiced, but that's very common. That's right, isn't it, Grace?'

She nodded but didn't say anything.

'I can't wait for you to see her, Iz,' Dan said. 'She's perfect.'

'Well of course she is,' I said. 'Fifty per cent of her DNA is *our* DNA. Twenty-five per cent of her DNA is *my* DNA.'

Dan laughed.

Grace put an arm over her eyes. 'I'm feeling really tired.'

'Of course, darling,' said Dan. He stood up and stretched his arms above his head and his shirt rose up, exposing his stomach.

He gave Grace a kiss on her forehead. 'We'll go and grab a coffee, let you get some sleep. Can I bring you anything?'

She shook her head.

'Well, it's been lovely to see you, Grace,' I said. 'You're looking great.'

That was bullshit. She was wearing a pale grey T-shirt which was not only completely shapeless but made her look really washed out, plus it had a stain on it that looked suspiciously like vomit. No matter what life might throw at her, you could always rely on my sister-in-law to make absolutely no effort whatsoever. She didn't deserve my brother. She never had. She never would.

Grace didn't bother to say goodbye to me, or show any gratitude for my visit, or thank me for the gigantic fluffy hippopotamus which I'd lugged all the way up to the ward and was now lying spreadeagled across the end of her bed.

When we were out of earshot, Dan said, 'Don't take it personally, Iz. She's still exhausted. She'll be so pleased you came. I know she will.'

I could not have cared less what Grace thought but it *was* annoying not to have seen my niece. As I followed my brother along the hallway towards the lifts, I thought back to the day Danny was born. I remembered how I had my first glimpse of this tiny little human and knew, absolutely and without a shadow of a doubt, that he was mine. And how, for a long time, that's all that mattered. Me and him. Mine. That was ... until *she* came along.

I had only just turned four when Dan was born. Even I, precocious and brilliant as I was, could only achieve so much as a four-year-old. But now I had a chance to do it all over again and this time I could bring to bear all the experience I'd accumulated in the intervening years, the skills I'd honed and the weapons I'd developed.

Waiting for the lift, Dan opened his arms wide and I stepped into them. He gave me an enormous hug, despite my spiked leather jacket. 'I'm so glad you're here,' he said, his breath tickling my neck.

I wrapped my arms around his pleasingly muscular back. 'Me too,' I said.

I didn't mind not meeting my niece that day. It was enough to know she had arrived. Dan and I found a table in the café next door to the hospital, and he went to buy me a coffee. Watching him in the queue, grinning like a fool, I was already anticipating how I would teach his daughter, mould her, train her, same as I had with him, but this time no half-measures. I would not allow a space to grow between us, as it had with my brother. I was going to be the most important person in my niece's life.

She would completely adore me and nothing and nobody – especially not Grace – would stand in my way. I would do whatever it took – *whatever* it took – to make sure my niece grew up to be exactly like me.

Notes

Grace rang and said she had some news. It was the first time I'd heard her sounding happy but she wouldn't tell me anything over the phone so I arranged to meet her at the garden centre that same afternoon.

We'd barely settled ourselves at the table before she announced Izzy had been arrested.

'I reported her to the police ages ago,' she said, her tone triumphant. 'So long ago that I'd begun to think nothing was going to happen. But they've finally done it. They arrested her yesterday.' She laughed and, for the first time, I caught a glimpse of who Grace might have been before her life became mired in tragedy.

Having heard from Izzy herself about her so-called 'business', it wasn't that much of a surprise to find out she'd been arrested, but finding out that the person to report her had been her own sister-in-law? That *was* unexpected.

'And now other people are coming forward,' Grace was saying. 'She's finally going to get what's coming to her. I can imagine the lies she's been feeding you. I bet she's told you that she's brilliantly successful. Really wealthy. Well, she's not. She's just a common fraudster.'

Although I had listened to many outlandish stories from Izzy by then, a small part of me had been holding on to the idea that she was just exaggerating, playing to the audience. But that afternoon I finally saw what I should have seen from the beginning: there was something deeply, disturbingly wrong with Izzy.

Grace was positively voluble that day, more animated than she'd ever been, as if Izzy's arrest had somehow loosened the tight grip she'd kept on herself, and I scrambled to keep up with what she was saying.

'I'd suspected for a long time that she was doing illegal stuff, scamming people, ripping them off, and I feel bad that I didn't do anything about it sooner. The thing is, we'd gone through such a difficult time before Beth came along. I'd had three miscarriages in eighteen months. After the third one my GP offered to refer me for counselling, but it wasn't me who needed it. I was sad and grieving, but I never felt like I couldn't carry on.'

She reached over and brushed Beth's hair away from her eyes. The little girl pulled away from Grace's hand and kicked her legs until her mother lifted her out of the high chair and Beth toddled off. Keeping a close eye on her daughter, Grace continued.

'I can't say the same for Danny, though. After the miscarriages the line between him coping and not coping was stretched so taut it was barely there. His stress habits were worse and his emotions were something I routinely monitored – in the same way I looked out of the window each morning to check the weather. I suggested *he* see a counsellor. I thought it would be good for him to talk to someone other than me. But you know what he said?'

I shook my head.

'He told me, "I've got Izzy. I don't need anyone else to talk to."' Grace's voice was bitter. 'I was so concerned about him that I found any excuse not to upset him by talking about his sister. I told myself I was too tired, or he was too tired, or I didn't want to ruin plans we'd made by having a conversation about Izzy. Then I got pregnant again and we had Beth and for the first few months after she was born it was as much as I could do to get through each day.'

Her eyes had filled with tears. 'But that wasn't the only thing. Every time I thought about confronting him about Izzy's behaviour, I'd remember what she'd said at the anniversary party. How Danny had loved her first, and when our marriage fell apart, she'd still be there for him.'

The tears started to fall.

'Honestly, the truth is that I didn't want to put Danny in a position where he had to choose between me and Izzy. I was scared if I ever did that ... if I made him choose ... he might not choose me.'

She stood abruptly and went to bring Beth back from where she'd started making her way down an aisle of bedding plants. At the table, Grace fussed with her daughter, undoing her little coat, smoothing down her jumper, then zipping the coat back up.

She sat back in her chair, wiping her eyes with the back of her hand. 'Then Danny's mum died.'

Grace's Story

2019–2020

1.

By December 2019, it was impossible to ignore how ill Sarah was. She had made it to Christmas, but I think we all knew she wouldn't be making it to Easter. All these 'lasts' – her last birthday, her last Christmas – made it feel like we were already grieving for her, even while she was still alive.

Danny, Beth and I – together with Mum, Ian and Pops – arrived at Danny's parents' on Christmas Day to find Sarah feeling too poorly to get up, Izzy still in bed and Roger nursing a cold cup of tea, trying – and failing – to make a start on preparing the food. Mum took charge, making more tea and a mountain of buttered toast before sending Danny, Beth and me up to see Sarah and arming Ian and Pops with knives, peelers and bowls full of veg.

Beth – who was five months old by then – was spoilt rotten all day long, surrounded by toys and clothes and stuffed animals. When Izzy finally appeared she gave Beth a totally unsuitable electronic tablet loaded with educational games for toddlers, which my daughter wouldn't be old enough to play with for ages, but I knew how expensive those things were, so I smiled, thanked her and decided to ignore what she'd written on the label: *To my own Bella-boo.*

From the moment Beth was born, Izzy had called my daughter Bella – or Bella-boo – and no matter how many times I said, 'Her name is Beth,' Izzy either ignored me or said Bella was *her* name for *her* niece.

'Talk to her about it,' I said to Danny. 'It'll confuse Beth, being called by two different names.'

'I'm sure it won't,' he said. 'Kids often get called all sorts of pet names. Besides, I think it's kind of cute how Izzy has her own special name for Beth.'

I might have agreed if the 'special name' was something meaningless like 'pumpkin' or 'cupcake', but as far as I was concerned, Izzy calling my daughter by a shortened form of her own name was downright weird. I loved the name we'd given our daughter – I'd always wanted a girl called Beth – and it was disrespectful of Izzy to call her something completely different.

We all – even Sarah, albeit in pyjamas and dressing gown – had only just sat down to Christmas dinner when Beth started wailing. Danny and I both got to our feet, but Izzy was there first, scooping my daughter up and saying, 'You two stay right there. I'll sort out my Bella-boo.' She picked up the changing bag and swept out of the room.

'Lovely of her,' said Pops.

'Izzy adores Beth,' said Danny.

I forced a smile, picked up my fork and stabbed a piece of turkey. I looked up to find Sarah staring at me.

Izzy returned with Beth dozing on her shoulder, eyelids drooping.

I held out my arms. 'I'll take her.'

'It's all right,' Izzy said. 'You finish eating.'

'She needs a sleep,' I said. 'Can you put her in her travel cot?'

'I'll cuddle her,' Izzy said. 'It's better for babies to fall asleep to the sound of a heartbeat.' She said this with the assurance of a paediatrician, rather than someone who not only didn't have any children of their own but had never, in my hearing at least, expressed any interest in babies whatsoever.

'Nevertheless,' I said, 'we've only recently got her into a routine and we need to stick to it.'

Again I reached for my daughter, but Izzy kissed the top of Beth's head and tucked her more closely into her embrace.

I looked at Danny, wanting him to back me up, but he just speared another potato.

'I don't want her routine broken,' I said, my voice shrill. Danny put his hand on my arm, but I shook it off. Everyone put down their cutlery. The only sounds in the room were Beth's tired snuffling noises and Sarah's laboured breathing.

'Of course,' said Izzy, in a quiet voice. 'I only wanted to help. I can see how tired you are. But since it's Mum's last –' I watched her face shift through several expressions, before finally settling on sad. 'I thought it would be nice for us all to have dinner together as a family, with Bella-boo as well. I'm sorry that's not what you want.'

In January 2020 Sarah was admitted to hospital with a nasty infection, and although it took a while to get it under control, eventually she was stable enough to return home. A couple of days later, Mum and I took Beth to visit her. Within a few minutes, though, Beth started crying, and when she didn't settle, Mum offered to take her out for a walk. After bundling her up in several layers against the February winds, she held my daughter's cheek first up to mine then Sarah's for a kiss.

'We won't be too long,' Mum said. 'I'm sure our little chipmunk will settle down as soon as we get on the move.'

After they'd left, my gaze lingered on the empty doorway. I missed my daughter already. I felt Sarah's hand covering mine. Her skin was cool and I turned to look at her.

'Are you cold?' I asked. 'Shall I get you another blanket?'

Sarah shook her head. 'I'm fine. But, Grace, I want you to promise me something ...'

'Of course. Anything.'

'Promise when she's old enough to understand, you'll tell Beth how much her granny loved her?'

I swallowed hard before replying. 'Beth will always know that.'

'You and Danny are brilliant parents,' Sarah said. 'She's a lucky girl.'

'We learned from the best,' I said. Then, when Sarah shook her head, I added, 'You've done pretty well at the whole parenting thing. After all, I did marry your son.'

I was horrified to see tears on her cheeks. Upsetting Sarah was the last thing in the world I wanted to do.

As she reached for a tissue, I said, 'I didn't mean to make you cry.'

'It's not you, Grace,' she said, wiping her tears away. 'It's strange, knowing I'm going to die very soon. I mean, we *all* know we're going to die, yet most of the time we manage to trick ourselves into thinking we're not. But when you're told you've only got a few weeks left it's impossible not to think about all the things you're going to miss out on. Knowing I won't see Beth growing up is the most upsetting thing about all of this.' She waved her hand, the gesture making it clear that 'all of this' included the rented hospital bed and other medical paraphernalia cluttering the room.

I had absolutely no idea what to say. All I could think was how much I wished I had been the one to take Beth out for a walk and it was Mum having this conversation with Sarah.

She must have sensed how uncomfortable I was because she said, 'I'm OK, Grace. Really I am. It's difficult, but you help. You really do. Knowing Danny has you beside him gives me a great deal of comfort.'

'I love him,' I said, my voice cracking.

'I know you do, Grace. I know you won't let him down like I have.'

I wondered if all the drugs she was taking were having an effect on her mind. The doctors had said she'd be 'lucid until the end', but she was sounding so *un*-Sarah-like that maybe they had got it wrong.

'You've never let Danny down. You're a great mum,' I said, really hoping that might be the end of it.

She didn't look at me. She was tearing the tissue, small pieces fluttering down onto the blanket. 'Right from the beginning she never really needed me,' she said. 'She was entirely self-contained.'

'Who?' I asked stupidly.

'Izzy.'

Of course. Izzy. Always Izzy. Even when she wasn't around, she still dominated the conversation.

'If she fell over and hurt herself, she wouldn't want me to cuddle her – she'd just get angry with whatever had hurt her. She'd smack the floor over and over, and if I tried to comfort her, she'd give me a look. You know that look, don't you, Grace? The one Izzy gives you when she's calculating exactly what she can get from you.'

I knew that look.

'I'd compare myself to other mums and wonder what I was doing wrong. But then I started having these terrible thoughts. I was convinced Izzy was manipulating me. Even as a toddler, it seemed like she knew which buttons to press. By the time she was four or five, I was convinced she was playing Roger off against me, persuading him to gang up on me. What sort of mother thinks like that about her little girl?'

Maybe a mother who has a manipulative, egocentric nightmare of a child, I thought, but I didn't say that. Instead, I said, 'When Izzy was four or five, Danny was a baby. You must have been shattered all of time. It's hardly surprising you had some pretty dark thoughts ... I'm sure most mums feel the same.'

'I don't think they do.' Sarah reached for my hand and laced her fingers through mine. It was strangely intimate, but I left our fingers intertwined. 'I've never told anyone this, Grace, but the truth is I'm scared of her. I know it's a terrible thing to say, but I'm scared of my own daughter.'

I feel awful admitting it, but it was exhilarating to hear her say this. Nobody had ever talked to me about Izzy like this before. No matter what unacceptable behaviour she pulled out of the hat, all her family ever did was roll their eyes or offer something trite like 'She's at it again'.

But this threw a different light on things. I was trying to pull my thoughts into something coherent to ask her, but there was more Sarah wanted to say.

'When Izzy was much younger,' she continued, 'the worst thing was knowing I had absolutely no influence over her. I couldn't guide her behaviour, and I had no idea what she might be capable of doing. Then when Danny came along, it all became so much more complicated.' She squeezed my fingers surprisingly hard, considering how weak she was. 'Look after him,' she said. 'Look after my boy, won't you?'

I nodded. 'Of course, but I –'

'Danny adored his sister, right from the beginning, even though she was so unkind to him.'

'How was she unkind?'

'She would tease him remorselessly and taunt him about all the things he couldn't do because he was younger than her. And she was always so jealous of anyone else Danny wanted to spend time with. In the end I stopped suggesting his friends came round to the house, because Izzy would do whatever she could to make sure they were no longer friends by the time they left. The sad thing was, it only made him more desperate for her attention. He had her on a pedestal a mile high.'

'He still does,' I said.

Sarah unlinked her fingers from mine and patted my hand. 'It can't be easy for you,' she said, 'the way Danny has always been in thrall to his sister. Even when he was a baby, if he was upset, it was always Izzy he wanted. He'd hold out his arms towards her every time.'

'He craves her approval,' I said.

'I know. And it really worries me. You're so very patient, Grace. But I worry what will happen if your patience runs out.'

'At least they don't argue like some siblings.' I didn't know what else to say.

Sarah held my gaze until I looked away, then she sighed. 'It's not right, how they are. She's so possessive of him and it's like he's wilfully blind to her faults. You understand there's something very wrong with my daughter, don't you? I know you see it too.'

I nodded, not trusting myself to say anything.

'She was such a troublemaker when she was young, but I always hoped she'd grow out of it. We were constantly being called in by her teachers because of bullying and cheating and god knows what else. Did you know she was expelled from two different schools?'

I shook my head.

'We tried to keep as much as we could from Danny, so maybe he doesn't really remember much of what went on. Like the shoplifting, for example. She used to steal the most ridiculous things. One time she stole a set of spanners, for goodness' sake. She had absolutely no use for spanners, but she seemed to get a kick out of getting away with it. There were other things too.'

She stopped speaking and after a moment, I asked, 'What things?'

Sarah shook her head. 'Horrible things. Danny's guinea pigs were the worst. At the time, I told myself it was a fox, but I knew what had really happened. The thing was, it was easier to lie to myself than confront the truth. It's always been easier to lie to myself.'

'Maybe her behaviour's got something to do with her uncle.' The words were out of my mouth before I could stop myself. This might be my only opportunity to talk to Sarah about it. Perhaps if I understood what happened back then, I could work out how best to handle Izzy.

Sarah said, 'What are you talking about?'

'Danny told me about your brother ...'

'What about my brother?'

I took a deep breath. 'Danny told me how your brother sexually abused Izzy.'

Sarah didn't say anything at first. She struggled to push herself up into a proper sitting position, and although I tried to help her, she wouldn't let me.

Finally, when she'd settled herself, she said, 'What are you talking about, Grace?'

'I know I shouldn't have mentioned it, but you were telling me all these things about Izzy and ... well ... don't you think it could be the reason for her behaviour?'

Sarah stared at the foot of the bed. 'My brother didn't abuse Izzy,' she said.

'I know no one talks about it, but I assume that's why he hasn't come back from Australia to see you.'

'If I had a brother in Australia, don't you think I might actually have mentioned him at some point in all the years I've known you?' Sarah said, her voice so cold I almost shivered.

I was very close to tears. 'I guess I thought you didn't mention him because of what he did,' I managed to say.

She finally looked at me and there were tears in her eyes, too. 'I don't understand, Grace. What exactly did Danny tell you?'

'He told me your brother sexually abused Izzy but you and Roger agreed not to report him to the police if he moved to Australia.'

'Danny remembers this, does he?' she asked.

'No, no, he doesn't. He said he only knows what Izzy told him, which is that when she was eight or nine she told you – actually, I think he said she told Clare first of all – what was going on, and after you confronted your brother, he left the country.'

'Grace,' Sarah said, 'I did have an older brother, but he died in a car accident when he was six.' She lifted her left arm, pushed back her sleeve and pointed to a needle-thin scar below her elbow. 'I was only a baby and I fractured my radius, but I was the lucky one. My brother broke his neck. He was dead before the ambulance arrived.'

I had no idea what to say. Sarah took a deep breath, holding it for several seconds before letting it out slowly. 'After it happened, my parents never talked about him. They found it too painful. And I guess I learned to do the same. I was so little and I have no memories of him. When our kids were young, I told them they had an uncle in heaven – one of those stupid things we say to children – but Danny obviously chose instead to believe Izzy's horrible, disgusting lies.'

'I'm so sorry,' I said.

'My brother's name was William. I know from photographs that he had the darkest hair and the bluest eyes. Then he died and my parents never talked about him.'

The tears that had been threatening to come were running down both of our faces. I reached for a tissue and wiped first Sarah's cheeks then my own.

'I'm so sorry,' I said again, helplessly. What else could I say?

Sarah looked at me. 'Have you ever mentioned this to Izzy?'

'Only once.'

'And?'

'She refused to discuss it with me.'

'Because it never happened.'

I nodded. 'I understand that now.'

Sarah gripped both my hands in hers and leaned

forward so her face was only inches from mine. 'Grace. Listen to me. Promise me you'll keep Beth away from Izzy. Promise me?' Her voice was urgent. 'She must never have the sort of influence over Beth that she has over Danny.'

I nodded again.

'Say it, Grace. Say you promise.'

'Of course,' I said. 'I promise.'

It's easy to say with hindsight, but I'm certain this conversation with Sarah would have finally persuaded me to speak to Danny about his sister, about her lying and cheating and about the suffocating influence she had over him. I believe I would have convinced him he needed help, and in time, he could have learned to be less dependent on her. I was already rehearsing the conversation in my head when an even more urgent worry began to emerge.

There were reports on the news about a virulent 'novel coronavirus' spreading right around the world. The government urged everyone to socially distance. On 20 March 2020, all bars, restaurants and gyms were ordered to close.

Sarah died the following day.

The cancer killed her, not the coronavirus. She was at home and Danny was there with Roger. No one could get hold of Izzy. We rang, texted and WhatsApped her over and over, but in the end it was nearly twenty-four hours after Sarah's death when Izzy finally turned up, claiming her phone had run out of battery. When I asked Danny how Izzy had felt about not being there when her mum died, he said she was 'completely devastated'.

Somehow I doubted that.

2.

Danny's parents had a lot of friends. They belonged to several sports clubs and before Sarah became ill they were always having dinner parties with one group or another. Under normal circumstances, Roger would have invited all of their friends to Sarah's funeral. However, circumstances were not normal. Two days after she died, the country was placed into a strict lockdown and only eight people were permitted to attend the service.

The undertakers urged Roger to hold the funeral as soon as possible – horrifyingly, it seemed the authorities were expecting a huge increase in deaths – and on 2 April, Roger, Danny, Izzy, me, Beth, Sarah's aunt Molly and Sarah's closest friend, Liz, and her husband, Will, gathered together at the crematorium.

Although Clare's service had been held in the same place, the occasion couldn't have been more different. Where the chapel had been packed for Clare's funeral, this time, with only seven of us, plus Beth, the building was freezing cold and cavernous, so every sound, no matter how slight, was amplified and distorted.

A man wearing a mask instructed us to sit in our separate household groups, then insisted Danny and I move because everyone was too close together. In the end, Roger and Izzy were on the front left-hand side, Molly was two rows behind them, Danny and I were on the front right-hand side, with Beth asleep in her buggy beside us, and Liz and Will two rows behind us. No one talked. At the back of the room something electric – a fan, perhaps – clicked on and off every couple of minutes.

I held Danny's hand and looked along the row of chairs at Izzy. She turned her head, meeting my stare. Neither of us smiled. My heart thumped faster and I felt a bit queasy. Not like I was actually going to *be* sick, just a sort of roiling nauseousness in my stomach.

I leaned back, letting Danny's body shield me from her gaze, and looked out of the floor-to-ceiling windows at the front of the chapel, rain smudging the view of the tree-lined meadow which lay beyond.

The service was short. Roger spoke from the lectern, standing alone, tears coursing down his face. The coffin slid away, the curtains closed, and we headed out into the rain, keeping our distance from each other. Danny's great-aunt Molly was anxious to get home before dark and left immediately, while the rest of us looked at each other, unsure what to do or what to say, and I realised why there's usually somewhere to go and be together after a funeral because this – standing around in the rain in a car park – simply felt cruel. Roger and Danny – and Sarah – deserved so much more. Even Izzy looked uncomfortable, although it didn't stop her making a fuss when I refused to unstrap Beth from her buggy so Izzy could 'hug my Bella-boo'.

'It's not allowed,' I said, relieved there was a genuine reason to refuse.

'All these rules ... you do realise they're a complete overreaction, don't you?' she said, taking a step towards the buggy.

I took a step back, pulling the buggy with me. 'The rules are there to keep us safe, Izzy.'

'Are they, though? Or are the government using this virus as an excuse to curtail our civil liberties?'

I'd seen this sort of attitude on social media and I knew some people really did think like that, but I had no doubt Izzy was being provocative for the sake of it.

'This virus is no worse than the flu,' she was saying. 'We don't stop people cuddling their nieces when there's a flu outbreak, do we?'

'Maybe we should,' I said. 'Flu kills thirty thousand people in the UK every year.'

'Does it, though? Don't be one of the sheep, Grace, blindly doing whatever you're told. One little hug with my best girl. What harm can it do?'

'No,' I said. 'It's not safe.'

'Can you believe this?' she said to no one in particular.

Will gave Liz a pointed look. 'I think we need to be heading off. Roger, you know where we are if there's anything we can do. Anything at all. I mean it.'

They got into their car and through the window I could see Liz wiping her eyes.

We watched them winding their way along the narrow lane and when they turned onto the main road Roger said to Danny, 'You OK, Dan?' at the same time as Danny said, 'You OK, Dad?'

They both attempted a smile but the weather was getting worse and it felt like there was nothing more to say. I put Beth into her car seat and waved at Roger, which was awkward and inappropriate. He got into his car with Izzy and they followed us out of the crematorium grounds. As we turned to the right, I looked behind me as Roger turned to the left. Awful though it was, I couldn't help feeling there was a silver lining to this whole lockdown business: I would not have to see Izzy again for some time.

Beth screamed for most of the journey home, making any conversation between Danny and me impossible. She needed her nappy changed, but we didn't want to risk going into a service station so we carried on without stopping. By the time we arrived home, Beth was overtired and in desperate need of a feed and a bath.

After she was finally asleep, I came downstairs to find Danny sitting on one of the bar stools in the kitchen, staring through the window, although it was too dark to see anything outside. He was tugging the hair behind his ear. I checked the baby monitor was on then made us both a cup of tea and sat on the stool next to him. I put my palm on the nape of his neck. Goldfinch required all male pilots to keep their hair short and I loved the feel of the bristles as his hair started to grow back.

'It's been a long day,' I said. 'Let's go to bed.'

He didn't reply and when I asked, 'Do you want me to sit here with you?' he just shook his head.

I went upstairs, but I didn't fall asleep. I could hear Danny moving around. He watched TV for a while, then I heard nothing. Sometime after midnight he came into our bedroom.

'Are you asleep?' he said, in a whisper.

'No,' I replied, and he switched on the bedside light. I could tell he'd been crying because his eyes were swollen.

There was blood on his lip from where he'd been biting it, and when he turned his head, the bald patch behind his ear was larger than it had been that morning and ringed in red where he'd been tugging on his hair. He sat on the edge of the bed, but when I held out my arms he shuffled over into my embrace.

'Today was the worst day of my life,' he said. 'Worse even than the day Mum died.'

'I know,' I said.

'It's so wrong not to have a proper funeral.' He reached for my hand, drawing it down so he could link his fingers with mine. I held fast to them, hoping to pull his focus away from his thoughts and onto me.

'I keep thinking about how Beth won't have any memories of Mum,' he said. 'She'll just be a person we talk about, which is so sad.'

'We'll make sure Beth knows all about her,' I said.

'But now Dad and Izzy won't see Beth either, because of this stupid pandemic.'

'We can FaceTime them,' I said. 'And Roger could read Beth a bedtime story every evening, as well. Other grandparents are doing that.'

'It's not the same.'

'I know, darling, but we have to do what we can.'

'It really upset me today when Iz wanted to give Beth a cuddle. It's not right, having to say no.'

'No, it's not right,' I said.

We didn't say anything more for a while and I thought he had fallen asleep but then he spoke again, his voice hoarse. 'I know I've got another week of compassionate leave, but I'm going to go back to work. It's the only thing that's going to make me feel better. I'll ring HR in the morning and ask to be rostered back on straight away.'

'Are you sure you're ready? Maybe it would better to have another few days at home.'

'I need to fly, Grace. You know what I'm like. You understand. I know you do.'

We lay in silence. With my arms tight around my husband, I forced myself to focus on the good things in our lives: I loved him and he loved me, I was certain of that. We had survived my miscarriages and we had a beautiful, healthy daughter. We had a lovely home and jobs we enjoyed.

I could be strong for Danny, strong enough to hold his vulnerabilities together. He would go back to work and he'd start to feel better. With this awful coronavirus I would have the benefit of time and space on my side: time to work out what to do about Izzy and the space to put a plan into place. No matter what happened, I would find the strength to deal with her.

Danny and I would be fine. I would make sure of it.

While we were sleeping Goldfinch Airlines emailed Danny. They were grounding all planes with immediate effect. The only exceptions were flights to repatriate customers stranded abroad and they would be complete within thirty-six hours, using planes flown by pilots already rostered to fly. After that, there would be no further Goldfinch flights for the foreseeable future. No matter how much he needed to be in the air, Danny would not be going back to work.

Notes

When Grace talked about those early days of lockdown, it was clear how challenging she found it. She told me about bulk-purchasing industrial-sized hand sanitisers to leave on the shelf by the front door and wiping down all parcels and food deliveries with bleach, and washing her hands with antibacterial handwash, and mopping the floors with disinfectant several times a day. Whenever she took Beth out for the permitted daily walk she'd leave a pack of wipes by the front door to clean the handles of the buggy and a bucket of warm water with bleach to swill over the wheels.

She was obsessed with the news bulletins, pouring over the graphs and charts, appalled by the daily death count. They had gone through so much to have Beth, and Grace was terrified when she imagined the future that might await their daughter. What sort of life would be possible if each interaction with someone could result in death?

Grace said she tried to talk to Daniel about her fears, but after the planes were grounded he became more and more withdrawn, spending most of his time in bed. He was mired in grief. Grief for his mother, obviously, but not flying was a very real grief for him, too. Grace knew how unhappy Daniel was, but she was looking after Beth and doing all the usual household chores pretty much single-handedly, not to mention barely controlling her own spiralling panic about the pandemic, so she had very little spare energy or emotional bandwidth to focus on him.

It was against this backdrop of grief and exhaustion that what Grace described as the 'worst possible thing' happened.

'I was expecting a food delivery,' Grace explained. 'So when the doorbell rang, I opened it and stepped back to give the delivery driver plenty of space. But instead of bags of food on the doorstep, there were two enormous suitcases. When I looked up, *she* was there, twisting her face into that awful smile of hers and shouting, "Surprise!"'

When I found out that Izzy had been arrested I sent her a text, fully expecting her not to reply, but she got back to me immediately, suggesting we meet at her father's house. I didn't realise it at the time, but it was a condition of her release on bail that she stayed there.

Her childhood home in Richmond was exactly as I had imagined it: light and airy with walls painted in muted shades of blue and grey, stripped wooden floors covered with thick rugs, expensive furniture and sofas piled with colourful cushions. I could hear the noise of the planes preparing to land at Heathrow, just as Izzy had described in one of our first meetings.

I didn't see Roger, who remained upstairs the whole time I was there.

I began by asking Izzy about her arrest, but she refused to give me a straight answer. She kept fiddling with her phone and met each of my questions with an insistence that the arrest was a 'routine thing' and a 'mix up' and that she was 'helping the police with their enquiries'. It was only later that I found out she had already been charged and was awaiting a trial date.

Accepting I wasn't going to get anything out of her about the arrest, I instead asked her if she'd like to explain why she had told Daniel that their uncle had abused her. Why lie about something like that? And why let him believe it for so many years? But I might as well have not spoken. Izzy ignored me – she actually appeared to be playing a game on her phone.

I was feeling very uncomfortable and wondering why on earth she had agree to meet me, but before giving up completely, I asked her why she had decided to go and stay with Daniel and Grace during lockdown?

Sighing, she put her phone down and looked up. There was no sign of the charming, friendly Izzy that I'd seen so many times before – in fact, her expression was curiously blank, as if I was a stranger or she was trying to see through me to the wall behind. I shifted in my seat uncomfortably, forcing myself to meet her gaze, letting the silence grow until eventually she said, 'Where else was I supposed to go?'

I looked around her father's generous living room, which was bigger than my whole bedsit. 'Here? Help your dad? Give him some support?'

She laughed. 'No way. Not with how miserable Dad was after Mum died. I had to get out and, in the absence of any better options, I went to stay with Danny.'

Izzy's Story

2020

2.

I was made to sleep in their basement. Grace refused to consider my perfectly reasonable suggestion that Bella went in with them so I could have her bedroom.

'We've got Beth into a proper night-time routine,' she kept saying, ad nauseam. I suppose it wasn't too bad: after they'd moved in they had tanked the whole basement, had a carpet laid and painted the walls yellow (or 'buttercup white', as Grace insisted on calling it), although my bed, which was a blow-up double mattress, was crammed between the desk and a wall, which meant I had to approach it from the bottom and shuffle up to the top to sleep.

As well as the bed, desk, chair, bookshelves and Danny's model aeroplanes, they'd put a television down there but I preferred watching TV upstairs in the living room, and whenever Grace said something like, 'It's absolutely fine if you want to go and watch your own thing downstairs,' I'd give her one of my smiles and stay where I was.

Obviously, I would rather have been back in my flat, but I was dealing with a temporary cash-flow issue after the misunderstanding over my Astatine business. I have never understood why anyone had a problem with it. It's not like I put a gun to my investors' heads and forced them to give me money. I've never even held a gun. It's far more fun to keep people alive. You can't play games with corpses.

And that's what I mean: no one was killed by investing in Astatine. The way I see it, I was doing them a favour. People like my investors understand nothing about the way the world works. They are clueless and careless with their money, and if it hadn't been Astatine, it would have been something else. You can be certain they'll take more care in the future. Rather than complaining, my investors should have been *thanking* me for teaching them such a valuable life lesson.

When I checked the vip@astatine.org email address for the final time, the mailbox was full of emails from my investors demanding proof that there really was an actual business behind the Astatine name. I clicked on the automatic reply function and typed a message: *Astatine has ceased trading. This mailbox is no longer monitored.*

The problem was I'd spent all the money. The cost of living in London was so high, and what with the rent on the flat, and paying for underground parking for the new convertible, plus all my clothes and jewellery, there was nothing left. Before I moved out of the apartment I had a party, inviting a load of people I met in a club, which only ended when the police turned up because a chair had been thrown off the balcony, narrowly missing a kid on a bike, and when I was kicked out a couple of weeks later the entire place was trashed and I couldn't get my deposit back. Which was how I found myself living in Danny's basement.

I can't stand routines. Grace *adored* routines. Her entire week revolved around the supermarket food delivery, which arrived on a Tuesday between 4 p.m. and 5 p.m. On one occasion, when there were no delivery slots available at 'her' time, she went into meltdown because the food would be arriving an hour later than usual. Our evening meals were similarly organised – there was an unchanging weekly menu – and when I suggested she make something different one evening to alleviate the monotony, I thought she was going to throw the Wednesday-evening lasagne at me.

Grace inflicted her obsessive routines on Bella, too. She had laminated (actually laminated!) a daily schedule and stuck it on the fridge. My niece was to be fed at specific times, whether she was hungry or not, put down for naps, whether she was tired or not, taken for walks, bathed, even abandoned in her playpen at specific times for specific durations.

Meanwhile, Danny was spending a lot of time in bed. He said he was tired and missing flying, but it was obvious the main issue was *her.* She controlled *everything.* But I had his back. Same as always. And I would sort it out. Same as always.

I started taking my niece with me when I went for my 'permitted' hour of daily exercise, although Grace was reluctant to let me at first. I heard her and Danny arguing about it. She was saying she didn't 'trust' me to 'keep our daughter safe', but Danny told her she was 'being unfair' because 'Izzy *loves* Beth', and in the end Grace grudgingly agreed to let me take the baby with me when I went for a walk.

Within a matter of days, I was on first-name terms with most of their neighbours. As I wheeled Bella's buggy around the village I was, as far as the residents were concerned, friendly and charming and was soon shopping for the old people who had no one nearby to do it for them. I always handed over a receipt with their bank card, so they could see how much they were paying for their groceries.

After a bit, I suggested to Danny he might like to come with me on my walks. 'You need to get away from the house,' I said, although what I actually meant was 'You need to get away from *her*'. I insisted and eventually he agreed to come out with me.

It was the middle of a heatwave, so before we left we had to endure Grace fussing over Bella, issuing instructions to us about keeping her hat on, not letting her overheat, not exposing her to direct sunlight, like my niece was some sort of vampire baby. Eventually, we made it out of the front door.

As we turned onto the pavement, I reached into the buggy and very gently pressed my forefinger against the tip of Bella's nose. 'Your mummy would rather I didn't spend time with you, wouldn't she, my little Bella-boo?' I said.

Beside me, Danny shook his head. 'That's not true.'

'It is,' I said, adjusting the hood of the buggy. 'You know she's always tried to come between you and me. And now, with little Bella-boo, it's the same thing. It makes me feel –' I paused to select the optimal word '– *sad*. It makes me feel sad.'

Dan frowned. 'She doesn't mean it.'

I turned towards him, making sure he saw my brave half-smile. 'It's OK. I mean, I can see how difficult she's finding things. She hides it well, of course, but it's clear she's struggling.'

'Do you think so?'

'Hundred per cent. But then you're not having the best time either, are you?'

On the other side of the road an old woman lifted her walking stick and waved it in my direction, calling, 'Lovely morning, Isabel.'

'It certainly is, Mrs Fletcher,' I said, crossing the road. 'You're doing well with your walking today. How are you feeling? Is the pain any better?'

To Danny, I said, 'Have you met Mrs Fletcher?'

He shook his head.

'Mrs Fletcher lives down the road at number seventy-three. That's right, isn't it, Mrs Fletcher? Her arthritis has flared up but her hospital appointment was cancelled two weeks ago. Isn't that right, Mrs Fletcher?'

She gave me a smile behind her mask, which was over her mouth but below her nose. Then she turned to Danny. 'Are you Isabel's husband?'

'No, Mrs Fletcher,' I said. 'This is my brother.'

'You're very lucky to have such a wonderful sister, young man. So rare to meet someone who is prepared to stop and chat these days. Most people don't want to give an old lady the time of day.' She turned back to me. 'Now then, Isabel, are you sure you really don't mind getting my shopping for me?'

'It's no problem at all, Mrs Fletcher. I don't know how you're expected to manage if you don't have the internet.'

She fumbled around in her bag, eventually producing her bank card and a piece of paper. 'Here's the card and a list of groceries. The number for the card is on the bottom of the paper. Is that what you need?'

'That's great,' I said. 'As soon as we've finished our walk, I'll go to the shop and pop round later.'

'Your sister is an absolute angel,' Mrs Fletcher said to Dan. 'I'll see you later, Isabel.'

She resumed her slow pace along the pavement.

We walked on in silence for a while, then I said, 'I'm only saying this because I care about you both, but –'

I left the sentence hanging, and as I knew he would, he said, 'What? What were you going to say?'

'It's nothing,' I said. 'Seriously, forget about it. I'm probably wrong anyway.'

'Come on, Izzy. Tell me.'

'It's nothing,' I repeated. 'Really. Look, hopefully you and Grace will get things back on track, but if she needs to lash out at someone in the meantime, then I'd rather it was me than you. Besides, no matter how much she tries to turn you against me, you know I only want what's best for you. Whatever happens, I'm here for you. I've got your back, Dan. Always.'

He had taken to wandering around the house in the middle of the night, which I found irritating because, although I never have any problems sleeping, the sound of his clumping footsteps overhead would wake me up. I would hear him flick the television on, only to turn it off five minutes later. Often I would go and join him in the living room.

And then one afternoon, when Grace was out for a walk with Bella, I found Danny pacing alongside the fence separating their garden from their neighbours' garden. He was slamming the fist of one hand into the palm of the other and muttering something under his breath. Three times I had to ask him what he was doing before he stopped and looked at me, blinking as if I had woken him up. He made an odd movement with his shoulder, bringing it up to touch the underside of his chin and looked up, tilting his head back. I tried to see what he was looking at, but there was only blue sky, dabbed here and there with cirrus clouds.

Behind his ear a large hairless area of scalp gleamed in the sunlight.

'You're going bald, little bro,' I said.

He frowned at me and I indicated the same place on my own head. 'Here,' I said. 'Bald.'

'Iz,' he said. 'It's just ... it's difficult ... you know ... with Mum gone ... and not flying ... I *hate* not flying. And Grace is being kind of weird with me too. It's a lot.'

'I know, Dan. I feel the same. I've lost my mother too and the person who I thought was my closest friend obviously doesn't want me here, and I have no idea why.' I gave a little sob, pleased with how genuine it sounded.

He put his arms around me, and I leaned into him, letting his strength take the weight of my distress. When I spoke, I felt the vibrations in his chest. 'At least we have each other little brother.'

My hair muffled his reply. 'I don't know what I'd do without you.'

One day when we were wheeling Bella round the village, he stopped to kneel on the pavement so he could fiddle with the front left wheel, which was making a clicking noise when it turned. With his face pressed against the side of the buggy, he asked me why I thought Grace was being so weird.

'It's none of my business,' I said.

'You must have a theory.'

'It's better if I stay out of it.'

Ahead of us, where the road led into a small cul-de-
sac, I could see Mrs Fletcher. She lifted her walking stick
in our direction, as if to flag down a taxi.

'You can sort the wheel out at home,' I said. 'Let's go
the other way.'

He straightened up. 'We always go this way.'

I turned the buggy round. 'Let's vary the routine. Live
life on the edge.'

I waited until we were in the park, and there was no
chance of Mrs Fletcher catching us, before I said, 'I'm
sure Grace'll tell you herself in the end.'

'Tell me what?'

'What she's up to,' I said, lifting Bella out of her buggy.

'You know something, don't you?' he said, as I handed
my niece to him.

'Nothing. It's nothing. Not really.'

'What is it?' He shifted Bella to his other arm.

'It's between you and Grace ...' I started walking
towards the baby swings, Danny following behind.

'What is it, Iz? What has she said?'

'Nothing. Forget it. Shall I go and get the coffees?'

While one of us pushed Bella in the swing, the other one
would always buy coffee from a mobile cart next to the
kids' playground. The guy who served the coffee was really
fit – he obviously worked out and I had every intention of
finding out if, behind the mask he wore, his face was as fit
as his pecs. Pandemic or no pandemic, I had needs.

Danny gave me his card and I walked over to the coffee
cart, but the guy wasn't there.

The girl who was serving the coffee in his place told me he had Covid.

I'd have to wait a bit longer to see his face.

When I got back to the swings, Danny was immediately on at me again about Grace and I said, 'I don't want to get involved. She's already so jealous of how close you and I are. If she knew I was telling you stuff ...' I let the half-sentence hang between us, shaking my head and arranging my face into a sad, troubled expression. Then I put my coffee cup on the ground and took over pushing Bella. 'Don't ask me, Dan. It's not fair.'

He was silent then, but out of the corner of my eye, I saw him kick over my coffee.

'Hey, I was still drinking that.' I turned, intending to tell him to go and buy me another, but his face was damp, covered in sweat, like he'd been running several miles rather than sitting on a park bench.

He pressed a hand to his chest. 'I'm going to faint,' he said.

'You're not going to faint,' I said. 'Sit down. Go on. Sit on the ground.'

While he did that I lifted Bella out of the swing and knelt on the ground next to him. I shifted Bella onto my hip and put my free hand on his arm. His skin felt hot and he was trembling.

'You've not got Covid, have you?'

He shook his head slightly and mumbled, 'My heart.'

He was breathing in shallow pants.

'Heart,' he repeated.

'It's a panic attack, Dan. It'll pass. Breathe nice and slow,' I said. 'In through your nose. And out through your mouth.' I demonstrated, breathing slowly and regularly, rubbing his back in small circles. 'It's OK, Dan. All OK. In through your nose, out through your mouth. You're going to be fine. I'm right here.'

After a few minutes, he lifted his head from his knees and gave me a shaky smile. I pulled him close, wrapping my arm tightly round his shoulders. Bella made a cute little noise and reached up, patting his face.

'You OK, little bro?' I asked.

He nodded uncertainly.

'First time that's happened?'

He nodded again.

I shook my head. 'I can't believe what that woman is doing to you.'

He didn't say anything, and we sat in silence for a while.

Eventually I said, 'You don't deserve this, Dan.'

'She's not going to leave me, is she?'

'I don't know,' I said. 'But you should think about speaking to a lawyer. Understand your rights.'

He made a sort of moaning sound, but when he didn't say anything, I continued, 'Better to be prepared. I mean, it's her house, isn't it? You don't want to end up homeless.'

'It's *our* house. It's in both our names.'

'*She's* the one with the rich grandfather. And *she's* Bella's mother. You might *think* you've got rights here, but you don't. Not really.'

'I own half the house.'

'OK,' I said. 'But this isn't really about a piece of paper, though, is it? She'll get her rich grandfather on board and you'll be forced out of "her house", then she'll stop you seeing Bella, and before you know it, you'll have no home and no daughter. It's how people like her operate.'

'Grace wouldn't do that to me,' Dan said, and I thought he was about to start hyperventilating all over again. 'She wouldn't ... You don't really think she would, do you?'

'I don't know. I mean, I used to think I knew her, but she's being so horrible to me, who knows what she's capable of.'

'I couldn't bear not seeing Beth.' He looked down at his daughter, who chose that moment to give her father the biggest smile.

Good girl, I thought. *You're learning.*

Dan kissed the top of her head. 'You're my whole world, little girl. I love you more than anything.'

He was mistaken of course.

I was his first love and I would be his last.

Notes

Before I left her father's house in Richmond, I had one final question for Izzy: had she been able to speak to any of her supposed contacts for me? I watched her closely, curious to see her reaction.

For the first time since I'd arrived, she smiled. 'Not yet,' she said. 'But I will.'

Of course she wouldn't.

I doubt she even knew anyone who worked in journalism, other than me.

After I'd completed the final *Planet Home* article, I redoubled my efforts to find more work. I'd submitted pitches to god knows how many publications, without any success. I'd had fruitless conversations over coffee with the few contacts from my old job who were still prepared to be seen with me. I'd offered to write short pieces for free for various websites, and although a few of them had been published, none of them led to any paid work. Not to mention that all I had to show for the hours and hours I'd spent speaking to Izzy and Grace and the time I'd spent following things up was a lot of seemingly irrelevant material, many unanswered questions and no coherent story.

Despite the pressure from my parents I was desperate to stay in London until after the inquest. Apart from anything else, I was *very* curious to see Izzy and Grace together in the same room, but more importantly, I owed it to Luke to be there. If nothing else, maybe the inquest would provide me with some closure. Maybe it would stop me lying awake for hours each night, tormenting myself with memories of Luke and thoughts of *what if?*

I'd completely run out of money, been turned down for another credit card, couldn't face another toast-based meal and had reached the point where I could see no other option but to call my parents and ask them to buy me a ticket home when a friend of a friend told me about a job going as a content creator for an online toy company. They needed someone to start immediately and offered me the job on the spot. It was a full-time role, which would mean far less time to focus on my journalism, but at least I would be able to pay the most urgent bills and attend the inquest.

A few days before the inquest reopened, on a warm spring Saturday, I made the journey back to the garden centre where Grace and Beth were waiting for me.

After buying our usual drinks – green tea for her, coffee for me – and waiting for her to stop fussing over Beth's coat, I explained to Grace that I'd been to see Izzy in Richmond and that she'd told me about living with Danny and Grace during lockdown.

Even while I was speaking, Grace was shaking her head. 'Whatever she told you, it's all lies. I bet she made me out to be some sort of monster while she was the perfect house guest. She did, didn't she?'

I said I'd really like to hear her side of things. What had it been like for Grace, having her sister-in-law living with them? And, I asked, was there was any truth in Izzy's suggestion that Grace been planning to leave Daniel.

Needless to say, it wasn't that straightforward.

Grace's Story

2020

1.

At first, I hoped she would only be with us for a couple of days, a week at most. And at least having her there meant Danny was making more of an effort to get out of bed. She even persuaded him to go for walks with her and Beth, which I hadn't been able to do. But as the days became a week and a week stretched into a month and there was no sign that Izzy had any intention of leaving, I decided enough was enough.

'I know she was kicked out of her flat,' I said to Danny one evening in the privacy of our bedroom, which, as long as Izzy was in the basement, was the only place I was certain we couldn't be overheard. 'But why can't she go back to your dad's? He needs company far more than we do.'

'She wants to be here,' he said. He was lying flat on the bed, arms over his head muffling his voice.

'But your dad's by himself.'

'She can't go, not with the Covid rules.'

'That didn't stop her coming *here*.'

'She had to go somewhere –'

I put my hands on his arms and pulled them away from his face. I needed him to listen. 'Surely it would be better if she was with your dad. It must be so difficult for him by himself.'

'Dad's doing OK.'

'Really? Are you sure?'

He closed his eyes.

His lack of energy and the ever-present apathy was really beginning to wear me down. I was trying to be patient, but we were in the middle of a global pandemic and I was doing everything around the house and looking after a very energetic toddler, all while putting up with an unwanted guest.

'Please will you speak to your dad?' I asked. 'See if he'd like Izzy to go and stay there.'

He finally sat up. 'Why can't you be honest?'

'What?'

'Regardless of how much *I* might want her to be here, how much Beth loves her being here, why won't you admit the real reason you want Izzy to leave? You're jealous of how close she and I are. It's ridiculous. She's my sister, for goodness' sake.'

'That's unfair,' I said, suddenly on the verge of tears. In the silence that followed, I watched Danny's shoulder lift to brush his jaw over and over. Forcing him to talk about it would only make things worse.

I rang Roger the next day.

My father-in-law listened while I explained why I thought it would be a good idea for Izzy to go and stay with him. I was careful not to criticise either Danny or Izzy, and when I finished speaking, there was a long pause.

'It's really thoughtful of you, Grace, but I'm OK,' Roger said. Since the funeral he was sounding older and more tentative. 'I'm just thankful Sarah wasn't ill during all of this. Imagine if she'd been in hospital and we hadn't been able to visit her.'

'It can't be easy being by yourself at the moment, Roger.'

'I appreciate your concern, really I do, but you don't need to worry about me.'

Despite my best efforts, Roger showed no inclination to ask Izzy to go and stay with him, so I was left with no choice but to endure her presence in our house, at least until the restrictions were lifted. That didn't mean I had to be happy about it, though. As I saw it, her appearance on our doorstep had been a declaration of war.

She refused to respect the steps I took to safeguard against infection, and at least once a day she would hold up one of the bottles of hand sanitiser I had placed around the house and say, 'This is antibacterial. *Bacterial.* Covid is a virus, Grace. A *virus.* What's the point of rubbing your skin raw with something to prevent bacteria, when what you're trying to prevent is a virus?'

'Good hand hygiene?'

The unintentional question mark at the end of my words annoyed me. This was *my* house, why should I justify my precautions?

'There's a bottle of hand sanitiser by the front door,' I continued. 'Please use it when you go in and out.'

Of course she didn't.

With Izzy there, our house – perfectly sized for me, Danny and Beth – felt cramped and claustrophobic. I did my best to avoid her as much as possible. The weather was lovely and I spent a lot of time sitting in our little garden, only heading inside when she came outside. But it was impossible to avoid her altogether and when the two of us found ourselves alone I would sometimes catch her looking at me, the corners of her mouth twisting up.

Once I said, 'Are you're smiling? It's not entirely clear.'

She let her face relax.

'There's a mirror in the bathroom,' I said, 'if you want to put in some practice.'

On one occasion I was outside in the sun, reading, with Beth asleep in the shade beside me. I caught sight of Izzy looking at us through the bathroom window and a minute later she appeared in the garden, noisily dragging a chair over the paving slabs.

'Shhh …' I said. 'Beth's only just fallen asleep.'

Izzy ignored me and pulled the chair a little further into the sun, metal legs scraping unpleasantly, and sat down.

I turned my attention back to my book.

'What are you reading?' she asked.

I reluctantly lifted my head. '*The Vanishing Half.*'

'Who wrote it?'

'Brit Bennett.'

'Never heard of her,' she said. I had realised long ago that the claims Izzy made about being a big reader were simply not true. She liked people to think she was well read, but I knew for a fact she read reviews of popular books then regurgitated them as her own opinions.

'What's it about?' she asked.

I stifled a sigh and laid the book on the table. 'It's about twin sisters. They're Black, but one spends her adult life "passing" as white.'

'Any good?'

'It's the best book I've read for ages.'

She didn't reply and I watched her lift her foot over a small blue butterfly fluttering on a tuft of weed growing between two paving slabs. She lowered her foot to the ground. When she lifted it again, there was the faintest smear of blue.

'Why did you do that?' I asked.

'Why shouldn't I?'

'For one thing they're endangered.'

'Are they? Really? I didn't realise you were a lepidopterist.'

I picked up my book determined to ignore her, but irritation got the better of me and I said, 'I'm not a lepidopterist. But I read the paper, I watch the news. I *engage* with the world around me. I'm not entirely consumed with myself.'

Izzy leaned over, putting her mouth close to my sleeping daughter's head. 'Are the vast quantities of antibacterial handwash affecting your poor mother's mind?'

'What *are* you talking about?' I said.

She ignored me and continued to speak to Beth. 'Is she a teeny, weeny bit unstable?'

Beth's eyelids flickered. Typical. Izzy had woken her up.

I got to my feet abruptly.

'*Stop it,*' I said. 'Stop talking like this.'

I scooped Beth up, holding her close, and stalked into the house.

The more time passed, the more difficult things became. It seemed ridiculous that I still hadn't told Danny what Sarah had told me. I'd never kept secrets from him before, and this one – how his sister had lied about being abused by their uncle – was enormous, but the atmosphere in the house was already so tense and he would need time and space to be able to get his head around what Izzy had done. I felt like I had no choice but to wait until she'd moved on.

In Danny's presence Izzy was weirdly solicitous towards me, behaving as if I was recovering from a long illness. She would make comments about 'how tired you must be, Grace' and 'how well you're coping' before pausing for a beat, then adding, 'despite everything'. Her fake concern was cloying and claustrophobic. She would pretend to be helpful, although, in reality, she was undermining me at every turn.

'It was really stuffy in Bella's room so I opened the window,' she'd say and Danny would thank her, even though I wanted Beth's window closed at night because I worried about foxes getting onto the fence and into her room.

'I noticed Bella's nappy needed changing, so I sorted it out for her,' Izzy said one afternoon and I saw Danny frowning at me, because I'd told him only ten minutes earlier that I'd changed her nappy. Izzy looked between us. 'It can be difficult to keep track of things,' she said. 'It's not surprising you're forgetful.'

'I've put them in the top cupboard,' she said to me in the kitchen, while I was looking for the macadamia nuts I'd become addicted to during lockdown. 'You left them out and Bella-boo got hold of them. She had some in her mouth but I managed to get them all out.'

'Oh god,' I said, visions of my daughter choking to death flashing in front of my eyes. I was always so careful – I was sure I'd pushed them to the back of the countertop.

Danny and Izzy wore identical expressions of concern.

'I thought I'd put them away,' I said.

'Obviously not,' Danny said.

'Come on, Dan,' Izzy said. 'We all make mistakes. No

harm done. It's difficult for Grace to remember every little thing.'

'What does that mean?' I said.

Izzy held her hands up, palms outwards, in a gesture of surrender. 'Nothing, Grace. Sorry.'

'You left the nuts lying around, Grace, not Izzy. Beth could have got hold of them,' Danny said.

'She didn't, though, Dan. Bella's fine,' Izzy said. 'I'm sure Grace won't do it again.'

I felt like a little girl being chastised by her parents.

Beth was teething – all crimson cheeks and ever-present tears – and I was already awake when I heard her whimpering. I slipped out of bed and into her room, picking her up and settling us both into a chair by the window. I massaged Bonjela into her sore gums, rocking her in my arms, willing her to go back to sleep.

Almost an hour later, I had just got her back into her cot when I heard the sound of the front door opening then, a few seconds later, closing. I went to the top of the stairs but there was no sign of anyone.

It couldn't have been Danny – he was asleep in our room – so it must have been Izzy. Why the hell was she going out in the middle of the night? Then I heard the sound of the microwave.

In the kitchen Izzy had her back to me, wearing only a long T-shirt. As I watched, she lifted her hair, twisting it into a messy bun. The back of her neck was slick with sweat and the T-shirt rose up, clinging to her backside, her buttocks firmer than mine had ever been.

She turned to face me, hands still tangled in her hair. Her nipples were hard, pressing against the fabric of the

T-shirt, which I realised with an unpleasant jolt was one of Danny's.

'Oh, hi,' she said.

'What are you doing?' I asked.

'Microwaving a jacket potato.'

'It's the middle of the night.'

'I'm always starving after a booty call.'

'What do you mean?'

'Sex makes me hungry.'

'You're joking, right?'

'No. It really does. I'm always starving afterwards. Aren't you?'

'I don't mean about being hungry. I mean, you haven't been out to have sex, have you?'

'Of course not,' she said. She opened the fridge and took out a block of cheese.

'So why was the front door open?'

She reached into a drawer for the grater, pushed a bowl of fruit out of the way and started grating cheese directly onto the countertop. 'How else was he supposed to leave?' she said.

'Who?'

'I think his name began with R. Richard, maybe? Ronan? Ryan?'

She grated the entire block of cheese, then opened the cupboard where we kept the plates. When she bent over Danny's T-shirt pressed tightly against her body and I could see the cleft between her buttocks.

'Tell me you didn't bring a strange guy into our house in the middle of a global pandemic,' I said.

'OK,' she said, taking the lid off a jar of Branston Pickle.

'OK, what?'

'OK, I didn't.'

'But did you?'

'Jesus, Grace. What do you want me to say? I did or I didn't. I can say either. Makes no difference to me.'

The microwave pinged, she opened the door, speared the potato with a fork and lifted it onto the plate she'd taken out of the cupboard. She cut the potato open and piled some of the grated cheese onto it, leaving the rest scattered over the countertop. She dug her spoon in the jar of pickle, taking scoop after scoop until it was all gone. Then she dropped the spoon into the fruit bowl, picked up the plate and headed down into the basement.

Since Izzy had moved in, I had rarely been down there and I missed spending time with my books. I had always wanted to have my own library and a few months after we'd moved in Pops had spent an entire weekend building shelves along the whole of one wall. Mum had bought me a squishy armchair in a lovely burnt-orange colour, perfect for curling up in, and I'd found a floor lamp that shone a light directly over my shoulder. It was a perfect spot for reading and I had loved it down there.

She was already in my chair by the time I followed her downstairs. Her plate was balanced precariously on one arm of the chair and she was using an upturned wastepaper basket as a footrest. She was shovelling food into her mouth, barely swallowing each mouthful before shoving in another loaded forkful. The smell of warm cheese made me feel a bit sick.

She couldn't be that hungry, surely? Izzy had the annoying ability to eat as much as she wanted, seemingly without putting on so much as a pound. If I ate even a quarter of what she did, I'd have been the size of a house.

The room was a complete tip. The floor was strewn with clothes and make-up was ground into the cream carpet. Half my books, which I'd spent a wonderful weekend organising into alphabetical order, were pulled off the shelves and dumped on the floor or shoved back onto the shelves in any old order. I was looking at the carnage around me when I saw it.

By the side of the mattress.

A condom.

Very obviously used.

'I *knew* it. You *did* have had someone down here,' I said.

Izzy didn't look at me, just continued to shove food into her mouth.

'Fuck's sake.'

Her gaze flicked up and held mine, but I refused to look away.

'No need to swear,' she said.

It was impossible to argue with Izzy because she always remained frustratingly calm, no matter what the provocation. Not so me, which is why I replied, 'There is reason to fucking swear. You've put us all at risk.'

'You're overtired. Why don't you toddle off back to bed?'

'Don't tell me what to do in my own house.'

'*Your* house. Yes. As I thought.'

'I know you lied about your uncle,' I found myself blurting out. If I was going to do this, I might as well get everything out on the table.

She looked utterly unconcerned. 'I've no idea what you're talking about.'

'You said he abused you.'

'I never told you that,' she said.

'Not me, no. But you told Danny.'

She shrugged. 'He must have got his wires crossed.'

'Bullshit. He's believed it for years. And you let him think it was true. What sort of person does that?'

Again she shrugged. There was no hint of shame. No flicker of embarrassment. My words simply slid right over her. I had an almost overwhelming urge to hit her or, better still, drag her up the stairs and shove her out onto the pavement. She had to leave – I didn't care where she went as long as it wasn't here.

'You've put us all at risk by bringing some guy into the house,' I said. 'You're so fucking selfish. You need to self-isolate, but after that, I want you gone.'

'Is that really what's bothering you?' she said.

'That we might die from Covid? Yes. The fact you're a pathological liar? Yes. That too.'

'Hmmm ...' she said. 'I think it's something else. *I* think little Grace is jealous.'

'Of what? I don't know what you're talking about.'

'That's it, isn't it? You don't like the idea of me being with someone.'

'What *are* you going on about?'

She didn't reply immediately – she had finally finished eating and she walked over to the bed, sitting down and scooting back until she was leaning against the wall, her legs straight, ankles crossed. The hem of Danny's T-shirt barely reached the top of her thighs.

'Why don't you admit it?' she said.

'Admit what? I have no idea what you're talking about.'

Izzy didn't say anything. She shifted slightly on the bed, uncrossing her legs, letting them fall apart slowly. I wanted to look away, but I couldn't.

'I know you think about me,' she said. 'About us.'

She slid one hand up her leg, slipping it between her thighs.

I should have turned away immediately, rushed up the stairs, put as much space between her and me as possible, but I didn't. I couldn't move. My blood hammered in my ears.

Izzy's hand started moving, slowly. 'I know you've wondered what it would be like.'

My mouth was dry.

'It's better with a woman. More intense.'

She opened her legs wider and still I watched.

'You like this, don't you?'

I couldn't drag my gaze away.

'You want to do this, don't you?' she said. 'Why don't you come over here?'

Finally, *finally*, I forced my legs to move and as I ran up the stairs, almost slipping on the top step in my haste, all I could hear was the sound of her laughter.

I shook Danny until he woke up.

'You've got to make her leave.'

He rolled over and picked up his phone to check the time. 'It's the middle of the night.'

'She has to go.'

When he didn't reply, I said, 'Your sister is bringing people into our house and having sex with them.' Stupidly, I felt the need to clarify. '*Men*. She's bringing *men* here.'

'What are you going on about?'

'She had a man here earlier.'

'Why'd you wake me up? I'd only just got to sleep.'

'No, you hadn't. I was up with Beth ages ago and you were fast asleep.'

'I'll get Beth next time.' He closed his eyes.

I tugged the edge of his pillow. 'Danny,' I said. 'You've got to tell Izzy to go.'

His only response was to pull the sheet over his head.

'Danny.' My voice was sharp.

He groaned and rolled over to look at me. 'It's driving me mad,' he said.

'What do you think she's doing to me? She's *your* sister.'

'I'm not talking about Izzy. *You're* driving me mad. This obsession you have with her.'

'*Me?*' I was incredulous. 'You think *I'm* the one obsessed with her?'

'Yes. You. You're obsessed with my sister.'

I took a deep breath, trying to focus on what I needed him to do. 'You have to tell her to go.'

'No, Grace. *You* have to stop this. Please. For me. I can't deal with it.'

He turned his back on me and, unbelievably, fell asleep. For two long hours, I lay in bed beside him, confused, ashamed but most of all angry about what had happened. It was a relief when Beth started crying.

I put my mouth against Danny's ear. 'Beth's awake.'

He pulled on a T-shirt and tracksuit bottoms and went to our daughter.

I waited until she was changed and fed and back in her cot before I went to find him and said, 'Come with me.'

'Where?'

'Please. Just come.'

He followed me down the stairs. I stood aside to let him go into the kitchen first.

'Go on. Go in and see the mess she made last night.'

I followed him in. The room was spotless. The countertops were wiped down and everything had been put away. I opened the cupboard where we kept the glass for recycling. The jar of pickle was there, rinsed out and ready to be put outside.

I couldn't read Danny's expression.

'She must have tidied up. But go and see the state of the basement. You'll see what I mean.'

'Grace –' he began, but I didn't let him finish.

'She's bringing strangers into the house – we're all going to get Covid.' I opened the door to the basement. 'Go on. Go down there.'

Izzy was fast asleep. The floor was clear, the books that had been strewn around were back on the bookshelves, and the cushions on my chair were plumped, a blanket neatly folded over one arm. There was no sign of her midnight feast or the condom. Izzy blinked in the light, then sat up. She was wearing cotton pyjamas with a picture of a teddy bear on the front.

'What's up?' she said.

'Where is it?' I asked.

Izzy yawned. 'Where's what?'

'The condom. Where's the condom?' I looked around the room. Where had she put it? I lifted a corner of the mattress, then I emptied the contents of the wastepaper basket onto the floor, but there were just chocolate wrappers and some balled-up paper. I dug my hand down the back of the chair, feeling around.

Danny and Izzy were staring at me: the same curve of their eyebrows and set of their jaws. But although Izzy looked amused, Danny's expression was grim.

'What the hell are you doing?' he said.

'It's here somewhere.'

'What?'

'The condom. She must have hidden it.' I turned back to the task at hand, pulling books off the bookshelves – she must have stuffed it somewhere.

'For god's sake, Grace,' Danny said. 'Stop it.'

'No. It's here somewhere. She had someone here last night. I *know* she did.'

Danny crossed the room and caught hold of my arms. 'Stop it. Please. This is mad. I don't know what you're trying to prove but stop it, please, stop it. I can't take it any more.' He rubbed his face. His left eye was twitching.

'It's OK, Danny,' Izzy said, getting to her feet. She pulled a dressing gown on over her stupid teddy-bear pyjamas. 'You're such a worrier anyway, Grace, aren't you? And now with the baby and the pandemic and everything, it's not surprising if you're imagining risks everywhere.'

'I'm not imagining anyth–'

'Why don't you take it easy today? Stay in bed, read a book. Danny and I can take Bella out, can't we, Dan?'

'Her name is *Beth* and I don't need to take it easy,' I said, the anger in my voice bouncing off the walls. 'What I *need* is to have *my* house to *myself.*'

Danny looked stricken.

'I wasn't talking about *you*,' I said. 'I meant –' but before I could clarify what I meant, Beth began wailing. I turned for the stairs, but Danny beat me to it.

'*I'll* go,' he said.

I turned to follow him, pausing briefly to look back at Izzy.

'You bitch,' I said, quietly.

Izzy raised her hand, licked her forefinger, then put her it between her legs. She flashed me the most genuine smile I'd ever seen from her and I fled upstairs, the sound of her laughter once again ringing in my ears.

The Inquest

The Guardian
4 May 2022
Live news feed
12:43 BST

As the inquest continued this morning into the deaths of the two pilots on board Goldfinch Airlines flight GFA578 on 9 September 2020, the court was played a recording from the flight deck in which it could clearly be heard that at 18:19, approximately twenty-six minutes after the flight took off from Stansted Airport, Captain Daniel Taylor locked his co-pilot out of the flight deck before rerouting the Airbus A320 from its intended route to Glasgow and setting the automatic pilot to descend from its cruising altitude of 34,000 feet. As Taylor increased the aeroplane's speed on three separate occasions during its fatal descent, First Officer Luke Emery can be heard shouting and hammering on the door to the flight deck. At 18:58:23 both pilots were killed instantly when the aeroplane smashed into the south-east face of Big Crag mountain.

I told my new employer I had Covid so I could attend every day of the inquest. The coroner's court was a bleak, airless room with no natural daylight and flickering strip lights that gave me a headache.

After the cockpit voice recording was released, copies appeared all over the internet. I've listened to it over and over, hearing Daniel's voice saying, 'No worries, mate,' in response to Luke saying, 'I've got to use the bathroom.' That was last thing I would ever hear him say. Of course, later in the recording you can hear Luke screaming on the other side of the door, although his actual words are unintelligible.

I've heard the recording so often I can recite it word for word. Each time I listen to it I promise myself it'll be the final time, but I find myself returning to my laptop, opening YouTube, pressing play and listening to the last minutes of Luke's life, willing something, anything, to change. But nothing ever does.

In the forty minutes between Daniel locking the cockpit door and the moment of impact, there is repeated communication from civilian air traffic control. The disembodied voice says things like: 'Goldfinch 578, this is London Centre – how do you read?' and 'Goldfinch 578, this is London Centre – contact me on frequency 121.5'. You can also hear other pilots in nearby airspace trying to contact the non-responsive plane.

Finally, five minutes before the plane hits the mountain, the voice of an RAF pilot can be heard: 'Goldfinch 578, you have been intercepted by a British military fighter. You are to comply with my instructions.'

While all of this is going on Daniel is doing the following: clearing his throat repeatedly, humming the theme tune to *Alphablocks* (Beth's favourite TV programme, according to Grace), saying several times 'I'm Danny', and shouting 'Go away' and 'Leave me alone' (it is not clear whether he is responding to the communications from air traffic control or to Luke banging on the door, begging to be let in). There is also a tapping noise. There was a lot of speculation in the media about what this was but it's obvious Daniel is drumming his fingers.

It is the singing which is mentioned most often. For the last three minutes, Daniel makes no other sound except to sing the refrain from Queen's 'Who Wants to Live Forever'. He repeats it over and over, until his voice is cut off at the moment the plane smashes into Big Crag.

Goldfinch employees (including 'Anthony') gave statements at the inquest which, along with the evidence from the air accident investigation team, left no room for doubt that the plane had been deliberately flown into Big Crag. And the cockpit voice recording proved what Jamie and I had known for months: Daniel Taylor was responsible.

There was intense focus during the inquest on the airline policies and procedures which led to an empty flight being in the air. The coroner also spent a considerable amount of time questioning Goldfinch's management team about how a pilot was able to be in the cockpit alone. But, of course, ghost flights were flown by skeleton crews, so it was perfectly usual for there to only be two pilots on board. If one of them needed to go to the bathroom mid-flight, as poor Luke did, there was no option but to leave only one pilot in the cockpit.

Another major area of scrutiny was how Daniel had been cleared to fly in the first place. The presumption was that someone who would deliberately fly a plane into a mountain must have had serious issues with their mental health, and the coroner wanted to know what checks and balances were in place to ensure this didn't happen. Even though I already knew from Jamie how little attention was paid to mental health by the Civil Aviation Authority in the annual medicals, I was shocked all over again to hear Goldfinch's human resources director explain just how easily a pilot can obtain their annual medical certificate. I find myself thinking about this every time I see a plane flying overhead.

The two pilots from the Typhoon jets scrambled from RAF Coningsby who had flown alongside the descending plane for the final few minutes of its flight both gave evidence. Squadron Leader Robert Sweeney explained that, although Daniel would have clearly been able to see him from the cockpit, he had failed to acknowledge the presence of the RAF planes. He went on to say, 'I also briefly saw First Officer Emery through the window beside the first row of passenger seats. His arm was banging on the window. I believe he was aware of our presence and was indicating his distress.'

The image of Luke at that small window, minutes from death, terrified, desperate, will haunt me for ever.

If the first RAF pilot's testimony wasn't harrowing enough, the second pilot – Flight Lieutenant Lucy Caves – explained how she was flying a little further away, allowing her to take photographs of the unresponsive aeroplane. There was utter silence in the coroner's court when the final picture, taken moments before impact, was displayed on the large screen. At that moment, Luke had been alive. A few seconds later, he was dead.

The families were called to give statements. Luke's mother was first. Mary told the coroner how, because of Covid, she hadn't seen Luke since December 2019 but that at the start of the first lockdown they'd made a pact to read the same books and have a fortnightly Zoom call to chat about them. It meant they would always have something to talk about, she said, tears falling as she explained how they'd had to postpone their call on 9 September 2020 because he had been rostered to fly at very short notice.

Luke's father was next and while he was talking I noticed how, in the months since I'd been to visit them, the tremor in Doug Emery's hands had worsened. I felt guilty that I hadn't been back to see them. I would go again soon and take Jamie with me.

Finally it was the turn of the Taylors.

Grace was first. She was wearing a black skirt suit which hung off her hips and shoulders. The grey of her blouse matched the pallor of her face and she cried as she told the coroner how her husband loved flying and how he was never happier than when he was in the air. She explained how miserable he'd been during furlough and how desperate he was to get back to work. She spoke about how much he'd struggled after Sarah's death, but Grace was adamant she had no reason to believe he was planning to do what he did.

Roger was next. He was in a terrible state and was pretty much incoherent. Because of that, and also because he hadn't seen his son for five months prior to the crash, there weren't many questions for him.

Then it was Izzy's turn. At the time of the inquest, she was out on bail, awaiting trial. Her make-up was as immaculate as ever and she was wearing an off-the-shoulder emerald-green dress. She looked like she was at a film premiere rather than an inquest. After her name was called, she fished a little mirror out of her handbag and took her time reapplying her lipstick before navigating her four-inch stiletto heels up to the front of the room.

The coroner asked her more or less the same questions she'd asked Grace. Izzy was composed, answering each question confidently and without hesitation. But then the coroner asked her how Daniel had seemed the last time she'd seen him. Izzy didn't reply immediately. Instead, she reached into her sleeve and produced a little cotton handkerchief of the kind I hadn't seen anyone use since my grandmother had died. She touched the corners of her eyes, delicately, first the left then the right. Then she briefly held the handkerchief over her face. When she dropped her hands back to her lap, her eyes were downcast and her lips were trembling.

'I understand this is terribly upsetting for you, Ms Taylor,' the coroner said. 'Would you like a short break?'

Izzy gave a little sob. When she spoke, her voice was barely above a whisper. 'I'm sorry. It's all so painful. Please continue.'

The coroner said, 'I'll try not to make this ordeal longer than it needs to be. The question I asked you was: how did your brother seem the last time you saw him?'

Izzy considered the question at length before saying, finally, 'It's very difficult to answer that.'

The coroner made a little noise of sympathy before urging Izzy to try her best.

'On the one hand, Danny was very happy to be getting back to flying. My brother loved flying aeroplanes more than –' Izzy paused, staring right at Grace '– more than anything or anyone in the world.' For a moment the whole room was utterly silent as the two women stared at each other, then the coroner prompted, 'On the other hand ...?' and Izzy turned back towards her.

'I don't like to mention it,' she said, 'but Danny and Grace were going through some difficulties in their marriage.' The coroner glanced at Grace. 'They had invited me to live with them during lockdown and I heard them arguing. My brother was convinced Grace was going to leave him, although, in reality, I think she probably wanted *him* to leave. Grace was very possessive of their house and she often gave me the impression she wanted both of us – me and Danny, that is – to go and leave her alone with Beth.'

Grace got to her feet, shouting that it had been Izzy who she had wanted to leave, not Danny. The coroner told Grace to take her seat. Izzy didn't have much more to add, just that her brother was upset and very worried about his marriage. The last thing she said was 'What happened probably wasn't Grace's fault, though.'

The coroner's criticism of both the Civil Aviation Authority and Goldfinch Airlines was coruscating. Urgent recommendations were made regarding the introduction of rigorous mental-health and wellbeing checks for aircrew and the immediate implementation of measures to ensure no pilot would ever be left alone in a cockpit.

The coroner also recommended an industry-wide review of the policies requiring airlines to fly ghost flights. She mentioned figures which indicated that in recent months alone there had been more than 100,000 empty flights across Europe, and it was particularly gratifying to hear her refer to a growing public campaign to ban them. Perhaps my *Planet Home* articles were having an effect after all.

Inquests don't determine blame, but the conclusions were clear. Daniel had suffered some sort of catastrophic breakdown which resulted in him killing both himself and his co-pilot. There was nothing to suggest he had specifically targeted Luke. He was simply in the wrong place at the wrong time. Daniel would have done what he did regardless of who was flying the plane with him on 9 September 2020, including my brother Jamie.

Notes

Shortly after the inquest was over, Grace contacted me and asked to meet one final time, but when I arrived at the garden centre she was distracted, convinced that people were staring at her. We moved tables twice and she still hadn't told me why she wanted to see me, so I asked her something I'd been wondering about.

'When did you find out Daniel was alone in the cockpit?'

She frowned. 'Shortly before the start of the inquest. Why?'

'Were you surprised? Or did you always have a feeling he was responsible for what happened?'

'Oh my god, Carly. You're actually asking me if I was *surprised* that my husband would deliberately crash a plane. Why would you even ask me that? *Of course* I was surprised. All this time I've spent talking to you, all the really personal stuff about our relationship that I've shared with you, and you ask me if I had a *feeling* that Danny was capable of killing himself and another man. Of course I didn't have a *feeling*. Of course I didn't.'

She stood and went to find Beth who had made it as far as an aisle of dwarf trees. Watching Grace cuddling her daughter it was clear how much she was struggling and I thought she might leave, but after a couple of minutes she returned to our table, settling Beth into a high chair and giving her a rice cake.

I apologised and she shook her head slightly, as if to bat my apology away. 'I wanted to talk to you about what Izzy said about me at the inquest.'

'Which bit?' I asked, tentatively.

'About me wanting to leave Danny. She knows that's not true.'

'Maybe she believes it was?' I suggested.

'Of course she doesn't.'

'So why do you think she said it?'

'To hurt me. Same as always. But she had no right saying what she did. It's all on public record now and for Roger's sake, for Beth's, she should have just kept her mouth shut.' Grace glanced at me, her expression unreadable. 'Like I did.'

Instantly, the hairs on the back of my neck stood up and I felt my jaw actually drop as she continued, 'Something happened that day. The day he died.'

I listened in silence, letting her speak without interruption, as she told me how, a fortnight before Daniel's death, she'd had Covid. Daniel had slept on a blow-up bed in Beth's room while Grace quarantined herself in their bedroom. Although she felt much better after a week, she remained isolated from the rest of the household for another few days because she didn't want to risk infecting them.

During that time Daniel had been called in to work to do the necessary flight-simulator sessions in preparation for resuming flying. On the last day of her husband's life, after almost a fortnight alone in their bedroom, Grace had gone downstairs.

Grace's Story

9 September 2020

1.

I waited until Danny had gone out for a walk with Beth before I went downstairs. Izzy was playing music in the basement, but I didn't care about infecting her – she was the reason I'd had Covid in the first place.

Shoes and unopened mail were strewn all over the floor by the front door. I paired up the shoes and replaced them in the rack before gathering up the envelopes and taking them with me into the kitchen, where I was met with a scene resembling a disaster movie. As far as I could tell, every single piece of crockery and cutlery had been used then left unwashed on the countertop. There were pieces of what looked like a smashed jar of pasta sauce in the corner by the kettle, which was smeared with the sauce. The door of the washing machine was wide open, a huge pile of laundry dumped on the floor. There was a revolting smell coming from Beth's used nappies which were next to, but not actually *in*, the bag where they were supposed to go.

Three adults lived in this house, but clearly it was too much to expect two of them to maintain even the most superficial levels of hygiene. The mess was revolting, but I couldn't summon the effort it would take to clean it up, so

I poured myself some water – after choosing the least filthy glass and washing it twice – and turned my back on the carnage. I paused for a few moments at the door to the basement but Izzy's music was making my head throb and I couldn't face a confrontation so I headed upstairs, taking the pile of unopened envelopes with me.

With the bedroom door closed, I could barely hear the music from the basement and I got back into bed, plumping up my pillows and making myself comfortable before sorting through the envelopes.

I had always been the one to manage our finances, keeping meticulous records, just as Pops had taught me, with spreadsheets to track every penny coming in and going out. Each month our salaries were paid into a joint account, from which I transferred a small amount to Danny's personal account for him to do with as he wished.

There was a gas bill and an electricity bill for Danny and me and everything else was for Izzy. Most of the letters had been sent to Roger's address and forwarded on to us. I looked through them: three were from Companies House addressed to Izzy as director of a company called Iz Bells Limited, another one was to her as director of Iz Bells Limited trading as Astatine. There were letters from three different firms of solicitors and a number of bills addressed to her at her old address in London, forwarded on to her dad's address, then on to us, and several demands from credit-card companies, sent directly to our address.

What on earth was she playing at? Why had she left them all on the floor by the front door? It was never a good idea to avoid dealing with official letters and demands. And I was really *not* happy to have our address linked to her credit cards.

I was still sifting through them when the bedroom door opened. Danny was back from his walk.

'Look at these,' I said, holding up a fistful of Izzy's letters. He barely glanced at them, or me. There were dark circles around his eyes and he looked like he'd lost weight while I'd been ill.

'You don't look great,' I said. 'Is it Covid?'

'I'm fine. I've heard from work. I've finally been called in. They want me to fly this afternoon.'

I knew I should be delighted for him – he'd been waiting for this day for so long – but he really did look very unwell. 'I'm not sure you should go, Dan,' I said. 'Maybe leave it a day or two?'

'Jesus, Grace. I'm fine.' His tone was harsh.

'Look,' I said, trying to keep my voice level, 'you need to tell them if you're not well enough to fly.'

'I told you, I'm fine.' The fingers of his right hand snaked up to tug the hair behind his ear and I decided to let it go.

'While you were out I went downstairs,' I said. 'There was post all over the floor and look … Izzy's got all these bills and official letters.'

I held the envelopes out towards him but he made no move to take them.

I selected one at random. 'Iz Bells Limited trading as Astatine UK. Have you ever heard of Astatine?' When he didn't reply, I continued, 'Apparently Izzy's a director, according to Companies House anyway. She's also got letters from solicitors, utilities companies and a debt-collection agency. She's used our address for credit cards, too.'

He looked at me but didn't say anything.

'This is serious,' I said. 'I mean, *really* serious.'

'I know,' he said.

I took a deep breath. 'Will you speak to her about it?'

'I'm not talking about some stupid letters, I'm talking about *you*. About what *you've* been doing.'

'What?' I said, totally confused. 'I haven't done anything. I've been stuck by myself in here.'

'Why don't you admit it, Grace? You're using all this stuff about Izzy as an excuse to kick us both out. You want the house to yourself. You want Beth to yourself.' His voice cracked when he spoke our daughter's name.

'What *are* you talking about? I don't want to kick you out. Why would you even say that?' I started coughing, heaving, painful coughs that wouldn't stop. Danny didn't say anything, just stood there, a blank expression on his face, while I tried to get my breathing back under control. When I was finally able to speak again, I said, 'You're worrying me, Dan. What's going on?'

'I know what you've been up to.'

'I've no idea what you're talking about.'

'You want to get a divorce.'

Of all the things he might have said, I would never *ever* have thought it would be that. 'What the hell are you talking about?'

'At least be honest, Grace. I know you've been searching for lawyers and about custody and stuff on your laptop.'

'No, I haven't,' I said. My laptop was beside me on the bed. I opened it up and turned it towards Danny. 'Here, look for yourself.'

At first I thought he wasn't going to move from the doorway, but then he crossed to the foot of the bed and picked up the laptop, balancing it on one arm and tapping on the keys with the other hand. When he found what he was looking for, he dropped the laptop back onto the bed beside me, saying, 'Your search history.'

Divorce lawyer.

How do I keep my house in a divorce?

How do I get sole custody?

Getting a divorce.

Lines and lines of similar searches.

'Dan. No. These aren't mine.'

'Who the hell else's are they? It's your laptop.'

He was close to tears, and so was I.

'At least be honest with me,' Danny said, 'rather than treating me like an idiot, like you always do.'

'I never treat you like an idiot. How can you say that?'

Izzy appeared in the doorway, holding Beth in her arms. 'Would you two keep your voices down? You're upsetting Bella-boo.'

'For god's sake,' I said, my voice definitely not quiet, 'her name is Beth. Beth. OK? Can you remember that? Not Bella. Or Bella-boo. Beth.'

Right on cue, my daughter started crying. Izzy put her hand on the back of Beth's head and kissed her cheek.

'Give her to me,' I said.

Izzy turned away. 'What if you're still infectious?'

'She's *my* daughter. Give her to me.'

I got out of bed, marched over to the door and put my hands on either side of Beth's compact little body. 'Let go of my daughter,' I said, wrestling my baby out of Izzy arms. Beth's crying cranked up into full-blown howls.

Using my foot, I slammed the door, leaving Izzy out in the hallway.

I turned to Danny. 'We need to talk about this.' I raised my voice to be heard over Beth's wails.

'*Your* daughter is she?' he said.

'You know that's not what I meant.'

He studied my face and for a moment his expression softened, but then he glanced down at the laptop and shook his head. 'I don't know what to think any more.'

'I didn't look up those searches. It must have been Izzy.'

'For God's sake,' Danny said. 'This obsession you have with my sister. Jesus. You think she ... what? Snuck in here, took your laptop, worked out the password, then did a load of random searches for divorce? Seriously, Grace, you're obsessed.'

'I think that's exactly what she did. I bet it was Izzy who told you to look on my laptop, wasn't it?'

'That's not the point.'

How could he not see what was right in front of him? I couldn't bear it any more. 'You want to know what your precious sister is really like? Do you?'

Beth was still whimpering, and I sat on the side of the bed rocking her, looking up at Danny. 'Everything Izzy told you about being abused was a lie. None of it happened. You don't even have an uncle in Australia. She made it all up.'

He didn't reply at first, just stood there, raking his tooth over his lip, then he shook his head, sadly. 'I don't know who you are any more, Grace. How could you say something so awful? Where's your sympathy? Your compassion? What sort of horrible game are you playing here?'

'*Me?*' I said, struggling to keep my voice calm for Beth's sake. 'I'm not playing a game. Your mum told me. She had a brother who died when he was little, but that's it. No uncle in Australia. Your sister has lied to you your whole life.'

'You're crazy,' Danny said.

'*I'm* crazy?' I shot back. 'I'm the only sane person in this house.'

Danny looked at me like he had no idea who I was, then he turned his back on me and left.

I lay on the bed cuddling Beth, trying to calm her down, trying to focus my thoughts on her, but I couldn't help going over and over it all, stunned my marriage had come to this – the two of us yelling over our daughter's head about whether or not I wanted a divorce. I didn't. Of course I didn't. I loved Danny, more than anyone in the world except the hot little bundle in my arms.

Izzy must have come into the bedroom when I was poorly. My laptop password was easy enough to work out – Beth's name and date of birth. Stupid, stupid me. God knows what sort of poison she'd been dripping into Danny's ears while I'd been ill. And now, when I'd finally told him about her lies, he didn't believe me.

I had just got Beth to sleep when the doorbell rang. Then it rang again, and again. I looked out of the window – Danny was in the garden with his headphones on and obviously Izzy would never bother to answer the door. The doorbell rang again. The last thing I needed was for Beth to wake up, so I went downstairs.

Outside was a middle-aged woman, brandishing a sheaf of papers.

I wondered if she was canvassing for some political party or other, but before I had a chance to speak, she said, 'How dare you?'

'I'm sorry?' I said.

'Stealing from an old lady. How did you think you'd get away with it?'

'I'm sorry,' I said again. 'I've absolutely no idea what you're talking about.'

'My mother is Mrs Fletcher. The old lady you've been stealing from.'

'What?' I said, totally confused. 'I've never stolen anything from anyone.'

'Don't play the innocent with me. This is number 31 isn't it?'

'Yes, but –'

'And you live here?'

'I do.'

'I've got her credit-card statements,' she said, thrusting the pieces of paper towards me. 'Hundreds of pounds on clothes and make-up. Deliveries from Selfridges, for god's sake. My mum's devastated. She thought you were an absolute angel for doing her shopping.'

Feeling faint, I leaned against the door jamb. 'You've got it wr–'

'You live here, right?' Disgust was written all over her face.

'Yes, but –'

'And you've got a young baby?'

'Yes, but it's not me who –'

'I didn't come to listen to excuses. I only came to say you're not going to get away with your despicable behaviour.'

She turned and marched down the path.

For the second time that day, I'd been accused of something I hadn't done. I thought about following her, explaining, making her listen, but there was another, more urgent confrontation I needed to have.

First, I took myself upstairs to the pile of unopened letters. One by one I opened them. Pleading letters from individuals, demands from lawyers, default notices from credit-card companies, official letters from Companies House and from HMRC, allegations of fraud from previous employers – the scale of Izzy's lying and cheating was worse than anything I could have imagined. Gathering them all up, I made my way downstairs.

In the basement the music was deafening, so loud the speaker was distorting the sound, and Izzy was sitting on her bed with her back to me, doing something on her laptop. Using stolen credit cards to buy more stuff, perhaps? I called her name, but she didn't hear me so I crossed the room to where the speaker was sitting on a pile of books. I jabbed at the buttons until I turned it off.

Izzy displayed absolutely no reaction, glancing towards me then carrying on with what she was doing.

'You need to leave,' I said.

'I was listening to that.'

'I don't care. You need to leave.'

'Leave what?' she said, tapping away on her laptop.

'Leave here. Leave our house.'

She looked up at me. '*Your* house, you mean.'

'No, *our* house. Mine and Danny's. I want you to go.'

'Danny wants me to go, does he?' she asked.

'*I* want you to go.'

'Shall we see what Danny wants?'

'For fuck's sake, Izzy. This isn't about what Danny wants, *I* want you to leave.'

'My little Grace has really grown up, hasn't she?'

'I'm not *your little* Grace.'

'Yes, Grace, you are.'

'I'm not –' I began, then realised she was doing what she always did – controlling the conversation. 'You need to pack up your stuff and leave. Today.'

'Why? Why should I?'

'Let's see. How about the conversation I just had with someone who said you've stolen her mother's credit-card details?'

Izzy shrugged but said nothing.

'How could you? She thought it was *me*. I was so embarrassed.'

'Life's not all about you, little Grace.'

'Stop calling me that.'

'Why? You'll always be little Grace to me. Little Grace. Little Grace. Little Grace.'

'For god's sake, grow up.' I waved the stack of letters in her face. 'All these demands, Izzy. Letters from solicitors. All these people you've ripped off.'

'You've been going through my private mail?'

'It's not private when you leave it all over the floor.'

'It's illegal to open someone else's post.'

'Are we really going to talk about what's legal and what's not? These letters, they're full of awful things you've been up to. Not to mention ripping off some poor old lady up the road.'

She shrugged. How many times over the years had she lifted her shoulders to indicate she had absolutely no interest in what I was saying? I couldn't stand it any longer.

'Stop fucking shrugging,' I said. 'You need to leave and, Izzy, honestly, I think you need help.'

'Do I?'

'Yes.'

'Why?'

'Because this isn't normal. *You're* not normal.' My voice was shrill, but it was impossible to remain calm in the face of Izzy's complete lack of concern.

'This is interesting,' she said. 'What do you mean by *normal*?'

'Everything. Everything about you is fucked up. You seem to think it's fine to steal from an old lady –'

'She was too trusting –'

'See? That's what I mean. That's not a normal response, Izzy. Where's your shame? Where's the guilt? You behave as if you haven't got a care in the world but you haven't even got a place of your own – you're sleeping in our basement, for god's sake.' Out of nowhere, I heard myself laugh.

'Shut up,' Izzy said, and I laughed harder. It was all she deserved. She behaved as if she was so successful but, really, she was pathetic.

'Shut up,' she said, and her voice was no longer calm.

Finally, I'd found a way to get to her. I laughed and laughed, tears rolling down my cheeks.

'Shut up,' she said again, and when I didn't she got up from the bed and stood right over me. 'Don't you dare fucking laugh at me. Don't you fucking dare. Shut up. Stop fucking laughing.'

I dug my nails into my palms and faced her, my back to the staircase. We were eye to eye and I stared into her blank, expressionless gaze. 'You're pathetic,' I said. 'You've got nothing of your own, have you? That's why you want to split me and Danny up. Your whole life is a lie. You lied about your uncle. You made up a disgusting lie because you're a pathetic waste of space. No job, no house, no relationship. I can't believe it's taken me so long to see what you really are. And to think I used to look up to you. Loved you even. Not any more, Izzy. You're a liar and a fraud, but other than that, you're nothing. I'm not scared of you. In fact, I have no feelings towards you at all. When Danny realises I don't want to leave him – and he *will* realise – he'll see you were feeding him lies, like you've always done. Then he'll abandon you too, and you really will be alone in the world and everyone will see what a joke you really are. An insignificant, unimportant, pathetic joke.'

'Stop it. Fucking shut up.' She was shouting. Finally, I'd found a way to get under her skin.

'You know what I'm going to do?' I said. 'I'm going to take these letters to the police. All of them. And I'm going to tell them what you've done to Mrs Fletcher. I'm going to tell them everything. You're going to jail. And when you're behind bars, Danny will finally see who you really are.' I laughed again, right in her face this time.

Her hands were balled into fists, her knuckles white. She leaned close. I wondered if she was going to punch me, but then she pushed her head even closer so her breath tickled my cheek. 'Danny won't abandon me,' she said, her voice small and hard. 'Have you still not got it? My brother doesn't exist without me. But you? You should have let him go years ago. You should have listened to that voice telling you you're not good enough for him. You've learned to ignore it, but you know. You've always known. You were never good enough for him. Christ, I gave you the best excuse, but you were too stupid to use it. Too clingy and desperate to hang onto something that was never even yours.'

'I won't let you gaslight my relationship. Danny and I have always been happy. We've always wanted to be together.'

'Really? *Always?* Are you sure about that?'

At first, I had no idea what she was talking about, but then it dawned on me. 'You mean *that*?'

'What?'

'That time he cheated on me?'

'Did he?' she said.

'You know he did.'

'Do I?'

'You know I saw photos,' I said. 'So you're saying – what? I should have left him after all?'

'Should you have left him after he cheated on you with a gorgeous girl called Libby? Yes. You should have. That was the plan.'

'What do you mean the plan? And you don't know she was called Libby. Danny could never remember anything about that night.'

'If you say so.'

'You know he couldn't. Because of his problem with alcohol.'

'My brother doesn't have a problem with alcohol.'

'He *does*. You know he does.'

'Poor naïve little Grace. The reason Dan can't remember anything about that evening has got absolutely nothing to do with alcohol.'

And it was then she told me the truth.

The truth about the thing Danny had never been able to forgive himself for.

The thing he hated about himself above all else.

The thing that cast a deep, deep shadow over his life. Over both of our lives.

God knows I have tried to block out what she told me. I feel sick every time I think about it. I'd do anything to be able to forget what she told me, but I can't.

When she finished speaking, I heard a sort of half-cough, half-sob and spun round to find Danny standing at the foot of the stairs, staring at us.

Izzy said, 'You deserved better than her, Dan. You still do.'

Danny sank onto the bottom step. I rushed over to him but when I put my arms around him he flinched, and when I tried to kiss him he pulled away.

'Don't,' he said.

'Danny,' I said urgently. 'You heard all of that? You can see now, can't you? Her lies? Everything she said about me?'

'No, Danny,' Izzy said. 'She's the one who's lying. Trying to make this all about me, when she's the one who came down here flinging accusations around, telling me how she's going to leave you.'

'I didn't,' I said, shouting now. 'It's all you. You're a monster, a sick, twisted monster. And now Danny can see it too.'

He stood up then. He wiped his eyes on his sleeve. He didn't look at either of us, just said, so quietly I barely heard his words, 'I'm going to work.'

Ten minutes later, my husband left our house for the last time. I would never see him again.

Notes

Daniel may have been flying the plane, but as far as Grace is concerned, it is Izzy who is responsible for both his death and Luke's. She believes what Daniel overheard utterly shattered his already fragile mind. He chose to fly a plane into the side of a mountain rather than live with the knowledge of what he heard that day.

Grace refused to tell me what Izzy had told her. She was adamant she would never repeat the words, not for me, not for anyone.

I had one final question for her. Grace had made it clear that she had her back to the staircase, so she didn't know Daniel was listening. But was it possible, I asked her, that Izzy knew her brother could hear what she was saying?

Grace's reply was unequivocal. Izzy was facing the stairs. She must have known.

I tried several times to get in touch with Izzy but with her trial imminent she was either unwilling or unable to talk to me.

The Trial

On 7 November 2022, Izzy walked into the court room for the first day of her trial looking extraordinary. She was wearing a hot-pink dress which was all sharp folds, pleats and protuberances. It was unlikely the expensive barrister who Roger had paid to defend her would have recommended it as suitable court attire. She spent at least a minute arranging the outfit around her. Then, before proceedings got under way, she turned and scanned the faces on the benches behind her. When she saw me she smiled and waved as if I were a friend she'd spotted across the street. I returned her smile but I didn't wave. She then turned towards the jury, smiling and nodding. She looked like the star of a film, attending a premiere, greeting her adoring fans. Two or three of the jury members smiled back, before remembering where they were and looking away.

The prosecutor set out the charges, explaining that as they were all offences of dishonesty, they were being tried together. There was the credit-card fraud, relating not only to Mrs Fletcher but also to two other elderly residents of the village. Then there were the charges relating to Astatine. Even though she'd told me about it, I was taken aback to hear she'd conned investors out of almost

£280,000. But that wasn't the end of it. There were five charges of theft and false accounting relating to HCAssist, her friend's mum's charity, and, finally, three individuals, two men and a woman, whom Izzy had been in brief relationships with, had come forward with claims that she had stolen money, jewellery, a car and, in one instance, an expensive piece of art, totalling almost £150,000.

Despite the gravity of the charges Izzy never once looked anything other than relaxed and unconcerned, exuding confidence and charm and being scrupulously polite to anyone who spoke to her. Indeed, when she heard the prosecution barrister describe Astatine as 'a sophisticated and complex fraud' she positively beamed. For much of the rest of the time, as far as I could tell from where I was sitting, she was taking notes. Either that or doodling.

I couldn't risk taking more time off work so I was only there for the first day, until a fortnight later when I returned to watch Izzy being found guilty of all but one of the charges (she was acquitted of the theft of a watch from an ex-boyfriend).

Although she must have known she was about to go to jail, Izzy looked as blithely untroubled as usual. For her final day in court, she was wearing a dark grey trouser suit and could easily have been mistaken for one of the lawyers.

Before she handed down the sentence, the judge addressed Izzy directly. 'What is particularly striking is the profound impact on others, which has been utterly devastating. You lived a lavish lifestyle from the money and misery of your victims. I have read nine personal statements and a business impact statement with regards to HCAssist. I heard about financial hardship, depression and anxiety. You should be ashamed of bringing such misery to so many innocent people. You undertook a prolonged and sophisticated fraud; you engaged in relationships based on deception and elaborate lies defrauding people out of significant amounts of money. Your actions were callous and calculated and a contemptible breach of trust.'

When Izzy received a custodial sentence of six years and four months there were no histrionics; there was no crying, no shouting. As she was led out of the court to begin her sentence, she displayed no reaction at all.

Notes

I caught Covid, which took me some time to recover from, so Izzy had been in HMP Downview for nearly three months before I went to see her. I booked my visit for a Sunday afternoon and made sure I arrived in plenty of time. Although TV dramas give the impression that investigative journalists are forever popping in and out of prisons to interview people, I'd never been to one before and, perching on an uncomfortable plastic chair screwed to the floor, I hoped I never would again.

Clearly I watch too many crime dramas myself because I had expected Izzy to be wearing a prison uniform. However, when she walked through the door she was in jeans, trainers and a green T-shirt. When she saw me waiting, her face arranged itself into its familiar smile.

'My favourite journalist,' she said loudly enough that people sitting at nearby tables turned to look at us. It was only when they turned away that Izzy sat down.

I asked her how she was finding life in prison. She was surprisingly cheerful even as she complained about the clothes she was allowed to wear ('dull'), the food ('shit'), the other prisoners ('morons') and the prison staff (also 'morons').

'I'm finding interesting ways to keep busy,' she said, and tempting though it was to ask her what she meant, I only had a limited amount of time.

'Did you like my dress on the first day in court?' she asked, before I could speak. 'Cost a fortune. Issey Miyake. Practically named after me.'

I had no idea what she was going on about and I cut to the chase. 'You ripped off so many people, Izzy. Do you feel guilty?'

'I can always rely on you to jump in with the feelings, Carly. Why on earth would I "feel" guilty?' she said, putting air quotes around the word *feel*. 'I taught all those people an important life lesson. If you're too trusting, you'll get ripped off. If it wasn't me, it would have been someone else – I was just smart enough to do it first.'

I looked around the room, which was lit by harsh strip lights, imagining how horrible the cells must be. 'Do you have any regrets about what you did?'

'Sure, I've got regrets.'

'What are they?'

'Getting caught, obviously. Which would never have happened if that bitch hadn't opened my post, which is illegal. They never said that in court, but they should have done. The whole case was built on her doing something illegal. *She's* the one who should have been in court. My case should have been thrown out. Useless piece-of-shit barrister – I'd have done better defending myself.' She smiled. 'That's another regret. Not defending myself.'

'You told Grace something the day your brother died,' I said, 'something he overheard. What was it?'

Her smile vanished. 'How disappointing,' she said. 'And here was I thinking you came to see me because you missed me, Carly.'

'She said Daniel overheard something you said right before he left for work. What was it?'

'Did you see her at the inquest? Lapping up the attention. Putting on the grieving-widow act.'

That wasn't at all how Grace had appeared to me.

'I know you told her something awful that day. Will you tell me what it was?'

'Depends on your definition of awful.'

'Are you going to tell me?' I said, determined not to let her sidetrack the conversation.

She gave me one of her flat, unblinking stares, and I forced myself to hold her gaze, refusing to be intimidated by it. She shrugged and said, 'You're going to write a book, yes?'

'I am.'

'And you'll put in all about my businesses, that I'm an entrepreneur, all of that?'

'Yes,' I said.

'You'll make it clear how successful I've been – much more than that pathetic sister-in-law of mine?'

I told her it would all go in.

Her smiled reappeared. 'OK, I'll tell you what I told her.'

When she'd finished speaking, Izzy stretched her arms above her head, clasping her hands together. She looked up at the grubby ceiling tiles and yawned.

I thought I might actually be sick and I pushed my palms hard against the sharp plastic edges of the prison chair, hoping pain would help me focus. I took a couple of deep breaths before I spoke. 'How could you do that to your own brother, Izzy?'

She didn't answer. She stared at the prisoner sitting at the table next to us, then at their visitor, who was crying.

Eventually her gaze returned to me. 'I just did what any sister would do.'

'I don't know *anyone* who would do what you did to Daniel.'

'Maybe they would, maybe they wouldn't,' she said, and shrugged. 'Or maybe they only say they wouldn't.'

'How do you live with yourself?'

'What do you mean?'

'Right after your brother heard you telling Grace what you'd done, he got in a plane and flew it into a mountain, killing himself and murdering his co-pilot. Are you saying you feel no responsibility for that at all?'

'Did I fly that plane into the mountain? No, I didn't. It's not *my* fault.'

'Do you at least agree that your brother might still be here, that Luke might still be alive, if Daniel hadn't heard what you told Grace?' I was trying, and failing, to keep my voice calm.

Her.

It was *her.*

She was the reason Luke was dead. *She* was the reason I hadn't had the time to make things right with him, the reason Grace had no husband, Beth had no father. The woman in front of me was a monster, just as Grace had said. An evil, sick, twisted monster.

'Look, it's simple,' she said. 'If Danny had believed me when I told him Grace wasn't the right woman for him, or if Grace had stuck to her supposed principle of never forgiving a cheater, or if the pair of them had simply accepted I *always* know best, then yes, sure, my brother would still be alive and so would your boyfriend.'

'So you're really saying you don't have any guilt at all?' I said, ignoring her reference to Luke. 'He was your *brother*, Izzy.'

'I told you the very first time we met – Danny was alive, and now he's dead. I had a brother, and now I don't. That's all there is to it. Why would I feel guilty about that?'

'Surely you can understand that's not normal?'

Izzy made a sound I'd never heard her make before. A sort of weird *hee-hee*.

She did it again. And again. I realised she was giggling. The hairs on the back of my neck stood up and I swallowed, trying to force down the nausea in my stomach.

She stopped abruptly and focusing her unblinking gaze on me said, as mildly as if she was asking me if I wanted a cup of tea, 'How dumb do you have to be to expect normal behaviour from a psychopath?'

Hearing her give a name to what she was, there in that horrible place, every instinct in my body was telling me to run screaming from the room, and it took all my will power to stay where I was. Even when she smiled her weird, creepy smile, staring through me with her thousand-yard gaze, I remained in my seat, pushing the rigid edges into my hands like my life depended on it, and said, 'Have you always known what you are?'

She shrugged. 'I've always known I was special.'

'*Special?*'

'Why don't you talk to my psychologist? You'll like her. Her name's Fiona Mackie. Talk to her. Then you'll understand.'

I mumbled something about an appointment, about how I was going to be late, and got to my feet. Izzy shrugged and, forcing myself not to break into a sprint, I stumbled towards the exit. Just before I left the room, I turned to look at her for a final time.

Izzy arranged her mouth into her familiar smile, lifted her hand and gave me a jaunty wave, looking utterly unconcerned.

Interview with Fiona Mackie: Part I

What follows is the first of two parts of a transcript of a conversation between Fiona Mackie, BSc (Hons), MSc, PgDip, and Carly Atherton which took place on 27 April 2023.

The conversation took place in Fiona Mackie's office. One wall was lined floor-to-ceiling with shelves crammed with books, while the other walls were decorated with black-and-white photographs of the sea. Beneath the window, a narrow bench was covered with colourful ceramic pots each containing a cactus. Although Fiona was seated at a desk when I was shown in, for the duration of our conversation we sat in two armchairs at the other end of her office, and before I began recording, Fiona made us a cafetière of coffee.

Carly Atherton (CA): Perhaps you could start by introducing yourself?

Fiona Mackie (FM): Sure. I'm a forensic psychologist registered with the Health and Care Professions Council, which is the organisation regulating health, psychological and care professionals in the UK. I'm also the head of clinical services here at our practice.

CA: And can you tell me what exactly a forensic psychologist does?

FM: I work in the branch of psychology that applies psychological theory to criminal investigations. Broadly speaking, I identify psychological problems associated with criminal behaviour and use psychological theory in the treatment of people who have committed offences.

CA: It sounds fascinating.

FM: I'd prefer the word 'challenging', but yes, it's certainly interesting.

CA: So, Fiona, you kindly agreed to meet me today to talk about one of your clients, and for the record we should clarify that we've received written consent from them to say they're happy for us to discuss their case history and also for you to disclose your psychological evaluation of them.

FM: That's correct.

CA: Can you tell me how you came to meet Izzy Taylor?

FM: She was referred to me for psychological evaluation by her solicitor.

CA: Is that where you usually get your clients? From lawyers?

FM: I receive a lot of referrals from legal representatives. It's not unusual for the question of mental illness to be raised with regard to someone facing criminal charges, and often it's the point at which an illness is formally recognised for the first time.

CA: Before we move on to talk about Izzy specifically, maybe you could speak more generally about diagnosing someone as a psychopath.

FM: I'll start by saying that strictly speaking I *can't* diagnose someone as a psychopath. Practitioners use certain manuals, principally one called the DSM-5-TR, to diagnose mental disorders, and those manuals don't contain the term psychopath. However, there's no question that psychopathy is a mental disorder, and a relatively common one at that.

CA: What do you mean by relatively common?

FM: There's broad agreement that at least one in every hundred people has symptoms of psychopathy severe enough to cause significant impairment. The number might actually be as high as four out of every hundred, although personally I think it's nearer the lower number. Either way, it's common enough that almost everyone, at one point or another, will cross paths with a psychopath.

CA: Between one per cent and four per cent of people are psychopaths? That's terrifying. And the main thing about them is that they lack empathy, is that right?

FM: Reduced empathy is certainly one of the characteristic traits, yes, but it's a lot more complicated than that. For example, someone with psychopathic traits will have low levels of remorse and they'll also be prone to uninhibited behaviour.

CA: And violence?

FM: Not necessarily. In fact, this is one of the biggest misconceptions about psychopaths. Not all psychopaths are violent. For example, someone who is very charming, but also glib, cold and callous, who lies a lot and exploits others, may well be psychopathic. That's the thing about psychopaths – they'll manipulate and exploit people while appearing to be friendly, engaging and well adjusted. They may devastate your relationships, shatter your self-esteem, destroy your entire life, even, but to everyone around them they may seem perfectly sane. It's often said that they wear a mask of sanity.

CA: But if they're all walking around wearing this mask of sanity, surely there's no way to tell if someone is a psychopath or not?

FM: Some people do appear to be more able to sense that something's a bit ... off, but obviously most people aren't assessing everyone they meet for potential psychopathic traits. In any case, psychopaths are experts at pretending to be interested in people and they'll often be very charming, although the reality is that their only interest in someone is in assessing the value that person has to them.

CA: If they're so good at pretending, how can *you* tell if someone is a psychopath?

FM: There are various tools, but we mainly use something called the Hare PCL-R or the PCL:SV, which is an abbreviated version of it.

CA: What does that stand for?

FM: Psychopath checklist screening version. When I'm assessing someone for psychopathic traits, I interview them, look at their history and, for each criterion, give them a score. With the PCL:SV, the maximum score is twenty-four, and anyone who scores eighteen or above is probably a psychopath.

CA: Did you use this with Izzy?

FM: I did.

CA: And what was her score?

FM: Against the PCL:SV, Izzy's score was 21.

CA: So she's definitely a psychopath?

FM: A score of 21 is a very strong indication that she has the traits of a highly psychopathic individual.

CA: That sounds pretty conclusive. What's on the checklist? What are you looking for?

FM: Superficial charm, a grandiose sense of self-worth, lying, shallow affect – which means not experiencing the normal range and depth of emotions – promiscuous sexual behaviour, a lack of long-term goals, failure to accept responsibility for their own actions, behavioural problems in childhood …

CA: It strikes me that a lot of those would apply to plenty of people. Surely they're not all psychopaths?

FM: You're beginning to see why it's not an easy disorder to identify. It's a spectrum disorder, too, like many others, which means psychopathic traits vary from mild to extreme. But it's like anything else – the more experience you have working with people who have a psychopathic disorder, the more able you are to identify it. Hopefully, anyway.

CA: Would I know if I was a psychopath?

FM: [*laughs*] You won't be surprised to hear that that's the question I'm asked more than any other. The thing to bear in mind is that psychopaths don't really experience anxiety, so if you're worrying about whether you're a psychopath, you're probably not a psychopath.

CA: [*laughs*] Well, that's reassuring. I know we've only got a limited amount of time, so shall we move on to talking about Izzy? I assume her solicitor referred her to you because he was hoping you'd be able to get her off the charges?

FM: I wouldn't put it like that. Izzy had a very experienced legal team defending her and they wanted to pursue all angles.

CA: But it didn't work?

FM: What do you mean?

CA: Well, she's in prison.

FM: Izzy's mental illness wasn't a defence to the charges against her.

CA: But she's a psychopath.

FM: Mental illness is only a defence to criminal charges if it means a defendant doesn't know the difference between right and wrong. Psychopaths know the difference between right and wrong. They just don't care.

CA: So when Izzy lied and stole from all those people, she understood that what she was doing was criminal, she understood she was hurting people, and she knew if she was caught she would go to jail, but she just didn't care about any of that?

FM: That's right. Psychopaths have no concern about the consequences of their actions, either for themselves or for their victims. There's a complete absence of shame or guilt. In most instances, psychopaths will actually feed off the humiliation they cause other people. Izzy didn't – actually, she *couldn't* – care about how upset or violated someone might feel as a result of her actions. She's simply not interested in anyone, beyond how they might benefit her.

CA: But she's so convincing. I mean, for a while I genuinely believed she wanted to help me. I'd lost my job not long before I met her and I really thought she wanted to help me get my career back on track.

FM: I'm not surprised it seemed that way to you. The feeling of being understood to an unusual degree is very common for people whose paths cross with those of a psychopath. Izzy is an expert in mimicking patterns of behaviour, but she was only pretending to be friendly. She understands the definitions of feelings and emotions, but the reality is that to her they're only words. They don't *mean* anything. A useful way of trying to imagine it is as if her emotional playing field is completely flat and featureless in all directions. No ups, no downs. Nothing. Izzy doesn't have any concept of what being friendly *feels* like – she just knows what to do to make people *believe* she's friendly.

CA: Why would she bother?

FM: As I said, she's a highly skilled imitator and an expert in making people believe she's interested in them. She does that in order to gather information to determine if someone is worthy of her investing her time in them. For people like Izzy, it's a constant calculation. Is this person useful? Are they going to provide me with entertainment? With opportunities? Are they relevant or pointless? A winner or a loser? Predator or prey? Psychopaths are really, really good at identifying victims. You've heard of Ted Bundy?

CA: The serial killer? Of course.

FM: That's the one. Well, he claimed he could identify a 'good' victim simply by watching them walk, so a psychologist in the States devised an experiment to test his claim. They used the PCL-R to identify which members of a group of volunteers had psychopathic traits. A second group of volunteers filled in a questionnaire which included a question about whether they'd ever been victimised, and then each person in the second group was filmed walking along a corridor. The first group, both those with psychopathic traits and those without, watched the video and were asked to rate each person according to how vulnerable to mugging they thought they were. And every single person in the first group who had scored high on the psychopath test picked out every single person in the second group who said they'd been victimised, just by watching them walk.

CA: That is completely terrifying.

FM: It is. But that's not all. The same video was shown to psychopaths in a maximum-security prison, and they not only picked out the victimised people but said they could identify them precisely *because* of the way they walked.

I paused the interview at this point because Fiona Mackie had a scheduled phone consultation. As she walked me to the reception area to wait, she asked me how holding eye contact with Izzy had made me feel. When I described her intense gaze, Fiona called it the dead-eye stare and explained that it's extremely common for people to find it uncomfortable to maintain eye contact with psychopaths. She said one of the ways we manage stress is by blinking, which gives our brains a tiny period of rest, but because psychopaths don't experience anxiety or stress, they don't need to blink as much, hence the intensity of their stares.

Interview with Fiona Mackie: Part II

What follows is the second part of a transcript of a conversation between Fiona Mackie, BSc (Hons), MSc, PgDip, and Carly Atherton which took place on 27 April 2023.

CA: One of the questions I wanted to ask you is whether psychopathy is something people are born with? Was Izzy born a psychopath?

FM: Well, before I get into the whole subject of nature versus nurture I should make it clear that there's a great deal of reluctance to label children as psychopaths. If you give a child a label like that, they are far more likely to become what you're calling them. But keeping that in mind, there is a recognised conduct disorder among children displaying what are called callous-unemotional traits, which are traits very similar to those displayed by adults who are psychopathic.

CA: And these kids, the ones with these callous-unemotional traits, are they born like that?

FM: It's not possible to say categorically, but the behaviours have been observed in children as young as two or three.

CA: And so does that mean it could be inherited? As far as I understand, neither of Izzy's parents were like her, but it's possible that her grandmother was.

FM: There's been a lot of research into the heritability of psychopathy, including by a neuroscientist called James Fallon. He was analysing brain scans of serial killers when he discovered that he himself had the same abnormalities in his brain as psychopaths. He started researching his family tree and it turned out he was descended from a long line of murderers, although he himself was a respected scientist and happily married with children – to all intents and purposes, completely normal, as far as we can ever say anyone is.

CA: A normal psychopath? I didn't know that was even possible.

FM: The thing to understand is that not everyone who is a psychopath is a criminal. There's so much we still don't understand but, like many other things, it appears to be the case that nurture plays as significant a role as nature. When James Fallon started examining his own thoughts and actions more closely, he realised that throughout his life he'd displayed many of the same emotionally distant and controlling behaviours as the psychopaths he was researching, but in his case he believed his upbringing, particularly his relationship with his family, meant he followed a path leading him to a distinguished career, rather than the alternative.

CA: Right. So that's the nurture part of it – what about nature? If he realised he was a psychopath because his brain scans had the same abnormalities as serial killers, what were the abnormalities?

FM: Well, another neuroscientist used a mobile scanning unit to take images of the brains of convicted criminal psychopaths in prisons around the United States. His research indicates that all psychopaths have atrophied amygdalae.

CA: I don't understand – can you explain what that means?

FM: The amygdala is part of the brain's limbic system and, among other things, it controls emotional responses. If it's atrophied, it would mean a significantly reduced capacity to experience emotional responses in the same way as the rest of us.

CA: But why would some people with these ... atrophied amygdalae ... go on to become serial killers, while others are like that scientist?

FM: Well, that's where the interplay between nature and nurture is probably important. We don't know for certain, but it's likely to relate in part to their experiences in childhood. For example, children who will go on to display psychopathic traits as adults are unresponsive to timeouts or other threats of punishment, so they'll have absolutely no effect on their behaviour. That's only one minor example, though. As with so many things, it's a hugely complex area and there's so much more that needs to be understood.

CA: This is all great background for my book.

FM: You do realise that Izzy will probably change her mind? I wouldn't be at all surprised if she suddenly decides to withdraw her cooperation.

CA: She's never shown any signs of that. In fact, she's said she's delighted that I'm hoping to write a book.

FM: I'm sure she has, but psychopaths are the epitome of fickle and unreliable, saying one thing, doing another. I imagine you've invested a lot of time into this project. Just as long as you're aware it could all be for nothing.

CA: Let's hope not ... Something else I wanted to ask you about was why so much of what Izzy told me puts her in a bad light. I mean, there's all her fraudulent behaviour, of course, but there's other things she's done that are probably criminal, not to mention some really terrible behaviour towards her friends and family, particularly her brother. She told me about something totally sickening that she did to him – I still can't get my head around it. I mean, if I had done any of the things she said, or hurt the people she hurt, then the last thing I'd be doing is telling a journalist.

FM: That's not how Izzy will see it. She will have told you things to feed her sense of grandiosity. She'll believe they make her appear more intelligent or more attractive or smarter than others. She thinks she's a winner and she wants everyone else to think that too. Of course, there's a very strong possibility that some of what she's said simply won't be true.

CA: I've found fact-checking her stories really difficult.

FM: I'm not remotely surprised. Look, any interaction with a psychopath comes with risk. Izzy's priority is always Izzy. She wants to come out on top, no matter what the cost or who she hurts.

CA: Actually, that brings me on to my final question. From what you've said and what she told me she did to her brother, I assume the whole predator-or-prey mentality includes her own family?

FM: Well, it's not uncommon for psychopaths to actively subdue their impulses and behaviour around their families, although they'll only do this to make sure they continue to receive the benefits they derive from being part of a functioning family unit.

CA: You make it sound so calculating. So you mean they don't actually love their family?

FM: Not in the abstract way that you or I would understand love, no. They generally equate love with sex – so if you ask a psychopath if they've ever been in love, they'll usually tell you about sexual relationships. However psychopaths might also believe themselves to be expressing love by forging all-consuming, selfish, obsessive connections. Having a relationship of any sort with a psychopath can be devastating, but having a psychopathic sibling presents a unique challenge. Tragically, it's not uncommon for it to be fatal.

CA: So Izzy *is* responsible for Daniel's death?

FM: I'm not saying that. I didn't know her brother and I'm not going to speculate about why he did what he did. But what I can say is that victims of psychopaths experience an erasure not only of their self-worth, but also of their entire self. Psychologists who work with victims are primarily trying to help them reconnect with who they were before they fell into the psychopath's orbit. If you understand that you can see how someone with a psychopathic older sibling may well never have had a sense of self that's truly independent of their sibling.

CA: That's totally terrifying.

FM: Yes, it is.

CA: So Daniel's entire sense of himself was wrapped up in his relationship with Izzy?

FM: It's very possible.

CA: And if something happened to make him question the whole basis of their relationship …?

FM: The psychological effects could be catastrophic.

Notes

After I left Fiona Mackie's office I walked to the nearby railway station. When the train arrived, it was already full and I had to stand. In my research on ghost flights, I'd looked at the carbon footprint of planes versus trains which is why I knew if every seat was taken and passengers were standing then there was likely to be about a thousand people on board.

And what that meant was that, even with the most conservative estimate, I was travelling with ten Izzys. Ten people on the train who did not feel emotions yet were experts in pretending they did. Ten people who knew the difference between right and wrong but simply didn't care. Ten people who would do whatever it took to get what they wanted, no matter who they hurt, even members of their own family.

I finally had my story. However, in many ways, I'd had it all along. It was obvious from the beginning that Izzy was a psychopath, if only I'd known what I was looking for.

But that's not entirely true, is it?

If only I hadn't allowed myself to be charmed by her lies and flattered by her interest in me. I was grateful for her attention, naïvely eager to believe she wanted to help me, but if only I'd been more professional and done my job properly from the outset then I believe I would have seen what Izzy was.

Thanks to my conversation with Fiona Mackie, I now understand how Izzy's whole life is based on a constant calculation of the value of other people to her. She has a complete absence of everything that makes the rest of us human. She's a yawning abyss of unchecked ego, all her desires free to run rampant, regardless of the consequences to anyone else, including her own brother. She is absolutely terrifying. She is a monster.

And even if only one per cent of us are psychopaths, that means there are at least eighty million Izzys in the world.

I had my story, but you don't, not all of it. I spent months trying to decide whether or not to share what Izzy told me that day when I visited her in prison. Even as I curated my interviews with her and Grace, turning them into the narratives that you've read in this book, I remained undecided as to whether I should include it.

I was concerned that it was disrespectful to Daniel's memory. After all, if I made public what she told me, it would be there for anyone to read including, one day, his daughter. Daniel murdered Luke, but there is no doubt that Daniel himself is also a victim and perhaps the details of what happened to him should be allowed to die with him.

However, understanding what Daniel overheard on the day of his death is necessary to complete the picture. Without it, Izzy Taylor will be known only as a convicted fraudster – which she is, of course, but that is not all she is. Not by a long way. This is why, in the end, I decided I had no choice but to include the final part of the story.

Izzy's Story

15 December 2012

1.

Danny and Grace had been together far too long. She'd had her fun and now it was time for her to move on.

I had a plan – there was no problem getting hold of the Rohypnol from my usual source – and when a final-year history student called Libby contacted my essay business, wanting to buy a dissertation on Charlemagne, I knew I'd found the right person to help.

No problem, I replied to her text, I had a couple that had never been submitted by anyone at her university. I told her how much it would cost.

She texted back: *Great! Can I pay in a couple of months?*

No. Payment in full upfront.

I haven't got the money now. Can I pay later but with interest?

It was then the idea occurred to me. *Maybe we can do a deal. Send me a photo.*

WTF? No!

Not that sort of photo. Send me a normal photo of your face.

A photo arrived almost straight away. She would do. I replied saying if she was prepared to travel to meet me and give me half an hour of her time she could have a guaranteed 2:1 essay on Charlemagne for free.

She didn't agree immediately and I had to speak to her on the phone to convince her that I wasn't a pervert, that I was, in fact, only a few years older than her and posed no threat to her whatsoever. She faltered again when I explained what I would need her to do, but in the end, with a looming deadline and a promise to supply her with a first-class dissertation, Libby agreed to help.

Next thing was to arrange to meet Danny, so I sent him a text: *Fancy a beer tomorrow night? Just you and me.*

Sorry Iz, too much studying to do. I've got an exam coming up.

C'mon. Only for an hour. You can't study the whole time.

I've got some extra shifts at work so I really need to study tomorrow night.

Please D. Work's really tough and I'm feeling really down. One drink. Please.

I deployed the 'I'm upset, boo-hoo, poor me' shtick sparingly, but it never failed to work, and sure enough, he agreed to meet me the following evening.

I made sure I arrived at the pub first so when Danny came in I was already at the bar, poised to order.

'You find us a seat and I'll get them in,' I said. 'Guinness?'

'Go on then, but I'll only have one.'

Yes. Indeed.

I ordered his drink first and when the barman put the glass on the bar I asked for a vodka, lime and soda for myself. I chose vodka because the bottle was empty and while the barman was changing it I dropped two Rohypnol tabs into Danny's pint. They had completely dissolved by the time I carried our drinks over to the table and put the Guinness in front of him.

'Cheers,' I said, raising my glass.

Danny clinked his drink against mine and took a big swig. 'Ahhh,' he said, putting his glass on the table. 'That's hit the spot.'

'Thanks for coming out,' I said.

'Nah, you were right. Grace thought it would be good for me to get away from studying for a bit.'

Grace. Grace. Always bloody Grace.

'Did she?' I said, taking a tiny sip of my drink. Best to keep a clear head.

'Yeah. She's worried about you, too.'

Ha. If only Grace knew what I was planning, she really would have something to worry about.

He took another gulp of his drink. 'So how are you really?'

'I'm fine,' I said and smiled at him.

His face twisted into an expression I recognised as concern and he said, 'It's OK, Iz, you don't have to pretend with me.' Reaching across the table, he put his hand on top of mine and I linked my fingers through his, trying to think of a plausible reason to be sad.

'I still miss Nan,' I lied.

'I know,' he said. 'She was such a big part of both our lives.'

After another few minutes of waffle Danny had finished his pint. He yawned. 'God, I'm knackered. Sorry, Iz.'

'It's fine,' I said. 'You've always been a lightweight.'

He tried to smile, but he was having a problem coordinating his lips, and the effect was more of a grimace.

He yawned again, then folded his arms on the table and put his head on them. ''S'need a little sleep. Be OK in a minute.'

I stood up. This was always going to be the most difficult part. Danny was bigger and heavier than me and getting him to where we needed to go was going to be tricky. I lifted his head off the table and pushed him upright in the chair.

'Feel weird,' he said.

I ducked my head under his arm and tried to get him onto his feet. 'Up you come little brother,' I said.

'Don't wanna,' he said.

'Danny,' I said, careful to keep my voice quiet – last thing I needed was an interfering barman to get involved. 'Come on. Time to go. Get up.'

It took a couple of attempts, but leaning hard on the table, he pushed himself upright and, with his arm still around my shoulders, we left the pub.

We staggered down the street, lurching as he almost tripped over his own feet. My back and neck were killing me. Thank goodness the hotel was only three doors down. Also thank goodness for the automatic doors which swished open as we approached. As we staggered past the same receptionist who had checked me in earlier that afternoon, she looked up.

I laughed and rolled my eyes. 'Someone's been celebrating his promotion very hard,' I said.

She smiled. 'He's going to regret it in the morning.'

In the lift, I leaned Danny against a wall, holding my hand against his chest to keep him from toppling forward. He looked around, catching sight of himself in the mirrored wall opposite. 'Where're we? Wha's going on?'

'You've had a bit too much to drink, Dan. But I'm here.'

He squinted at his reflection, as if he wasn't sure whether he was looking at himself or someone else. 'Where's this place?'

'It's a hotel, Dan. You're too pissed to get home. I'm going to stay with you. You don't need to worry.'

His eyes closed and he started to list towards the doors, so I shoved my head back under his arm, bracing my legs against his weight to keep him upright.

The elevator pinged to announce we'd arrived at our floor and the doors slid open. Danny's eyes opened, too.

'That's it,' I said as we stumbled out. 'Nearly there. Just a few more steps.'

I touched the key card to the reader. It flashed red.

'Fuck,' I said. Now was not the time for the card to fail.

I tried again and this time, thankfully, it flashed green. I pushed down on the handle with my elbow, the door swung open and we fell through and onto the floor. Danny cushioned my fall and the carpet, hopefully, cushioned his. The door swung the other way, hitting me in the back of the legs and I rolled off Danny and shuffled round behind his head, put my hands under his arms and dragged him until he was fully inside the room, and the door, finally, clicked shut.

'Danny, Danny, Danny,' I said. 'The things I do for you.'

I got out my phone, swapped sim cards and texted Libby. *ETA?*

She replied almost immediately. *Be there in 20.*

Right. Twenty minutes. I could do this.

I bent down and started dragging Danny towards the bed. Fortunately, it was a small room, so we didn't have far to go.

'Can you stand up for me?' I said, but he didn't even open his eyes.

'Have I got to do everything for you, little brother?' I said, kneeling at the end of the bed, trying to heave him up. 'We could have avoided all of this if you'd only see that Grace is no good for you.'

I eventually got his top half onto the bed and started to hoist him up towards the pillows. 'You're worth a thousand of her, little brother. Ten thousand of her.'

His legs were still dangling off the end of the bed but I gave a couple of major heaves and he was finally on. 'The things I do for you,' I said again, chuckling.

I started removing his clothes methodically, piling everything up neatly on one of the two armchairs in the room. Shoes first, then socks. When he was little, Mum said Danny had puppy paws because his feet were too big for his skinny little prepubescent body. She said that meant he was going to be tall because eventually he'd grow into his feet. His toes were slender. Artistic toes, I thought. My Danny was perfect in every way.

I took his phone out of his jeans pocket. The notifications were already full of missed calls and texts from Grace, and as I looked at it, another one flashed up. *Where are you, Dan? Call me. I'm getting worried.* Good. Let her worry.

My brother had always preferred a button fly and I undid them one by one but when I tried to tug his jeans over his hips they got stuck. I ended up having to push them down a bit on one side then the other, one side then the other. His boxer shorts started coming down too, but it was too early for that, so I put one hand on the waist-band to keep them in place.

I looked at his face and his eyelids flickered. He said something, but it was just meaningless sounds.

'Shhhh, Danny, it's OK,' I said, in the sort of voice I'd heard people use with babies.

He fell silent and I carried on pushing his trousers down little by little. Once they were past his thighs, I was able to pull them the rest of the way without any resistance.

His jumper and shirt were easier to remove, although getting them off messed up his hair, so I spent a little time stroking it back into place, then lifted his head and put a pillow underneath. He was dribbling a little from the side of his mouth, and I wiped it away with my hand then sat quietly beside him, leaning against the headboard, our legs touching, looking at him, this extension of me. My baby brother. My little Danny.

My phone buzzed with a text from Libby: *I'm here. Come up. 7ᵗʰ floor. Room 712.*

I kissed Danny on the forehead, crossed the room and opened the door.

Despite the ugly old-lady raincoat she was wearing, I was pleased to see Libby was as pretty as she had looked in her picture. Slim, with glossy dark hair cascading down her back and pert little breasts. Much more my brother's type than Grace.

She stepped into the room and I shut the door behind her. When I turned back, she was staring at the bed.

'This is Rob,' I said. 'Rob, this is Libby.' She didn't say anything and, unsurprisingly, neither did Danny.

Libby turned towards me. 'I'm really not sure about this.'

I looked at her and she flinched. 'Look, you're here now,' I said. 'It'll take ten minutes tops. I'll forward you the dissertation before you even leave the room. We'll both get what we want, and he,' I nodded at Danny, 'will be none the wiser.'

'But who is he?' she asked. 'Why are you doing this?'

'All you need to know is this is absolutely for his own good. I've got his best interests at heart and no one else will know you've been here.'

'Promise?' she said.

'Yes. Now let's get on with it.'

She took off her raincoat and, glancing at the pile of Danny's clothes on the first chair, draped it over the back of the second armchair. She slipped off her shoes, leaving them where they were.

'I won't do naked,' she said. 'That's what we agreed. OK?'

I nodded. 'Bra and pants are fine.'

'And he definitely won't wake up? You're sure?'

'I'm certain.' I waved a hand towards Danny. 'But you can check for yourself.'

She approached the bed, hesitantly, looking down at my beautiful boy. She reached out and touched one finger-tip to his leg, then snatched her hand away.

'Go on,' I said. 'He won't wake up.'

She slowly slid a hand under one of his calves and lifted his leg a couple of inches. She withdrew her hand and his leg dropped onto the bed.

'See?' I said. 'He'll be out cold for hours. But the sooner we do this, the sooner you can go.'

Libby looked at Danny, then at me, then at the door, then back at me. 'And I'll definitely get a first?' she said.

I nodded.

'OK then,' she said, more to herself than to me.

To be fair to the girl, having finally made up her mind to get on with it, she shimmied out of her jeans and her jumper without any further delay and stood in front of me. I had told her to wear her sexiest underwear and she had chosen well; her bra and pants were a matching set made of translucent material with little pink hearts sewn along the seams. They left very little to the imagination. I would have liked to wear them myself.

'Nice,' I said. 'Right. Hop up onto the bed.'

She sat on the side of the bed, then slowly swung her legs up. She kept her back straight as if she was expecting a tray of food to be delivered to her lap.

'Lie down,' I said.

She looked at Danny. 'He's definitely not going to wake up?'

'He's definitely not going to wake up.'

She lowered her head to the pillow next to Danny's.

'Right,' I said. 'Turn on your side, put your mouth close to his, like you're about to kiss. Put your arm across his chest.'

She didn't move. Her gaze slid down towards his boxers.

'Look,' I said, calmly and politely, 'can we get on with it? On your side. Arm over his chest. Like you're about to kiss. Couple of photos. Change pose. Few more photos. Job done. Degree in the bag. OK?'

Libby rolled onto her side and moved her head so her mouth was a couple of inches away from Danny's.

'Closer. You're supposed to be about to kiss each other.'

She jerked her head back, but then lowered it really close to Danny. Her hair swung forward. She had lovely hair, so different from Grace's, but it was obscuring their faces and the tops of her breasts, which bulged appealingly over the top of her bra.

'Tuck your hair behind your ears.'

Libby did what I asked.

'Hold it there,' I said as I moved around the bed with the phone. I leaned over them both, finding the best angles, making sure it would look like Libby had taken the photos herself. When they arrived from an unknown number, I didn't want Grace thinking anyone else had been present in this little love nest. The last thing I needed was for her to start asking questions rather than dumping him. The pictures should simply show two people overwhelmed with lust and the excitement of photographing their beautiful bodies as they had incredible sex.

Which meant I also had to make it appear Danny's eyes were shut in pleasure and not because he'd consumed four milligrams of Rohypnol.

'OK,' I said. 'Nearly done. You can sit up for a minute if you like.'

I moved to the bottom of the bed, put my phone down next to Danny's feet, reached up to take hold of his boxers and tugged them down.

Libby made a noise in the back of her throat. 'Do I have to? Haven't you got enough already?' she asked.

'This is the last thing, then I'll email you the dissertation and you can leave. Put your head on his stomach and your hand on his thigh. And for god's sake, look like you're enjoying yourself.'

She moved slowly, but eventually she was in position. It took me longer than I thought to get exactly the right shot, to make sure the picture would show his lovely handsome face and her plump rosebud lips and her breasts spilling out of the bra, her hand, his pubic hair and a tiny bit of his penis. Just enough, but not too much. No point having a picture of a flaccid penis. I also made sure to include his birthmark – the one above his left nipple that looked like an owl – so there could be absolutely no doubt it was him.

'Right,' I said. 'All done. You can get dressed.'

Libby sprang off the bed and rushed over to her clothes, pulling everything on as quickly as possible. Then she picked up her coat and turned to me, saying, 'Will you send me the essay now?'

'Of course,' I said and scrolled through the emails on my phone, looking for the one I had sent myself earlier with an essay attached from the *History/Middle Ages/ Final-Year Dissertation/First Class* section of my database. I found it. *Charlemagne: Why Did He Become Known as the Father of Europe?*

'Some bits are highlighted,' I said. 'Change those. It's not difficult. As long as you're capable of stringing together half a dozen words, this dissertation will get between seventy-eight and eighty-two per cent.'

As I was talking, Libby's gaze kept flicking towards Danny's naked body. His legs were splayed, so I pushed his ankles together, then said, 'You listening to me, Libby? You have to make the marked changes in order to avoid the plagiarism checkers. OK?'

She dragged her attention back to me. 'Right, yes, I'll do that.'

'OK then,' I said and pressed send. 'It's all yours.'

'Thanks,' she said and picked up her bag.

'One more thing before you go.'

She looked at the door, then back at me. 'What?'

'If you ever tell anyone what you did here, or ever mention Rob to anyone, I'll forward the university the email I've sent you. They'll know you cheated and you'll be stripped of your degree. You'll be called a cheat and a liar for the rest of your life. Is that clear?'

She nodded, pushed past me, opened the door and stepped out into the corridor, leaving me alone with a well-stocked minibar and my handsome, naked, about-to-be-single brother.

Final Notes

I've never seen Izzy again, although we have been in contact, because when I was offered my publishing contract, it was a condition that both Izzy and Grace consent in writing to the publication of this book. As Fiona Mackie had predicted, Izzy changed her mind – but when I agreed to her demands that a greater proportion of the book would be devoted to her life than to Grace's and that I'd include references to her designer clothes (she sent me a list to make sure I referred to them correctly) and mention her twenty-first-floor apartment and convertible BMW, she changed her mind again and signed the consent. I suppose there has to be some benefit to dealing with a narcissistic psychopath.

But I haven't returned to HMP Downview. I have no wish to spend any more time with her. There is no point asking her what other poison she dripped into her brother's ears or going through her stories asking her to identify which ones are genuine. She wouldn't tell me the truth anyway. Or maybe she would. In one of our earliest conversations Izzy had told me 'Dan wasn't Dan without me', so maybe she was telling me the truth all along. How would I know?

For example, I don't know if, as an eight-year-old, she manipulated her classmates to bring about the sacking of a primary school teacher for 'touching' pupils, or if she blackmailed her colleagues at the insurance company for using cars she herself had authorised them to use. I don't know if she crept into Grace's bedroom while Grace was ill, took her laptop and filled the search history with divorce lawyers.

However, I do know she was not abused by her uncle because she does not have an uncle living in Australia or anywhere else. I have copies of the birth and death certificates for William Walker – Sarah's brother – who, as Sarah told Grace, died aged six in a car accident.

And I cannot prove whether or not Izzy did what she claims to have done to her brother in December 2010. Grace deleted the photographs years ago, and without them there is no way to even begin to try and find a student who may or may not have been called 'Libby' who paid for an essay by posing for photographs with a drugged and unconscious young man.

Finally, I will leave it up to you to decide whether or not you think Izzy knew Daniel was listening that day. Grace is adamant Izzy would have seen him on the stairs, but it is yet another element of this story that can never be confirmed.

Notwithstanding everything else, I always thought it was possible that Izzy felt at least some genuine affection for her brother, albeit in a twisted and warped way. If so, it is her only redeeming feature.

But if she knew he was listening, if she knew he could hear her telling Grace about the depraved thing that she did to him, but his wellbeing at that point was less important to her than 'beating' Grace, then truly she is beyond redemption.

Despite her initial reluctance, Grace is a willing participant in this project. She wants her version of the truth about her husband and his sister to be made public, so Izzy's version does not stand as the only one. She wants her experiences to be a warning to others. She doesn't want anyone else to go through what she has been through.

After the inquest was over, Grace took Beth to stay with her father in Canada for an extended visit, but we had two further conversations on Zoom and I told her about my visit to Downview and my meeting with Fiona Mackie. Afterwards, I emailed her a copy of the transcript. On our final call, she reconfirmed that I could include whatever I liked of our conversations in whatever form I decided to write this book. She provided her written consent without any conditions attached.

While I was still considering how to turn all the material I'd gathered into a coherent story, I found out that my *Planet Home* articles and the resulting Clean Skies Campaign had been nominated for the Bellinger Prize for Journalism. Some weeks later, I received the news that I had won.

It was a bittersweet accolade: winning the prize meant that I had my pick of jobs. I was once again a journalist, and for that I was – and still am – delighted. But the only reason I'd pursued the ghost-flight story in the first place was because during a completely unnecessary and environmentally damaging flight a pilot alone on a flight deck deliberately flew an aeroplane into the side of a mountain. In one way, it was as simple as that. But in so many other ways, what happened on board flight GFA578 was the final scene of a tragedy which had been inexorably unfolding since the day Daniel Taylor was born.

The greatest tragedy of all was that Luke was in the aeroplane. Kind, funny, affectionate, my brother's best friend and my love, Luke Emery was entirely undeserving of his untimely, violent death. I dedicate this book to his memory. We will always remember him.

Postscript

As I was completing my final edits, I received an email from Grace.

18 November 2024

Dear Carly,

The last time I saw you in person, after the inquest, when you asked me if I was surprised to find out that it was Danny flying the plane, I know I reacted badly, but even then, even after hearing all the evidence, I couldn't really believe what he'd done. I still can't believe he killed someone else. I want you to make it completely clear in your book that my husband never hurt anyone before the plane crash. Please, Carly, make sure people know that. Danny was *nothing* like his sister.

What that psychologist told you was true – I don't believe Danny knew who he was without Izzy. He was unnaturally bound to her from the moment he was born. Roger has always refused to acknowledge it, but Sarah knew, deep down maybe, but she knew what her daughter was.

I'm glad I reported Izzy to the police. I'm glad she's in prison. Hopefully she can't hurt anyone there, although I wouldn't bet on it. Knowing Izzy is in prison doesn't make me happy, though, because it's not justice. Izzy is responsible for what Danny did. She is responsible for Danny's death. She is responsible for poor Luke Emery's death.

I also have my own guilt to bear. The night before I left for Canada, before her trial, I saw Izzy at Roger's house and I asked her why she had gone to the trouble of planning something so elaborate to try and break me and Danny up all those years ago. And you know what she said? *It was fun*. She is pure evil. It wasn't *fun* that made her tell me what she told me that afternoon in our basement, though. I goaded her in a way I'd never done before. I *laughed* at her and she couldn't stand it. *That's* why she told me what she'd done to Danny. To hurt me. To win. To her, Danny's feelings were simply collateral damage. If only I had never gone down there. If only I hadn't confronted her. If I hadn't goaded her, she would never have told me what she did, Danny would never have heard it, and he and Luke would still be alive. I shall carry that guilt with me forever.

It wasn't *my* Danny who flew a plane into the mountain. It was a devasted and utterly broken man. God knows I experienced what Izzy was for myself. From the moment I met her in that church anteroom, my life's orbit was altered. It swung around her, sometimes closer, sometimes further away, but always around her.

I'm haunted by what Fiona Mackie told you about psychopaths being experts at identifying victims. Every time I think about it (and I think about it a lot) I feel sick. Did *I* walk in a way that marked me out as a target? Is that what Izzy saw when sixteen-year-old, chronically under-confident and desperate-to-be-liked me walked into that room at the church before Pops and Clare were married? Did she take one look at me and know I was a victim?

At the time, I was naïve and stupid enough to think we were friends, but Izzy never liked me. Not for a minute. I understand that now. To her I was just someone who was vulnerable and needy, perfect for her to toy with, until she got bored of me.

But – and this keeps me awake at night – do I still walk like a victim? Could this happen to me again? I choose to think not. I'm not the same person I was back then. Everything I've been through has made me strong. Very strong.

I'm using another name now. People no longer ask if I'm *that* Grace Taylor, the wife of *that* pilot. The thing is, though, no matter what name I use, as Izzy pointed out on the day my daughter was born, Beth shares approximately twenty-five per cent of her aunt's DNA. This is my greatest fear. Since you sent me the transcript of your conversation with Fiona Mackie, I've thought a lot about how she said psychopathy is a combination of nature and nurture. How someone might be born with abnormalities in their brain that might make them grow up to be a serial killer. Or grow up with completely socially acceptable behaviour. Or be born with the abnormalities and grow up to be like Izzy.

So I spend my time watching my daughter, looking for signs. Last week her teacher asked to speak to me when I picked her up from nursery. Beth had been bullying one of the other children, taking her toys, pushing her over, pinching the other girl through her sleeve where the bruises didn't show. The teacher was kind. She knows how Danny died – I didn't try to hide it from her new nursery; the grief counsellor I've been seeing said it was best to be open, at least in this regard – and the teacher said she was sure it wasn't serious; it was probably just Beth finding her feet. She was only mentioning it, she said, so we could work together to 'nip it in the bud'.

Maybe she's right – I know children are inherently self-centred – but I still worry. I recently found some of my jewellery in a little box under Beth's bed. When I asked her why she took it, she shrugged, which made my blood run cold.

Like Fiona Mackie said, I'm constantly searching for signs of anxiety – looking for evidence that Beth is not like her aunt – but my daughter is a confident, independent, self-reliant little girl. Her lack of anxiety makes me anxious.

I haven't tried to hide us away completely. Beth needs to be around my family, and so do I. When she gets out of prison, Izzy will be able to find us if she wants to. I will be honest with my daughter about her aunt and, in time, about her father. What Danny did will be there for her to see on the internet, so there's no point trying to pretend it didn't happen. In the meantime, although I will watch my daughter like a hawk, I have to accept that eventually she will be too old for me to shield her from her aunt.

All I can do is to give my daughter the knowledge she needs to resist Izzy's charms and hope that, should the need ever arise, my little girl is able to see through those charms to the psychopath lurking just beneath her aunt's skin.

With best wishes,
Grace

Acknowledgements

My first and biggest thanks go to my brilliant agent, Marina de Pass, and my wonderful editor, Sarah Hodgson, both of whom believed in this difficult second novel even while I was having my doubts about it. I am truly grateful to have two such wise, talented and thoroughly lovely people on my side. In particular, Sarah's vital editorial suggestions allowed Carly to step out of the shadows and become a character in her own right.

It's a peculiar quirk of the publishing industry that we must write the acknowledgements in advance of publication, so I would like to take this opportunity to thank everyone who worked on, read and reviewed my first novel, *The Silence Project*. The whole team at Atlantic Books was fabulous and I feel extremely fortunate that my début was launched by such an excellent group of people (with an extra special shout-out to Aimee, Kirsty and Kate).

I was overwhelmed by the support *The Silence Project* received from bookshops, booksellers and reviewers, as well as from Zoe Ball and the BBC Radio 2 Book Club. Sincere thanks in particular to Mel, Elin and Hollie at Griffin Books in Penarth, the Independent Booksellers Association and all the Welsh Waterstones shops and booksellers (particularly Kate, Rowan, Lauren and Steve) for taking me and my book to your hearts.

It was an absolute joy to be on the receiving end of so much support from book bloggers. I wish I had room to name you all, but by giving a huge thank you to just one – Clare Mason – for championing *The Silence Project*, please know that I am sending all of you my love and immense gratitude.

And so to the acknowledgements for this most difficult of second novels. When I set myself the task of writing a story about a female psychopath and her brother, I had no idea where it would lead me and I am hugely grateful to the following people for their invaluable input and without whom I could not have written this book.

To my brother, Andrew Hailey, a commercial airline pilot and former RAF fighter pilot, for answering so many questions, for plotting the route of flight GFA578 and for your patience while explaining to me over and over how the real-time warning system works.

To my sister-in-law, Dr Fiona MacLean, for your medical expertise and the idea for a missing arm, which was too good to leave out.

To Alex Abraham, for Izzy's glorious outfits (and mine, for my book-launch party!).

To Moira Lloyd, for checking the psychologist's language in the transcripts.

To Daniel Swan and Ali Rafati, for your advice on fraud trials and sentencing.

To Lindy Stephens, for help with the inquest process.

Any errors are mine alone.

A big thank you to Lucian Huxley-Smith, for your invaluable feedback on a very early draft of this novel. Thank you to Emma Dunne, for being the most meticulous of copy editors. And an enormous thank you to

Grace Nutland-Frankel, for lending me your beautiful name.

The final thanks must go to my friends and family. I am immeasurably grateful for your indulgence while I bang on and on about book-related things and for all the photos of *The Silence Project* that you've taken in various places. For your unconditional support, thank you to my parents, Gill and Terry; my brother and sister-in-law, Andrew and Fi; my nephews, Seb and Teddy; all the Cherries, for the Scottish support; Juliet Nutland, for the slow-chopped mushrooms; Lindy and Gaynor, for continuing to be my biggest cheerleaders and gin-drinking buddies; and last, but never least, to my husband, Pete, without whom I could not have embarked on a whole new career writing books.

For anyone interested in reading more about psychopathy, below is a short bibliography of the non-fiction books I found most interesting and informative while undertaking research for *Scenes from a Tragedy*.

Babiak, P. and Hare, R. D. (2006) *Snakes in Suits*, Harper
Cleckley, H. (1955) *The Mask of Sanity*, Echo Point Books & Media
Dutton, K. (2012) *The Wisdom of Psychopaths*, Penguin
Fallon, J. (2014) *The Psychopath Inside*, Portfolio/Penguin
Hare, R. D. (1993) *Without Conscience*, The Guilford Press
Kiehl, K. (2014) *The Psychopath Whisperer*, Oneworld
Ronson, J. (2011) *The Psychopath Test*, Picador
Stott, M. (2021) *The Sociopath Next Door*, John Murray Learning
Thomas, M. E. (2014) *Confessions of a Sociopath*, Pan Books